When the Getting Was Good

*To Alina Tugend
Writer, community leader,
and friend,*
Susan G. Bell

Susan G. Bell

11.20.10

authorHOUSE®

AuthorHouse™
1663 Liberty Drive
Bloomington, IN 47403
www.authorhouse.com
Phone: 1-800-839-8640

First published by AuthorHouse 6/1/2010

ISBN: 978-1-4490-8989-4 (e)
ISBN: 978-1-4490-8122-5 (sc)

Printed in the United States of America
Bloomington, Indiana

This book is printed on acid-free paper.

A Note about the Author

Susan G. Bell was born and grew up in northern California. She graduated from Stanford University and earned an MBA from Loyola University Maryland and an MFA from Sarah Lawrence College. Prior to writing *When the Getting Was Good*, she spent twenty-four years in the financial services industry. She was the first woman to be promoted to managing director at J.P. Morgan Securities. She and her family live in New York.

For Sam

Do the thing that's less passive. Do the active thing.
There's more of the human in that.

—Nuala O'Faolain
My Dream of You

Prologue

The year was 1985, and the Reagan Rally was well underway. For nearly three years, the American stock and bond markets had moved steadily higher, on the way to creating personal fortunes unimaginable at the start of the decade to even the most optimistic forecasters. Investors weren't the only beneficiaries of rising markets. The men and, to a far lesser extent, women who worked on Wall Street became wealthy too. Some partakers in the financial bonanza recognized their luck: they had been in the right place at the right time. There were others on Wall Street who thought that being extravagantly well paid was a logical outcome for people who had recognized the opportunity and gone after it.

Whatever the perspective, it felt good to have money and access to the new American dream.

Chapter 1

Kate Munro pushed herself away from the bank of screens, leaned back in her chair, and said out loud to no one in particular, "I'm out!" The guys on the trading desk whooped and whistled: they knew she had just completed the trade. A million dollars in profits on a billion-dollar trade, by far her best day as a trader.

"Nice going, Kate. You can take the rest of the day off," Jim Fletcher kidded from the far end of a row of desks in the center of the trading room. Jim was Kate's boss, the head of government bond trading at A. J. Matheson & Company. His praise made her blush.

She reached for her shoulder bag under her desk at the opposite end of the row. She loved getting the market right but wished she hadn't been so obvious. Her job was to trade and, win or lose, keep quiet about it. She had little respect for the hot-doggers in the business, who high-fived it all around when they made money and broke handsets against the phone turrets when they lost.

Kate fished in her purse for her wallet and stood up. She was tall and slim, her light brown hair pulled back from her face. She wore no make-up, though at the moment there was color in her cheeks. She had what her father described as good features: clear hazel eyes set the right distance apart, ears that didn't protrude, straightened white teeth. Her wide mouth made her smile generous, though her expression was usually serious. The double ridge of skin between her nose and upper lip was pronounced, like a crimp in the crust of a small pie. It was this feature and her full and unshaped eyebrows that gave her a boyish look.

She ducked around a marble-clad column and into an aisle of wide steps leading up and out of the trading room. Her workplace resembled a small stadium, with rows of desks rising on either side from where the traders sat. She glanced at the wall of windows in back of her and saw that the weather outside was nice: sunlight permeated recently cleaned glass. She would escape to the lobby and step outside for a moment before anyone came over to investigate the reason for Jim's compliment. Already the phone lines were lighting up as word spread about Matheson's success in the year-bill auction.

She couldn't have played this one better. She sold the bills she'd bought in the auction to dealers whose auction bids had been too low, not aggressive enough for the strong investor demand. The clients who had taken her advice and submitted bids alongside hers were rewarded with instant profits. The flurry of buying and selling after the auction results were announced had been awesome. She had never felt more powerful or up to the test of a trading job on Wall Street.

And now she was completely out, the revenue booked, her risk cut to zero. It was a quietly satisfying moment, the most rewarding part of the ride—and it wouldn't last. By Monday, everyone would have forgotten her winning trade; it probably wouldn't be mentioned again. And maybe that was better. Though she wanted the recognition, craved it even, for how well she had done, she was wary of drawing too much attention. She was the only woman on the trading desk and already stood out.

On that particular Friday afternoon, a steady buzz filled the trading room as the salesmen at A. J. Matheson wrapped up what for them had been a routine day in the government bond department. As she walked past them, Kate remembered her own days as a salesman, and the sense of closure that would come once her tickets had been written. She had always shared her clients' concern about their portfolios, and followed the trades she recommended to see how they worked out. But being conscientious about her clients' performance didn't approach the responsibility of taking trading risk of her own. People in sales might witness the action, but they were only spectators. The players were the traders.

She was a player. Her performance in today's auction had proved it. Anyone who made money could be a hero in this business, even a woman. She didn't have to say a word; her trading profits would do the talking. Feelings of bravado exhilarated and frightened her, like a ride on the back of a motorcycle.

Jim Fletcher's voice came over the intercom. "In honor of Kate Munro's successful coup of today's bill auction, she's offered to buy ice cream for everyone. Do we have any takers?" Cheers went up, and Jim made an elaborate show of counting hands. "Just buy the place out," he yelled across the trading floor. "I'll come help you carry them."

She watched her boss amble over. In his mid-thirties, a few years older than Kate, Jim still had the bearing of the college athlete he'd once been. His expensive cotton shirt, boldly striped in sapphire blue, fit snugly, accentuating what good shape he was in. As if to leave no doubt, he rolled his sleeves up to his elbows the moment he removed his suit jacket each morning.

As they waited at the elevator, Jim spoke to her seriously. "Nice call on the market." Kate mumbled her thanks and stared at a worn spot in the rug. Winning at a game men considered worth playing heightened her sense of accomplishment, but she wanted to keep her head the way Jim did whenever he made money in the market. "Don't get caught celebrating," he always said. "Opportunities come in bunches. You've got to be ready for the next one."

Kate liked working for someone who understood the challenge of trading, someone whose own trading skills were still sharp. Jim's promotion to head trader hadn't curbed his appetite for risk-taking. Bringing her onto the trading desk, for example. She couldn't think of another manager at Matheson who would have made that move. She was determined to prove Jim right, to justify his confidence in her.

In the snack shop downstairs, Kate loaded boxes of Häagen-Dazs bars into Jim's outstretched arms. "Can I borrow some money?" she said. "I'm short on cash."

"Sure," Jim said, shifting the ice cream onto the counter and peeling bills from a silver clip choked with currency. "I'll deduct it from your bonus." He grinned slyly and paid for the ice cream.

"What's up for the weekend?" he said in the elevator back to the trading floor. Kate rarely had plans and dreaded that question, though Jim wasn't singling her out. He regularly asked the same question of everyone in the trading room.

"Maybe go to the movies," she said. "How about you?"

"Claudia's got a list for me a mile long, but I'm sneaking out on Sunday to play golf." At the entrance to the trading room, he balanced the cartons of ice cream against his chest and leaned back into the door. "Ready to feed the animals?"

Kate had been surprised when Jim offered her a job on the trading desk, more than a year ago now. She had been happy in sales, the job she'd been hired to do at A. J. Matheson. She hadn't been a trading groupie either, someone who hung around the traders, fetching and carrying for them in hopes of becoming their assistant. As a salesman, she had avoided the traders and approached them only when necessary. Entering their domain could be unnerving. They dominated the room from the center row, like so many raucous crows on a line. Without warning or apology, a trader would leap up, slamming his swivel chair into whatever happened to be behind him, or bellow into the phone, punctuating his language with profanity, which didn't faze people in the securities business.

Kate had prepared herself to contend in this environment, and become a top salesman at Matheson. She was the first one in every morning, checking the screens and reading the overnight faxes from the bank's foreign offices. She followed the markets closely for her clients, the managers of money market mutual funds. Listening carefully to what they needed to accomplish, she soon developed her own market opinions and strategies. She could defend her views too, with an equanimity that set her apart. Eventually the traders sought her out, coming over to her desk during a lull to discuss the market, or calling her to check on a particular client.

Though flattered by Jim's offer to join the trading desk, Kate didn't rush to accept. It seemed better to remain a top salesman than to become a mediocre trader. If she tried trading and didn't cut it, moving back to sales would feel like failure. And once she gave up her customers, there would be no getting them back, at least not at Matheson. She would have to find another job, and she couldn't imagine working anyplace else.

When Kate asked Jim if she could think about his offer, he had stared at her, steely-eyed and silent, and told her to take all the time she needed, his ironic tone implying that he was having second thoughts. She worried that she had blown it, but she had to confer with someone before making a move this big. She knew of several women who had traded elsewhere on Wall Street, but none of them had lasted very long. Kate was cordial with other salesmen at Matheson, but what could they tell her about trading? She could think of only one person worth consulting before giving Jim her answer.

Ernie Hartnack. Self-described as Wall Street's oldest living trader, Ernie had traded Treasury bills for almost twenty years, more than a lifetime on Wall Street. He seemed to remember every ticket he'd ever written. He was an invaluable, if ill-tempered, resource. Never one to mince words, Ernie would tell it to her straight, and she would trust his opinion.

The gray-haired trader acted as if he had been expecting her. "You know why I think you can trade?" Ernie said. "You know when to get out."

"Get out?" Kate said.

"I've seen you do it." He settled back in his chair, warming to the role of advisor. "Let me put it differently.

You're at a bar, and you start to feel uncomfortable. I don't know, say the guy you came with turns out to be a bum… he gets drunk and disorderly." Head tilting, eyelids drooping, Ernie pantomimed her imaginary date's condition. "So what do you do?"

"Call a cab and chalk it up to experience?" Kate said, playing along.

"Exactly! You don't fool around with this jerk. You cut your losses and get the hell out."

She laughed softly. "If that's all there is to it, I'll be a trading genius."

"Don't underestimate how hard that is to do," Ernie shot back, as serious as she had ever seen him. He lit a cigarette and let it dangle from the corner of his mouth. "People ignore their better instincts, time after time, which can lose you a lot of money." He narrowed his eyes, studying her over exhaled smoke.

Kate sat silently, wondering if she really had that sort of perception. She knew she was empathetic. Her mother had taught her to always look at a situation from the other person's point of view. It was how she had become friends with Ernie in her early days as a salesman.

One Monday afternoon, shortly before the weekly auction of Treasury bills, a client told Kate that he had significant interest in that day's sale of three-month Treasury bills: he wanted to buy fifteen per cent of the issue, over a billion dollars' worth of securities. The client, who managed a huge money market mutual fund, was a well-known participant in Treasury bills, a key player whose actions moved markets. Excited to possess such an important piece of information, Kate had walked over to Ernie's desk and asked how he thought it would affect the pricing. If Ernie sounded on top of the situation, Kate would ask the client to submit his bids through Matheson for the first time.

Kate's information was news to Ernie, though he couldn't admit it. "That guy cheats at squash," he snarled. "You think he's telling you the truth?" What Kate read on Ernie's face was more fear than anger. For years, his greatest source of information had been a network of cronies, mostly middle-aged men like him, veterans of the securities business who had worked their way out of the back office, or landed jobs on the line because they knew someone in management. But now graduates of the country's top business schools, sensing that big money could be made in the bond business, swarmed over Wall Street, picking the brains of the veterans before shoving them out of their way.

Kate's client submitted his auction bids through another dealer, one more in touch with the last-minute interest. When the results were announced later that afternoon, Jim Fletcher summoned Kate to Ernie's desk. "I just got off the phone with Morgan Stanley," Jim said loudly, for the benefit of every salesman on the floor. "Your customer was huge in this auction. Lucky for us, Ernie squared our position or we would have been screwed. But we could have made money, if you'd known about his interest, which by the way is your job."

Her face burning, Kate nodded once and walked back to her seat. She knew better than to embarrass Ernie in front of his boss. No matter who dropped the ball in the trading room, the onus of picking it up was always on the salesman. The next week, she invited Ernie to dinner with the client. Ernie accepted, making the reservation himself at Smith & Wollensky. At dinner, he regaled Kate and the client with a self-deprecating story about his promotion to vice-president the day after a huge trading loss. Ernie said his boss couldn't justify any one lower than a vice-president losing that kind of money.

Kate reached for the leather folder when the waiter brought the check, but Ernie intercepted it. "You get it next time. This one's on the trading desk." Then he turned to the client. "I've seen a lot of salesmen over the years, and Ms. Munro is one of the best. We'd like a shot at working for you next time you're interested in the auctions."

"I think he was impressed," Kate said after they put the client into a cab.

"You too, I hope," Ernie mumbled. It was as close to an apology as she was going to get, and more than she had expected.

Kate looked steadily at Ernie, taking in his appraisal of her chances at trading. "You think that's why Jim's offering me the job?" she said. "Because I know how to get out?"

Ernie let his chair snap upright. "Who knows what the fuck Jim thinks?" he said, irritated that she needed an endorsement beyond his. "Maybe he's running for chairman and wants a female trader to show his commitment to equality."

When Kate accepted the trading job the next morning, Jim took the news matter-of-factly. "Good," he said, his eyes glued to the screen on his desk. "You'll be working with Hartnack on bills."

Kate immediately suspected Ernie's behind-the-scenes involvement. "When should I move to the trading desk?"

"If you have to ask that, I'm putting the wrong person in the job," Jim said, his eyes never leaving the screen.

Kate left Jim's office, deflated. She glanced at Ernie and caught him watching her. He rolled his eyes, as if he knew the way she'd been welcomed to the new job. When that didn't make her smile, he stuck his thumbs in his ears and waggled his fingers, which did. Later that morning, she spoke to the sales manager and set up a schedule for transferring her accounts. After lunch, she shoved a cardboard box containing her things under the unoccupied desk next to Ernie's and sat down.

"Are you having fun yet?" he said.

*   *   *

The wastebaskets on the trading room floor overflowed with empty Häagen-Dazs boxes. At quarter past five, Kate and Ernie were still at their desks, savoring their triumph in the year-bill auction, when Lloyd Keezer wandered over from his seat in the front row of sales. A short pudgy man of indeterminate middle age, Lloyd Keezer made his living calling on dozens of mediocre accounts, customers not even rookie salesmen coveted. Keezer had been at Matheson longer than anyone in the department, starting out when he was still in high school, part of the company's work-study program, though he kept this biographical detail to himself. Longevity was not the kind of credential you pointed out in a trading room, certainly not about yourself; the next thing you knew, someone would be checking your shelf life and suggesting early retirement.

Keezer was a dealer in information. Like the color commentator on a sports broadcast, he provided quips and analysis of life as it transpired on the trading room floor. For the past ten minutes, he had been pacing back and forth behind the front row of sales desks, talking on the phone with the third largest bank in Missouri, one of his better accounts. Keezer had managed to procure a special phone cord, three or four times longer than the standard issue, from his brother-in-law, who worked for the phone company. The longer cord allowed Keezer freedom of movement during the hours he spent on the phone, which, with his lousy book of accounts, occupied most of the day. He was still tethered, like everyone else in the trading room, but at least Keezer had found himself a longer leash.

"We shut Salomon out of the auction," Keezer commented nonchalantly, as if Matheson besting Salomon Brothers, the most dominant bond shop on Wall Street, were an everyday occurrence.

Ernie, who had been leaning back in his chair, elbows crooked, hands cradling the back of his head, dropped his arms and sat up. "Where'd you hear that?"

"From Steve," Keezer said. "The portfolio guy at Missouri Trust."

"Oh, Steve," Ernie said dismissively. "Now there's an impeccable source."

But Kate was interested. Keezer learned a lot from his list of third-tier accounts, smaller banks around the country that were kept surprisingly well informed by the surfeit of salesmen at the big banks and dealers in New York. "Shut out totally?" she said.

"Yep," Keezer said.

Kate cringed. She hadn't given much thought to the specific losers in the auction.

"And this," Keezer went on, "after their head trader said he had the auction wired, and that customers had better bid through Salomon if they wanted to own year-bills."

Ernie beamed, relishing any fiasco that hadn't happened to him. "Salomon will be in the penalty box for weeks."

"Yeah," Keezer said, a satisfied look crossing his face, too. "Their head trader wanted to know who got in front of him with a bullet bid. Someone said it was us, and he went ballistic, no pun intended. He said, 'What the fuck would A. J. Matheson be doing in a year-bill auction with a bullet bid?'"

A bullet bid. Instead of scaling in auction bids at increasingly higher prices, a dealer would bid for all the securities he wanted at a single price, usually a price above the market. It was an aggressive move, and the right one to make in a rallying market. The winning bidder shut out other participants, who had to pay up to get the securities they needed.

Salomon sounded like a war zone, Kate thought as she listened to Keezer describe the scene.

"Steve says that other than looking like idiots to their customers, the salesmen at Salomon got a big kick out of watching Woody blow himself up," Keezer said.

"I would've paid a grand to see that myself," Ernie said. "Hee, hee, hee." He let out the high-pitched laugh he reserved for moments like this, when the market made the pros look like schmos, and reminded them what getting hosed felt like. Markets could be very democratic that way.

Kate felt her earlier sense of power vanish. She knew

who Woody was. Head Trader at Salomon Brothers, Morehead Woodson had celebrity status. She had been introduced to him at a brokers' party once, though she was certain he wouldn't remember. He had barely acknowledged the introduction before brushing past her in search of more important conversation.

Woody wasn't tall, but he was intimidating, his contemptuous expression marring what would have otherwise been a handsome face. People tended to forgive his unattractive attributes because of his position. The traders who worked for him were sycophants rather than colleagues. He chose his staff carefully, not so much for their market skills as for their willingness to curry his favor. He continually and publicly put them down no matter how obsequiously they behaved, and they took it because of the bonus dollars that accrued to those who did as he said.

He was something of a dandy. He had a collection of beautiful shirts, each embroidered on the left cuff with different letters and numbers distinctively Woodson: his monogram, his birth date, even his Social Security number. His clothes were custom tailored at a shop on Madison Avenue, which had once featured him in the store's catalogue. A dog-eared copy had kicked around the trading desk at Matheson for several weeks.

"Steve said to tell you thanks for your advice on the auction." Keezer directed the comment to Kate, who nodded absently.

Ernie noticed the change in Kate's mood and spoke quietly to her after Keezer went back to his desk. "What's the matter? You don't think it's funny about Woody?"

"I don't know. He probably got what he deserved. I just wish we hadn't been connected with it. I kind of like being anonymous."

"Come on, kiddo, no one who calls markets the way you've been doing lately is going to stay unknown for long. That's what's bringing in the clients. They want to know who the hot hand is. The only way to get your auction read is to do business with us. And the more business we see, the better read we give them, and so on and so on. This business is a very simple game."

"Yeah, I guess," Kate said, straightening the stacks of unused trade tickets on her desk. "But I'm not trying to tick anybody off either, especially someone like Morehead Woodson."

"Aaaah, Kate, be honest," Ernie said. "Don't you feel a little bit glad that we were the ones in the know this time?"

Kate was unable to suppress a smile. "Well, when you put it that way."

"That's the only way to put it. You love being right just as much as I do…maybe more than I do because everyone says women can't trade. There's nothing wrong with ringing the cash register."

Ernie had grown increasingly light-hearted all

afternoon and was now downright giddy. The way he smiled, his lips pursed together and turned up at the corners, made him look so much like a grizzled elf that Kate had to laugh. But Woody wasn't someone to shrug off what he took to be a slight, particularly when it was associated with public embarrassment. She worried that once he confirmed Matheson's involvement in the auction, he would be looking for a way to retaliate.

Chapter 2

It was still daylight when Kate got out of the taxi in front of her building that evening. Whenever she'd had a good week in the market, she would skip the subway on Friday, and take a cab all the way from Wall Street to the Upper East Side. She had used her first big bonus check to buy the apartment two years ago. She and Ted had still been married then. A chief resident at Cornell Medical Center, Ted spent most of his time at the hospital. He had been on duty the day they moved, and Kate had fended for herself. She slept there alone the first night, something she reflected on a year later when he told her he was leaving.

Kate's sister Liz had decorated the apartment. She worked for one of New York's patrician decorators, but promised not to make Kate's place look anything like what they did for their clients. The sisters met a few times in Midtown to select defining pieces, as Liz called them. Otherwise, Kate limited her involvement to signing the checks.

"I gave your mail and some dry cleaning to your sister, Ms. Munro," the doorman said when Kate came into the lobby. "She went up about ten minutes ago."

"Thanks, Frank," Kate said to the ruddy-cheeked man. His name and the address of the apartment building were stitched in gold on the breast pocket of his uniform. "With groceries or without?"

"With."

"Good. We're dining in." In the year since Ted had been gone, Liz visited almost every Friday night. The sisters had dinner together, sometimes at a place in the neighborhood, sometimes at Kate's apartment.

Kate crossed the marble floor of the lobby. Between the elevators, an arrangement of spring flowers sat on a console table. She could smell the lilies before she saw them amongst the other pink and red blooms. She put her face into the flowers and breathed deeply. Stargazers, her mother's favorite. Kate had carried them on her wedding day a decade ago. Liz had been critical of the choice—the flower's rust-colored pollen might stain the wedding dress—until the significance dawned on her, and she silently removed the stamen tips from her big sister's bouquet.

Kate straightened up self-consciously when the elevator door opened, but the car was empty. On the eleventh floor, she stepped out onto thick carpet and padded down the hall. At her front door, she smiled at the sound of Carol Channing belting out the lyrics to "Before the Parade Passes By." Liz took encouragement from show tunes, and her selection of music often telegraphed the conversational theme she intended to take up. *Hello, Dolly!* Kate prepared herself for advice about getting back into circulation.

She put her shoulder bag on the entry hall table and went into the living room. Natural light streamed in through casement windows and reflected off the glazed, ecru-colored walls. The comfortable chairs and sofas were upholstered in fabrics of red and yellow. Happy colors, Liz called them.

Kate's was an elite existence, though a tony lifestyle had never been something she had imagined for herself or even aspired to. She and her sister had grown up modestly in a stucco bungalow in Santa Cruz, California. When her father first visited Kate in New York, he had looked around the apartment with a polite smile fixed on his face. "Never let your possessions possess you" was one of his favorite expressions. Was he thinking that now? she had wondered, suddenly embarrassed for giving Liz so much leeway.

Kate rounded the turn at the end of the living room and saw Liz standing in the kitchen. She was tossing a salad and enthusiastically accompanying Miss Channing. "'For I've got a goal again! I've got a drive again! I'm gonna feel my heart coming alive again!'" She stopped singing when she saw Kate. "Hi! I didn't hear you come in." Kate plucked a lettuce leaf from the wooden bowl. "Not yet," Liz said, elbowing her away. "Look in the fridge."

Inside the refrigerator a split of champagne chilled in the bottom half of a fish poacher. "I think this is the first time that thing's been used," Kate said about the hammered copper pot she and Ted had received as a wedding gift. "What are we celebrating?"

"All the money you made today." Liz lifted her chin and gloated over the surprise on her sister's face.

Kate shook her head. She no longer bothered to ask which of Liz's sources had supplied her latest piece of intelligence. "You should be the trader," Kate said. "You really should." She watched as Liz removed the makeshift ice bucket from the refrigerator. Wrapping a dishcloth around the neck of the champagne bottle, she eased out the cork and released a vaporous mist.

Opening champagne elegantly: now there was a skill totally in keeping with Liz's repertoire. She took pains to make life gracious, both in her job as an interior decorator and with her family and those fortunate enough to be her friends. She was naturally good-looking, but the care she took with her appearance made her strikingly so. She had blue eyes and a creamy complexion, which she zealously protected from the sun, finding other ways to maintain the golden highlights in her hair. Her nails were always manicured and polished. She owned a drawerfull of neutrals. Delicacy, and Ballet Slipper. She was constantly pressing a bottle of polish on Kate, urging her to use it, and once and for all rid herself of the habit of chewing on her nails, a nervous tic from childhood that had resurfaced with the divorce. Whenever Kate admired an aspect of her sister's appearance, and there were many from which to choose, Liz would brush aside the compliment. "It's part of the image. If you can't pull yourself together, why would anyone hire you to decorate?"

Liz was good at her job and in demand for someone so young, but she made no bones about the depth and meaning of what she did for a living. She had never been much of a student, lacking patience for those subjects that required more than the application of her unerring common sense. Wasn't it logical to work at things that came naturally? Liz would ask, expressing one of her life's philosophies. Where was the harm in helping people make their homes look nice?

There was space enough between the two sisters—at 31, Kate was five years older—that they didn't compete with each other, not overtly anyway. They could even joke, after getting over the initial affront, about an elderly aunt's regularly expressed opinion that Kate had inherited their father's brains and Liz, their mother's good looks.

Now, over champagne, Liz revealed the source of her information about Kate's successful day in the market. "Ernie told me. He picked up your line when I called. You went out for ice cream?"

"Jim bought ice cream for everyone. He made a big deal of it."

"And well he should! You're making him look good, remember. Don't be too generous."

Too generous to Jim? Not likely. He was the man who had given her a chance; he was her lucky break.

Aside from Ernie, Jim was the person she felt closest to at work. He bragged about his decision to make her a trader and teased her about everything, particularly what he termed the refinement she brought to the desk. She didn't curse and posture, not to mention belch and fart, like the men.

Liz touched her glass of champagne to Kate's. "So, tell me how you did it."

"Did what?"

"Made all the money."

"You really want to know?"

Liz leaned back against the counter. "Give me an executive summary."

"All right," Kate said, pleased by her sister's interest. "Once a month the United States Treasury has an auction for year-bills, which are basically IOUs from the government to investors. People lend the government money, and the government pays it back with interest a year later. The Treasury bill is the security that represents that agreement."

"Go on, I'm with you."

"We had a lot of customers who wanted to do this—two of the orders were huge—and when we added them all up we had $3 billion worth of customer interest. These are mostly investors, not traders. It's called 'going-away' business because the bills are going to be put into portfolios and not get traded right away."

"Like you do, right?" Liz said. "Anything you buy is going to be sold right away?"

"It could be a few days, a few hours, or even a few minutes—like today. I was out of most of them within twenty minutes, and all of them by the end of the day."

"So why did the price go up so much?"

"There's a finite number of these bills for sale, and they go in order to the highest bidders. That's why knowing what investors want to do in the auction is so important. We had three billion dollars' worth of solid customer interest, so we decided to bid for a billion for ourselves, to trade. Now we have $4 billion worth of bids: three billion for our customers and a billion for us. That's half the auction."

"The auction was $8 billion?" Liz said.

"Right. We submitted bids for 4 billion all at one price, a little higher than the market talk. It's called a bullet bid. Dealers generally scale their bids because no one wants to pay too much. This time that strategy cost them. We got the four billion."

"But you made a million dollars."

"With bills, you've got to trade billions to make millions. It's different in bonds. You make a lot more in price movement with a bond. Of course, you can also lose a lot more, too. Do you want me to explain the math?"

Liz held up a hand. "I'll take your word for it. But what do the dealers who got shut out do?"

"If they want the bills, they have to pay up because the market's traded higher with all that demand. The worst part though is how they look to their customers, the ones who bid through a dealer like Salomon because of the firm's expertise. Believe me, it's humiliating. You look clueless, and that's bad for business."

"Have you ever been shut out?"

"Never in this sort of size. It's the best read on a bill auction we've ever had." Kate was boasting now, if only to her sister, but Ernie always said you had to take credit for your victories before someone else did.

"How about all the little guys out there?" Liz said. "Did they get screwed, too?"

"There's protection for smaller investors," Kate said, looking at the golden bubbles in her glass. "If anyone's afraid of missing out, they can submit non-competitive tenders and get their bills at the average auction price." Was Liz intentionally tweaking her? There would always be some of this between them, despite their close relationship. Once when they were little, the girls played happily on a seesaw, carefully launching each other to the top until Liz paused at the bottom and stared up at Kate elevated three or four feet off the ground. Kate remembered the change coming over Liz's face as she smiled and slipped off her end of the seesaw, bringing Kate down with a bone-jangling whack.

Liz had turned her attention to the stack of mail on the countertop. "This looks interesting," she said. Kate didn't recognize the return address on the heavy vellum envelope. She read the enclosed invitation and handed it back to Liz, whose interest seemed piqued by the large card embossed with an American flag.

"It's engraved," Liz said, checking the back of the card. "Pretty fancy for a barbecue. Jim must be doing all right. Clapboard Ridge Road is the best address in Greenwich."

Kate arched her eyebrows but didn't say anything. She was thinking about the handwritten note at the bottom of the invitation: *Bring a date!*

Liz read her thought. "Are you bringing a date?

"Would you like to come?" Kate said sarcastically.

"I don't think I'm what the Fletchers had in mind."

"Only married people think telling you to bring a date is a friendly gesture."

"There must be someone at work you'd like to know better. Tell him it's a work obligation. There's no commitment that way. Men do it all the time."

Kate topped up her glass with champagne. Her personal life seemed bleaker with every passing month. For a while, her lack of a social life felt justified; it was as if Ted had died and she'd entered a period of mourning. But the divorce had been final for almost a year, and Liz had started to push. She had excoriated Ted for the break-up, but held Kate responsible for reviving her own love life.

"It's no big deal," Liz said. "People try to fill the guest

list with unattached people. They're providing a service."

"I can find my own dates."

"Of course you can. I just wish you would." Liz took a gentler tone. "If you take someone to Jim's party, word will get around that you're available again. There are probably guys waiting for that cue. You've got to venture forth."

"I don't see *you* venturing forth," Kate said.

"I'm not going to venture forth with someone from New York. I'm going to marry a Californian. They're interested in things besides work. Every man in New York is obsessed with what he does for a living. It's so boring."

"But boring is all right for me?" Kate said, deliberately twisting Liz's words.

"You're serious, not boring. You're earnest, which can be misinterpreted until someone gets to know you."

"Do you think I'm obsessed with my work?"

"No, but you're letting it take up all your time. I understand why, I really do, but if there's one thing living in New York has taught me, it's that you've got to take action, and this party strikes me as a perfect opportunity to start getting on with your life."

Liz busied herself with dinner and let the subject drop, but her words lingered. After Liz went home, Kate went into her bedroom and opened the door to the walk-in closet. An overhead light came on automatically, illuminating a rarity in New York City: a closet with unused capacity. She moved aside hangers of winter clothes and

uncovered a set of recessed shelves where she kept her treasures. "The archives," Ted had dubbed this hidden section
of the closet, which contained her mother's recipe file and
jewelry box, Kate's high school yearbooks, a heart-shaped
candy box filled with her swimming ribbons, and a set of
oversized photo albums.

She removed a particular album from the bottom of
the stack and carried it over to her bed. On the first page
was a picture of Ted, tall and lean, standing next to a
U-Haul trailer hitched to the back of his white Camaro.
Already looking older than his years, he stared impatiently
into the camera, as if taking the picture were throwing
them off schedule. The caption below the photo was in
Kate's neat handwriting: "We set out for Baltimore."

Her chest tightened, but she ignored the customary
reaction. Slowly she went through the pictures that she
and Ted had taken on their cross-country trip. He had
been so eager to get started. They had driven practically
straight through and never stopped to see anything along
the way. The snapshots were either of her or Ted standing
in shorts and a T-shirt in front of the budget motels they
had stayed in. He had done most of the driving, but she
took the wheel for a few hours every afternoon to give him
a break. Otherwise she navigated.

Each day, as an August afternoon in a car without
air conditioning ended, they would pull off the highway
into a motel recommended by the car club. They would
eat dinner at Denny's or a pancake house connected with

the motel, then retire early so they could start at dawn the next morning. Every night they showered together and made love.

She winced and shut the book. She sat for a minute, staring at the album's cover, dark simulated leather stamped with the words "Ted and Kate" in gold block letters.

They had met on her first day of college. He had been one of a group of male students who showed up at the girls' dorms, ostensibly to help the incoming coeds with their luggage. After delivering Kate's matching blue suitcases to her room on the dormitory's top floor, Ted had lingered, pointing out the buildings she could see from her window. He was so knowledgeable that she assumed he was an upperclassman, though it turned out that he was a freshman, too, and enterprising enough to recognize an opportunity. Kate was elated when he called the next day to invite her to a movie. They were quickly an item on campus, and a serious romance by Christmas. Her life was under way. Finally she felt released from the burden of grief and responsibility that had accompanied the loss of her mother.

Kate ran her index finger over the names on the album cover, straining to remember, again unsuccessfully, the last time they had made love. Oh, how she wished she could remember. In the months preceding his departure, Ted had been on call every other night and slept on a cot at the hospital. That's what he had told her anyway.

On the nights he came home, they would lie together on the bed with their arms around each other. He would be asleep within minutes. He said he was just too exhausted, and she had believed him.

She took a deep breath and reopened the album toward the back, where she found what she'd been looking for, pictures from a harvest festival in the Maryland countryside. Kate had read about the event in the newspaper and suggested the outing to Ted, who had surprised her by agreeing to go.

Early on a Saturday in mid-October, during Ted's final year in med school, they drove the Camaro north on I-83. It had been raining steadily for several days, but the weather that morning was clear and crisp. Kate wore a yellow slicker and black rubber boots. "You look like Christopher Robin," Ted said good-naturedly, kissing her as they left their apartment.

She was prepared for the mud anyway. The sponsors of the festival, held at a farm just south of the Maryland-Pennsylvania line, had covered the area where the booths were located with a blanket of straw. But the ground was sodden and the straw a squishy mess by mid-afternoon. The light quality was perfect though, and Ted took an entire roll of Kate, whose yellow slicker complimented the orange of the pumpkin patch and the weathered red of the barn. As he directed her in successive shots, Ted said he was making the pictures tell the story of their day. Sitting in her Manhattan apartment, Kate could smell the wet straw under their feet, and taste the cider sipped from waxy paper cups.

She studied a photo at the bottom of the page, one of Ted sitting at a picnic table, a row of cornhusk angels arranged on the redwood planks in front of him. She could just make out the tiny musical instruments each figure held in pipe cleaner hands. She remembered how Ted had carefully sorted through bushel baskets of these dolls, making certain that Kate took home a perfect set of six. Smiling up into the camera in the flattering light of late afternoon, he looked proud of the treasures he'd gathered for his mate.

She shut the album, wondering when she would find someone to take his place, someone she could love as much as she'd loved Ted.

Chapter 3

Kate raced to work on Monday morning. All weekend she had felt superfluous in her perfectly decorated apartment. She preferred the hubbub of the trading room with its sense of controlled chaos. The market was bigger than anybody; she was veteran enough to know that. But her chances of figuring it out—the bill market anyway, now and again—were as decent as anyone's. She felt festive as she climbed the subway stairs and headed down Wall Street.

She got breakfast each morning from two brothers who operated a quilted aluminum coffee wagon stationed near the entrance to the bank. As if by pre-arrangement, the elder of the two, who was about Kate's age, always filled her order. Decelerating the rapid pace he used with other customers, he poured her coffee slowly, carefully sealing the I♥NY cup before placing it and an old-fashioned donut into a brown paper bag. The way he looked at her and smiled approvingly made her self-conscious, though not unpleasantly so. In the elevator ride to the tenth floor, she imagined asking him to Jim's barbecue.

What would Liz say to her taking a man who ran a coffee wagon? Not that a chief resident at New York Hospital had been any prize.

Jim was in his office when Kate came onto the trading floor at 6:30. "Yo, Kate!' he called, gesturing for her to join him. She dropped her things at her desk but took her coffee. Her boss was often expansive in the hour before the crowd showed up for work.

"Did you get the invitation?" Jim asked when she arrived in his doorway.

"I did. Thank you…I'll be there."

"Your name came up on the golf course yesterday. A guy, who shall remain nameless, was ragging me about the year-bill auction. He refused to believe he'd been shut out by a woman. 'Bullshit! No woman trades like that.' He couldn't sink a putt the rest of the afternoon. I should cut you in on my winnings."

"You want me to lie low for a while?"

"Lie low, and I'll fire you," Jim laughed, and sent her back to the trading floor.

Ernie arrived thirty minutes later. He pulled a leaky cup of coffee from a wet paper bag. "Every goddam day. The little piker leaves the lid loose on purpose."

"You should try the guys in front of the bank," Kate said.

"This *is* the guys in front of the bank."

Rosemary, a young, heavyset clerk, leaned over the desktop and waved a computer printout sheet in front of Ernie and Kate. "Who gets the position sheet today?" Rosemary was as diligent as a process server.

Ernie grunted.

"I'll take it," Kate said.

"Oh, that's right," Rosemary said sarcastically. "Kate has Monday through Friday, and Ernie takes weekends." Rosemary waited for Ernie to take up his defense; his years in operations made him an expert at back office banter. Instead he smiled benignly, and the disappointed clerk resumed her route across the trading room floor.

Kate added the position sheet to the stack of paper that had arrived overnight on her desk. Ph.Ds at Matheson, as well as those employed by other Wall Street banks and investment banks, inundated salesmen and traders with market commentaries. Churned out daily, much of the information was helpful—economic forecasts and technicians' charts—but a trader had to be selective. You could spend the entire day reading about the market instead of trading it.

Ernie spoke up. "You got any plans to get out of the city?"

Kate sorted papers, debating whether or not to mention the invitation to Jim Fletcher's barbecue.

"You think I'm not presentable enough for Greenwich?" he said.

Kate's wondering if Ernie had been included had more to do with his age than his presentability. She was only a few years younger than Jim, while Ernie was, well, not a baby-boomer. "I'd present you anywhere," she said.

Ernie let her off the hook. "I'm going too."

"Is everybody on the desk invited?"

"Nobody's said anything."

"Maybe people are being discreet."

"This crowd? You've got to be kidding." But instead of riffing on the deficiencies of the traders, most of whom he considered socially inferior, Ernie quietly drank his coffee and watched people arriving for work.

Kate glanced at him. "You're pensive this morning."

"I'm a pensive kind of guy."

"What are you thinking about?"

"Nothing."

She slid a pile of market reports into the wastebasket. "Maybe I should let you drink your coffee in peace."

"Go ahead, talk if you want. I'm listening."

It was like grade school, she thought: take it or leave it. If nothing else, trading was preparing her for motherhood.

She began again, watching for clues in Ernie's body language. "Let's see. There's something you want me to know without actually coming out and telling me. Am I warm?" He put his coffee down and folded his arms

35

across his chest. "Something to do with Jim's party…how we're the only ones going?" He unfolded his arms and shifted his posture. "The only ones from *here* going?" He folded his arms again. She thought for a moment, then her forehead creased. "Jim's not trying to set me up with some guy, is he?"

Ernie looked across the trading floor as if consulting an off-stage judge. "Not exactly."

"Come on, Ernie, tell me who's coming. I won't give you up."

Ernie's words tumbled out. "Morehead Woodson, that's who."

"Really," Kate said, stretching out the word. Morehead Woodson didn't seem like the type of guy Jim would like, let alone invite to his home. Jim was a family man, with pictures of his kids in his office and their Play-Doh sculptures on his desk. Woody chased skirts and ate dinner alone every night at a restaurant bar.

Ernie shrugged. "They know each other. Guess they'll be getting to know each other a lot better, too."

"Why is that?"

Ernie struggled a moment before capitulating. "Jim's getting promoted. He's going to run the whole show, sales and trading." Ernie sighed and sat back heavily in his chair.

"That's fantastic!" Kate said, though she wondered why Jim hadn't told her himself. He'd had the perfect opportunity in his office that morning. And Ernie, who loved gossip better than anyone, wasn't taking his usual pleasure in scooping her.

"Yeah, well, that's the good news. Since Jim's moving up, he needs someone to take his spot on the desk." Ernie looked at Kate over his glasses and waited for her to make the connection.

"Woody? No way! He'd never leave Salomon Brothers for Matheson."

"He's topped out there. They didn't can him or anything, but they told him not to plan on moving any further up the line. Those guys aren't the best in the business for nothing." Ernie pulled a pack of cigarettes and a disposable lighter from the pocket of his drip-dry shirt. Kate watched him light up and blow smoke rings into the air between them.

"Why can't he just stay where he belongs?" Kate said, a chill surrounding her heart. Surely it was Woody who had been Jim's weekend golf partner. They had probably sealed the deal over beers in the clubhouse.

"Management at Salomon thinks Woody is an opportunist," Ernie said.

"Since when is that a drawback at Salomon Brothers?"

Ernie flicked ash from his cigarette. "Maybe he got aggressive with the wrong people."

"Did Jim tell you all this?"

"Yeah, last night, when I called about the barbecue."

"Did you tell him what a jerk Woody is?" Her words came in a rush, as if her own sense of urgency might avert the calamity about to befall them.

"Tough saying that to the boss, particularly when he thinks he's making a brilliant hire."

Kate stared at Ernie and shook her head. "I don't get it."

"What's not to get? Woody's made Salomon a ton of dough, even if he isn't Mr. Congeniality."

"But he'll ruin everything! You've got to warn Jim. He listens to you."

"Only when I'm telling him what he wants to hear."

Kate stared at the glowing end of Ernie's cigarette. Was euphoria over his own success clouding Jim's judgment? People grew susceptible when they achieved a coveted goal. In the headiness of the moment, had Jim forgotten how long and painstaking getting there had been?

Thus far Jim's career at A. J. Matheson had been a succession of accomplishments. He was the bank's rising star, recruited from Harvard a decade ago and groomed for upper management since his training program days. Jim was smart and, more important, a strategic thinker. Kate had heard him say many times that Matheson could either change its clients—the *crème de la crème* of American corporations—or change what they *did* for those clients. Matheson was becoming less relevant as its clients financed themselves in the fixed income market by issuing commercial paper and bonds, underwriting services provided by investment banks like Salomon Brothers, and legally prohibited to commercial banks like Matheson. But the bank was fighting hard to change the law, and pursuing every avenue to level the playing field with the investment banks. Jim was convinced that the bank would win, and that one day he would run one of Wall Street's most powerful firms.

"Look," Ernie said, "Jim's got the talent and drive, but he lacks first-hand experience with corporate issuers of bonds and the investors who buy them. Enter Morehead Woodson. Get it?"

Kate swallowed hard. "So Jim's unveiling Woody at his barbecue?"

"Jim says it's important that you and I are comfortable. Woody knows everyone else on the desk."

Naturally, she thought: Woody would know who the men were. Then it occurred to her. "You know him too though, don't you, Ernie?"

"I've seen him around." Ernie stubbed out his half-smoked cigarette and didn't look up. Of course he had, she thought. The men in the bond business saw plenty of each other at the DAC—the Downtown Athletic Club—or at Harry's, drinking beer charged to someone's expense account.

"And you're supposed to convince me what a great move hiring Woody is."

"Believe it or not, Jim's got the idea that you and Woody are going to hit it off." Kate gave Ernie a sharp look.

"Not that way," he added.

"Not *any* way."

"I know. It's crazy. I told Jim he should just talk to you, but he wants you to think it's a good idea all on your own, not that it would change anything. I think Woody already accepted the job. They're working through the fine print of his contract." The personnel department claimed that the bank didn't have contracts with individual employees, but apparently in Morehead Woodson's case a precedent would be set.

Kate's dread deepened as she contemplated the impact of Woody cannon-balling into her pond. He was notoriously sexist. There weren't any women in his group at Salomon; even the clerks there were men. How long would it take for him to establish similar conditions at Matheson?

Ernie looked at Kate ruefully. "I did right telling you, didn't I?"

"Yeah," she said. "It would've been lousy if you'd held out on me."

Keezer's voice came over Kate's intercom, asking for an indication of where the bill market would open. She didn't answer, prompting Ernie to lean over and bark into the intercom. "We'll tell you at the sales meeting!" he said, and punched the release button.

"Sell everything and go home," Kate muttered. "That's my advice."

"Cheer up," Ernie said. "Maybe it won't be too bad. We're making money. That's all a guy like Woody is going to care about." Their eyes met for a moment, but Ernie quickly looked away, which made Kate think about the upcoming changes from his perspective. Jim tolerated Ernie's avoidance of risk because he respected his experience and valued his development of younger traders. Woody wasn't known for such broad-minded thinking. She and Ernie were anomalies on the trading desk: someone female and someone over fifty. Maybe Jim had invited them to his party as a show of special protection. If she was thinking along these lines, she suspected that Ernie was too.

"I'll do the sales meeting," Ernie said, volunteering for a job he hated. He slapped the top of his thighs with both hands and stood up. Kate stayed where she was and let him make his gesture. Gesture as closure: she knew Ernie had said all he intended to on this topic. With a woman, Kate would have gone on for hours. The night watchman would have had to kick them off the trading floor. But in telling her about Woody, Ernie had done more than honor his version of friendship; he'd also tipped his hand. He was going into this gig as worried as she was.

Chapter 4

Kate walked down the platform on track twenty-five, and the heat blasted up to meet her. During July and August, the encapsulated air in the tunnels running under Park Avenue into Grand Central Station would only get worse. But the lights in the 3:40 Stamford local were already on, and the air conditioning, working in at least some of the cars, would be close to refrigeration levels. She continued moving past the train's open doors, waiting until she felt warm enough to tolerate the frigid air.

Fifteen minutes early, Kate had her choice of seats. She had once overheard a man on a train say that the safer seats were the ones that faced backward. In the event of an accident, he had explained to his traveling companion, you would be slammed into the seatback instead of pitched indefinitely forward. Kate realized that avoiding injury in a situation like that would be almost completely random, but the advice had stuck in her head. She chose a window seat facing the rear of the train, on the three-seater side of the aisle.

Passengers streamed on board. A family with small

children and strollers sprawled across the seats that faced each other, nearest the door. An elderly couple, dressed in layers of dark clothing, debated where to place their suitcase. People Kate's age or younger, traveling back to their parents' homes in the suburbs, listened to Walkmans with their eyes closed. Kate could see her reflection in the train window. She wore the dress that Liz had helped her select for Jim's party.

As the train started to move, Kate thought about their shopping trip. They had been the first customers through the door when Bergdorf's opened at ten, not that they needed to worry about crowds. On a summer Saturday, the vacant, wide-open floor spaces at Bergdorf-Goodman seemed more like a Broadway set than an actual retail establishment.

Watching Liz flip through a rack of sundresses, Kate had pointed to a navy blue dress that had somehow got mixed in with the brightly colored prints.

Liz held up an aqua and pink dress with a print of parrots and palm trees. "I was thinking something a little more summery."

"It's a little bright," Kate said.

"It's a sundress. They're supposed to be bright. Let's try it on." Liz made a beeline for the dressing rooms, and soon Kate was considering her appearance in a three-way mirror, pleased with the becoming effect of the dress, one she would never have selected on her own. Looking at Liz, who stood with one hand on her hip, the other on the handle of the dressing room door, Kate was flooded with memories of the shopping trips they had taken when they were girls, back when saleswomen still waited on customers. Liz loved to shop and relished all the attention, discussing size and color options with store personnel, and including them in the decision-making. Kate, on the other hand, didn't want a saleswoman anywhere near her, and had insisted that Liz or their mother stand guard at the door—the way Liz was doing now—so that she could try things on in peace.

"Did you know that fifty percent of American women buy the first dress they try on?" Liz said.

Kate checked the back of the sundress in the mirror. "Where did you hear that?"

"I don't remember exactly, but it was a reliable source."

"How do they track it?"

Liz was silenced, though only momentarily. "Maybe it was fifty percent of wedding gowns purchased are the first ones tried on. It doesn't matter. The principle applies."

Kate wanted to ask which principle applied, and what the other fifty percent of American women did. Instead she said, "I like this dress," and Liz, with a look of accomplishment, had gone off in search of a saleswoman.

The train moved out of the tunnel and into the sunlight. Kate reached into the side pouch of her overnight bag and took out the magazine Liz had given her. A note in her sister's large handwriting was stapled to the cover: "Good article on skin care—page 75."

The setting for the Fletchers' summer barbecue rivaled any a doyenne of elegant lifestyles might suggest. Kate stood at the edge of the terrace and looked out over a large, perfect lawn on which tables with pink market umbrellas were clustered like water lilies. Birch trees bordered the perimeter of the garden, which was how Claudia Fletcher had referred to their two-acre backyard. It was a common affectation in the New York area, though even Kate could see that "backyard" was a misnomer for grounds such as these. Perennials bloomed everywhere in well-tended beds, and bouquets of these flowers decorated the tables. So far the good weather was holding.

Jim had taken up his position by the grill, but several men in chef's attire were doing most of the cooking. Kate watched Jim carry on animated conversation while keeping track of the steaks. Just like at work, she thought, where he recorded every bid and offer the desk put out no matter how engaged in other matters he appeared to be. She was beginning to feel self-conscious amidst the group of young suburban couples when Ernie and Marie Hartnack arrived.

"Some pad," Ernie said after he and Kate went through the away-from-the-office ritual of brushing cheeks, still awkward after a year of working together. He quickly took in the scene while lifting two glasses of wine from a passing tray. "So we're finally going to see if the chef lives up to his reputation."

"Jim's been talking about this all week," Kate explained to Marie, who smiled absently and patted her on the arm.

"That's nice, honey." Marie wore a hearing aid, and Kate was unsure how much of the conversation she was actually getting. With all the years Ernie had spent in the business, Marie had probably been to a hundred parties like this one. "Your dress is so pretty," she said.

Ernie appraised Kate openly. "Very smaht, very smaht."

Kate mumbled her thanks and hoped her bra straps were still safely positioned in back of her shoulder blades. Ernie pursed his lips into a fake smile and waved at Jim. "We've been noticed by the grillmeister. Don't look now, but I think there's someone he wants you to meet."

Kate gave Jim a furtive look. He had been joined by a man dressed in pleated khaki slacks and a pale blue polo shirt—the same shirt, different color, worn by every man present, except Ernie and the waiters, who wore white dress shirts and ties.

"That's Woody, right?" Kate whispered.

"I'll leave the introductions to our host," Ernie said.

Kate turned toward the two advancing men. Ernie ran interference by half a step, and shook their hands. Jim followed with a peck on the cheek for both women. He introduced Marie to Woody, then asked Kate whether or not she and Woody had ever met.

"I would have remembered that pleasure," Woody said before Kate could answer. He looked her straight in the eye and grasped her hand with just the right pressure—neither the bone-crushing grip some men subjected women to, nor the limp clasp of fingers that was even more offensive. Kate felt uncomfortable under Woody's intense scrutiny and hoped her sunglasses were hiding that fact. He released her hand and turned his full attention to Marie, engaging her in small talk about being married to one of Wall Street's senior statesmen, and letting Marie's responses steer their conversation. Woody seemed to have noticed that Marie was hard of hearing; raising his voice and facing her as he spoke, he gave every appearance of being engrossed in what she said.

He's good, Kate thought, really good. She looked at Ernie to see if he shared her reaction, but he was laughing at something Woody had said, and seemed as charmed as Marie by all the attention. Jim caught Kate's eye and winked, amused by the Woodson-Hartnack repartee, and how unnecessary he and Kate were to it. Then Jim tipped his head toward the French doors, indicating that she should follow him. They left Woody and the Hartnacks on the terrace and went into the house.

In the center of a spacious kitchen, Claudia Fletcher conferred with the catering captain. She gesticulated like a coach on the sidelines, lacking only the clipboard and headset. Jim and Kate curved around them and walked down a tiled passageway that opened into the front entry hall, large enough to be a living room in many homes.

"The joint is jumping," she said.

"Not exactly my idea of a backyard barbecue," he said, pleading the case of a regular guy, though Kate suspected that Claudia had taken her directions from Jim. "I've been wanting to bring you up to speed on something." He shifted his weight from one Gucci-clad foot to the other. "They've asked me to take over the department. Sales and trading." Kate responded with enthusiasm, and could tell that Jim was pleased by her reaction.

"I want to take the operation to the next level," he said. "Increase our market share to bulge-bracket status. I'll still direct our risk position, but I need a point man on the desk to manage the day-to-day, so Woody's coming in as head trader. He's got a tremendous client following and will bring a lot to the desk. He knows corporates, municipals, mortgage-backed's—everything we need for the future. This will be announced next week, but I wanted you to know ahead of time."

Kate kept smiling and nodding, grateful for Ernie's advance warning.

"Woody has a colorful reputation," Jim went on, "but there's substance there, too. I think you'll like working with him." With, not for: Jim was being diplomatic. "He's a trader's trader. He backs his team to the hilt. You have nothing to worry about."

As long as I'm making money, Kate thought, and against her better judgment, she let the words slip out. Jim looked surprised and thrown off by her negative take on his big news. "Well, yeah," he said, "keep contributing. That goes for all of us."

She was being perverse, qualifying Woody's support before he had even started, which was not her usual style. She remembered Ernie saying how psyched Jim was about his promotion and the acquisition of Morehead Woodson, a Wall Street ace by anybody's benchmark. Jim was expecting accolades from her, not whining.

"We're going to shoot the lights out," Kate said, recovering as best she could.

"Damn right! Let's go find Woody." Jim brought their *tête-à-tête* to an abrupt close. It was her own fault, she thought. Jim wanted to be around someone as bullish about his future as he was, someone who would confirm his choice of Woodson as inspired, someone with a positive attitude.

Kate told Jim that she would join them outside in a minute, then stepped into the powder room off the entry hall. She closed the lid on the toilet seat and sat down. The room had layers of ornamentation on its green and gold wallpaper. Framed pieces of silk hung over a towel bar, which was draped with lace-edged linens. A mahogany curio shelf held a collection of ceramic pieces, hand-painted cottages and shops from a Cotswold village. Hiding out in the Fletchers' powder room was like browsing through a fancy boutique.

Kate sighed, recalling the conversation she had just concluded with Jim. She knew the rules of the game as well as the next guy: you played by them or picked a different sport. Nothing irritated a boss more than a lukewarm response to his vision. It was like telling a guy who asked your opinion of the new suit he was wearing that the fabric looked durable. Stupid.

Stupid, stupid, stupid.

She sighed again and stood up. She took off her sunglasses and stared into the mirror's beveled glass. She practiced smiling, and then listening with rapt attention. "Get over it," she told herself, and rejoined the Hartnacks, who were seated at one of the tables on the lawn.

"I'm impressed," Marie said. "The waiters are taking orders for medium rare."

"Grandstanding," Ernie said. "Those steaks are either burnt or bleeding."

The women ignored him and watched as a waiter lit the torches surrounding the lawn. Soon the mosquitoes would be out, even in Greenwich, but the party wouldn't move indoors unless it rained. Though Kate was susceptible to mosquito bites, she didn't like slathering on repellent unless it was absolutely necessary, but a buzzing near her ear made her rise from her chair. "I've got to spray my arms and legs before the mosquitoes find me." She looked toward the terrace and noticed Woody standing in the arch of the French doors, scanning the property as if it were his.

"Too late," Ernie said as Woody spotted them. "Here comes the bugger now."

Woody arrived at their table with a solicitous look on his face and asked if he could bring them anything from the bar.

"Are you joining us?" Marie asked. "We could use a fourth, someone young so Kate won't be too bored. We're always the oldest guests at these parties, aren't we, Ernie? It makes us feel like chaperones." Ernie smiled mechanically and drank from the bottle of light beer that he'd switched to at Marie's request.

Woody turned to Kate. "Is that all right with you?" He was taller than she was, though not by much, and held himself stiffly. Even dressed casually, Woody didn't look relaxed. Standing this close to him, Kate noticed that his eyes were not dark like his hair, but blue. She remembered her powder-room resolve, and smiled at him.

"That's fine," Kate said, as a second mosquito buzzed her ear. She considered telling Woody that she would be right back, but his manner was so formal and unyielding, she decided not to. He touched the chair she had just vacated and pulled it out from the table. She felt the cool metal of the chair against the back of her legs before she sat down.

Woody sat down, too, and took up Marie's line of conversation about chaperones. Chaperones at proms. Chaperones in Shakespeare. Woody seemed to be an expert on the subject. Kate silently observed. Despite all she had heard and noticed about his rudeness, Woody had taken a different tack tonight. The attention he was paying to Marie was particularly surprising. There was nothing the older woman could do for him, and yet he was extending himself to her. Kate toyed with the thought that Woody's behavior was calculated to impress her rather than Marie. Maybe he wanted them to get off on the right foot. Was that a crime? If he was showing off, at least he'd chosen a praiseworthy method.

"I suppose the idea of a chaperone sounds pretty unnecessary to a woman of today," Woody said to Kate. He sounded disappointed.

"On the contrary," Kate said. "It's a jungle out there. My sister and I accompany each other everywhere." New boss or not, she was tired of men who reduced the concerns of women to nonsense issues like who opens the door and who pays the check.

Woody raised his dark eyebrows. "Is your sister here tonight?"

"She figured I'd be safe in the home of my employer," Kate said.

"Touché." Woody bowed his head. "And tell me," he added, lowering his voice. "Do you feel safe here?" The presumptuous look on his face made Kate feel ridiculous.

Ernie banged his empty beer bottle down on the glass tabletop. "I sure as hell don't. Those goddam tiki torches are smoking up the place. What are they burning, diesel?"

The torches did seem more smoke than flame, and the one nearest them was listing. Ernie shouted at a young man rushing by with a tray of empty glasses. The confused waiter stopped and looked around before identifying the source and coming over to their table. "You better douse that thing before we're all asphyxiated," Ernie said.

"I'll take care of it," Woody said, getting up from the table. He commandeered the waiter and strode off in the direction of the offending torch.

Marie patted Ernie's hand reassuringly.

"What a lot of bullshit. 'Tell me: do you feel safe here?'" Ernie imitated a Continental accent. "Sounds like a B-movie, for chrissake."

"It's all right," Kate said. "You can never have the last word with a guy like that. I keep forgetting."

"Yeah, well, he's a bigger asshole than I thought he was," Ernie said.

"He's a big one, all right," Kate said.

"Yeah, a big one," Marie chipped in. The sentiment coming from Marie made Kate laugh. Now there was loyalty for you. Woody could chat her up all he wanted and never work his way back into Marie Hartnack's good graces. The realization gave Kate her first sense of peace since learning she had to work for Morehead Woodson. She laughed harder, riding the release, and soon Marie was laughing too. "A great big one," she said, managing to coax a smile from her husband.

*   *   *

The fireworks display began around ten. "Those fucking torches weren't enough?" Ernie complained.

"Now, Ernie," Marie said, taking his arm and quickly looking around to see if anyone besides Kate had heard him. Marie was more concerned about her husband's drinking than his language, though neither vice was much of a liability on Wall Street as long as you showed up for work on time and did your job.

Two uniformed men flanked the fireworks launch pad, which had been assembled in front of the pool house. What money couldn't buy, Kate thought, wishing they would hurry up and get the show underway. She would be leaving with the Hartnacks as soon as the fireworks ended. She didn't like the way her conversation with Woody had gone; that whole exchange about chaperones felt wrong. Maybe things would be better when he started at Matheson, where their interaction could be focused on something impersonal, like the market.

The first Roman candles went off successfully and drew appreciative exclamations from the guests, who had gathered at the edge of the terrace. Marie and Ernie wandered onto the lawn and sat at one of the umbrella tables some distance from the group, but Kate remained on the flagstones with the other people her age.

"Not bad. Not Macy's, but not bad." The sound of Woody's voice made Kate start. Assuming his comment had been directed elsewhere, she didn't turn around, though she was acutely aware of his presence. Then he came alongside her and watched a few more rockets launch. "I need to speak with you."

"Right now?"

He nodded and stepped back from the group, clearing a path for her to follow him to the other end of the terrace. "You keep disappearing. You're not avoiding me, are you?"

"No," Kate lied, "just watching the fireworks."

He patted his pants' pockets, front and back, then held his hands out, flipping them palms up, palms under, as if frisking himself. "All right?"

She smiled and sat down on the stone bench, the only friendly gesture she could think of. He sat down, too, but left a space between them. "Jim said he told you about my joining Matheson."

Kate cupped her hands on her knees. "He told me today. Congratulations. When do you start?"

"I'm telling Salomon first thing Monday, which means I'll probably see all of you around ten o'clock." He grinned, though on Woody it looked more like baring his teeth.

There were no long good-byes on Wall Street. The minute someone announced he was leaving to join a competitor he became *persona non grata*. Kate had heard stories about people not being allowed to return to their desks to get their things. Within hours of such a departure, word would spread around the trading floor that management was relieved to see the guy go. He had been on the fade, losing his edge, not a team player. Quite frankly, he wasn't that bright. His decision to leave on his own accord had saved everybody a lot of time and trouble. The reaction was predictable.

"How long have you been at Salomon?" she said.

"Ten years. Ten years this month, to be exact."

"We'd throw you a party at Matheson."

Woody opened his mouth as if to say something, but seemed to think better of it. "I understand you used to cover bill accounts," he said.

"I was in sales before I moved to the trading desk."

"I'm close to a number of those accounts myself, and from what I hear, your successor is nowhere near the salesman you are."

"I don't know about that." Kate was uncomfortable receiving a compliment at someone else's expense, but she wondered which of her clients Woody had talked to, or if he was making it up. Maybe Woody wanted to get together with some bill investors, she thought, which wasn't a bad idea. Clients were usually flattered to meet the traders, particularly the ones in charge.

"We have an opportunity to completely dominate the bill market. It's staring us right in the face." Woody folded his arms across his chest and peered at Kate, as if waiting for her to read his mind.

"We're sure working on it," she said, glancing at her watch.

"You made that pretty clear in the last year-bill auction."

Kate looked up sharply, but Woody smiled with a teasing sort of respect, as though he bore her no hard feelings for his loss of money and face. She wished she could think of a clever—but not *too* clever—comeback that might keep their conversation rolling. The best she could do was wince and duck her head in the same joking manner he had used.

"What I'm thinking is that with me on the desk, we could free you up to cover bill accounts again," Woody said. "Hartnack could handle the day-to-day trading, and I'd run the big risk positions based on the intelligence you gather. We'd be unbeatable."

To sell from the trading desk would be unconventional and hard to juggle, Kate thought, not to mention the potential for conflict of interest. She couldn't imagine management approving such an arrangement, but that was for Jim and Woody to work out. "I never thought of covering accounts from the trading desk," she said.

"That'd be pretty tough," Woody said, "even for someone with your talent. What I meant was to have you sell full-time, back in sales. That's where our competitive advantage comes in."

Kate looked at him for a moment, then stared into the darkened recesses of the Fletchers' property. She could hear people behind her reacting to the fireworks. The volume and duration of their oohs and aahs crescendoed with the final stages of the display. She had kidded with Ernie about getting dumped from the trading desk, and how Woody's aversion to women as colleagues would do her in. And here he was, losing no time. He wasn't even on Matheson's payroll yet.

"Have you run this past Jim?" Kate said.

"Jim and I have talked about a lot of things. I don't remember whether this came up specifically."

In other words, no. An unexpected composure settled upon her, though she was certain it wouldn't last. "It's an interesting idea," she said, feigning serious consideration, "but the way it's set up now is working, and I'd like to stay with trading." She spoke definitively and nodded a couple times as if confirming a meeting of two minds.

"I think it's best to stay open-minded," Woody said, his tone now abrupt. "Our focus has to be what's right for the business and not the wishes of any one individual."

Kate studied him in the shadowy light of the terrace and thought how starkly anger had changed his hand-some face. "I'm all for open-mindedness, and I've never been someone who shoots from the hip."

Woody stood and looked down at her indifferently, like an animal turning its nose up at small prey. "We'll talk again next week," he said, and walked off.

*　　*　　*

The leave-taking seemed interminable. Kate tried to sound sincere when she thanked Jim and Claudia for their hospitality. By the time she slid into the back seat of the Hartnacks' old Mercedes, the control she had mustered during her final exchange with Woody was gone. She was agitated and eager to spill her guts to Ernie, but Marie's presence made her hesitate. Marie didn't need to hear any more of Kate's angst about their new boss. She might not even know yet that Woody was coming to Matheson. Many wives of men in the business seemed unaware of what their husbands did during the day, other than make a great living. The men left each morning before the rest of the household was up, and came home late at night, often after the children had gone to bed.

Ernie sat on the passenger side of the car's front seat and smoked, staring straight ahead, while Marie drove through the Greenwich hills toward the parkway to Rye, the Westchester suburb where she and Ernie lived. Several minutes passed silently. Kate regretted accepting the Hartnacks' invitation to stay overnight. If she had gone home, she could have called Liz.

Ernie rolled down the car window and flicked his cigarette butt out into the night. "Mind if I leave it open?" he said, turning his head slightly toward the back seat. Kate scooted forward until she hung on his shoulder like a parrot.

"The breeze feels great," Kate said. She waited a moment for Ernie's follow-up, and plunged in when none came. "Woody thinks I should go back into sales. He said we could dominate the bill market with a three-pronged approach. I told him I wanted to stay in trading, but he made it sound like that was up for debate."

Ernie grunted. "He's blowing smoke at you."

"Why?"

"He's throwing his weight around, showing you who's boss. He wants you slinking around like a whipped dog. 'Yessir, Mr. Woodson, sir, whatever you think is best.'"

"Well, I didn't say *that.*"

Ernie chuckled softly. "No, I don't suppose you did. I've got to teach you how to bullshit better."

"Don't you dare," Marie said, sounding appalled by the suggestion. "Kate was perfectly lovely. If you ask me, Morehead's the one who should worry about making a better impression."

"Yeah, but it doesn't work that way," Kate said.

"He's not going to take you on," Ernie said. "Not right away. He'll pick off the limping lambs first, the ones Jim will let him fire without an argument. That ought to keep him busy for a month anyway." Ernie spoke as though he had seen it all before, as if they could bank on his prediction. "We've just got to keep making money. That's our insurance policy."

Kate slumped back against the soft leather seat, only

mildly relieved. She thought about the people on the desk who could no longer pull their weight, particularly with the bank trying to break into the securities business and facing the kind of competition that had given rise to men like Woody. Ernie was right: firing people would be a dramatic way for Woody to communicate change. She could imagine him relishing the role, though it wouldn't prove much about his ability to build a business.

As they drove through the warm July night, Kate could hear the rumbling of fireworks through Ernie's open window. They seemed to be going off everywhere.

Kate woke up in the middle of the night not knowing where she was. Lying on her side, her cheek indenting freshly laundered linen, she saw the reddish glow of a digital clock and remembered that she was at the Hartnacks' house, sleeping in their daughter's old room, converted to a guest room after she'd married and moved away.

Kate rolled onto her back and thought about Woody and the way his expression had changed from charming to caustic. Despite what Ernie had said about their trading profits insuring their jobs, she knew there would be no immunity to the malaise Woody would introduce to the trading room. She chided herself for thinking she might approach him as an equal. Had he intended all along to move her back into sales, or had she precipitated the suggestion by rebuffing his so-called friendly overtures?

She would have to avoid interaction with him until she could learn to read him better. In the meantime, there was Ernie. She would lie low and run things past him.

She rolled onto her side and pulled the bedclothes up under her chin. "Things will look better in the morning," she whispered. It was what her mother had said whenever Kate was upset. And her mother's reassurance had always been accurate, a testament to her wisdom and experience. Or so it had seemed, until Kate got older and realized that the petty nature of her problems had something to do with how quickly she got over them.

Before the severity of her mother's medical condition was recognized, Kate's concept of trouble was simple: she didn't have one. In the early stages of what she had described as "not feeling herself," her mother had started taking a nap before dinner, but other than that, nothing seemed changed in Kate's life. Her mother saw them out the door in the morning and was waiting for them with a snack when they came home. Kate was completely unaware of the adjustments taking place in her mother's routine while she and Liz were at school.

Kate remembered when that had changed, or at least when, looking back, she could cite the beginning of the change. On that particular day, her father had driven her mother up to Stanford for a work-up by a specialist. Kate was told to pick Liz up after school and bring her home. Assuming their parents were still out, the sisters walked down the driveway to the back door, which was always left unlocked. To Kate's surprise, her parents were already home. Framed by the kitchen window, they were sitting across from each other in what the family called the breakfast booth. They didn't look up when the girls climbed the porch stairs, and when they came through the door, it was their father who spoke first, telling Liz that he was taking them for ice cream. Kate had glanced at her mother, a believer in before-dinner treats like fresh fruit or an orange juice bar. But her mother didn't protest, not even mildly. It was this indifference to a rule on her mother's part and her father's jovial taking-charge that introduced a new and different level of anxiety into Kate's life.

Ted's farewell phone call had been like that too, she thought, as she lay in the dark in Linda Hartnack's old room. Kate remembered every detail. That his call had come on a Saturday afternoon around four; that she had answered the phone in the kitchen, staring at her to-do list on the message pad. And after Ted had hung up, saying he was sorry for the tenth time, how she had started to set the dining room table for dinner, too stunned to absorb what had just taken place.

Where had Ted been when he called? A phone booth in the hospital, one in the row of booths made available for bearers of bad news? Or had he called from the woman's apartment after spending the afternoon together, discussing how he would break the news to his wife? It had occurred to Kate later, when Ted's whereabouts at the time of the call began to torment her, that she should have immediately called the hospital and had him paged. She could have hung up if he'd answered.

The end of a marriage wasn't life or death, her father had told her, trying to be a comfort about a situation he couldn't comprehend. But Ted's departure had produced an anxiety like the one she'd experienced when her mother was ill, the kind that carried over from one day to the next, the kind you woke up with and felt in your gut before the source registered in your mind.

Was her new boss going to make her anxious in the same way? Woody's comments at Jim's party shouldn't merit this level of concern; she didn't want them to anyway. She should be thicker-skinned by now. She would never have gotten this far in business if she had let every sexist piss-ant get to her. The business world teemed with types like Woodson; Kate had encountered her fair share. Her first boss in Baltimore, taking her for lunch at the Playboy Club to discuss her next assignment; the client who refused to shake her hand when she visited his office because—as he told her flat out, in front of the male associates accompanying her—he didn't believe in women's lib; the senior banker who said, "I enjoyed your little presentation," after she had salvaged their pitch for a new piece of business, one he'd almost blown with a rambling discussion of boilerplate instead of answering the client's questions. Other than a few notable exceptions—Jim and Ernie came to mind— Morehead Woodson was the same man Kate had been dealing with since she started working.

She sat up in bed and switched on the lamp on the

bedside table. She wished she had a cookie. It was her father's antidote for insomnia, and it always worked. When you ate a cookie, he had explained, your body had to concentrate on digestion, and the blood rushing from your brain to your stomach made you drowsy. This had seemed intuitively logical to the teenaged Kate. Throughout the final months of her mother's illness, Kate and her father would bump into each other in the kitchen several nights a week. Silently, he would pour them each a glass of milk while she got the Oreos down from the cupboard. They would sit across from each other in the breakfast booth, sometimes talking, but usually not. They drank their milk and ate the cookies and then went back to bed.

Kate leaned against the headboard and looked around Linda Hartnack's old room. It had a pre-Beatles feel to it. The dresser and desk were painted cornflower blue, the color of the flowers on the wallpaper. Pale green sashes tied back curtains of white eyelet cotton. A bookshelf still housed the paperbacks from a 1960s' high-school English curriculum: four Shakespeare, four Dickens, and four by various women writers—Austen, Eliot, Brontë, and Wharton. Kate thought about getting out of bed for a book, but the effort seemed too ambitious.

She reached instead for the magazine Liz had given her, and thumbed through it for a while. The air conditioning came on, its white noise lulling. She tossed the magazine aside and turned off the light. Despite her expectations to the contrary, Kate fell asleep and did not stir until Marie tapped on the bedroom door in the morning.

Chapter 5

As he had predicted, Morehead Woodson arrived at the bank around ten o'clock on the Monday after Jim's party. Stylishly dressed in a dark, pinstriped suit and a tie the color of butter, Woody stood out from the rumpled mid-morning look of the rest of the men on the floor. But he would have been spotted no matter what his attire. Little escaped the attention of the sales and trading staff, who were paid to take notice. On the threshold to the trading room, Woody paused a fraction of a second before crossing the width of the floor. He presented himself to Jim's secretary, who showed him into Jim's office, took orders for coffee, and shut the door quietly behind her. The drapes remained open on the office's interior windows, which looked out on the trading floor, allowing everyone to witness Jim's enthusiastic reception of his new head trader.

Lloyd Keezer, who had been on the phone, pacing behind the front row of sales desks, scrambled back to his seat. Tucking himself into his desk as if it were a cockpit, he lowered his head and announced in a pilot's monotone: "The eagle has landed."

Kate noted this first public acknowledgment of Woody's presence with an odd sense of relief. Keeping the news quiet had been a strain, and she had long since exhausted Ernie's willingness to discuss it. She was interested in fresh reaction to the big news. She thought she might feel better if others shared her apprehension.

Ernie was ready with a blasé response to Keezer's announcement. "Must be someone from the banking department," Ernie said.

"He's not a banker, but you're going to wish he were." Keezer sounded smug, though he had just heard the news on his last phone call. It wasn't much lead time, but the slightest jump was worth parading. "He's the pain-in-the-ass from Salomon Brothers—and your new boss." Keezer chuckled, his front teeth protruding slightly from his round, fleshy face, which made him look cartoonish.

Ernie sniffed with pretend indifference. In other circumstances, he would have pursued Keezer, prying the information out of him over the phone, even though they sat steps away from each other. Keezer would divulge all he knew, though he would toy with Ernie first. The two men had come into the bond business via the back office. That, and their subsequent years together on the line, made them comrades, particularly regarding the *arrivistes* on Wall Street, who were taking over the investment banks, and now it seemed, with Morehead Woodson at A. J. Matheson, the commercial banks too.

Kate sat at her desk and watched Keezer debrief several

salesmen huddled around him. She listened attentively, but did not speak; she wasn't ready to be engaged on the subject. Woody's parting words at the barbecue—that they would "talk next week"—had hung over her all weekend. Despite Ernie's reassurance, she worried what would happen when Woody showed up for work. She glanced at Jim's office. Maybe Woody was pitching his idea for the bill desk to Jim.

Kate brought herself up short: what was she thinking? Woody was a *bond* man, and not about to mention the bill desk in his opening minutes on the job. He would look like a fool, as if he didn't understand why he had been hired. His baiting her at Jim's party had been for sport, like pulling the handle of a slot machine on the way into a high stakes game in the back room. All this seemed obvious, now that she was physically at work, and out of the time warp of life away from the trading room.

Morehead Woodson's expertise was in bonds, and his relationships with the investors who bought bonds—both corporate and government—were what made him valuable to Matheson. Since the Glass-Steagall Act of 1933, the bank had been prohibited from underwriting and trading in stocks and corporate bonds, an activity that had contributed to bank failures during the Great Depression. That law still stood, though Matheson and other commercial banks were lobbying hard to repeal it. By recruiting Salomon Brothers' top bond trader, Matheson was signaling its intent to become a player in all sectors of the bond market as soon as it could find a way to do it legally. Kate imagined that this was exactly how Jim had positioned the idea to Phil Armstrong, Chairman of the Board at Matheson. Woody might want to get rid of her, but making changes to the bill desk his first official act was out of the question.

Now that she had grasped the essence of Woody's situation, Kate felt much better. "What have you got for us, Rosemary?" she said brightly to the heavyset position clerk, who had planted herself next to Ernie.

Rosemary handed them each a sheet of paper. "An announcement from senior management," she said, pleased to have a role in the breaking news.

Ernie squinted at the sheet and pretended to read from it. "'*The bank will be closed for the weekend*.' Christ, not again. Why do they keep doing this to me?" He looked plaintively at Rosemary.

"If you don't want to know what's going on around here, just say so." Rosemary put out an arm to retrieve the memo, but Ernie clutched the paper to his chest, which seemed to satisfy her. She jerked her head toward Jim's office. "The new guy's in there now."

Ernie swiveled in his chair and craned his neck to get a better look. "Have you met him yet, Rose?"

Kate watched Ernie's performance, admiring his sense of theater. He tried to have fun with whatever went down in the trading room. It sometimes crossed her mind that she was way too serious for this business.

"Not yet, but I'm looking forward to it," Rosemary said. "He's good-looking. Single, too, I understand." She glanced at Kate, who smiled gamely.

Ernie caught Kate's expression, and his eyes recorded surprise before he continued his teasing of Rosemary. "What would Albert say?"

Albert was Rosemary's husband. In the wedding photo that she kept on her desk, Rosemary appeared a foot taller than Albert because of the geyser of tulle rising from her head. Albert worked in operations at the Federal Reserve Bank on Liberty Street, a few blocks away from Matheson. The newlyweds commuted to and from work together. Rosemary had recently bragged to everyone in the trading room about Albert's rapid promotion from the accounting pool to staff accountant in the debt management department, the office that provided advice and analysis on the issuance of U.S. Treasury securities and financial markets.

"What Albert always says: just because I'm on a diet doesn't mean I can't read the menu." Rosemary threw her head back and laughed, but sobered up quickly. "Probably stuck on himself though. Men that good-looking usually are."

Ernie clasped Rosemary's hand and looked at her with beseeching eyes. "You think I'm stuck on myself?"

During the course of this play-acting, Lloyd Keezer had edged down the aisle of salesmen until he stood across from the bill desk. He positively twitched with impatience.

When he could stand it no longer, he reached over the top of the counter and grabbed at Rosemary's memos. Startled, then irritated, she pulled her hand away from Ernie and slapped at his arm. "Quit your nonsense now. I've got to get these out." She handed Keezer a memo. "Jim said to deliver them simultaneously."

"Simultaneously? With what? Is something else happening?" Ernie's head whipped from left to right, but Rosemary and Keezer had already walked off.

Kate skimmed the memo. "Did you know that Woody went to Yale?"

"Now isn't that nice. Does it say which eating club he belonged to?" Ernie crumpled his copy of the memo and arched it into the wastebasket.

"No mention of where he ate." Kate pulled open the lower drawer of her desk and placed the memo into a hanging file.

Jim and Woody emerged from the office around noon. Like Jim, Woody had shed his suit jacket, though he hadn't rolled up his sleeves. As he approached the center of the room, Kate tried to see if there was embroidery on his shirt cuff. Jim began to introduce him to the traders, each one standing in turn to shake Woody's hand. The traders seemed to take his presence in stride. Most still kept an eye on the screens as they exchanged pleasantries, then sat down when Woody moved on.

Kate stared at her screens without seeing them. Jim and Woody approached the desk of Adam Campbell, the two-year note trader who sat on the other side of Ernie, and two desks down from Kate. Adam was the most consistently profitable trader at Matheson. He made money on the minute-by-minute fluctuations in the market, movements he seemed to instinctively anticipate. But ask him to predict tomorrow's market, and he would invariably answer, "That's a tough call." When Kate was in sales, she thought Adam was evading her with that kind of response. But Ernie explained that Adam specialized in the near term—the *very* near term—and that it was a waste of time to ask him questions more forward-looking than the next hour.

Adam's narrow focus often proved useful. When Kate first came into trading, she remembered sitting with a three-month bill position that wasn't working out. Ernie had gone into the lunchroom, opening up the air space between her and Adam; when Adam looked to his right, he saw Kate instead of Ernie. This happened regularly enough, though Adam always seemed surprised. "How's it going, Kate?" he would say, as if they hadn't seen each other in months. She told Adam about her position in three-month bills, and how she thought the economic news expected later in the week would bring buyers into the short end of the bill sector and make the market rise. But she was losing money on the trade and beginning to wonder if her thinking was flawed.

"A lot of people I talk to have got that trade on,"

Adam said. In other words, Kate was positioned like every other dealer on Wall Street. Where would new bill buyers come from with everyone already long? She dumped the three-month bills and took a loss, but nothing like the hit she would have taken if she had held on—as it turned out, even for another hour. At the end of the day, when she thanked Adam for his advice, he had looked at her quizzically, seemingly unaware that he'd provided any.

Today, as usual, Adam sat hunched over his desk, oblivious to all but the screens.

Jim tapped him on the shoulder and gave him the news about his promotion, and Woody taking over as head trader. "That's great," Adam said, a lazy grin on his face. He looked from Jim to Woody and back at Jim again, then stood up and stuck out his hand in what appeared to be an afterthought.

Was there a more relaxed human being than Adam? Kate wondered about the impression he had just made, and whether she would fare better with Woody if she were more like Adam, though a woman like Adam would never have been brought onto the trading desk.

As Woody and Jim approached Ernie, an outside phone call was announced for Kate. Telephones didn't "ring" in the trading room. Instead the phone turrets on the desks of the sales and trading staff displayed a panel of lights that would flash as a call came through. Traders and salesmen picked up their own direct lines. For traders, direct lines were the ones that connected them to other dealers and brokers. In the case of the salesmen, direct lines were to customers whose volume of business justified the additional expense. The rest of the incoming calls were fielded by a trio of phone operators, who announced them over small intercom units on each sales and trading desk.

Judy, the senior operator, had discerned everyone's private life from these calls. She knew if you were in love or out of luck, and had suspected that Kate and Ted were separated long before anyone else. Kate could read it in her eyes whenever she dropped off a batch of phone messages, all from Liz and none from Ted.

"It's your sister," Judy now announced over Kate's intercom. Kate looked at the flashing cube that would connect her to Liz. To her left, Woody and Ernie were yukking it up over something. Should she take the call and duck Woody, or have the second encounter with him and be done with it? Over the intercom Judy's voice inquired: "Kate?"

"She'll be right with you," Woody said, stepping closer. The intercom went momentarily silent, then beeped off. "Talk to your sister." He gestured for Kate to stay seated, and she noticed the dollar signs embroidered in green on his cuff. "I'll stop by later." He smiled down at her in his superior manner, but she looked away, furious that he had pre-empted her decision about the call. She stared at the handle on her desk drawer, suppressing an impulse to jerk the drawer open and into Woody's kneecap.

"We really should be going up to lunch," Jim said, checking the overhead clock. "The Chairman usually arrives about now." Jim smiled and thumped the top of Kate's chair in a sign of goodwill.

A few minutes later, she watched them leave the trading floor together. They were wearing their suit jackets.

Woody came back from lunch in high spirits. He stopped by Kate's desk to ask how the bill auctions had gone, put in his two cents about the market, then headed off to Personnel to be photographed and fingerprinted. Rubbing elbows with senior management seemed to have a cheering effect on men. On women too, Kate imagined, though she had yet to experience the phenomenon. The only time she'd seen the executive dining room was on a tour of the building for new employees.

Woody attended the afternoon trading meeting in Jim's office. At first he didn't say much. When Jim asked for his opinion, Woody offered an innocuous comment: he was the new guy on the block and still figuring out where the men's room was. The first trader to arrive, Kate sat in the corner of the sofa closest to the door, though most traders sat on the floor, their backs against the wall and their legs jutting out into the center of the room. They wisecracked and spouted opinions unguardedly, as if nothing at work had changed. But after ten minutes, Jim rose from his chair and announced that Woody was officially oriented and would begin to earn his keep. Jim joked about getting in nine holes of golf before the sun went down. He slung his suit jacket over his shoulder and left to a chorus of envious groans. Through the window that looked out on the trading floor, Kate watched him go.

Woody stood up and made his way through the traders seated on the floor to Jim's desk. He sat down in Jim's high-backed swivel chair. The meeting proceeded, though the mood was subdued. Each trader recounted what had happened in his sector of the market, describing the trades he had seen and the ones being done away. One or two traders ventured predictions for the trading week ahead. Kate stayed quiet, observing how the discussion never veered from the market or erupted in laughter the way it did with Jim behind the desk. Eventually the traders started shifting in their seats; there wasn't much left to say. The two traders sitting closest to the door assumed that the meeting was over and stood up to clear the exit.

"Did a bell ring?" Woody said. He looked around the room as though searching for a phantom source. Sheepishly, the two traders sat down.

Woody said he was giving them all an assignment. He wanted them to rank the trading staff, from first to last, according to each trader's contribution and importance to the desk. They were to complete this task by the end of the week. "Any questions?"

Adam Campbell spoke up. "You mean put together

a batting order?"

"A batting order. Now that's interesting. Who sets the table? Who bats cleanup?" Woody looked from trader to trader as though considering them for the various positions. "I think we'd better keep it simple: little steps for little people. Just do it from top to bottom—and rank yourselves in there, too. In writing, on my desk, by the end of the week." He leaned back in Jim's chair in a proprietary manner. No one moved. "You can go now," he said, and watched them file out of the office.

Back at their desks, the traders barely looked at each other and said even less. Woody's directive felt like the request of a tyrant.

"Talk about a camaraderie killer," Kate said quietly to Ernie.

"Ignore it," he said. "That's what I'm going to do."

Dodging the assignment had never occurred to Kate. She watched Ernie switch off his screens and put away his pencils. "You think you'll get away with that?"

"It's worth a try."

On the subway ride home, Kate toyed with the notion of following Ernie's lead and ignoring Woody, but she quickly abandoned the idea as a solution only her partner could pull off. The patriarch of the bond department, Ernie often exempted himself from this kind of directive. Over the years, he had tested his theory that management wasn't paying attention, and discovered how easy civil disobedience could be. Kate had the opposite problem: she always did more than what was expected. Ignoring authority figures was not in her make-up. Despite her disdain for Woody, it bothered her to be on his bad side, where she would forever remain if she disregarded his first official request.

She decided to walk the final leg of her commute and exited the subway at 42nd Street. The sidewalks outside Grand Central were filled with office workers in lightweight suits and tourists in T-shirts and thick-soled athletic shoes. She went up Lexington to 46th Street and crossed one block west to Park Avenue. Moving into the school of people heading north on the wide sidewalk, Kate felt anonymous and safe, so different from how she felt at work, now that she reported to Woody instead of Jim. She worried that dislike for her new boss might undermine her performance.

"You trade with your head, not your heart," Jim Fletcher had once told her, and meant it as a compliment. She wondered if every profession placed a premium on holding emotions in check. Veteran traders claimed it was key to survival in their business; certainly Jim would never have put her on the trading desk if he considered her emotional. As for men slamming down phones and cursing at the sales force? That wasn't emotion; it was part of trading room color.

Only to Liz had Kate confided how much she relied

on feelings to do her job. It took courage to make a bet on incomplete information, and then keep her nerve through uncertainty, hoping the market would prove her right. And it was fear that drove her to reduce or eliminate her exposure when she thought she'd been mistaken in her judgment or timing. Though she would never admit it to Jim or even to Ernie, emotions were behind her every decision. The trick was looking calm even when her gut was churning, something she had been doing for as long as she could remember, behavior she would have to keep up.

As Kate walked past the Waldorf and St. Bart's and into the residential blocks of Park Avenue, she grew more conscious of her surroundings. The weather was beautiful, warm and dry, a light breeze blowing. Well-tended flower gardens bloomed in the center of the avenue. Such tranquil, unhurried moments were rare in her day. She did everything in the most efficient way possible, measuring a day's success by how much she had accomplished, even away from work. She would tell people she was going to relax over the weekend, then start every Saturday by making a to-do list. When she found herself completing something she hadn't previously listed, she would write the job down and put a line through it.

She turned the corner at 72nd Street and walked through the entrance to her building. "Good evening, Miss Munro," Frank said, touching the visor of his hat. She slowed her pace slightly for the exchange of pleasantries. When she first moved in, she had tried unsuccessfully to get him to call her "Kate." But now she liked being greeted this way every evening. It was a grace note in a city that didn't offer many.

When Kate was summoned to Woody's office at the end of his first week at Matheson, she assumed it was to discuss her memo about the trading desk. She had met his Friday deadline, though not the specification to rank the traders in order of their contribution and value. Her first attempt had been an alphabetical listing in which she described each trader's strengths and suggested an "area for development."

When she showed the memo to Ernie, he had immediately skipped to the lines about him. "You think I could show more patience with the sales force?" he said incredulously. The notion that people in business preferred the direct approach was completely false.

"I had to put something down."

"No, you didn't."

"You want me to take it out? Here." Kate reached for the memo, which Ernie handed back with a look of disgruntled resignation.

"Go ahead, leave it in. I *am* impatient, and who gives a fuck?"

Kate obliterated the offending lines with a flair-tip pen. "I'm sorry. I sound like an ass in this memo. I don't know what I was thinking."

Ernie seemed somewhat soothed. "What you wrote is accurate, as far as that goes, but you're missing the point. Why make it easier for him? Name, rank, and serial number, Kate. Name, rank and serial number."

Kate had revised the memo, limiting it to praise for her co-workers. But as she approached the cramped, windowless conference room that Woody used as an office, she worried about his reaction. She heard Woody's voice and stopped short of the doorway. He was talking on the phone to the portfolio manager at the World Bank, a man whose clout and unusual first name were well known on Wall Street. "The way I see it, Svem," and "That's a good point, Svem." Woody had a habit of repeatedly mentioning a person's name when he wanted to impress.

Kate moved into the doorway and saw Woody sitting at the small, round table he used as a desk. He looked up and gestured for her to come in. The only vacant chair was wedged into a corner directly opposite him, so she stood waiting for him to finish his conversation. Instead he turned on the speakerphone. Making her an eavesdropper seemed an odd thing to do, but maybe he wanted to introduce her to Svem. Kate waited a minute longer, but the conversation continued. "I'll come back later," she mouthed when Woody looked up, but he pointed his finger at the empty chair and pulled the table back a few inches so she could squeeze into the space.

Kate sat down and studied the room. The walls were

covered with a simulated grass cloth and the framed hunt scenes that hung everywhere in the bank. A screen, a phone, an intercom unit, and a gym bag emblazoned with the DAC logo and *Home of the Heisman*, sat on top of a credenza. On the table in front of Woody were an unlit cigar and two pieces of silver and black smoking equipment. His left hand rested on her memo.

"Svem, I love you," Woody said and got off the phone. He slid the memo across the tabletop. "What did these guys do, pay you?"

Name, rank, and serial number, Kate remembered, and smiled noncommittally.

Woody picked up the cigar and slowly went through an elaborate ritual of preparing it to smoke. After cutting, lighting, and turning the cigar, he snapped the lighter shut and laid it on the table. Smoke flumed from his rounded mouth. It was inexcusable, Kate thought, the way men smoked cigars in quarters as close as these. She had once observed a visibly pregnant secretary taking dictation from a man smoking a cigar. The woman had sat in the office doorway, leaning her head into the hallway to avoid the nauseating smell.

Woody stared at Kate, waiting for a response. "We've got a good group," she said.

"Yeah, a real bunch of all-stars. You know how long they'd last away from here?" He took the cigar from his mouth and laid it on the side of the ashtray. "By the way, none of them had any trouble ranking you."

Woody was baiting her again. The few traders who would actually make his Friday deadline were probably still writing their memos back at the desk.

"Really?" she said. "How'd I do?"

Woody maintained his pose for a few seconds before succumbing to a guilty grin. "Jim suggested that I meet with everyone, so that's what I'm doing."

"Did he suggest the memo too?" Kate said.

"No, that was my idea." He picked up the metal lighter, repeatedly snapping it open and shut. He seemed as uncomfortable as she was. "Tell me something," he said, dropping the confrontational tone. "When was the last time someone around here got fired?"

"I don't remember anyone getting fired. One or two people left on their own, but otherwise things have been pretty stable."

"That's one way of putting it." He set the lighter aside. "Have you worked anywhere else?"

"Not in New York."

"You realize what a joke this place is, don't you? It's the laughingstock of the securities business." Woody spoke collegially, like one scientist sharing his theories with another, though his characterization of the bank struck her as unfair. The push into the securities business *was* fairly recent, but Matheson was a highly respected institution, regarded by many as the best commercial bank in the country.

"I thought we were considered a sleeping giant," Kate said, quoting the backhanded compliment she had heard about her employer.

Woody looked amused. "It's like a country club around here. The shoeshine guy who comes around? And the way they give you all new currency when they cash your checks? Meanwhile you could fire off a cannon at five o'clock and not hit anybody on the trading floor." He shook his head. "This place pays attention to all the wrong things."

If Woody meant his comments to be insulting, Kate didn't take offense. She understood what he was talking about. Matheson did have a clubby atmosphere, and its share of employees with more pedigree than talent, especially in the bond department. But that state of affairs was probably why she had gotten a break. If there had been a man with comparable skills available for the bill-trading job, Jim would have undoubtedly selected him.

And why tell her all this? Was Woody looking for empathy from someone who didn't fit the profile, someone without connections who worked past five? Maybe it was because she was female, someone he didn't consider a competitor, someone unlikely to capitalize on his tacit admission of poor judgment. Salomon had told Woody that he didn't figure into their future management plans, not an easy thing to hear, but he had overreacted, and his hasty departure from Salomon Brothers now seemed to be troubling him.

"I didn't leave Salomon to manage a bunch of light-weights with well-connected parents."

Kate gave a little start: it was eerie to be on the same wavelength. "No," she said, "I don't suppose you did."

"What's that supposed to mean?"

"Nothing," she said quickly. "Just that it's hard to know a place from the outside. I remember when I first got here, I went home every night, took two aspirin, and went to bed. The trading room was so loud and big. It made where I came from look like a dollhouse."

"Yeah, well, I'm used to loud and big." Woody studied the screen on top of the credenza. "What would you do, if you were me?" He glanced at Kate, then started fidgeting with the lighter again.

She hadn't expected his candor, or the twinge of sympathy she felt. She wanted to encourage this kind of exchange, or at least make him think that asking for her advice wasn't a waste of time. What would she do if she were Woody? She would be more like Jim, who had shown that trading success didn't have to exclude fairness and decency. But Woody would probably find that advice insulting, and she couldn't tell him what she really thought: that in leaving Salomon Brothers for A. J. Matheson, he had already made his biggest mistake.

"I need to give it some thought," she said.

Woody flicked the ash from his cigar. "Let me know when it comes to you."

Kate leaned forward to explain, but the phone rang and she sat back in her chair. Woody grabbed the receiver and launched into conversation, laughing into the mouthpiece. She waited for him to signal whether or not she should stay. When he leaned back and put his feet up on the credenza, she got up and quietly left the room.

Chapter 6

Woody fired two traders at the end of July. Word spread rapidly through the trading room that the bank had been generous with the severance package, giving both men a year's salary and the use of an employment agency until they found jobs. "Where do I sign?" Ernie said when he heard the terms of the deal. But he wasn't serious. He would never volunteer for a retirement package.

Kate listened without comment as the men on the trading desk protested. It was hard to see people get fired, though in her unvoiced opinion, Woody had correctly identified the two weakest contributors. That she could formulate such a thought made her feel guilty, but the departing traders seemed relieved to be going after the hazing that Woody had put them through. In the weeks leading up to their dismissal, he had badgered and be-littled them in the morning meetings, attended by every-one on the floor. One trader would express his opinion only to have Woody cut him off and contradict him. When the other trader played it safe and stuck to the facts of the market's previous session, Woody disputed the account. Intimidated by their new boss, the surviving traders became cautious and restricted their commentary to rote recitations. The sales force complained that the meeting had become a waste of time; they claimed they got a better briefing from the *Wall Street Journal.*

"Quit bellyaching," Ernie told a knot of salesmen hanging around the bill desk late one afternoon. With Woody on the prowl, people had begun to stay past five. "Try selling vacuum cleaners door-to-door if you think you've got it so bad," Ernie said.

Though Woody had steered clear of the bill traders, Ernie rarely attended the sales meeting any more, leaving it to Kate to deliver the bill report from the doorway, then exit under the guise of pressing business. She tried to remain positive. At least once an hour, she got on the intercom with trade suggestions and comments on the intra-day movement in the bill market, which gave the salesmen a reason to call their customers. The extra attention was paying off. Bill transactions increased, and the number of customers who bid through Matheson in the auctions was also on the rise.

"Now Albert and I both have to stay late on auction days," Rosemary said, proud about the increased activity she was processing for the bill desk.

But it was sad to watch the atmosphere in the trading room deteriorate. There had been such a spirit of camaraderie and fun when Jim ran the show. Kate wished he were around more, but he spent an increasing amount of time away from the trading floor, briefing the bank's senior management and strategizing about Matheson's expansion into the securities business. The only time she saw Jim now was the occasional afternoon when he meandered through the rows of desks in the trading room, hobnobbing with the salesmen and traders and picking up facts about the operation that he might otherwise miss.

"Yo, bill traders!" Jim shouted on one such afternoon from the far end of the row, where he'd been conferring with Woody. Jim held up a sheet of paper and waved it. "Looking good in the bill auctions. The Fed's got us at 10 per cent."

"That's dated information," Ernie yelled back. "We're fifteen per cent. Show him your diary, Kate."

Kate shot Ernie a look, but it was too late. A disembodied falsetto voice rose from behind the phone turrets: "Dear Diary, you'll never believe what happened today in the bill market."

Woody led the laughter and seemed to be enjoying himself for the first time in weeks. Kate caught his eye, but he kept laughing, not bothering to restrain himself or even to look away. Her body burned with embarrassment. A trader's skill was supposed to appear natural, not the result of some drone-like taking of notes.

"You keep a journal, Kate? I did too, when I was on the desk." Jim's comment silenced the room. Did he really keep a journal, she wondered, or was he being like Eleanor Roosevelt, who drank from her finger bowl to cover a dinner guest's gaffe?

"It's more like a log," Kate soft-pedaled the effort. "It helps me keep track."

"We need a tracking system like that for every trader," Jim said, walking down the aisle to her desk. Not one for idle musing, he took a small manila card from his shirt pocket and scribbled a note to himself. "Can I take a look? As long as there's nothing too personal in there." He smiled and pumped his eyebrows at Kate. It seemed like a long time since she had experienced Jim's graceful form of praise.

She pulled out the bottom drawer of her desk and removed one of several speckled notebooks. She found the entry for last week's auction, which listed the amount of bills bid for and awarded to each customer. Her eye moved to the bottom line, and she quickly calculated. Ernie was right: their participation had been close to fifteen per cent of the last auction, ranking Matheson first among the thirty-six primary dealers who underwrote the government's debt.

Kate handed the notebook to Jim, who read through the roster of auction clients, asking about each new name on the list. He listened closely, smiling as if vicariously experiencing her successful business development. "Well done," he said, handing the notebook back.

As soon as Jim was out of earshot, Keezer's voice came over Kate's intercom. "Seven minutes: that's almost a record." Keezer had a practice of timing how long Jim spent with various individuals on his afternoon walkabouts.

How quickly they turn, she thought, certain now that Lloyd Keezer had been the falsetto voice with the dig about her journal. And after all the odd lot business she had helped him with! She started to say something smart, but held herself in check, remembering the criticism leveled at women: that they took everything personally instead of shrugging off slights, part of the give-and-take of business.

Kate leaned over the intercom to make sure that Keezer could hear her laugh. "Thanks for the post, Lloyd." She put her journal back into the drawer and picked up the phone to call Liz. She felt like spending the evening with someone indisputably on her side.

The cool, dark interior of JG Melon, an Upper East Side restaurant known for its burgers and cottage fries, was a relief after the steamy subway ride from downtown. In the past year, Kate and her sister had dined here frequently. As her eyes adjusted to dimmer light, Kate saw the hostess nod a greeting.

The restaurant's floor plan was like a keyhole, with a rectangular front room connecting to a rounded room at the back. Checked cloths covered the tables. On each, a sheaf of napkins was propped between a votive candle and a pair of salt and pepper shakers. Various representations of watermelons—water-colored, needlepointed, and woodcut—covered the walls. A framed still of a movie scene shot in the restaurant hung over the table where the actors had actually sat.

Seated by the window, Liz seemed lost in thought.

"Have you been here long?" Kate said, hooking her bag on the back of her chair.

Liz shook her head. "I wasn't far from here…a job on Fifth Avenue. A penthouse in a beautiful pre-war building. There's a view of the park from most of the rooms and an express elevator that opens into the foyer. The kitchen is top-of-the-line everything. The cabinets alone are $50,000."

"That's outrageous," Kate said.

"But good for the economy, right?" Liz unfolded a napkin and smoothed it across her lap. "This guy is trickling down the big bucks. He's related by marriage to Sally Townsend. Remember my first solo client? Sally's a big fan of mine."

"All your clients are big fans," Kate said.

Liz smiled, as if acknowledging her due. "It helps with referrals. There's no stated budget. Morehead Woodson the Third. Who'd do that to a kid?"

Kate felt a twist in her gut. "I suppose Morehead the Second."

"He's great-looking, like a *GQ* cover."

"If you like that type."

"What type is that?"

"Arrogant, condescending, completely out for himself."

"You know him?"

Kate waited a moment, reluctant to disclose the connection. "He's my boss," she finally said.

"You've got to be kidding! What happened to Jim?"

"He got promoted. Jim's running the whole department now. He brought Woody in to be head trader."

Liz's eyes narrowed. "What about you for that job?"

"Oh, Liz." Kate looked around for a waiter. "Woody has ten times more experience."

"Still, I'll bet you'd have gotten the job if you were a man."

Kate shook her head. "Jim wanted a marquee name, someone from an investment bank, someone who'll put us on the map."

"Can Woody do that?" Liz said, admiration in her tone. "I've got a key to his apartment, if you'd like to see it. He's away most weekends."

Kate pressed her lips into a disapproving line.

"I'm *kidding*!" Liz said. "Give me a little credit."

But Kate knew they would be there in a heartbeat if she had shown the slightest inclination. She shifted in her seat, looking for the waiter.

"And by the way, he's not my type," Liz said. "Sounds like you had a good day though. What happened, exactly?

You were pretty cryptic on the phone."

Kate provided a brief description of the Fed report and Jim's compliment, which hardly seemed worth mentioning now.

"What did Woody say?" Liz's interest in his reaction was irritating. Kate's good news was Jim's recognition of her success in Treasury bills, and not how Woody had reacted. Why did everything that happened lately seem to lead back to Morehead Woodson?

"He'll never fit in at Matheson," Kate said. "I think he's sorry he came to the bank."

"Maybe he'll go back to Salomon Brothers."

"That's not going to happen. Matheson's the only place that takes people back." Kate knew several bank employees who had tested the waters elsewhere and come running back to Matheson, which welcomed them back like prodigal sons. Cut the cord at Salomon Brothers, and it stayed cut.

A waiter finally arrived at their table. It was the same man who usually took their order. He was tall and lanky, good-looking in a burned-out sort of way. He had an efficient manner and didn't joke around or announce himself as their server, though tonight Kate would have welcomed the distraction.

"Things are going well at work though, aren't they?" Liz said, after the waiter left.

Kate thought a moment about Jim's public support

that afternoon on the trading floor. "It's not as fun as it used to be and Woody is a jerk, but as long as Jim's in charge, I guess things will be all right."

Liz watched the hostess as she seated a couple at the movie scene table.

"And I'd just as soon keep Woody in the dark about our being sisters," Kate added.

Liz looked back at her. "I take it you haven't mentioned me."

"He's the last guy I'd share anything personal with," Kate said. "It gives me the creeps to think of you working with him."

"Well, *you* work with him. What's the difference? It's not like either of us had a choice in the matter." Liz studied the menu, even though she always ordered the same thing.

"No, I guess not." Kate hadn't meant to give the impression that she mistrusted Liz, though her sister did let things slip. Liz didn't consider information as something to be held back: you knew it, you told it. They were different in that way. Kate held back even with those closest to her, even with Ted, though she had shared more with him than anyone, except for her mother, who had always seemed to know what was on Kate's mind whether or not she'd divulged it.

Liz turned the menu face down on the table. "Did I tell you I'm going to see Dad tomorrow? It's a spur-of-the-moment trip."

Of course she hadn't, Kate thought, hurt not to be invited to California, no matter how unlikely her acceptance. "I'm sure he's looking forward to seeing you."

"He sounded pleased. I'm on the first flight out, and I haven't packed."

"You should have said something."

"It's fine. I had to eat, and you kept me out of the kitchen."

Chapter 7

Light had begun to seep through the gap in the bedroom drapes. Kate turned away from the window and tried to fall back to sleep. It was too early to start a weekend in which she had nothing to do and no one to be with. She hadn't minded being alone when she was married. Even though Ted spent most of his time at the hospital, his eventual return had been something to build around, like planning a party once the guests have accepted. Then he left for good, and Liz stepped in. But her sister was in California for the weekend.

Kate slid her leg into the cool, unoccupied portion of her bed and quickly pulled it back. Sleeping alone in a big bed was depressing. She took a deep breath and forced herself upright. For a moment she sat there, fatigued by the effort, as if she were recovering from illness.

By mid-morning, she had exercised to a Jane Fonda videotape, eaten a bowl of cereal, taken a shower and dressed. She went out for the newspapers and read them, then looked around her pristine apartment, which never got messy now that Ted was gone. She didn't know what to do next. At work there were markets to watch, a continuous flow of new economic data to consider, commentary and analysis to absorb. The salesmen always had a bid list for her to price or a trade problem to work out.

She wandered from room to room, looking around at all that Liz had assembled. Kate remembered feeling proud that she could afford such beautiful things, though she couldn't recall how they had come into her possession. Except for the silver. Sitting on a butler's table in front of the sofa were a small bowl and a lidded box, part of a dresser set that had been her mother's and, before that, her grandmother's.

Kate brought the silver pieces into the kitchen. Taking a jar of polish from under the sink, she sponged the pungent cream onto the silver, its ornate trim an embossed leaf and scroll pattern. She lathered the pieces and set them to dry on the countertop.

She started to dial her father's number, then remembered how early it still was in California, and replaced the receiver. She rinsed the polish from the silver. The smoother surfaces gleamed, but the narrow grooves of the trim remained shaded with tarnish. She buffed each piece with a linen tea towel softened by hundreds of trips through the wash. "These are for you," her mother had told her a month before she died, "and the mirror and perfume bottle are for Liz."

Kate returned the silver pieces to the butler's table and scanned the room for anything else that might need attention. When her mother got sick, Kate would come home from school every day and furiously vacuum the living room, dragging the Hoover Upright back and forth, and scolding Liz when she left her things around the house. "You're taking such good care of us," her mother had said.

Kate took the silver pieces into her bedroom and placed them on the dresser. Then she got into bed and cried. She drifted off to sleep and woke up an hour later with a headache. She went into the bathroom, took two aspirin and splashed cold water on her face.

In the kitchen she opened the cupboards, looking for something to eat. There was a box of Uncle Ben's Converted Rice—"Converted from what?" she mumbled—and the cardboard canister of oatmeal that Ted had eaten to ward off the bad kind of cholesterol. She checked the oatmeal's freshness date and felt a pang to see it long since passed. She dumped the container into the garbage, and tried calling her father's house, but there was no answer. She went back into her bedroom and slipped some money and her house key into the pocket of her Bermuda shorts. In the mirror, her face was red and blotchy. She put on sunglasses and took the elevator downstairs.

The streets looked dirty, the way even clean neighborhoods do when it's muggy. She walked to a grocery store on Lexington and browsed the aisles, depositing items into a red plastic basket until it became heavy. A six-pack of cream soda, barbecued chips, a box of Oreos and a quart of skim milk. Waiting her turn at the checkout counter, she thumbed through a copy of *People* with Michael Jackson on the cover. The hell with it, she thought, and tossed the magazine into the basket.

Outside the store she stood on the sidewalk, immediately regretting her impulsive purchases. Two boys on skateboards approached. She thought about offering them her white plastic bags, but they banked around her and into the next corner.

On the way back to her apartment, she passed the church where she and Liz occasionally attended the Sunday service. They both liked the minister, and Liz was a patron of the church's annual rummage sale. On a bulletin board encased in glass and planted in a small patch of green between the church and the sidewalk, Kate read:

Sunday Worship Service

August 4, 1985

11: 00 A.M.

Sermon: "The Time for Trust"

Rev. Thomas Barlow

All are Welcome

It was the same minister. Maybe she would go. She was glad to have something to do, but surprised when her eyes began to tear.

*   *   *

The next morning, Kate sat at the far end of a pew near the back of the church and waited for the service to begin. The gray stone sanctuary was austere, except for the double row of stained glass windows that ran the length of the nave, one row at eye level and the other twenty feet above the ground. On a hot August morning, the church was as sparsely populated as the rest of the Upper East Side, with congregants scattered mostly in pairs across the pews. There was no air conditioning, though several fans installed along the center beam of the vaulted ceiling revolved at top speed. The ground-level windows were opened to the extent that this was possible; except for a narrow section at the bottom, the windows were fixed in their frames.

Kate wasn't a member of this church or even a regular visitor. She had become a fallen away Catholic since her divorce. She still believed in God, though not like when she was younger. "God's will is sometimes hard for us to discern," the parish priest had said in an attempt to be consoling after her mother's funeral. Kate had smiled wanly and kept silent. What was there to say? She didn't resent the fact that her prayers for her mother's recovery hadn't been answered; she had simply misunderstood. God was a listener, an inspirer, but he left the doing to others.

Kate liked being inside a church, around people who appeared to be making an effort. The quiet of an empty church was equally appealing, though it was hard to find an unlocked church other than the hours during services. Her attraction to this particular church, beside its proximity to her apartment building, was the minister. Thomas Barlow, an unassuming man in his sixties, carried himself with humility and delivered sermons that were more like discussions with a good friend.

From somewhere beyond Kate's line of vision, an organ began to play. She referred to her program. *Sonata in A by Mendelssohn.* She listened to the music and watched the people assembling, mostly well-dressed, gray-haired women, a few with their husbands, but most with other women their age.

Kate thought about her father and sister, and how they would be spending the day in Santa Cruz. Her father would watch baseball on television, and Liz would clean the house, tackling the grittier jobs, like scrubbing the grout in the shower and defrosting the freezer compartment of their old refrigerator, which her father still called "the ice box." When the ball game ended, Liz would suggest they go out for fresh air. They would end up strolling along the Boardwalk, her father stopping to talk to everyone walking a dog. He would ask the dog's name, then pet and praise the animal, using the compliment as an entrée into further conversation. Her father and Liz would pass the late afternoon this way, then go for dinner at the family-style Italian restaurant he liked so much. There he would consume large quantities of ravioli and garlic bread, and ask for the rest to be packaged for home.

The church seemed fuller when the congregation rose to sing the opening hymn. Kate was pleased to recognize the melody. A woman in the next pew handed her a hymnal opened to the correct page, a hymn that Cat Stevens had recorded when Kate was in college.

Morning has broken like the first morning,
Blackbird has spoken, like the first bird.
Praise for the singing! Praise for the morning!
Praise for them springing, fresh from the Word!

The selection seemed to be a favorite of the minister's, who had entered the chancel and stood in front of a high-backed bench fitted with velvet seat cushions. His sincere, off-key singing of the opening bars, picked up by a tiny microphone clipped to his lapel, could be heard over the speaker system. In deference to the heat, Rev. Barlow was wearing a black suit and shirt with white clerical collar instead of the robe he had worn on other Sundays. He was a refined looking man, with the slightly stooped posture of someone who coped with a bad back. His hair was silver and still plentiful enough to be parted. He smiled often, but his eyelids were hooded, which gave him a wistful expression.

Although they had been attending services off and on for several years, Kate and Liz had met Rev. Barlow just a few months ago, after the Easter Sunday service. He had stood inside the main entrance to the church and spoken a few words to everyone in a line of people waiting to greet him, something he did every Sunday. On their previous visits, Kate and Liz would slip out the side door, but the minister's sermon on that Easter Sunday was about eternal life, a promise that meant more to Kate now that her mother was gone. As she waited her turn in line, Kate watched Rev. Barlow listening and responding in an unhurried manner to the members of his church. No one paid that kind of attention anymore. Suddenly she wished she could vacate the line, but Liz was introducing herself, and then Kate. The minister shook Liz's hand and looked at Kate expectantly, smiling with lips parted as though eager to connect. "That was a good sermon," she said self-consciously. He had smiled and redirected the compliment to his subject matter: "There's no greater theme than the Resurrection."

Now Kate watched as Rev. Barlow climbed the short, circular staircase built into the back of the wooden pulpit and looked out over his congregation. If he was displeased with the light turnout, he didn't show it. Taking up his subject, he spoke earnestly about trust and its varying degrees in different people. He quoted a psychoanalyst who had theorized that the ability to trust begins in the first months of life. Kate thought about her position on that spectrum. She took people at their word and, until events proved conclusively otherwise, gave them the benefit of the doubt. Like Ted, in the final weeks of their marriage, saying he was too tired to make love. Since when? she should have asked.

"I believe," Rev. Barlow said from the pulpit, "that no matter how we got our start, there are in all of us enough kernels of trust to affirm the goodness of life, of God's presence in each of our lives."

I'm with you, Reverend, Kate thought, but we're outnumbered. She thought about Woody, and the story he had recently told in the trading room about learning how to swim, a reminiscence prompted by Jim saying he'd hired a lifeguard to teach his kids. Woody's father had stood his five-year-old son on the side of the pool, held out his arms and said, "Jump! I'll catch you." But when Woody jumped, his father stood back and let the small boy plunge into the water, where he flailed unsupported for several moments before his father grabbed the back of his swim trunks and steered him to the ladder. "'Never trust anyone,' my old man told me." Woody had quoted him proudly.

Reverend Barlow's sermon had moved from developmental psychology to Biblical characters. Kate didn't grasp the transition until the names Abraham and Isaac came up. She remembered how as a devout ten-year-old, a picture of Pope John XXIII taped to her bedroom wall, she had lain in bed one night, fretting over Abraham's willingness to sacrifice his son as a sign of trust in God. The illustration in her catechism book had been graphic: Abraham standing over Isaac, a knife raised in his hand, stayed by an angel swooping in at the last possible moment. With that image flashing through her head, Kate had been too terrified to even glance at Liz asleep in the adjacent twin bed.

Reverend Barlow stood silently in the pulpit. Kate had a momentary panic that he was waiting for her attention, though he had simply paused to empathize a point: "There's no formula for trust. You just have to go ahead and do it."

Kate's shoulders sagged. She needed a formula, frankly, some truism that always applied. Her job was full of them. Buy low, sell high. Cut your losses, and let your profits run.

She shifted in her seat, the back of her dress sticking to the varnished pew. Her eyes wandered from the minister. On the arched wall behind the pulpit, high above the minister's head, sunlight coming through an upper window had dappled the stone with the clear, jeweled tones of the stained glass. As she watched, the elliptical pools of color deepened, then receded, pulsing with the wavering source of light. This simple beauty seemed a kind of consolation.

A swell of organ music interrupted her thoughts. Rev. Barlow had moved across the front of the altar to the lectern, a less stately podium than the pulpit. They were nearing the end of the service. A Caring Community, the program read. The minister reported that several members of their church had been hospitalized, and that one had been discharged and was resting comfortably at home.

"A final announcement Peter Hanley asked me to make," Rev. Barlow said. "He's away this weekend at a marching band convention in Michigan." There was soft laughter from the congregation. "Let's hope the weather there is a bit less steamy. Peter is looking for volunteers to help with the youth group's trip to Shea Stadium, which he's organized again this year with a church in Queens."

That would have to be the case, Kate thought, looking around the sanctuary; she was the closest thing to youth by several decades.

"There's a need for at least one adult to make certain that we, as sponsors of the event, are providing proper supervision," the minister continued. "Peter told me he'll take any offer of help, but he would prefer a woman."

Hearty laughter rose from the congregation, but it tapered off when Rev. Barlow held up a hand.

"Many of our guests will be girls," he explained, "and a woman can be a positive role model as well as see to the girls' needs at the stadium. I hope I've made this invitation sound attractive."

Not quite, though Kate appreciated his refusal to milk the situation for laughs.

"Last year's trip was so worthwhile," he said. "We established friendly ties between our church, which has much to share, and a wonderful group of people in Queens." He looked down at the lectern, checking his notes. "Did I mention that Peter promises all the refreshments his volunteers can consume?" Rev. Barlow sounded tentative, as if following someone else's script. "If you're interested, please speak to me after the service."

Kate looked doubtfully at the congregants as they sang the recessional hymn. They didn't strike her as a baseball kind of crowd, but she couldn't fault them. Sweltering in the afternoon sun might spell death for some of these people.

At the end of the service, Kate lingered a moment, debating whether or not to speak to the minister, who was greeting people a short distance from where she stood. If past Sundays were any indication, they would be telling him about their ailments and their friends' ailments. How could he listen to it all with such a genuine look of concern on his face? He was a saint, she thought, an anomaly to be admired but difficult to emulate.

She decided to slip out the side exit. Stepping into the aisle, she heard the minister shouting a welcome to someone who was probably hard of hearing. When she glanced back, Rev. Barlow was looking right at her, as were those waiting to speak with him. "It's Kate, isn't it?" he said. "Your sister is Liz."

"You have a good memory," Kate said, walking toward him. She glanced at the people waiting in line, who seemed more interested than surprised by the special treatment.

Rev. Barlow smiled warmly and shook Kate's hand. "I was wondering if by any chance you might be a baseball fan?"

Chapter 8

Kate took the Wall Street Express bus to work on Monday morning so she could go through the newspapers in a civilized manner. Reading the paper on the subway at rush hour was impossible, though she had seen men do it, folding the entire length of the paper in half, then reading the long narrow strips.

She hurried through the *Wall Street Journal* and the business pages of the *Times* before settling back in her seat and gazing out the window. Heading south on the FDR Drive, the express bus passed the New York University Medical Center, then curved toward the river where the island of Manhattan reached its widest point. Runners jogged along paths in East River Park. Other early risers sat on benches and read the paper or drank morning coffee.

A yellow school bus, headed in the opposite direction on the FDR, reminded Kate of the field trip she would be taking on Saturday. Rev. Barlow's gentle manner had been disarming, and the reason she had agreed to help. She wondered about Peter Hanley. Rev. Barlow told her he was a high school teacher. She should have asked more questions, though maybe Peter Hanley wouldn't call. Life would be simpler if he didn't.

She took out the sports section of the *Times,* part of the paper she never read, and skimmed its pages. There were several articles about the Mets, who were having a wonderful season. She read a report on the previous day's game and a story on one of the players. It was refreshing to see something other than the market rally commanding so much ink.

The bus pulled off the FDR onto Fulton Street. Kate got off at the first stop with most of the other passengers, three times as many men as women. Everyone was dressed in tailored suits of gray, navy, black and, now that it was summer, khaki. Several women wore socks and running shoes over their stockings, a practice that had caught on during the last transit strike. Liz abhorred the look, and Kate had to agree that a pair of Reeboks spoiled the camouflage effect of dressing like men.

At seven in the morning, Wall Street was filled with people on their way to work. They grabbed breakfast from coffee wagons and hole-in-the-wall delis that kept financial market hours, closing on weekends when the area was deserted except for scattered tourists, who wandered by after visiting the Statue of Liberty or the twin towers of the World Trade Center.

Kate stopped at the silver coffee wagon near the entrance to the Matheson building. The younger man saw her first but stepped aside for his older brother, who smiled presumptuously. Avoiding eye contact, Kate looked instead at his baseball cap. "Is your cap Mets or Yankees?" she said.

"Yankees," the older brother said, his tone smug like his smile.

"How can you tell the difference?" she said. He seemed taken aback by the question, as if she had challenged his authority. "In the hats," she said. "They both have 'NY.'"

The younger brother leaned into the open window. "The Y is below the N on the Mets hat, and the letters curl," he said, pointing to the hat he was wearing. Kate looked intently at both caps, committing the distinction to memory. "And the Mets letters are usually orange," he added, treating the key difference as an afterthought.

Kate took the paper bag from the older brother and thanked him, but he was already looking past her, barking the next order into the wagon's cramped interior.

Shortly before eight o'clock that morning, Woody's voice came over the trading room intercom: "I trust everyone is ready to underwrite and distribute the nation's debt." The salesmen and traders were silent except for Keezer, who started to hum "The Star Spangled Banner" under his breath.

"Woody *does* make it sound like a patriotic duty,"

Kate said to Ernie. "You think he's sorry he came here?"

"He bought the biggest house in a so-so neighborhood," Ernie said. "There's no changing that fact, no matter how often he waters the lawn."

Woody appeared more wired than usual. Throughout the morning, he punched buttons on his phone turret and smacked the handset on the desktop when he couldn't get the right parties on the line. He jumped up from his chair and paced in the space behind his desk.

Kate felt a vague twinge of sympathy for the new head trader. She could imagine Jim negotiating the hire, telling Woody that he was getting in on the ground floor of the securities business at one of the most illustrious firms in American financial history, and how together they would establish a trading operation bigger and better than Salomon Brothers. Jim often spoke like that, and it wasn't a line with him; he believed every word. And maybe his prediction would prove to be true, though Woody didn't strike her as a builder, and his susceptibility to such a rah-rah pitch surprised her.

At lunchtime, Kate bumped into Lloyd Keezer on his second pass through the cafeteria. She set her empty tray next to his full one on the thin metal bars of the food line. "What's going on in bill land?" he said.

Kate selected a salad and put it on her tray. "Not much…just watching the auctions."

Keezer smiled uncomfortably. "I was wondering if any of your customers need coverage on the long end.

I'm trying to add some accounts to my list, and I figure an introduction from someone you talk to might be a way in."

Keezer didn't write big tickets. Whether or not the dozens of smaller trades he executed were profitable was an issue perpetually under discussion by department management. Should they expand Keezer's effort with these smaller, "retail" accounts, or shut it down completely and cover only the largest institutions? It would be like Woody to get rid of the small-fry accounts, a move that might cost Keezer his job, one he couldn't afford to lose because of the bank's generous medical benefits. His wife and daughter had asthma, and one or the other always seemed to be in the emergency room.

"I can ask," Kate said, "but it might be hard to get their attention with the auctions going on." Keezer nodded, as if accustomed to news of his poor timing. She watched him add a fistful of cookies to his tray. He would never find another job on Wall Street, not with all the MBAs running around.

"Or now could be the perfect time to call," she said. "I'll get you some names and start the ball rolling."

"That would be great." Keezer caught her eye, then quickly looked away.

"You're a Mets fan, aren't you, Lloyd?" Kate said, knowing full well that he was. For months now, he had led the growing contingent of Met fans in the department, who reveled in the fact that for once their team was doing better than the Yankees.

"Since 1962," Keezer said, noting the franchise's first year.

"I might be going to the game on Saturday."

"I've got a program, if you want to see it."

"Since when are you interested in baseball?" Ernie asked later as he flipped through Keezer's Mets program.

Kate told Ernie about her tentative plans for Saturday.

"You realize there isn't an entrance exam," he said.

"I like to be prepared," she said.

"Tell me about it. Who you going with?"

Kate explained about the field trip, glossing over the church connection.

"If you really want to enjoy a game, you need to go at night," Ernie said. "The bank has great seats. I might even go with you."

"We could invite some customers," Kate said. At Woody's prompting, Jim had recently mandated a twenty per cent increase in face-to-face sales calls with clients, an edict that had elicited Ernie's usual oppositional response.

"The ballpark's better at night, is all I'm saying. It'll be hotter than hell out there on Saturday afternoon. You better wear a hat."

"Yes, Mom."

"There's more than you chaperoning these kids, I hope."

"The guy who's organizing it is going, too. I'm helping him out. I take the girls to the restroom, that kind of thing. Are you serious about going to a game?"

"Not if you're going to spoil it with customers."

"What if it's a customer you like?" She gave Ernie her most beguiling smile.

"Submit a name, and I'll get back to you."

The prospect of putting events on her calendar lifted Kate's spirits, despite Ernie's disparaging comments. At the first opportunity, she walked over to see Rita Jones, who was, in Kate's opinion, the department's best salesman.

Rita held the phone between her shoulder and chin, and scribbled numbers onto her sales blotter with a lefty's back slant. "Uh-huh, exactly," she said. "I'll certainly keep you posted." She was gauging interest in the three-year note, the first auction in the Treasury's refunding.

"Taking a break from Ernie?" Rita said when she got off the line.

"Actually, Ernie's feeling hospitable," Kate said. "He wants to invite you and a client to a baseball game."

Rita's look was half skeptical, half intrigued. "You're going, too, right? I can take Ernie only if you're there to

115

handle him."

"It would be you, me, Ernie, and your customer."

"I don't know, Kate. What about you having a drink with Wayne Kimmel and me? We're getting together after work one day next week. Wayne's always glad to see you."

"Maybe he'd like to go to a game," Kate said, reluctant to give up her original plan. "Ernie says the ballpark's beautiful at night."

Rita sighed, but if she was tired, her appearance belied it. Like many black women her age, Rita's skin was completely unlined. She was married with two children, a boy in high school and a one-year old daughter she had given birth to at the age of forty-two. "My menopause baby," Rita called the surprise pregnancy. She spent the final trimester in the hospital, hooked up to an IV to prevent premature delivery.

Rita went at her job in workmanlike fashion, confiding once to Kate that selling securities was not all that different from her previous job in Investigations, the department of the bank that tracked down problems too time consuming for the customer service desk. Rita was direct without being offensive, and persistent too, qualities that had eventually landed her a transfer to the line. She started in the trading room as an assistant to a disorganized senior salesman. Rita wrote his tickets and gave his clients first-class service. When he left for a competitor, she established herself as his successor before management got around to reassigning the accounts to someone more senior.

If a trader asked, Rita would call a customer ten times a day to propose the same deal, something many other salesmen wouldn't do, claiming that their customers weren't interested, and in essence making the decisions for them, a habit the traders hated. When Rita's production surpassed that of her predecessor, the sales manager congratulated himself for taking a chance on her, and bragged about the decision in his annual performance review.

Rita eyed Kate warily. "Ernie said the ballpark's beautiful at night? The old grouch," she said, though her tone had softened. "I've got to make sure Charles can watch the baby before I go anywhere."

"We'll have a car at the stadium to take you home," Kate said.

Rita waved off the suggestion. "I'll take the train and be home before you clear the parking lot. You sure this is Ernie's idea? I've been working with that man a long time, and this is the first customer entertainment he's ever initiated, other than paying for drinks at some bar."

"I think he's turning over a new leaf."

Rita rolled her eyes. "Lot of leaves turning over around here," she said, and got back on the phone.

Kate was enjoying the novelty of being away from her desk and the constant stream of inquiry from salesmen. She drifted over to the phone operators for a social visit, one she hadn't made in quite a while.

"There you are," Judy said, handing her a message slip. Peter Hanley had called. Kate looked at the phone operator, whose expression was sphinx-like.

"Can you buzz Ernie for me?" Kate said. Judy dialed Ernie's number, and Kate leaned over and spoke into the intercom. "You there, Ernie?"

"I thought you left for the day," he said.

"Rita will let us know after she talks to Charles."

"Who's Charles?"

"Rita's husband."

"Why is she talking to him?"

"About the baseball game, remember?"

"Oh, yeah, the game."

"OK if I make a quick call off the desk?"

"Just be back before the sales meeting. I've had enough of these morons."

Kate called Peter Hanley from a reception room that shared a glass wall with the trading floor. Salesmen met with customers in this room. Observing the trading floor was supposed to make outsiders feel like part of the action.

When Peter came on the line, Kate identified herself and waited for him to take the lead.

"Tom Barlow spoke to you about the game on

Saturday?" Peter's voice was friendly and young.

"That's right, I'm the female role model." Kate was surprised when Peter laughed; her thoughts were generally funnier than her words.

"I'm glad you can make it. The kids are great. Tom says you're a baseball fan."

"Well," Kate said carefully, not wanting to contradict the minister, particularly since he and Peter Hanley were on a first-name basis. "That might be stretching things a bit."

"I hope Tom didn't twist your arm too much."

"Oh, no," she said, remembering how Rev. Barlow had lassoed her in.

"Have you ever been to Shea?"

"No, I never have."

"You're not a Yankees fan, are you?" Peter had lowered his voice with what she read as feigned hostility.

"No, I'm a Giants fan." She couldn't believe she'd said that. Her entire life she had been to one, maybe two, Giants' games, and that was more than twenty years ago.

"National League anyway," Peter said. "Who are your favorite players?"

Kate couldn't name a single player on the current Giants team, but she hated to answer "I don't know" to any question. "I guess I'd have to say Willie Mays. Willie

McCovey, too, and Orlando Cepeda." She reeled off a list of players from her youth, names she had heard on the car radio, which was tuned to sports whenever her father got behind the wheel.

"The '62 Giants, right? They were an awesome team. You have good taste." She was ridiculously pleased by his comment. "Did you ever see Mays in the field?"

"Yes, I did," she said, finally telling the truth. "We sat in the bleachers behind center field. My dad told me it was the best vantage point for watching Willie Mays line up a catch."

"Smart man." Peter's raspy laugh was pleasant, but she hoped he wasn't a smoker. "I saw Mays play for the Mets."

"Mays played for the Mets?" She had never followed baseball, and before this week had only a vague notion of the Mets, the butt of sportswriters' jokes when she was in grade school. She wondered how old Peter had been when he saw Mays play for the Mets.

"The Giants traded him. Can you believe it?" Peter spoke as if the wound were still fresh, as if he shared in the slight.

Kate matched her tone to his: "I had no idea."

"Yeah, pretty bad, but it worked out well for Met fans. I think Willie got a kick out of being back in New York. We can trade stories on Saturday. Let me walk you through the drill."

Kate had been right about the lack of youth in Rev. Barlow's congregation, at least during the summer months. Peter explained that most of the children were away at camp or summering with their parents outside the city. It looked as though she and Peter would be the only representatives from Manhattan. He told her he would pick her up a few hours before the game, then drive to the church in Queens, where they would board the bus with the kids.

"How many kids are going?" she said.

"Twenty so far, but there'll probably be some last-minute interest."

"Will two chaperones be enough?"

"The minister from the other church is coming too. I've got plenty of tickets if you'd like to bring someone along."

Kate looked through the glass wall of the conference room, imagining the response she would get in the trading room to such an invitation. And Liz had extended her stay in California, not that her sister would have agreed to all those hours in the sun.

"A lot of people are away in August," she said.

"We'll manage. I know some of these kids. We can draft a few junior counselors to help out."

"Battlefield promotions."

"Don't worry, it'll be fine. A couple of the little kids brought their grandmothers last year. It all works out." He sounded like an old hand.

"It's a nice thing you're doing."

"You, too." He took her address and told her he would see her on Saturday. "No bailing out on me now."

"Oh, I wouldn't do that," she said, before realizing that he was probably teasing.

Kate checked the screens when she got back to the trading desk. "Market's strong," she said to Ernie, who was still reading the Mets program. He grunted, but didn't look up. "You want me to do the sales meeting?" she said.

He tossed the program aside. "I've got to show up, too. Woody wants everyone in there, but you can do the talking." Ernie looked at her and smiled sweetly.

The rectangular room in which the sales meetings were held ran the length of the hall separating it from the trading floor. The meeting room had two entrances. Just inside the room, situated between those entrances, was an elevated platform that faced several rows of tiered, upholstered banquettes, arranged in the shape of an opened staple. From either doorway, it was possible to keep an eye on the action in the trading room as well as the meeting room, which was why the traders clustered there, awaiting their turn to address the sales force before returning to work. The market was the traders' permanent, built-in excuse.

At four-thirty sharp, Woody walked down the hall-way. Traders standing in the first doorway cleared a path for him. He stepped onto the raised platform and sat behind the long wooden desk. The salesmen, who had been lounging on the banquettes and shooting the breeze, came to attention.

"I don't need to tell you what an important week this is." Woody looked at the sales force as if he believed the opposite to be true. "Particularly to a shop where govern-ments are the only action. You have little credibility with corporate bond buyers or mortgage-backed buyers or even long agency buyers, for that matter. And your influence with equity investors is zero." He tapped his cigar on the edge of the desk, and ash fluttered to the floor.

Pig, Kate thought, any sympathy she had felt for him vanishing.

"But you do have a handle on the economy and loan demand," Woody said. "You're a top player in money markets, especially bank paper, and you're a respected Fed watcher. You've got to start treating these strengths like products: forecasting the economy, Fed watching, predict-ing the direction of short-term interest rates. You've been giving this information away and getting little in return. Salomon wouldn't do that, and it's got to stop happening around here."

Woody had accurately described Matheson's position vis-à-vis the competition, Kate thought, but he packaged the information so negatively, and used "you" instead of "we." From her position in the doorway, she watched the faces of the salesmen who, despite their business attire, looked like school children being reprimanded by the principal. Though the salesmen technically worked for the sales manager and not Woody, everyone knew where the power was vested.

"Buyers don't like to pay for intangibles," Woody said, "but they'll pay up for product. That's why a mediocre salesman can make a good living at Salomon Brothers. There's always product on the shelves there—so much product that customers have to take the Salomon call. You don't have that kind of inventory, so you've got to live off how much you know." Woody looked around the room, making eye contact with every salesman who hadn't ducked his head. "Tell your customers if they want access to Matheson's thinking, they have to show us their auction business."

Again Kate found herself agreeing with Woody. Providing good information was the reason she and Ernie were doing so much auction business, and why profits on the bill desk had risen. She caught Woody's eye. Was he going to point to their example?

"And not just in Treasury bills either," Woody said, his eyes still on Kate, a sardonic smile playing around the corners of his mouth. "Bills are peanuts compared to the money made in coupons. Most dealers run their bill desks as a loss leader. Bill trading isn't even a profit center. It's a cost of doing business, like the glass of water they put on your table in a restaurant." He paused and let the image sink in before looking back at the salesmen.

"The days of customers parking money in the short end for double-digit rates are over," he said. "Inflation is dead. Volcker killed it. Money is pouring back into stocks and bonds, and it's going to stay there for the returns. When serious bond investors get involved—I'm talking size—they do it in the auctions. You need to start seeing that business, or you'll be left behind. Maybe you're used to that around here, but I'm not someone who gets left behind."

Kate could feel perspiration forming under her arms and along her sides. Woody was right about the relative worth of bills to the longer end of the market—in an across-the-board rally, a dollar invested in bonds made more money than a dollar invested in bills—but he could have made his point without putting down the bill business. Why disparage something that was going well, particularly when he could take credit for it up the line? He was toying with her, dangling the prospect of a compliment, then converting it to an insult once he had her attention.

"Why are you frowning?" Woody said. "Don't you agree?"

Who was he going after now? Kate looked at Woody, who was staring at her. He had belittled her work as a loss leader and called her profits "peanuts." Now he expected her to publicly agree with the assessment. The traders around her stirred the way horses do when a stranger comes into their midst.

"That wasn't a rhetorical question," Woody said.

"Auctions are critical," Kate said, confirming the indisputable part of his statement. "It's why we're a dealer." Somehow she managed to speak steadily, though she could feel her face burning.

Woody turned back to the sales force. "You hear that? It's why we're a dealer. Even a bill trader knows that. Any two-bit outfit can trade around in the brokers' screen, but underwriting and distributing the government's debt is why we're in business. It's why you have a job. If your accounts aren't buying their bonds through us, you're just taking up space in the trading room." His eyes moved to the cluster of traders in the doorway, and Kate felt her chest tighten further.

"Where's Campbell?" Woody said.

Emerging from the group of traders, Adam Campbell exchanged places with Kate, who stepped into the hallway. She could hear Adam's voice, but his words were only sounds. She felt a tap on her elbow. It was Ernie, offering a can of soda. They walked to the end of the hall so they wouldn't be overheard.

"Sometimes this job sucks," he said.

Kate's eyes widened with agitation. "Did you hear what he said?"

"Yeah, I heard. It was a sucker punch. Consider it a

compliment."

"A compliment?" she said, forgetting to keep her voice low. "He's scaring off all our business. What salesman's going to do bill trades with him calling it peanuts?

"Calm down. You're overreacting."

"Please don't tell me to calm down, Ernie. I'm frowning? I'm overreacting? What do you expect? I'm being attacked."

"All right, he lobbed one in. He's taking out his frustrations, and you were a convenient target." She started to protest, but Ernie held up a hand. "You really think short-term investors are going to stop buying bills because Morehead Fucking Woodson says they ought to be in bonds?"

Kate held the cold aluminum can of soda against her face. "My head is pounding."

"There's aspirin in my top drawer. Wash 'em down with Coke. It'll give you a buzz."

She started to go, but stopped and swung around. "What if he wants information on the bill market?"

Ernie waved her off. "He wouldn't ask now, even if he did." He laughed quietly, shaking his head. "If he calls on you, I'll say you're going through people's desks, looking for loose change."

"It's coming to that."

"Go do some drugs."

Kate watched Ernie shuffle back to the huddle of traders in the doorway. Turning on her heel, she nearly collided with Jim, who was coming around the corner at a fast clip.

"Whoa!" he said, raising his arms in an exaggerated gesture of self-protection. "Aren't you heading the wrong way?"

"Probably. Where have you been?"

"At the Fed," he said, unfazed by her blunt tone. "Didn't pick up much, but schmoozing with the *federales* never hurts." He grinned and re-accelerated down the hallway.

Kate found the aspirin in Ernie's desk and swallowed two tablets with the soda. She had been eager to get away from the sales meeting, but felt left out now that she had. She considered going back, but couldn't risk another exchange with Woody.

She sat by herself in the empty trading room, listening to the hum of electricity from the overhead lights and the screens. She found the white noise comforting, like a tumbling dryer or the refrigerator coming on, though people joked that the extended exposure to cathode ray tubes would eventually sterilize them all.

She took out her trading journal and flipped through entries from earlier in the year. Some of her commentary was familiar, recorded on both good days and bad, but more of it seemed as if someone else had recorded it. She ran her palm over the ball-pointed words, which felt like a rash on the paper. Six million dollars in trading profits would be a record-setting year for Matheson's bill desk, a number Woody would undoubtedly include in the total he took credit for at bonus time. If bill trading was so inconsequential, why didn't he just ignore it *and* her?

The way Woody had jumped at the chance to belittle her work reminded her of Ted. At a reception for incoming med students and their wives—there had been a few women in Ted's class, though none had been married—a professor had asked Kate what she planned to do while her husband went through school. When she answered that she was a banker, Ted had laughed.

"You work at a bank," he said, his derisive tone making her feel as if she had been caught in a lie.

The professor had patted her reassuringly on the shoulder. "You'll have to forgive your husband," he said. "Sometimes doctors forget that there are careers other than medicine."

Kate wanted to do her best; why did that bother men? Their defensiveness seemed universal, except for Ernie and Jim. She wondered if Jim realized how his new head trader carried on. She couldn't imagine that Jim would approve. She had considered speaking to him about her concerns, but now that Woody had publicly gone negative about the bill business, her comments would appear biased. It would be different if Jim asked for her opinion, or sought her out for one of the informal chats they used to have before his promotion. If that happened, she would tell him exactly what she thought about Morehead Woodson, and how he was ruining the bond department. But Jim would have to come to her. If going around Woody had seemed presumptuous before, now it was completely out of the question.

Ernie was the first to return from the sales meeting. "You find the aspirin?"

Kate nodded. "I'm still waiting for the buzz. Maybe it doesn't work with Diet." She drank the last of the soda. "Did I miss anything?"

"Woody took it down a notch when Jim came in, but the heat's still on for the auctions. Woody is going to be pissed when he sees how light we are on coupon bidders. The fact that most of our customers are banks and don't buy longer-dated securities hasn't sunk in yet. I hope Keezer's scrounged up a few orders."

Remembering her commitment to Keezer, Kate phoned Rita to explain his request. "You know anyone at Amalgamated who needs coverage on coupons?"

"Not from Lloyd Keezer, I don't," Rita said.

"He's actually very good with his clients. They're active and tell him everything they're doing. They're just small."

Rita sighed through the phone line. "Can't Joel throw Keezer a few names?" she said, referring to the sales manager. "It's not like we cover the world."

"I think Lloyd's afraid to draw attention to himself.

It's too risky."

"Making money seems to be risky now too," Rita said, making light of Woody's earlier comments. "I guess I can find someone at Amalgamated who would talk to Lloyd. We're still respected outside of New York, no matter what Morehead Woodson says."

Kate added some names to the one Rita gave her, and took the list over to Keezer. He sat staring at his blotter, penciling over his customers' orders, as if bolder print might make the numbers bigger. "I think these are the best bets," Kate told him. "We could call now," she said, glancing at the clock, "though it is after five."

Keezer looked up, the wispy strands of hair on his head in need of a comb. "People always say they're too busy, no matter what time I call."

"Let's make the calls in the morning. People are usually in early on refunding days."

"I'll get here by seven," he said. Kate nodded with more optimism than she felt, wondering what arriving at seven entailed for a man with Keezer's complicated home life.

"Did you get the Mets program?" he said.

"I did. Thanks. Can I keep it overnight?"

"It's yours. You're going on Saturday, right? Doc Gooden's pitching." Keezer looked pleased, as if he had arranged the star pitcher's appearance for her benefit.

Chapter 9

Kate woke up on Saturday with a sense of purpose. In a few hours she would be on the field trip, escorting a busload of kids to the baseball game. Peter Hanley had called the evening before to confirm a ten-thirty pickup. He was enthusiastic and had a voice like a cheerleader.

She went downstairs at ten-fifteen to wait in the lobby. Frank was standing outside the doorway and turned when she came up behind him. He quickly took in her attire—Bermuda shorts and a sleeveless white shirt—as if determining which service to offer.

"Do you need a taxi?"

She shook her head. "Someone's picking me up."

"I can let you know when the car's here, if you'd rather wait inside."

"I'm looking for a red Honda," she said, not wanting to seem unfriendly.

"Accord or Prelude?"

"I'm not sure."

"Are you getting out of the city?"

"I'm going to Shea Stadium. Does that count?"

"Sure it counts. Doc Gooden's pitching."

Kate listened as Frank recounted the young pitcher's accomplishments. She would have preferred to wait by herself, but there was no way the doorman was going back inside now. What a lot he knew about her, she thought, as they watched for the red Honda. She remembered telling him that Ted would no longer be getting his mail at this address, her roundabout way of informing the staff about the divorce. Frank had dropped his eyes and nodded, discreetly focusing on the change-of-address card she'd handed him.

"Prelude," Frank said. "Your ride's here."

Kate stayed in the doorway and watched the sporty red car come to a stop in front of the apartment building. The car's front windows were down, and she felt a pleasant jolt when she saw the profile of the driver, a good-looking man her age. He seemed familiar, though she had that re-action to many people now that she lived in New York.

Frank crossed the wide sidewalk and waited for Peter Hanley to get out of the car. He was a big man, six-two or six-three, with the kind of husky, athletic build that's hard to maintain past thirty-five. He looked younger than that, though his jaw line had begun to soften. When he came around the front of the car, she noticed that his baseball jersey wasn't tucked into his cut-offs. If he was developing a paunch, it was well disguised.

He asked Frank if he could leave the car for a moment.

The doorman inclined his head in her direction, and she stepped forward. She shook Peter's hand, which wasn't as bulky as the rest of him.

"Good to meet you," he said, his voice deeper in person than it had sounded over the phone.

Before she could respond, Frank spoke up. "I've been a Mets fan since 1962."

In the past week, Kate had learned that rooting for the team since the first year of the franchise was a badge of honor for Met fans.

Peter smiled conspiratorially, as if he had read her mind. "Did you know Kate's been a Giants fan that long?" Frank looked at Kate, who felt obliged to nod her assent; the interplay seemed to amuse Peter.

He opened the car door for her. The bucket seat was filled with three-ring binders, and a jumble of shoes and empty deli bags covered the carpeted footwell. "Hang on a sec," he said, transferring the clutter to the car's back seat.

"My car's the same," she said, before trailing off. She hadn't owned a car in more than a year. The Camaro had gone with Ted.

"You work in the city?" Peter said.

"I work for a bank downtown."

"Making loans, that sort of thing?" His tone was casual, but she recognized a New Yorker sizing up the situation.

"I'm on the securities side. We deal more with investors." She got into the car, wondering if the subject would change by the time he got around to the driver's side. But after steering away from the curb, Peter continued the same line of questions.

"Stocks or bonds?"

"Bonds. We're not allowed to deal in the stock market yet."

"Are you in sales?"

"I was, but now I trade Treasury bills."

His eyebrows rose slightly. "Buy low, sell high."

"That's the goal anyway." She waited for more questions, but he seemed finished with the subject. "Rev. Barlow said you're a teacher."

"Yep," he said, minding the traffic.

"Where do you teach?"

"Stuyvesant. It's a high school downtown."

"Do you teach music?"

"I teach *band*," he said. "There's a distinction, according to the school board."

They drove along in silence, and Kate wondered why he had stopped talking. He had seemed unfazed about where she lived, though an address in Manhattan could typecast you. New Yorkers always wanted to know the cross street, even when they weren't picking you up. Maybe her job had put him off. She looked sideways at him. He was much better looking than she had imagined.

They waited for the light to change on York Avenue, near the entrance to the FDR. A young man with a squeegee approached the car and began washing the front windshield, an action that always made Kate uneasy. She didn't want to stiff the guy for his work, but she didn't want to roll the window down either.

Peter's window was already down. "Thanks, it needed it," he said, handing a dollar to the young man, who took note of Peter's jersey.

"You going to the game?"

Peter nodded. "Gooden's pitching."

The young man stepped back from the car as the light changed to green, and raised the squeegee over his head in a kind of salute.

"Everyone's talking about Doc Gooden," Kate said. "I feel lucky to see him."

"He's impressive. You could build a championship around a player like that."

"Is he as good as Sandy Koufax?"

Peter gave her a long look, as if to determine her sincerity. "There are similarities," he said. Warming to the subject, he discussed the two pitchers all the way into Queens.

*   *   *

There were a dozen children already waiting when Peter and Kate pulled up in front of Mount Zion Church, a small stone building wedged between a business college and a Chinese laundry. A black man, dressed in a short-sleeved shirt and jeans, waved from the top step.

"That's Lawrence Parker. He's pastor here," Peter said, leaning across Kate to open the car door. "I'd do this properly, but the kids tend to mob you once you're out of the car."

The kids did run up to Peter. "Hey, buddy," he said to the boy who reached him first. Peter threw a light shoulder punch at one of the older boys. "You're taller, man."

Kate followed Peter to the bottom of the church steps, where he bear-hugged the minister, dislodging the shorter man's glasses.

"Lawrence Parker," Peter said, "may I present Kate Munro?"

The minister adjusted his glasses and shook her hand. When a yellow school bus rumbled to a stop at the curb, Peter climbed aboard and spoke to the driver.

"He has a lot of energy," Lawrence said, watching Peter open and close the emergency door at the back of the bus.

More children arrived, and Lawrence put Kate to work writing nametags. She was grateful for a job that gave her a reason to interact with the kids. She hadn't spent much time around children. When she was a teenager, she had been too busy caring for her sick mother and younger sister for neighbors to ask about babysitting.

Sometimes Kate was troubled by her lack of interest in children. She didn't peek into carriages or gush over new babies shown off at work by their mothers. "Can I hold him?" other women would beg while Kate kept a comfortable distance. She contributed to the collections for baby showers, a social staple among the bank's clerical staff, and studied the photos they passed around the trading room. But she did so without envy or maternal twinge. She had assumed that she would eventually have children, once Ted had finished his training, though motherhood hadn't been something she longed for. It was more part of Ted's plan than her plan, and both plans had changed.

At noon, the bus pulled away from the church with twenty-six kids, Peter and Kate on board. Lawrence Parker drove the adult guests—two grandmothers and an older man who worked as a custodian at the church—in Peter's car, back-up transportation, he explained, in case someone needed to leave before the rest of the group. Peter sat in the back of the bus with the boys, and Kate sat up front with the smaller contingent of girls. The kids were enjoying themselves, especially the older boys, whom Peter had drafted to assist him.

Everyone cheered when the bus pulled into the parking lot and circled the perimeter of Shea Stadium. Concrete ramps zigzagged up the sides of the building like laces in a gigantic shoe. Over these concrete lacings was a scattered pattern of confetti-like shingles. What an ugly building, Kate thought, until she looked into the open end of the stadium and took in the grandeur of the place.

The kids were up before the driver turned off the ignition. Peter came down the aisle looking relaxed and unflustered despite the commotion. He stood near the front door and grinned, his cheeks forming parentheses around the rest of his features. "It's a perfect day for base-ball," he said.

"That's what you said last year," a boy in a Yankees shirt said.

"Did I?" Peter caught Kate's eye and shrugged. "If you need anything, ask one of the adults, or one of my assistants." The junior counselors raised their arms over their heads like boxers announced in the ring. "We'll stick together, but our section is written on your nametags in case you get turned around. Just ask an usher. They're the guys with the orange bow ties. Or ask a policeman."

"My uncle got arrested here once," the boy in the Yankee shirt said.

"That's 'cause he's a Yankee fan," a junior counselor said.

They got off the bus and trooped toward the entrance gate, where Peter handed the tickets to the usher and counted the kids through the turnstile. A young woman distributed souvenir give-aways, foam hands with index fingers extended. Kate reached for one, but the woman shook her head: "Twelve and under." Peter whispered something to her, and she gave him a souvenir, which he passed to Kate.

"What did you say?" Kate asked quietly.

"I'll tell you later," he said.

They rode the escalators to the upper deck, where warm breezes blew through the stadium corridors. Kate smiled down at Christina, her seatmate from the bus, and tapped her on the head with the foam hand. An usher showed them to their seats in the front rows of the upper deck, just to the right of home plate. Peter tipped him—generously, from the expression on the man's face. Minutes later he returned with a hot dog vendor, the first of a stream of vendors that would visit them over the course of the afternoon. Kate looked out over the emerald grass and felt contented. In the early innings, she tried to follow the game, though she couldn't distinguish everything the crowd reacted to. Each time Doc Gooden struck a batter out, the kids taped a sheet of paper with a "K" on it to the front railing; Lawrence had brought quite a stack. When Darryl Strawberry, the Mets' star offensive player, hit a home run, the crowd roared, and a gigantic apple rose from an equally large top hat in back of the center field fence.

"What do they do for the other players?" Christina asked. Kate looked puzzled and then laughed: the apple did look a lot like a strawberry.

During the seventh inning stretch, Peter walked up from his seat, a few rows down from hers. "You're getting burned," he told Kate. "Better wear this." He took off his hat, and she noticed for the first time that his eyes were green. The front of his hair was matted and spread back from his forehead, exposing a narrow strip of un-tanned skin just below his hairline. She put on the cap, which was damp at the base of the crown.

"It fits," she said with some surprise because he was so much bigger than she was. He stepped closer, as if to share a confidence, and she took in the grassy smell of a clean body sweating.

"I do have kind of a pinhead," he admitted, his face so close that she had to tilt her head back to see what he was talking about.

"I don't know," she said. "Maybe it's me."

He knit his brow and studied her. She turned her head, partly to show him her profile and partly to avoid looking him straight in the face. When she turned back, he was nodding seriously.

"I think you're right," he said, a small smile on his lips as he went back to his seat.

The rest of the game passed quickly. All the while Kate thought about the exchange over Peter's hat. She couldn't tell if it meant anything. There were men who flirted that way all the time, and she didn't know him well enough to categorize him, one way or the other. But the sensation of his face close to hers lingered, and she was still wearing his hat. She reached up and secured it.

The driver had the engine running and the windows opened when they got back on the bus. They left the parking lot slowly, stopping and starting as the traffic cleared in different directions. Most of the kids were quiet, except for the older boys who discussed the highlights of the game with Peter. It was pleasant, listening to their conversation on the otherwise silent bus. She was impressed by how closely they had followed the action, recapping plays and at-bats that hadn't registered with her.

"Windows up on the highway," Peter said. The bus picked up speed, but the air conditioning didn't. Kate looked down at Christina, who leaned against the side of the bus.

"Are you OK?" Kate asked. Christina made a coughing sound, her small frame shuddering. Kate quickly took off Peter's hat and held it in front of the girl, who proceeded to throw up an afternoon's worth of refreshments. The particulars of someone being sick wafted through the bus. Uncharitably, the kids vocalized their disgust. Kate looked over her shoulder for Peter, who was already coming up the aisle. He squatted next to them. She thought she saw him raise an eyebrow as he took the hat and held it down by his feet.

He spoke gently to Christina, clasping her small hand in his fingers. "Too much cotton candy?" The girl hid her face against Kate. "It gets me like that too, sometimes." He pulled a folded handkerchief from his pocket and gave it to Kate. "We're almost there," he said, his voice soothing. He patted the top of the child's shoulder before going back to his seat.

Their car ride together back to Manhattan went more quietly than Kate had anticipated. She had hoped that Peter would be talkative, but he seemed focused on the road. She glanced at him and remembered where she had seen a profile like his: in an ad for a mail-order art school, which had run in the back pages of magazines in the '60s. "Can You Draw This Man?" the caption read. The idea was to instill confidence in potential students by offering a simple figure to replicate. She had done so herself, many times, sketching the thick eyebrow; the straight nose rounded at the tip; the nostril slightly arched and flared; the evenly proportioned lips and strong chin. Peter even had the model's longish sideburn, cut almost to the base of his ear, a popular look when the ad had run, though not so much anymore.

Kate didn't want the day to come to an end, and wondered about asking him in for a soda. Should she say something now or wait until they got to her building? Which way would seem more spontaneous?

"That was quick thinking with the hat," Peter said. "You've got the reflexes of a shortstop."

"I owe you a hat," she said.

"I've got a dozen just like it," he said, slowing down

for the tollbooth. "Well, not *exactly* like it."

"I threw up on a bus once," she said.

"How you feeling now?" He was teasing her again, which made her happy.

"It was so embarrassing. I was in high school, on the way home from a swim meet. I went to a girls' school, but this one time we were sharing a bus with the boys' school down the block. We had to pull over at a gas station on the highway, and everyone had to get out so the driver could hose down the bus. It was bad. I went into the restroom and changed back into my swimsuit and a pair of sweatpants. I would have walked home, if it hadn't been so far away. For years I carried a barf bag in my purse."

"Where'd you get a barf bag?"

"I took a lunch bag and lined it with a plastic bag."

Peter nodded, his lower lip jutting out. "Very resourceful. Were you by any chance a Girl Scout?"

"I was a Camp Fire Girl."

"Your troop would be proud. Don't worry about the hat."

"I liked that hat. I was going to keep it."

"I'll give you another one. We're the same size, remember?" He paid the toll and accelerated into the Manhattan-bound traffic.

"Would you like a cold drink?" she said. "I have cream soda and I think maybe a beer in my refrigerator."

"They both sound great, but I've got to be going. Thanks a lot though. We'll do it another time."

Suddenly, she felt self-conscious. Her skin was sticky with perspiration, especially down her front, and the scent of someone being sick seemed to linger on her clothing. It was probably her imagination, or maybe it wasn't. She edged closer to the car door and cracked open the window, even though Peter had the air-conditioning on. She was grateful that Frank wasn't on the sidewalk when they stopped in front of her building.

"Thanks for coming today," Peter said. "Tom was right about you."

A minister's praise wasn't exactly what Kate had in mind, but she smiled anyway. "It was nice to meet you." She stuck out her hand, and Peter grasped her fingers, the way he had held Christina's hand on the bus.

"Maybe I'll see you in church tomorrow. My grandfather and I sit up front on the left, right below the pulpit." He let go of her fingers and turned to open his door.

"Don't get out," she said, opening the door herself.

"Don't forget your souvenir," he said, retrieving the orange puffy hand that had slid into the space beside her seat.

Kate took it from him. "What did you say to the woman at the turnstile?"

"I said I was trying to impress you and asked her to help me out."

Chapter 10

When Kate got to work on Monday, Woody was sitting in her chair and having his shoes shined. Scott Pratt, whose primary function at the bank was shining the shoes of its officers, looked up from the Gucci loafer he was buffing, and winked. Kate put her hand up in silent greeting. Usually she exchanged a few words with Scott, but Woody's presence put her on guard.

Kate had been stunned the first time she encountered Scott kneeling in front of a trader to polish his shoes. She had glanced around the trading room, but no one paid the slightest attention. Even Ernie shrugged off her amazement that the bank would provide an employee to shine shoes.

"Why not?" he said. "It saves the bank money. Guys keep working while they're getting a shine."

"But what about Scott?" Kate said.

"What about him? He's paid a good salary, and the tips are gravy. Hell, he's doing better than most of the bankers. He's got a house on the Jersey shore. He told me last week he's buying the place next door for his kid."

"But it seems so demeaning, his kneeling in front of them like that."

"He doesn't kneel. He sits on that little case he pulls around."

"And they list him in the directory under 'Shoeshine.'"

"He gets more calls that way. They can't list him as 'Scott.'"

"What about 'Scott Pratt'?"

"His last name is 'Pratt'?" Ernie said, which had brought their discussion to a close.

Woody made no move to get up from Kate's chair. "Ernie and I are talking about the two-year auction," he said. "You got bill buyers ready to extend?"

"Not really," Kate said. "Our customers buy two-year notes for a trade sometimes, but they've got to be very bullish to do it, and even then they get nervous. The two-year is like the long bond to bill buyers." She realized that comparing the two-year note to the long-bond, with its 30-year maturity, was a bit of a stretch, but she wanted to make her point.

"What are they worried about?" Woody said. "Interest rates aren't going higher, and the curve is going to stay steep. The arbitrageurs will short the hell out of the new two-year every month, like they always do, and make it special in the repo market. Your customers can lend their two-years, pick up yield, roll into next month's auction, and do the whole thing all over again. The trade's a fuck-ing lay-up."

Was he naturally condescending, Kate wondered, or did he have to work at it? "A lot of customers think the Fed's finished lowering interest rates for a while," she said. "Our customers don't like to buy longer-dated securities unless they think the market's really going to run."

"Since when is putting on a trade only the customer's idea? God forbid one of you proposes a trade that's in *our* best interest." Woody looked from Kate to Ernie, and seemed disgusted with them both.

"So you'd be extending in here," Ernie said.

Kate hated to see Ernie playing the game, but Woody brought out the defense in everyone.

"I think it's the kind of trade you've got to watch," she said, "and some portfolio managers might not want to get aggressive before they go on vacation."

"Markets don't rally in August?" Woody asked sarcastically.

"We can ask at the sales meeting and see what they say," she said.

"You do that," Woody said. He handed Scott Pratt a dollar and went back to his desk.

"Now that was a pleasant little exchange," Kate said, after Scott had moved on to his next customer.

"This is a lose-lose proposition," Ernie muttered,

taking off his glasses and rubbing his eyes. "We put people into this trade and it works, Woody's going to take the credit, and if it craters, we'll be off their list for months. We'll be begging Keezer for odd lots. Were you serious about proposing the trade to the sales force?"

Kate didn't agree with the timing of Woody's trade idea, though bold strokes were the ones that made big money. It was fine for her to approach trading in a steady, cautious way—her bullet bid in the June year-bill auction notwithstanding—but a head trader had to think bigger, and push those around him to do the same. She understood that Matheson would have to become more aggressive if it wanted to compete with the investment banks, which took much larger risks when it came to trading securities.

Woody needed to pick his spots though. The yield curve had already steepened dramatically in the past year, with interest rates falling furthest on securities with short maturity dates. More to the point, she and Ernie were sitting on $6 million in profits. Six million might be spare change to Woody, but this would be a record year for the bill desk, even if they didn't book another dime. If Woody was so convinced about the curve steepening further, she thought, let him put the trade on in his own account.

"Earth to Munro." Ernie jiggled the armrest on Kate's chair. "Do we pitch the trade or not?"

"There's pitching, then there's Doc Gooden pitching," Kate said.

Ernie blinked at her once or twice before putting his glasses back on. "How was Saturday?"

"The Mets won."

"I read that much in the paper. How'd the guy from the church do?"

Ernie's suggestive tone threw Kate off. She had never participated in that kind of trading room innuendo. A seemingly innocuous comment could be a trap, a way to draw you into a crude story or practical joke. Even announcing that you were hungry could get people started.

"God Squad?" Ernie said.

"Not at all," Kate said, abandoning her principle of non-engagement. "Even you would like him."

"Is that some kind of shot?"

"I'm just saying he was likeable, that's all."

If Kate wanted to talk about Peter Hanley, Ernie would have to do. She was still annoyed with Liz for not inviting her to California, and for her sister's sketchy explanation of why she had extended her trip to visit her employer's San Francisco office. When Liz called Sunday evening to say she was back, Kate didn't mention the ballgame on Saturday, or seeing Peter at church the next morning either.

Kate had arrived early and stood at the back of the sanctuary, unsure if Peter had meant for her to sit with him or to meet after the service. A gray-haired man with a carnation boutonnière approached and asked if she was looking for Peter Hanley. "He said to keep an eye out for you," the usher explained, before leading her down the center aisle. She hadn't felt so on display since her wedding.

Peter sat in the third pew, his head bent toward the older and much slighter man on his left. She slid into the pew next to Peter, who seemed surprised to see her in this different setting. He introduced his grandfather, Arthur Etheridge, who wore a crisp white shirt, knitted tie, and navy jacket. Peter was similarly dressed, but otherwise the two men didn't resemble each other. Peter was big and handsome in a conventional way, while Mr. Etheridge, apart from his age, seemed more delicately formed.

When they stood to sing the opening hymn, Peter shared his hymnal with her. He had an enthusiastic tenor voice and sang every word. After the service, he invited her to join them for a glass of iced tea in the church social hall, a large musty room below the sanctuary. Its décor was tired, with patches of flaking paint around high-set windows and faded blue curtains unlikely to survive another cleaning. But the crowd was lively and chatted amiably. Kate spotted Rev. Barlow, who waved at their small party from across the hall.

Accepting the offer of a ride home, Kate waited on the sidewalk with Mr. Etheridge while Peter got the car, this time a dark blue sedan and not the red Prelude. When they arrived at her building, Peter told his grandfather and then the Sunday doorman that he would be right back. Inside the empty lobby, Peter fidgeted with a button on the sleeve of his jacket. The button came off in his hand, which seemed to perplex him.

"I want to collect on that drink you mentioned yesterday," he said. "I was thinking Saturday night?"

Pleasure flooded through her. "Saturday's good. Or sooner, if you'd like."

"I was thinking Saturday, but if sooner is better for you…"

"That's fine."

"Saturday, or sooner?" He pointed left, then right, which made her smile.

"Either way. I'll look forward to it." She spoke encouragingly, to make up for her own lack of clarity.

He nodded as if deep in thought and slowly backed up toward the door. "I think I'm better on the phone. I'll call you."

Which is what he did early Monday morning, just as Kate was deciding how much of her weekend to share with Ernie.

"Peter Hanley?" Judy's voice came over the intercom, crisply enunciating the "t" in his first name.

With a show of indifference, Ernie picked up his newspaper.

Kate spoke as quietly as she could into the mouthpiece.

"You got past the operator."

"It wasn't easy," Peter said. "She gave me the third degree."

"Judy's tough."

"Her name's Judy?" Kate pictured him writing the name down for future reference. She liked that he wanted to know the phone operator's name, and that he realized how things worked. "I said I was from your church."

"Did you really?" Kate said. "Church doesn't come up very often in the trading room."

"That's all right, religion's not for everyone. So, how's the Treasury bill market?"

He was saying all the right things. She wouldn't describe herself as religious, and most people outside the business never remembered what she traded. They thought stocks were the only market. On the rare occasion when their knowledge extended to fixed income securities, they mentioned bonds, not bills.

Kate assumed her best update voice: "We've got the weekly auctions today. Three-month and six-month bills. Any interest?"

"Only in the trader. You want to get some dinner tonight?"

He *was* good on the phone. "Dinner sounds great."

"Any foods you don't like? Wouldn't want you queasy on our first date."

"Sushi wouldn't be my first choice."

"Raw fish? No worries. Is seven too early?"

Kate thought rapidly. "Can we make it seven-thirty? We have a sales meeting, and sometimes it runs late."

"Seven-thirty then."

Kate slowly put down the receiver and looked at Ernie. Neither of them bothered to pretend that he hadn't been listening.

"That went rather well," he said.

Late that afternoon, Kate perched impatiently on the seat nearest the door of the large conference room and watched the salesmen assemble. She usually enjoyed the Monday afternoon meeting. It was one of the few times when the department convened without the time pressure of markets about to open, and the only time that sales, not trading, set the agenda. She suspected it was this reversal in leadership roles that gave the meeting its relaxed atmosphere. Of course, the sales staff was expected to make the meeting worth the traders' time. Every salesman reported on his customers, and predicted how they would react to a particular offering or scenario, though only a few salesmen were actually privy to their customers' thinking. The rest of the salesmen faked it, falling back on clichéd comments to disguise the fact that their customers told them next to nothing.

Kate looked around the room, noting which salesmen were there. Fred Manning, the oldest salesman in the department, whose well-established clients always told him what they were doing, though not until moments before the auction; Lloyd Keezer, who knew well in advance what his customers were doing, though their trades weren't large enough to make much difference; and Rita Jones, the best salesman of all. Rita had big customers, always knew what they were up to, and never revealed that information in the sales meeting. Despite continuous warnings that discussions in the sales meeting were proprietary and shouldn't leave the room, most salesmen leaked what they heard because they wanted to appear in the know. Burned in the past, Rita had learned to reserve what she knew for private conversations with the traders.

The sales meeting started with the usual updates from Nick Bhattacharya, the bank's economist, and Stuart Gerard, its Fed watcher. Kate tapped a pencil against her thumbnail. How many times did they have to listen to the breakdown of the employment report and the money supply figures? She could give the report herself, she'd heard it so often.

Woody appeared in the doorway just as Joel Eckman, the sales manager, completed his wrap-up. He started to repeat it, but Woody cut him off and pointed at Kate.

"Have you talked about the trade?" Woody said.

"Not yet," she said.

"Well, are you going to, or should I?"

Be my guest, she felt like saying, but the way he'd put it didn't leave her much choice. As objectively as she could, Kate laid out the curve-steepening trade for the sales force. When she noticed the salesmen taking notes, she sped up her delivery and completed her comments without an endorsement, an omission that Woody pounced on.

"We're actually recommending this trade, in case you couldn't tell," he said. His eyes panned the room, but he didn't look at Kate, making it clear that questions about the trade should be directed to him.

Kate felt her face flame. Which was worse? Being associated with a trade she didn't endorse or being publicly disassociated from it? She wanted to retreat to her desk, but that would only reinforce Woody's message that her opinion didn't matter.

After the meeting, Rita stopped Kate in the hall outside the conference room. "I'll show the trade, but I'm not going to sell it, you know what I mean?"

Kate smiled weakly. "My luck, it'll be the trade of the century, and I'll never hear the end of it."

"You didn't badmouth it," Rita said.

"I didn't get behind it either, which amounts to the same thing in his eyes."

"Difference of opinion is what makes a market, isn't that what Jim always says?" Rita rolled her eyes. "Or some such pearly wisdom."

"Pearls of great price," Kate said solemnly.

"Pearls before swine is more like it," Rita said.

"A stitch in time saves nine."

"One if by land, two if by sea."

"Damn the torpedoes! Full speed ahead!" Kate grabbed the top of her head with both hands. "I feel giddy."

Rita shook her head. "Now there's something I thought we'd never see."

That evening, Kate and Peter took a cab to Le Refuge, a French restaurant on East 82nd Street, where the atmosphere was cozy rather than elegant. Patterned fabric from Provence covered the tables, and there were little vases of wildflowers. The restaurant had two dining rooms, and the waiter led them to the one in the back. Peter ducked his head to avoid a low-beamed doorway; he seemed too large for the quaint space. The waiter took note and showed them to a table with an oversized wing chair.

"You look like Old King Cole in that chair," Kate said.

Peter eyed the spindly chairs at the other tables. "I think they're protecting their investment."

They were shy with each other, paying undue attention to the place setting and flowers. The menu was entirely in French, and they distracted themselves with translations of the various culinary terms. The conversation loosened up with the wine. Peter talked about the teachers' meetings that would begin soon at his school. He said the meetings were a drag, though he liked getting back to work in September.

"The place is all spruced up. There are decorations on the bulletin boards and new chalk in the trays. Then the kids show up, and football season begins, and there are pep rallies and concerts to plan."

"I miss the way September used to feel," Kate said. "All the seasons run together in business. September isn't autumn anymore. It's the end of the third quarter."

"What do you like best about your job?" Peter leaned forward, his arms resting against the edge of the table. She noticed a small nick on his chin where he had cut himself shaving.

Kate gave him her standard response: how she had to follow what was happening in the world because of the possible impact on the market; how the rapid pace made the day fly; how she knew exactly where she stood because trading was so measurable; how she could read the credit column in the newspaper the next morning and know whether the reporter had gotten it right; how she was always on the spot and had the chance to be right or wrong a hundred times a day. It was a spiel that had always seemed sufficient proof of what an exciting job she had.

But the moment she finished, she wished she had been more reflective and open with Peter. What she actually liked best about her job didn't have much to do with the intrinsic workings of the market. She liked feeling included and wanted to show her competence at work that was considered difficult. And she liked being part of a team—part of the celebration when things went well and the commiseration when they didn't. That these aspects of work had placed her in a trading room on Wall Street seemed almost peripheral to the satisfaction she got from her job.

Kate changed the subject to Peter's work. He was starting his tenth year as a high school band instructor, the past five years at Stuyvesant, where he had once been a student and marched in the band. He had gone on to Princeton, where he'd majored in religious studies and played drum in their band, too. He told her he'd always been interested in religion, his and everyone else's, and that Princeton's department was one of the best in the country. He believed his degree qualified him to teach a high school course on world religions, though he thought the subject an unlikely addition to the city's high school curriculum.

"Did you ever think about becoming a minister?" Kate said.

Peter laughed softly as if she had caught him out. "I did a year of divinity school, but I didn't finish. I didn't think I had a calling. I was relieved about that, too. I'm not interested in running anything, especially a church."

"You ran a pretty great field trip on Saturday."

"That's different. No one else wants that job. I'm fine running that kind of thing."

The night air felt wonderful when she and Peter left the restaurant. Walking west on 82nd Street, she felt lightheaded, particularly when he took her hand in the crosswalk at Lexington. They turned left at Park Avenue, which was so brightly lit it could have been daytime. He chatted away, about the great weather they had been having and about baseball. He took her through the Mets' line-up, dropping her hand so he could demonstrate the batting stances of Darryl Strawberry and Gary Carter, two of the Mets' offensive stars, and the rituals each player went through at the plate. She enjoyed listening to him and was content to let him do most of the talking. She could sense him watching her, checking for her reactions the way he had done at the baseball game when he teased her about the hat.

He took her hand again. When they reached her corner, he asked if she would like to keep walking awhile. She felt increasingly relaxed in his company, and happy that he wanted to extend their time together. They walked all the way to 46th Street. In the arcade running alongside the Helmsley Building, he guided her to a recessed part of the walkway. He put his arms around her and kissed her. His lips were so soft. She had forgotten that about a man's kiss.

"You smell good," he said, his cheek against her temple.

"I'll take that as a positive," she said into his collar, thinking the same about him. He held her at arm's-length a moment as though to admire her. He seemed unaware of the people passing them, commuters on their way to Grand Central after working late. She felt the warmth in her face spread through the rest of her body as he pulled her back into his arms. He was more physically at ease than she was.

"I guess I'd better get you home," he said, still holding her close. "What time do you have to get up in the morning?"

"Five-thirty," she said, which made him groan.

Chapter 11

The next day, Woody's curve-steepening trade and the two-year note auction were the focus of the morning meeting. Woody badgered the Fed watcher into supporting his position, that there was little chance of short rates rising. He cut the economist off midway through his update with, "We've heard this all before." Woody didn't bother to call on the traders for their input, not even Adam Campbell, who traded the two-year note. Joel Eckman, the sales manager, repeated his report from the sales meeting the afternoon before. Kate knew the book of business was light when even Keezer's small orders were mentioned. But instead of exploding, Woody reacted stoically, as if he had resigned himself to the paltry book of business and the magnitude of the task ahead.

Jim appeared briefly in the doorway of the trading room and listened as Woody made the summation of his case for the curve-steepening trade: a friendly Fed biased toward lowering short-term rates, and a new supply of securities coming to the long end of the market, which would temporarily raise long-term rates. Jim was wearing his suit jacket, a sure sign that he was leaving the floor.

Kate kept her eyes on him. When he slipped out of the doorway, she rose and quickly followed him out to the elevators.

Jim seemed pleased to see her. "Are you psyched for the two-year?"

"Not really," Kate said. "The risk-reward isn't there for short-end buyers. Do you like the curve-steepening trade?"

Jim checked his watch and frowned before looking up. "Do I like the trade? I'm not as close to it as Woody is. You keeping him posted on bills?"

She wondered if Woody had mentioned her comments or complained about her lack of support. "I told him what I thought."

"Good. Remember: there's no 'I' in team...though there is in 'Jim.'" Kate smiled, just barely. She had heard Jim make that comment before. "Got to get myself a new cliché," he said as the elevator door opened.

"Will you be back in time for the auction?" she said.

The elevator door closed on Jim shrugging an answer.

The afternoon price run-up in the market made it clear that there had been big interest in the two-year note auction, but Kate was amazed to learn that the demand had actually come from A. J. Matheson. Had there been some last minute investor interest that hadn't been shared with the trading room? Maybe one of Rita's accounts had stepped up. Maybe Woody had convinced one of his old Salomon customers to bid through Matheson, or maybe Woody was buying two-year notes outright for a trade. Whatever reasons had prompted Woody to dominate the bidding, he wasn't sharing that information with anyone on the desk, though he must have told Jim. Shortly after the auction results appeared on the screen, Jim was out on the trading floor, clapping his new head trader on the back. Woody seemed to take it all in stride. There was certainly no offer to buy everyone ice cream.

With all the demand in the short end of the market, the yield curve steepened dramatically. Kate was embarrassed to have been so wrong on the trade, though Woody didn't gloat. He didn't need to. The spotlight in the government bond department had definitely shifted to him, a development reinforced by a visit that same afternoon from Phil Armstrong, the bank's chairman, who stood chatting with Jim and Woody on the edge of the trading room floor for everyone to see.

"I don't remember the Chairman down here after the year-bill auction," Ernie said as he watched the congratulatory scene.

Kate had been thinking the same thing, but she also understood that Armstrong's visit was more than male chauvinism. The bank's investment in Woody went beyond all the money they were paying him. In recruiting an outsider for a high-profile position, Matheson had dipped its toe in unfamiliar waters, and was eager for the new hire to make good, and relieve the anxiety that bringing him onboard had created.

Kate thought about how well she had traded in the months before Woody's arrival. Spring had been her season. But now that it had passed, she was more reflective than disappointed. She had never coveted the role of bellwether trader, and it didn't bother her to be one of the regulars again, as long as people remembered what she could do. She told herself there would be other chances to shine, though watching Woody gather accolades from Phil Armstrong was annoying.

"Ready for a little customer schmooze?" Kate said to Ernie, as they closed down the bill desk for the day. A blank look from Ernie. "We're having drinks with Wayne Kimmel, remember? Instead of the baseball game he couldn't make?" A pained expression was her partner's only response. "It's on your way home," she said reproachfully. "That's why we picked Grand Central."

"You go," Ernie finally said. "You're the one Kimmel wants to see. Besides, I promised Marie I'd cut back on the drinking."

Rita was pleased when Kate told her that Ernie wasn't coming. "Fine with me," Rita said as they headed for the subway station at Broadway and Wall. She had dismissed the idea of taking a taxi, with all the rush hour traffic on the FDR Drive. "Let's switch to the local at City Hall.

We've got time, and we might get a seat."

They did get a seat on the local. As it pulled out of the City Hall station, Rita handed Kate a pink message slip. "Judy asked me to give you this. She wanted to make sure you got it today."

Kate read the message that Peter had called. "Thanks," she said, folding the message slip into her pocket.

"Judy said he's a God-fearing man with a sexy voice. I *told* Keezer it wasn't Woody."

"Woody?" Kate said, loudly enough to make the woman seated opposite them glance up from her copy of the *New York Post*.

Rita straightened her pocketbook on her lap. "There were rumors."

"Based on what? The way he puts me down in front of the entire department?"

Rita shrugged. "Well, he is good-looking, and you're both single."

"You can't be serious."

"No, I guess not." The subway doors opened and closed at Bleecker Street. "Weren't you even a *little* tempted?" Rita said, leaning into Kate. "Before he got on your case."

"No," Kate spoke firmly, "I never was. Besides, he's my boss."

"I married *my* boss," Rita said, sounding slightly

defensive. "Did I ever tell you the story?"

As the subway rolled north, Rita reminisced about how she had met Charles, but Kate didn't pay much attention. She was thinking about the rumors linking her to Woody. She found him repellent and suspected he felt the same way about her. Had others seen an attraction that she hadn't noticed? She dismissed the thought as trading room speculation, the kind that cropped up on boring afternoons about anyone single.

Kate and Rita reached the Sun Garden Bar at the Hyatt Grand Central ten minutes early, and learned from the hostess that Wayne Kimmel had already been seated. She led them up several carpeted stairs to a space that looked onto 42nd Street, through a two-story wall of plate glass. Wayne Kimmel was seated on a small sofa, reading through a sheaf of papers that looked like market reports. He stood up and shook their hands.

There was nothing flashy about Wayne, who wore a brown suit and nondescript tie. A native of Rochester, New York, and a SUNY Binghamton grad, he had been managing fixed income assets in Manhattan since the 1970s, long before portfolio management and securities sales became glamorous occupations. Wall Street would have ignored the plainspoken, methodical manager if not for the $10 billion in assets under his control. Well aware of this fact, Wayne remained refreshingly uninfluenced by the salesmen and traders who tried to ingratiate themselves. He had portfolios to manage. If you could legitimately help him do a better job, he was more than happy to take your call.

A waitress took their order and left. Wayne returned his reading material to a scuffed leather briefcase and set it down by his feet. He moved the way he spoke, calmly and deliberately. Rita regularly put Kate on the phone with Wayne to discuss technical matters in the Treasury bill market. He would listen closely to her ideas, ask a few questions, then either execute the trade through Matheson, or politely explain why her recommendation didn't fit. He wasn't like those in the business who took a trade suggestion from one firm, and shopped it with others for a better execution price. Wayne's old-fashioned ways had endeared him to the handful of dealers who still valued that kind of integrity, and who wouldn't exploit a customer's loyalty.

Eventually, as Kate knew he would, Wayne brought up the two-year note auction. "I gave your curve-steepening trade some thought, but we didn't put it on. We've been feeling more cautious about the market." *We've been feeling more cautious about the market.* It was the kind of comment she would record in her notebook about a customer's outlook.

Wayne paused while the waitress set glasses of beer and a bowl of pretzels on the table. So, Kate thought, Amalgamated hadn't gone into the two-year note auction earlier that afternoon, through Matheson or any other dealer. She felt vindicated by the fact that Wayne Kimmel had shared her more neutral stance.

"You must have made a bundle though," Wayne said. "The curve really steepened."

"Actually," Kate said, "the curve trade was the head trader's idea, not mine."

"Well, then," Wayne said, lifting his glass. "Here's to us both catching the next one."

After Wayne and Rita headed into Grand Central to take their respective trains home, Kate stopped at a pay phone in the hotel lobby to return Peter's call.

"You want to get some dinner?" he said.

"I should make you dinner," she said.

"Sounds good. What time should I come over?"

Kate had been thinking about some night in the future, a meal that she would plan for days in advance. It was almost 7 o'clock. "I need to go to the grocery store first," she said.

"Let me do that. I've got unit pricing knocked."

"I've got to go through the aisles myself."

"Or we could go together." Kate hesitated. She wanted to be with Peter, and was charmed by his confidence and spontaneity, but she couldn't plunge ahead with quite the same fervor. "Or maybe you wanted to surprise me," he said.

"I *do* want to surprise you." They agreed on dinner at eight-thirty.

Peter arrived on time, with a bouquet of flowers and a box of candy under his arm. He wore a pair of olive green slacks and a white Oxford cloth shirt, which handsomely set off his tan. Kate felt a return of her contentment from the evening before, and wondered if Peter's attire and traditional gifts were a purposeful tack, a reassurance that he wasn't moving too fast. She admired the flowers, an elaborate bouquet from a shop on Park Avenue. When, at her request, he took down a vase from the top shelf of a cabinet, she noticed again how broad his shoulders were.

"Can I help with anything?" he asked.

Kate opened the refrigerator and took out two bottles of beer. "You can open these."

While she prepared dinner, Peter leaned against the kitchen counter and ate from a plate of antipasto she had taken from the refrigerator. He seemed at ease in the kitchen—he seemed at ease everywhere—and pitched in without taking over. She handed him a colander filled with green beans, which he started to trim.

"*Haricots verts*," he said in an exaggerated French accent. "I had a book growing up that tried to teach you French by hiding French words in the story. Harry Covair was the hero. Get it? *Haricots verts*?"

"Well, it seems to have worked," Kate said. "You're practically fluent."

He feigned tossing a bean at her.

"*Haricots verts,*" she said. "They're on the menu in the guest dining room at work. I think the bank likes to see which customers know the proper pronunciation."

"If they pronounce the 't', they don't get the loan?" Peter popped one of the beans into his mouth.

"It's not that bad, but there is a kind of setting apart. I mean, why not just say 'green beans'?"

"And waste all that refinement?"

"You'd make a good banker."

"Oh, don't tell me that."

"What have you got against bankers?"

"Nothing."

Kate smiled as if she didn't believe him.

"Really," he said. "There's just an awful lot of them around, you know? Where did all these bankers come from?"

Their conversation continued to flow easily over dinner. Peter complimented her cooking and accepted second helpings of everything. He asked whether these were family recipes, and she explained about the recipe file her mother had put together.

"My mother died when I was in high school," she said, hoping to head off an uncomfortable comment or question.

"But your dad is still living?"

"Oh, yes, my dad is still living."

Peter nodded thoughtfully, and Kate found herself telling him about her mother's death, and the way her father insisted that they all immediately resume a regular schedule. She and Liz had gone back to school the day after the funeral. Liz was only ten years old. She had torn up the sympathy cards, and would burst into tears over seemingly unrelated slights, like their father bringing home the wrong flavor of ice cream.

"What about your dad?" Peter said, his voice quiet.

"My dad?"

"How did he deal with it?"

Kate started to remember out loud, without her usual filter. "After dinner, I would put Liz to bed and ask my dad if there was anything else I could do. He would thank me and say that he was going out for some air. Then he would walk to the garage in back of our house. He installed a punching bag out there. I could hear it when I took a bath. Dá-da-da, dá-da-da. It went on like that for hours. Sometimes I can still hear it pounding."

She stopped talking. Not even Ted knew that story. As she set cheesecake and coffee on the table in front of the sofa, it occurred to her that she might be hurting her chances with Peter: unguarded reminiscences were not usually the stuff of dream dates. But then he told her that both his parents had been killed in an automobile accident when he was very young, and that his mother's parents had raised him. He spoke dispassionately, as if explaining his personal history for the hundredth time.

"Do you remember them?" she said.

"I'm never really sure if my memory is what I experienced, or what I've been told over and over." Peter smiled. "I think I remember one time though. I woke up in a crib in a room with my parents. We must have been away from home because it was one of those portable cribs. I was pretty large even then, and I remember standing up in this crib I barely fit into, and watching my parents asleep about three feet away. They woke up and smiled at me. I said, "Tiny, tiny crib," which they thought was hilarious. I remember all of us laughing. After that, our family referred to anything small as 'tiny-tiny.'"

Kate felt her eyes sting. If she had taken a bite of the cheesecake, she might have been able to compose herself, but looking at Peter, so long removed from anything tiny, made her cry. He set his dessert plate on the coffee table and produced a folded handkerchief from his pocket.

"Some mood we're creating here," he said. "I had a very happy childhood. I think it was hardest on my grandparents."

Kate blotted under her eyes with Peter's handkerchief. "I was married before," she said.

"I figured you might have been."

"You did?"

"Women like you get taken pretty early."

"What about men like you?"

"I've never been married, if that's what you mean, though I was engaged once."

"What happened?"

"She met a banker." Kate looked at him incredulously. "No kidding," he said. "I'm trying not to hold it against you."

She relaxed against Peter's shoulder. He wasn't male in the way she had encountered it; he didn't seem put off by emotional subjects, or the way sharing his own sorrows might make him look. Still, she was relieved when he changed the subject to the upcoming weekend. He mentioned an invitation to go dancing at Roseland with Lawrence Parker, his minister friend who had gone on the field trip to Shea Stadium.

"I've never been to Roseland," Kate said, intrigued by the idea.

"Me neither, but Lawrence and his girlfriend are regulars. I think you're the reason I'm finally getting the nod."

Kate couldn't remember the last time she had danced, though it probably hadn't been with Ted. He hated to dance, and would palm her off on single men at parties while he talked shop with the more gung-ho medical types.

Peter lightly touched her cheek. "You're pretty when you blush."

She shook her head. "I wish I could control it, but I can't."

"Who's asking you to?"

Chapter 12

On Friday, Kate arrived at work to find Rosemary waiting at her desk. Kate wondered what sort of operational problems she might be untangling with the position clerk that morning. "Isn't it Ernie's turn?" Kate asked, only half kidding.

Rosemary didn't respond with her usual good-natured sarcasm. It was only seven o'clock, but beads of perspiration had already formed on her forehead. "I need to talk to you off the floor."

"All right," Kate said, stowing her bag in the bottom drawer of her desk. "Where to?" She expected that they would confer at Rosemary's workstation, one of a dozen steel gray desks lined up like ships in dry dock on the edge of the trading room. But Rosemary kept walking, beyond the Xerox room and around a corner into unfamiliar territory. It wasn't like the level-headed clerk to be so mysterious.

Rosemary opened the door to a long, narrow closet filled with office supplies. "Wow," Kate said, eyeing the floor to ceiling shelves. "So this is where Rita gets all her

No. 2 pencils."

Rosemary sighed and lowered herself onto a stepstool in the corner of the closet. "Close the door and pull up a chair," she instructed, pointing to a box of copy paper. "Sorry to be so secretive, but I swear, the people out there have X-ray hearing."

"And they can read lips, too," Kate said from her cardboard box chair. "They jump on the least little tidbit." She felt an odd conspiratorial sensation; this clandestine meeting was so unlike her usual routine.

"Like a flock of filthy pigeons," Rosemary said, her tone harsh. "I can't have anyone tracing this information. Albert could lose his job."

It was hard to imagine Rosemary's mild-mannered husband getting into trouble. "Is there a problem?" Kate said.

"It's not Albert who has the problem. He just can't have his name turning up as a source."

"A source of what?"

"A source of information, in case the press gets hold of the story."

"What story?"

Rosemary sighed again. "Albert stayed late last night going over bids in the two-year note auction. He didn't get in till midnight." Despite her worries, Rosemary also seemed proud of her husband's special assignment.

"Why are they going over the bids?" Kate said, though the idea that the bids were being checked wasn't completely astounding. Demand like that coming from Matheson must have caught the Fed's attention. But why was Rosemary telling her? The two-year note auction was Woody's deal, not Kate's.

"I guess you could call it an audit," Rosemary said, "but it's not routine. Albert's boss is head of debt management. He doesn't get involved in anything low-level."

"No, I guess not," Kate said, looking over Rosemary's head at the abundance of supplies on the shelves.

"They're also checking the June year-bill. The one you did so well with, remember? You bought everyone ice cream. You went out and got it yourself, too. None of that 'You fly and I'll buy' jive."

Kate felt the prick of adrenaline under her arms. "But didn't you say they were auditing the two-year note auction?"

"That's the one people have been talking about, but Albert's checking the year-bill, too."

Kate had heard that dealers were complaining about the two-year note auction, but they often complained when they lost money. Dealers would go short the new securities, when the sale of those securities was announced, with the intention of buying them back cheaper in the auction. But if the auction went stronger than expected, dealers had to pay up for the securities, and often lost money in the process. And price wasn't the only concern;

sometimes the newly auctioned notes simply couldn't be found, even on a temporary basis in the financing market, where dealers could lend and borrow securities from each other. When that happened, dealers failed to make delivery and were forced to go to the Federal Reserve Bank for help. The Fed was understandably concerned: dealers failing to make on-time delivery upset the smooth functioning of the government securities market, one of the Fed's most important charges.

But there hadn't been a delivery problem in the June year-bill, Kate thought. Dealers who missed in that auction had paid up for the bills and squared their positions. There had been no market dislocation, nothing lasting beyond an hour or two. She remembered being pumped by her success, and then worried about retribution from Woody for making him look bad. But nothing that could be described as a problem for the government securities market had occurred in the June year-bill auction.

"I don't understand why they're looking at the year-bill auction," Kate said. "There weren't any delivery problems on that issue."

"Maybe because we bought so much of it, and it wasn't that long ago," Rosemary said. "Woody can cover his own raggedy ass, but I thought you and Ernie deserved a heads-up."

The warning threw Kate. She and Ernie had followed the standard procedure, reading their bids over the phone to Johnny B, the Matheson employee who stationed himself at the Fed an hour before the auction, phoning the traders for their final bids, which usually came minutes before the 1 o'clock deadline.

Had Johnny B screwed up? Kate immediately dismissed the notion. Johnny B was a back-office veteran, a walking operations manual for how to move money and securities through the financial system. He would have caught an operational error long before the Fed. Kate considered the possibility that Albert and Rosemary were overreacting, the way junior employees sometimes did when a senior official showed interest in their work. Kate had done that a time or two herself.

"What exactly did they tell Albert to look for?" Kate said.

"They told him to get the facts because they wanted to be absolutely sure before proceeding further," Rosemary said.

Kate nodded slowly. "Check the facts and follow wherever they lead. That's exactly what Jim would do."

"Well, Jim's not getting this from me. He'd put two and two together and nail Albert for the leak."

"I think you can trust Jim to keep this quiet."

"The old Jim maybe, but the one strutting around here lately?" Rosemary leaned forward, squaring her forearms on her knees. "I'm not trusting him with my husband's job." Her tone and expression were fierce.

Kate pictured the Federal Reserve Bank building on

Liberty Street, a fortress of tan-colored stone. Its very architecture intimidated. She had been introduced to senior Fed employees on their visits to the bank. They clearly considered Matheson a model of probity, a partner in preserving the stability of the country's financial system. If Matheson had done something illegal, Phil Armstrong would go berserk. His aversion to publicity of any kind was well known. He wouldn't permit the bank to advertise because he found the practice crass.

"But this is the *Fed*, Rosemary. Jim's got to be told."

Rosemary sat back hard, as if she'd been shoved against the shelves. "Why? If something bad went down in that auction, there's nothing he can do about it now."

"But if there's a problem, it's much better if Jim points it out to the Fed, instead of waiting for them to come after us. Something bad might happen again if we don't tell him."

Rosemary shot Kate an accusing look. "Ernie wouldn't tell Jim, and I shouldn't have told you. Albert warned me not to, but I told him you were different."

I *am* different, Kate thought, though Rosemary's warning implied that there might be tracks to cover. Had Rosemary intended to be helpful, or was she simply unable to keep the information to herself? People were born to blab; it was right up there with eating and breathing. And yet Rosemary had come to her, not Ernie, who was the better choice if gossip had been the clerk's only objective.

Kate stood up from the cardboard box and offered Rosemary a hand. "I've got to get back to the desk."

Rosemary didn't budge. "You're going to tell Jim, aren't you?"

"I wouldn't say where I heard it."

"What are you going to say?"

"I'd say it came to my attention anonymously."

"Like in a note?" There was vulnerability on Rosemary's upturned face, which gave Kate an unwanted feeling of superiority.

"A note or a phone call. Please don't worry. You haven't done anything wrong."

Rosemary hauled herself up from the footstool, refusing Kate's hand. "Since when has that been a reason not to worry?"

When Kate got back to the trading room, Ernie was talking to the agency traders, leaning against the elevated row of desks behind him like a neighbor over the back fence. Kate looked at the overhead clock. 7:20. She had lost more than half her usual preparation time. She lifted her coffee from the brown paper bag, but the cup was already cold. She took a half-hearted bite of the old-fashioned donut and dropped the rest into the trash. What if she had done something wrong in the June year-bill auction? The question gnawed at her. Matheson employees were instructed to act ethically at all times, to do the right thing and avoid even the appearance of conflict of interest. Now, several blocks away, the Fed was working overtime, poring over the bank's participation in the most recent Treasury auctions, including the one in which she had made her name.

Ernie ended his chat and acknowledged Kate. "Working a half-day?"

"I wish."

"Trouble in paradise?"

"I've got to tell you something."

He jingled the coins in his pocket. "Come on, I'll buy you a drink."

They left the trading floor and walked past the elevators to the soda machine just beyond the women's room. Ernie fed quarters into the machine, flipped open a Coke, and handed it to her. "A guy buys you a drink, you tell him your troubles."

Kate noticed someone coming out of the women's room, and moved beyond the soda machine to the stairwell door. With a quizzical look, Ernie followed her. "What gives?"

Quickly Kate told him what she had heard from Rosemary, including the clerk's proviso about secrecy and protecting Albert's job.

"Wild horses couldn't drag it out of me," Ernie said. "You should dummy up too." Ernie patted his shirt pocket for a pack of cigarettes that wasn't there.

"Do you think we might have accidentally done something wrong?" Kate said.

"Relax. The June year-bill auction was a textbook case of a strong retail book driving a bid. We nailed it, fair and square, so calm down. I don't see striped pajamas in your future."

Aren't you worried? Kate wanted to ask, but her partner's soporific expression seemed anything but. "What do you think happened in the two-year note auction?"

Ernie grunted. "Maybe Woody tried to jump-start his career at the bank."

"So you *do* think there's something wrong with the two-year."

"It's possible. It ought to be interesting, watching Jimbo pitch his way out of this one."

Kate's eyes widened. "You think Jim's got something to do with this?"

"Maybe."

"But why would Jim do anything wrong? He's already on his way to the top."

"Maybe he wants to get there faster."

Kate shook her head adamantly. "Jim would never fool with an auction. Tampering with a Treasury auction is a federal offense."

"Cheating the government does seem more Woodsonesque," Ernie said.

"What do you think he did?"

"There's a hundred ways to cheat."

"But how, specifically?"

"Maybe he bid for another dealer? That's collusion to corner the market. How should I know? I don't possess a criminal mind."

Kate slowly shook her head. "I can't believe this could happen at Matheson."

"Matheson is exactly the kind of place where stuff like this happens," Ernie said. "All these trusting souls. The situation here was ripe, when you think about it."

Kate watched him buy a cup of coffee from the machine. She had mentally conceded that Woody could have been sloppy with the bidding process, something for which the Fed might issue a reprimand or fine, but Ernie made it sound as though fraud was just as likely. He didn't seem shocked by the possibility that Woody might be the loose cannon people always worried about. She remembered the month she started at Matheson, when a money market trader lost a half million dollars on a futures trade. He had been fired—the size of the trade had been way over his limit—and so had his boss, for failing to properly supervise.

Ernie started back to the trading room. "Let's go. We were still employed, last time I checked."

"Wait," Kate said, catching up to him. "Do you think I should talk to Jim?"

Two salesmen came off the elevator, and Ernie waited for them to go through the trading room doors.

"I like Jim," he said. "He's kept me around a lot longer than anyone else would have, and I appreciate that. I always try to give him an honest day's work, and I like to think I've had a hand in training a future all-star. But my obligation to the bank doesn't include passing on pillow talk some nice lady from the back office tells me."

"I wouldn't mention her name. I'd say I got an anonymous tip."

Ernie snickered. "You're a great trader, Toots, but a lousy liar."

"But I'd be telling the truth."

"What makes you think Jim would let you keep your source confidential? He'll want proof before he tells Phil Armstrong and the boys that the Fed's got their bean counters working overtime on our records. Jim could turn the tables on you, if he's antsy enough, and make you give up your source as a test of loyalty. Is Munro on the inside or the outside? Are you ready for that kind of question?"

"You think he'd put it like that?"

"Maybe. I don't think Lord Jim's ever been in a bind, not around here anyway. It's hard to predict how someone will react when he feels threatened. Fairness to others is not usually the first consideration."

Kate looked away, then back at Ernie. "I don't know what I should do."

"Then don't do anything. The big boys around here can take care of themselves. Hell, they'd flick Rosemary and Albert off the table like a couple of crumbs, if push comes to shove."

"Maybe Jim would be grateful for the tip-off and leave it at that."

"Maybe, but I don't take chances like that with people like Rosemary and Albert. They need their jobs more than I do."

Kate set aside her dilemma for a moment and smiled fondly at Ernie. "And you voted for Reagan."

Ernie's eyes rolled left, then right, then left again, like the plastic orbs of a Kit-Cat Clock. "Who says I did?"

Kate stood on the threshold of the trading room and watched Ernie shuffle back to his desk. Then her eyes shifted to the glass office in back of the room. Jim still wasn't in.

It was a busy morning, and for stretches of twenty minutes at a time Kate didn't think about the Fed poking around in the bank's auction records. She made prices for customers, spoke with Nick about the flash report for third quarter GNP growth, and listened closely to Adam describe a Long Island golf course as though she was considering membership.

But the distraction of work had its limits, and snatches

of her morning conversations with Rosemary and Ernie kept surfacing. Maybe he was right: Jim Fletcher was a big boy, with even bigger boys looking out for him. The more Kate thought about it, the less likely it seemed that Albert was the only one with this information. For all she knew, someone may already have tipped Jim off. He could be in the back office now, checking the auction sheets for himself, or even over at the Fed, setting matters straight.

That had to be it. She imagined Phil Armstrong taking Jim aside and telling him about the call that had come in from the Fed. A discreet internal investigation would be conducted. If Woody had knowingly broken the rules, then the firm's relationship with him would be severed. The company would tolerate a mistake in judgment—Matheson employees were human and, alas, prone to error—but a breach of principle was a grave offense. If Woody had betrayed the company and everything it stood for, then dismissing him would be in everyone's best interest. Putting an outsider in a key position had been an unsuccessful experiment, a practice to avoid in the future. Surely that was it. Kate had to get over the feeling that she was the designated rescuer, and acting as if the powers-that-be didn't have the situation under control. She would follow Ernie's advice and let the process play itself out.

But as the day wore on, the comfort of Kate's newly adopted isolationism disappeared. It started to crumble when she took out her trading journal and checked her notes on the June year-bill auction. She had carefully recorded every detail about the auction and the clients who had bid through Matheson. It was all there: the names of the institutions and their representatives; the specific amounts of bills bid for at various yield levels; the actual results; even a line or two about the client's stated reason for bidding. *Swapping out of the old year-bill. Covering a short. Going long for a trade.* Kate smiled like an athlete flipping through a scrapbook of favorable newspaper clippings.

Jim Fletcher had made her success possible. Giving a woman a chance on the trading desk would never have occurred to anyone else. There was no precedent for it at Matheson, a company steeped in tradition, with little inclination to veer from established practice. But Jim had stuck his neck out, and here she was playing it safe, making convenient assumptions that might well prove wrong. What if she and Rosemary *were* the only ones at Matheson who knew what the Fed was up to? Shouldn't Jim have the chance to conduct his own review before the Fed pre-empted him? If Woody had tampered with the auction, it would be far better for Jim to make that discovery than be caught flat-footed. Once he had the facts, Jim would concede that hiring Woody had been a mistake, and deal with the head trader's dismissal. Jim might even come through this ordeal with an enhanced reputation as a steady head in a crisis. Surely he wouldn't press Kate for her source if he understood that a man's job was at stake.

But which man's job would be more important to Jim—his or Albert's? Kate could almost hear Ernie answering the question.

There had to be some middle path. If she could somehow manage to get Jim talking about auctions, the subject of the investigation might naturally come up. He had recently complimented the journal she kept, and mentioned the need for a system that would provide the same sort of statistics for every trader. She would follow up with him on that idea, which could lead into a discussion about bidding in auctions. It wasn't a perfect plan, but it was better than doing nothing.

Kate went over to Jim's secretary and asked when he was coming in.

"He's at an orientation meeting for parents at his daughter's preschool," Lorraine explained. "He should be in shortly." She seemed proud that her boss was spending time with his family. "Is there a message, or do you want to see him?"

"I probably should see him." Kate watched as Lorraine completed a message slip, filling in blanks and checking boxes. *Kate Munro* written in perfect Catholic school cursive. Stopped by your office. ✓ Would like to see you. ✓

Lorraine looked up, her pen poised over the last row of little boxes. "Does it need to be today? Fridays are busy, and he's getting a late start."

Kate froze, suddenly gripped by the thought that the future might turn on which little box got checked. In that moment, she understood what Ernie had been trying to explain. How would she handle a probing question from

Jim when she was having trouble telling his secretary which box to check on a message slip?

Lorraine dropped her pen to the space provided for more detailed messages. "Can I say what it's in reference to?"

"Jim wants to develop a system to track auctions," Kate said. "I'm following up on that." Lorraine turned the message pad around for Kate's approval. "You'd better check 'Today,'" Kate added. "This tracking system is pretty important."

Lorraine put a check the size of the Nike swoosh in the designated box.

But Kate's request to see Jim didn't lead to a meeting. He arrived midday and stood behind Woody's desk for a moment before Lorraine herded him into his office to meet with visiting clients. Kate lost track of him after that.

On her way out for the weekend, Kate bumped into Rosemary on a crowded elevator. The clerk gave her an anxious look, and smiled beatifically when Kate shook her head.

Chapter 13

Roseland, an essential part of New York nightlife in the 1950s, was considerably less grand thirty years later, though there was still a festive feel to its red décor. A mirrored ball revolved over the center of the room, and tables ringed the polished wooden dance floor. The space had seemed overly air-conditioned when the two couples first arrived, but by ten o'clock it was as sultry as the August evening they had come in from. New Yorkers of various ethnicities crowded the floor, moving to a selection of pop, salsa, and R & B introduced by a disc jockey.

Peter sat with his arm resting across the back of Kate's chair, laughing at stories Lawrence was telling about his days as a high school basketball coach, before he had become a minister. Kate watched the give-and-take between the two men, occasionally catching the eye of Muriel Williams, Lawrence's girlfriend, who smiled amiably and sipped from her ginger ale, the only one in their party not having a beer. A shy, shapely woman dressed in a sarong-style dress, Muriel managed to appear both modest and voluptuous at the same time.

"That's a nice shirt, Peter," Muriel said. "Very colorful."

"You like it? It was either this or an old aloha shirt." Peter's cotton button-down shirt had patchwork sections of blue, yellow, green, and pink stripes. It looked like a preppy quilt.

"Muriel," Lawrence said. "Be honest with the man now. He looks like a narc in that shirt."

Peter pulled his head back and stared at Lawrence. "You don't think these stripes are kind of funky?"

"I'd lend you one of mine, but even with the stretch it would never fit you." Lawrence's shirt was a tapered mauve knit, a disco holdover from the '70s, and practically a uniform on the dance floor.

Peter looked down at the front of his shirt. "I could wear it open, but I don't have a gold chain." He smiled at Kate.

"Maybe roll the sleeves up a little." Kate unbuttoned his cuff, turning it back twice. "Like that." She looked up at Peter, whose rapt expression sent heat rushing through her.

"You can take him out, but you can't dress him up," Lawrence said, while Peter saw to the other sleeve. "I'm warning you about this, Kate, because I like you."

Peter stood up and reached for her hand. "Are you going to give advice all night, Lawrence, or are we going to dance?" Not waiting for an answer, he led Kate through the tables and chairs to the middle of the hardwood floor. He turned her once slowly under his arm until she was facing him, then reeled her in close. Over the top of his shoulder, Kate smiled at Lawrence and Muriel, who had joined them on the dance floor.

Kate hoped Peter wouldn't spin her around too much or show off any intricate steps. She couldn't keep up with that kind of dancing, which might have explained her tendency to lead. Ted had always accused her of leading, though she couldn't tell when she was.

"What are you smiling about?" Peter said.

"Honestly?"

"Of course! Unless it's going to hurt my feelings."

"Have I ever hurt your feelings?"

He smiled and shook his head.

"I was hoping I wouldn't start leading," she said, though Peter was so large and holding her so close that she didn't think it would be a problem. The way he held her hand, his fingers curving around the back of her wrist and his thumb in the center of her palm, felt incredibly intimate.

"Do you like to lead?" he said.

"I've been called on it before, but I can't tell when I'm doing it." Peter was smiling at her now, tenderly it seemed. "I know men hate it."

"I'll keep my eye on you."

Kate listened to the synthesized opening of a song she had heard on the radio dozens of times. Now, because it was their first dance, she paid attention to the words.

> *Acting on your best behavior*
> *Turn your back on Mother Nature*
> *Everybody wants to rule the world.*

Not exactly the sentiment she was looking for, she thought, smiling at her own romanticizing.

"*Now* what are you smiling about?" Peter said.

"I was listening to the lyrics."

"Tears for Fears. They're very big at Stuyvesant. The kids use this song for background music on projects."

"For what subject?"

"Doesn't matter. It's anti-Me-Generation."

Kate couldn't tell whether or not Peter was joking, but the song's repetitive phrasing made it easy to dance to, or maybe it was the skill of her partner. Peter had confessed to several years of dancing lessons with Miss Louise, an Upper East Side matron whose instruction in ballroom dancing was an institution in the neighborhood. What other finishing touches had he received in his youth? He made no attempt to hide his privileged upbringing, though he joked about it too, as if to lighten its impact and the distance it might have produced. On the drive to Roseland that evening, he had recounted some of his dancing school mishaps, like the time he blew out the seams of his pants doing the limbo.

But Peter had clearly paid attention in dance class, his stories notwithstanding. Kate sensed that he was toning it down for her now, which made her wish she had been taught something beyond the hokey-pokey. It got easier when the disc jockey shifted up-tempo, playing a medley of Madonna's hits. *Get into the groove, baby, you've got to prove your love to me.* Peter closed his eyes and turned his head to the side as if jamming on a set of drums. His light brown hair gradually darkened with perspiration, and when he held her during the next slow dance, his shirt felt damp.

"You want to take a break?" he said after almost an hour on the dance floor.

"Not unless you do."

"You want to lead?" She smiled, and he pressed his cheek against hers. "I thought I'd offer the car to Lawrence and Muriel so they don't have to take the train home. Lawrence has to work tomorrow, so they may leave a little early."

The two couples said their good-byes. Peter and Kate danced again, but after the first number, they looked at each other and walked off the floor. Taxis were lined up outside the entrance. They climbed into the spacious back seat of a Checker cab and were in each other's arms as soon as the taxi pulled away from the curb. Before long, some sense of propriety made them pull apart and sit up straighter. Peter cracked open a window. The cab sped up Park Avenue, and Kate ticked off the numbered streets as if in a trance: 65th, 66th, 67th.

The cab turned right at 72nd Street and stopped at the first entrance. Peter paid the fare. "Keep the change," he said, the first words he had spoken since giving the driver her address. They got out of the cab without touching each other and were stone silent as they went into the building. Kate was glad that Frank wasn't on duty.

She unlocked her apartment door, and Peter followed her into the foyer. The moment the door closed, he kissed her, his lips warm and moist. She turned to chain the front door and felt his arms encircle her from the back. He nuzzled her neck and shoulders, and desire threaded up through her.

Slowly she turned to face him. "Would you like a beer?"

"A beer?" A kind of confused agony came over his face, which made her sorry that she had teased him, though not enough to stop.

"Your eyebrow's twitching a little," she said, smoothing it with her finger.

"It is?"

She nodded. "Like a cat."

*   *   *

In the morning, Kate woke up facing the empty space next to her. The pillow was indented and the covers turned back. She noticed that the bedroom door had been pulled shut, and the thought that Peter had left without saying good-bye made her sad. When she heard the muffled sound of a voice coming from the kitchen, she stretched and smiled like a baby waking from a nap. Her nakedness felt good against the sheets as she lay there, thinking back on the night before and how naturally it had unfolded. Part of her wanted to stay in bed all day and think about their lovemaking, but she wanted to see Peter more.

She got up and went into the bathroom to get her robe. In the mirror, her face had the high color of exercise. She brushed her teeth and ran a comb through her hair.

Peter was dressed in his clothes from the night before and talking on the phone in the kitchen. He had obviously attempted to comb his hair with his fingers, and there was a new growth of beard on his face. He looked up and pointed toward a pot of coffee on the counter. He already had a cup, which Kate refilled before pouring one for herself. Standing next to him, she leaned against the edge of the kitchen counter.

"I'll see you soon," he was saying into the receiver. Again she felt a twinge, and then the delayed reaction of curiosity. *To whom was he talking?*

Peter hung up the phone and put an arm around her waist, rubbing the side of her hip with his palm. "Was I too noisy out here?"

She shook her head. "Do you have to go?"

"I have to drive my grandfather to church. He told me to invite you for lunch at our house after."

She tried not to look surprised that his grandfather knew they'd spent the night together. "Do you live together?"

"I have the ground floor of his house on 80th. He had a small stroke not long after my grandmother died, and I moved back in for a while. I guess I'm still there most of the time. He has a housekeeper and a driver. He's really pretty independent, but I was uncomfortable being all the way downtown."

"Is that where you lived before?"

"I still have a place there, but I've been up here most of the summer. It's not like I have to tell him where I'm going or anything, but his driver has Sundays off, unless we set something up beforehand."

"I think it's nice that you have a close relationship."

Peter seemed to relax now that explanations were behind him. "He likes you, by the way."

"He said that?"

"Not in so many words, but I can tell. You're both hard-working and honest."

"Not to mention clean and thrifty."

Peter smiled and pulled at a loose strand of her hair. "And you're both game, in a formal sort of way." He sounded serious, as if he were taking his first real measure of her.

She liked his praise, but it embarrassed her too. "You think I'm gamey?"

"I'm the one who's probably gamey."

"No," she said, slowly shaking her head. She set her coffee down, then stepped between his feet and leaned into him.

He put his arms around her. "Will you come to church?"

"Yes, but I'll probably be late. I'll sit in the back and see you afterwards."

"You'll come to lunch?"

She nodded.

"Kate?"

"Yes?"

When he didn't continue, she drew back to look at him. His green eyes glistened and he was smiling, the parentheses in his cheeks framing his handsome features. She smiled back inquiringly, but he didn't give voice to his thoughts.

"I've got to go," he finally said. "I've got to take a shower and change clothes."

She touched the front of his wrinkled shirt. "If I didn't know better, I'd think you slept in these."

Kate lingered in the shower. She felt golden and silky, as if she were still lying next to Peter in bed. She ran her hands over her body the way that he had, and thought about the way they had been with each other. He seemed so comfortable and completely open, calling his grandfather like that from her place so early in the morning.

She poured out a capful of conditioner and lazily massaged it through her hair. She felt as if she were showering in the open, with the temperature of the air and the water and her skin perfectly in balance. She loved the way Peter made her feel, though she wanted him to speak first. Words like that came easier for some people, and she thought he was one of them. She had grown up in a loving family, but it hadn't been a demonstrative one. Maybe it was why she had fallen so hard for the first man she'd met. The chance to be natural and uninhibited the way that lovers are had been liberating, and the best thing Ted had given her.

But Kate didn't want to think of Ted or anything unpleasant. The Fed investigation flashed through her mind, but she pushed away that thought too, and got dressed for lunch with Peter and his grandfather.

Chapter 14

At work on Monday, Kate hummed softly as she bent over a stack of trade tickets. Her day had gone perfectly, one they didn't have to pay you for, as Jim sometimes said. She had won the business she wanted and barely missed on the rest. Like a carnival barker, she revved up interest in the weekly Treasury bill auctions, and the salesmen rewarded her with orders just to get in on the fun.

Jim came over to the bill desk around auction time and watched as Kate handled the last minutes before the one o'clock deadline. He seemed to get a kick out of the way she was making an event of an otherwise routine auction. If he was concerned about how she was conducting herself, he didn't show it, nor did he mention her Friday request to see him. Then she noticed the pink message slip in his hand, and the large check mark that Lorraine had put in the box marked "Today." Jim frequently walked around with a handful of message slips, sometimes to delegate a next step and sometimes to respond in person to those who had contacted him.

But Kate was no longer certain that she wanted Jim's

attention. The more she thought about it, the more likely it seemed that Rosemary had exaggerated the importance of her husband's review of the auctions. That kind of checking by lower-level employees must happen all the time at the Fed, and if it actually was a serious investigation, others more senior would know. Kate didn't need to risk getting Albert and Rosemary into trouble by redundantly pointing out a problem.

And what if she and Ernie had made a technical mistake in the year-bill auction? Alerting Jim to that possibility seemed excessive, like flagging down a cop because your parking meter has expired. Any error, no matter how unintentional, would diminish her success in the auction and tarnish her reputation.

Keezer wandered over from his desk in the front row of sales. "Did you see the Mets game yesterday?" He had directed the question to Kate, though seemed pleased when Jim jumped into the conversation.

Lorraine appeared at Jim's elbow; there was a phone call he needed to take. Jim showed Kate the message slip. "Can this wait?" He was already walking away.

"Sure," Kate said, silently letting out her breath. She waited until Keezer went back to his desk, then turned and smiled broadly at Ernie.

"Only one explanation for a mood as good as yours," he told her.

"Can't a person like her work?"

"Three out of four don't, and that's the national average. It's got to be worse in this business."

"You sound like my sister. She's got a statistic for everything."

"I don't need statistics to make sense of the way you've been acting."

"And how am I acting?" she said, playfully taking him on.

"Well? Am I wrong?"

Kate couldn't suppress a smile. "Hand me your lunch tray."

"Shouldn't we start saving the silverware?" Ernie noisily gathered up the utensils on his tray. "Does Madame prefer service for eight or for twelve?"

After work, Kate took the subway to Bloomingdale's. Liz had come back from California the night before, and called to suggest that they check out the summer sale and have dinner. Kate had told Liz next to nothing about Peter Hanley, though she didn't feel guilty. Liz hadn't exactly been forthcoming: with a single, five-minute phone call, her sister had stretched a weekend visit with their father into a nine-day stay on the West Coast.

Kate daydreamed about Peter on the subway ride up from Wall Street. The lunch with his grandfather the day before had been pleasant. Despite the patrician setting of his home—dark woods and faded fabrics, and lunch served in the dining room by the housekeeper—Mr. Etheridge's actual manner was unassuming. He asked her opinion about the fixed income market and listened closely to her response. He was still an active investor, mostly in equities but also in bonds, and Peter seemed happy when she and his grandfather connected in this way.

Liz stood inside the revolving door at Bloomingdale's metro entrance, reading her Filofax and looking every bit the upscale New Yorker, cool and refreshed and every hair in place even after a day at work.

"Are you wearing blush?" Liz said by way of greeting, studying Kate's complexion like a dermatologist.

Kate gave her sister a hug. "It's hot in the subway."

"I wouldn't know. I took a cab. Are you shopping for anything in particular?"

"Let's just see what strikes us. It doesn't have to be on sale."

Liz eyed her suspiciously but couldn't pass up the green light. "For fall or right now?"

Kate shrugged. "Now is good."

"You realize we're off-season for summer."

"That's good for bargains though, isn't it?"

"Not if you're size ten. Let's start on the fourth floor."

Kate felt comfortable in Bloomingdale's. The store stayed open late on Mondays and Thursdays, and when Ted had worked those nights, she would stop in on her way home and browse through the different departments. Bloomie's had a younger, hipper feel than the city's other department stores. Its ever-changing shopping bags doubled as billboards all over Manhattan. Kate knew that her sister felt superior to the store's mainstream-trendy image, but shopping was shopping, and Liz was enjoying herself.

"I did your colors on the plane," Liz said over her shoulder as they rode the escalator. "You're an Autumn." She handed Kate an envelope filled with strips of color, clipped from the back of a *Color Me Beautiful* book.

Kate squinted at the colored strips. "Are you sure? I don't wear any of these colors."

"You have a camel's hair coat," Liz said. "That's your most becoming neutral."

"What about navy blue?"

"Nope, no navy. You shouldn't wear white either. Or black."

"What else is there?"

"You've got plenty of nice colors…lots of wonderful greens and earth tones."

They stepped off the escalator and huddled over the color strips. "It looks like camouflage," Kate said.

"Your sundress doesn't look like camouflage."

Kate smiled, thinking about the dress she had worn twice in Peter's presence. "Were those my colors?"

Liz gave her a knowing look. "Don't think you're evading me with all this shopping. I'll grill you later." Holding the color swatches in front of her like a divining rod, she waded into the racks.

The sisters had dinner at the Isle of Capri, an Italian restaurant a block north of the store. The place was only half-full, and the waiter seated them by the window, at a table large enough to accommodate their shopping bags. "I can't remember a more successful shopping trip," Liz said after they'd ordered.

"That's because I said 'yes' to everything," Kate said.

Liz smiled regally, accepting the natural order of the universe. "Your skin looks great."

"It's the lighting." Kate pointed out the pink light bulbs in the wall sconces.

"Pink lighting should be mandatory." Liz offered the bread to Kate, then put the basket out of reach on the empty table behind them. "So tell me: it's the guy from the church, right?"

They spent the next hour talking about Peter. As far as Liz was concerned, no detail was too small to mention. "He sounds great," she said. "The opposite of Ted."

"I'm not looking for Ted's opposite," Kate said.

"Well, you're not looking for his twin either. Peter sounds atypical for his background."

"What do you mean?"

"How many Princeton grads teach high school?"

"I'll bet plenty of them do."

"Not at a public school. They teach at Exeter or Farmington, places like that. It doesn't matter, as long as you're all right with it."

"Why wouldn't I be?"

"You know, the stigma of teaching, especially for men. Peter sounds like a rock, but the men teachers we had were all kind of weak."

"Peter's not weak."

"I know that. I'm talking about the stereotype, which by definition is oversimplified and unfair, but it must have crossed your mind."

It had crossed Kate's mind, but she wouldn't say so to Liz. "It's a relief being around someone who's not out to prove he's better than everyone else. Ted didn't know how to relax."

Liz's brow furrowed, as if Peter had hit his first snag. "Do you worry that he's not a hard worker?"

"He jumps right up and helps with the dishes. He trimmed the green beans."

"Well, that's something," Liz said, missing Kate's ironic tone. "You couldn't get Ted to pre-heat the oven."

Kate smiled. "I'm not worried about Peter's work ethic."

"I wouldn't. You've got career enough for two."

"Peter has a career. He's been teaching for almost ten years."

"Of course he has a career, but it's not like what you and Ted were holding down."

"I was home by 6:30 almost every night, and I never worked on weekends," Kate said. "My job never got in our way."

"Maybe not time-wise, but your doing so well must have had an effect on Ted."

"I could have been cashing checks at the bank, for all Ted knew. He wasn't remotely curious about how I spent my day. He didn't pay attention."

"He paid attention when you bought the apartment. You couldn't have done that on a teller's salary, or a chief resident's either. That had to hurt his pride."

"Are you feeling sorry for Ted?"

"Of course not. I hate Ted."

"Your empathy was throwing me off."

"I'm trying to say all this while you're still unattached, which from the sound of things won't be much longer. You're a high-powered person. No, hear me out. You are, which is fine, but if you work all day with arrogant, male chauvinist types like Morehead Woodson, you can't afford to come home to a guy just like him."

"Ted wasn't like Woody."

"You're right, he was worse, because he was supposed to be on your side. Isn't that the deal with a spouse? You back each other 100%?" Liz fastidiously arranged her knife and fork on the side of her plate and aligned the salt and pepper shakers with the vase and votive candle. "Maybe you need the kind of relationship where the woman has the dominant role."

"You make me sound like some kind of ball-buster."

"Well, you're no pushover."

The comment intrigued Kate, who stared out the window at a couple walking hand in hand up Lexington Avenue. People saw her as strong, but she had always yielded to Ted, and let him treat her like the junior partner in their marriage. "Is there nothing in between?" she said, looking back at Liz. "What about equality and mutual respect?"

"In *your* line of work?"

"I'm not talking about work. I'm talking about a relationship."

"And I'm saying that they go together. The only way you can walk into that snake pit trading room every day is to have the most supportive mate on earth to come home to. Isn't that what Jim Fletcher has? And what about Ernie? Why shouldn't you get the same treatment when you come in the door at night? What's good for the goose is good for the gardener."

"Gander," Kate said.

"What?"

"Good for the gander."

"You know what I mean. You're angry now, aren't you?" Liz said.

"I'm not angry, but it doesn't sound like progress."

"But if Peter's happy teaching, it's a perfect match."

"The fact that Peter's a teacher doesn't influence me one way or the other."

"Good. Letting it get in your way would be foolish." Liz ordered *crema catalana* and two spoons and watched the waiter walk off. "Well," she said, taking a deep breath, "I've got some news of my own. I've been offered the job of senior designer in our San Francisco office."

It took Kate several moments to register what Liz had just told her. "Are you interested?"

"Of course I'm interested! It's my dream job. I'm younger than they'd like, but they know I can handle it. Remember Sally Townsend, my first solo client? She called the head of the firm and recommended me. She played up the fact that I'm a Californian. She's a native too, and still very connected in San Francisco. She volunteered to host an introductory cocktail party and invite all her friends. She practically guaranteed a year's worth of business if I'm out there to handle it."

"Is that why you were in San Francisco?"

"I thought I'd make sure it was going to happen before I said anything to you or Dad."

"Dad knows?"

"He figured it out. They called me at his house a couple times to set up the week in San Francisco."

Filled with emotions she couldn't express or even properly identify, Kate carried on the conversation as if Liz were recounting a story about someone else. "When are you leaving?"

"San Francisco wants me the day after tomorrow, but Manhattan insists they don't have anyone to replace me here."

Liz was as good as gone. No sane boss was going to ignore that kind of entrée into San Francisco society. Liz could easily be replaced in New York, where the connection that mattered most was the one you had to money.

"They're just stalling," Kate said. "You're perfect for the job—and you deserve it."

"Thanks," Liz said, sounding relieved. "It's been great in New York, especially with you here. I hadn't been thinking about going back so soon, but then this came up and I couldn't say no. It's not only the job, though it really is a boost. My salary will double, well almost, and I'll get a car and a travel allowance. So don't worry, I'll be back in New York a lot. There's a chance for a percentage deal too, if Sally's referrals come through. The whole thing would make what I do seem more substantial, more like a career. Like what you've accomplished. And I want to go home."

She ate a spoonful of dessert and closed her eyes, as if savoring her future along with dessert. "It's funny, but now that it's really going to happen, I can't wait to leave. I'm afraid if I stay any longer I'll start thinking like a New Yorker, saying stuff like I'd miss the change in seasons if I left. If that isn't the most overrated reason to live here! Like we all have a view of a tree."

Liz giggled and took another bite of dessert. Giddy with having broken the news, she had moved into that conversational territory where sparing the feelings of others gives way to assuming that whatever you say will be taken the right way. In this vein, Liz babbled on about the advantages of living in California: the great weather, the informal lifestyle, the beauty of the Pacific coastline, the Academy Awards show ending before ten o'clock.

"Congratulations, Liz," Kate said, keeping her tone positive.

"I feel like I've finally arrived, you know? Well, of course you know. You arrived ages ago."

That's right, Kate thought, I arrive early everywhere. Marriage. Divorce. "How was your visit with Dad?" she said, changing the subject.

"The usual. I cleaned the house while he watched some game on TV, and then we went to the Boardwalk."

"Did you go to Adolph's?"

Liz nodded. "Can you believe it's still there? I swear, the same waiters too. We've got to have a talk with Dad about portions. He kept piling the food onto my plate. He said I looked thin."

Kate felt an intense longing for her family, who would soon both be 3,000 miles away. Her jaw clenched and her throat tightened.

"There's a ton to wrap up before I go, mostly Woody's apartment," Liz went on. "That job has been a pain, though it probably helped me get this one. Things have a funny way of working out, don't they?"

Half an hour later, Liz handed a shopping bag from the back of the cab to Kate's doorman. "That's the last of them, Frank."

"Nothing for you, Ms. McCord?" Frank glanced at Kate for confirmation.

"Not this trip," Kate said. Frank shut the car door, and Liz waved from the taxi as it drove off.

"You had a visitor." Frank's tone shifted the way a parent's does once the children have left the room. Inside the building, he set Kate's shopping bags down and gave her an envelope. She immediately recognized the hand-writing. "He was here around eight. He waited awhile and then asked if I knew when you'd be back. He wanted to know if you'd gone out with your sister. I said I didn't know, and he left you the note."

Kate looked up from the envelope. "How long was he here?"

"Fifteen, maybe twenty minutes."

Kate nodded absently and was halfway to the elevator before she remembered her shopping bags. Frank already had them and insisted on taking them all the way to her door. They didn't speak in the elevator, though she thought he looked uncomfortable.

Once inside, Kate abandoned her packages in the foyer and went into her bedroom. She sat on the bed and read the note, her heart aching at the sight of the familiar cramped handwriting.

Kate—I was on your block and thought I'd drop by. Sorry I missed you. Hope you are well. Ted

She left the note on the bed and retrieved the shopping bags. Carefully, she took her new clothes from the tissue paper wrapping and hung them on the vacant side of the closet. Why had she let Liz talk her into all this greenery? She had purchased a small forest.

She reread Ted's note and felt her shoulders start to tremble.

Chapter 15

"You're late," Ernie said when Kate got to work the next morning. He looked up from his newspaper to give her the once-over. "Are you hung over?"

"No," she said as she dropped into her chair, "but I feel that way."

Kate had been awake half the night, thinking about Ted stopping by and Liz moving away. There was nothing she could do about her sister but try to be happy for her; Liz's dream job had come through, and she was going for it. But the matter of Ted stopping by was tricky. He seemed to be holding out an olive branch, which she could either accept or ignore. Maybe he didn't deserve much consideration, though her bigger concern was her own reaction: would it be healing or wrenching to speak with him again?

She told Ernie about Ted's note. "Ignore it, and he won't bother you again," Ernie said.

"It might be important, if he came by," Kate said.

Ernie looked at her askance. "He's going to call you with the bimbo eavesdropping in the next room?"

"Maybe she's not a bimbo."

"Oh, yeah, I keep forgetting. She's Mother Teresa with tits."

"You're incorrigible," Kate said, though sometimes she really appreciated the way Ernie saw everything as black or white.

"And so is the good doctor. He probably spotted you with the Mets fan somewhere and wants to know who he is. No guy likes to see his wife with another man."

"*Ex*-wife." Ernie rolled his eyes at the quibble. "Maybe he was just passing by, like he wrote in the note," Kate said.

"Yeah, maybe that's it." Ernie folded his newspaper and tossed it under the desk. "Listen, Toots, do yourself a favor. Don't call him. The guy's got a bad track record."

"But ignoring him seems a little cold."

"And walking out on you wasn't? You were a wreck for months. Dragging yourself in everyday, looking like you'd lost your best friend."

"I didn't drag myself in, and you would never have known if my sister hadn't told you." Kate had been furious with Liz, though grateful in the end that someone at work knew what she was going through.

"Don't you think Pete deserves a little consideration?"

"Pete? A minute ago he was 'the Mets fan.'"

"Yeah, well, Pete's a good guy."

"When did you form this opinion?"

"I talk to him every day, don't I, while he's waiting for you to get off the phone? He calls it 'circling O'Hare.'" Kate smiled, thinking how much that sounded like Peter. "Your ex-husband would never wait, the few times he actually called."

"He waited last night. Twenty minutes, the doorman said."

Ernie sniffed, unimpressed. "Maybe Mother Teresa kicked him out of the house. Ever thought of that?"

Kate hadn't thought of that.

Like the operation of a motor vehicle, a trading job required attention even at slow speeds. That day, Kate welcomed its demands, which kept her personal life at bay and gave her the excuse to further put off talking with Jim. She met with Keezer and one of his Midwestern clients, a session that had run a little long when Woody reneged on the scheduled meet-and-greet.

But Kate's thoughts returned to Ted the minute she left work. On the express train uptown, she wondered if he might have been "kicked out of the house," as Ernie had so delicately put it. She didn't think so. A doctor with his training behind him was too good a catch to be thrown back this soon. But Ted wasn't someone who stopped by simply because he was in the neighborhood. The more Kate dwelled on his note, the more she read into it. Maybe he missed her. Maybe he regretted the way he had left, with nothing but an apology over the phone.

Should she call him? He hadn't asked her to, but she felt she should acknowledge his gesture. Ernie was adamantly against it, and certainly Liz would be too. Liz would seek a restraining order and instruct the doorman to shoot first and ask questions later. She would accuse Kate of being a moth to the flame if she had anything to do with Ted. But Kate didn't plan on discussing Ted's note with her sister, who had accepted a cross-country transfer without even a token consultation.

Kate got off the subway at 59th Street and stopped at a florist on Lexington to buy herself some lilies. Coming out of the shop, she noticed a man in the long white jacket of a physician. She felt a little leap, though he wasn't anyone she recognized.

The truth was that Ted's note and overture of stopping by had touched her, reminding her of everything she had been drawn to in him. How smart and accomplished he was. How witty he could be when he was in a good mood. Even his tremendous drive was attractive, the way he set ambitious goals and pursued them with daily discipline. No one got the better of Ted Munro and, by extension, his wife. In the early years of their relationship, when Kate was still getting her bearings after her mother's death, Ted had engaged the world for them both. His achievements became hers. In theory, Kate didn't endorse that kind of lopsided arrangement, but Ted's sense of purpose and the structure it brought to their lives had been comforting and protective.

Kate often wondered if she had become too much like Ted for their attraction to last. Since college, his schedule had always set their agenda, but when she began to have work commitments of her own, he had protested. He didn't understand why she couldn't cancel her plans whenever he had a rare evening off. She tried to explain that client dinners and occasional travel were part of her work. Only after their break-up did Kate plot Ted's behavior against advances in her career, and the arrival of ambitions separate from his. In many ways, she was no longer the woman he had married, or thought he'd married. Maybe Ted wanted a more traditional arrangement, with the husband earning the living and the wife taking care of everything else, the kind of marriage Kate had once thought she wanted too. Why hadn't he embraced the more complete and equal partner she had become?

Or maybe she was over-thinking the situation. Ted left her because he fell in love with someone else, not because he had consciously analyzed his marriage and found it wanting. Though that didn't explain why he was contacting her now. Had his new romance cooled to the point of remorse? Everything about Ted was so complex.

Peter was different; he was intelligent and well educated, though not ambitious in the current fashion. He made her laugh, but he was more good-natured than witty. He knew his way around a ballpark and the dance floor, but seemed to negotiate more aggressive situations by avoiding them. He was full of plans, though agreeable to her suggestions too. It didn't take a genius to figure out that her attraction to Peter had something to do with how different he was from Ted. Liz had put that much together without ever having met the new man in Kate's life.

That situation was rectified several days later when Peter took Kate and Liz to dinner. Liz had suggested Le Cirque, one of the few top restaurants she hadn't been to, a choice that embarrassed Kate since Peter was picking up the tab.

"The Reagans were here last month," Liz said *sotto voce* in the small dining room tightly packed with patrons the age of the President. "It's their favorite New York restaurant." Peter asked a question about the preparation of an entrée, and the waiter responded as if it were an imposition. Kate wondered how old you had to be to feel comfortable in such an establishment, though Peter paid no mind to the waiter's condescension. Neither did Liz, but she was focused on other matters. She had begun the process of selling her apartment, and asked Peter about pricing. Kate could tell that Peter's block-to-block assessment of real estate values impressed Liz, who paid him the highest of compliments by taking notes in her FiloFax.

"I can't believe what prices have done in just two years," Liz said. "It's doubled what I paid for it."

"It's the stock market," Peter said. "Everything in New York does better when stocks rally. Fixed income, too," he said, with a nod to Kate.

"I owe it all to my big sister," Liz said. "She lent me the down payment so I could buy instead of rent. Now I can pay her back with interest. Everything Kate touches turns to gold." Flushed with her newfound financial well-being, Liz smiled magnanimously at the waiter topping up their water glasses.

"Liz," Kate said quietly. Their parents had taught them never to talk about money, and here was her sister, toting up profits at the dinner table in front of someone she had just met.

"It's true," Liz said, mistaking Kate's mild reproof for modesty. "She's always been good with money. She was the banker when we played Monopoly. She was the banker for our family, too. She was the only one with cash when the newspaper boy collected, or when we needed money for something at school. She kept her money in a little safe with a combination lock. You'd hear 'brrrii-ing,' which meant that Kate was going into her safe. We weren't surprised when she ended up in banking."

Peter's eyes widened with mischief, but he didn't say anything. Liz's unflattering disclosures made Kate sound mercenary, and had nothing to do with her ending up in banking. She had needed a job, and the bank offered a training program. But her childhood interest in money was factual. She looked around the restaurant and felt a degree of complicity with the other well-to-do diners.

Over coffee and dessert, Peter asked Liz about her work. She told him about her jobs in Manhattan, lowering her voice when she dropped names, as if whispering made the practice all right. Kate was thinking how to change the subject when Peter asked Liz which designers she admired, then ably held up his end of the ensuing discussion.

"I didn't realize you knew so much about designers," Kate said later that night, when she and Peter were alone in her apartment. He lay on his side next to her on the bed, lightly stroking her arm. "I thought Balenciaga was a baseball player."

"Very good," Peter said, laughing softly. "I was just rattling off stuff I remembered my grandmother saying."

"Did your grandmother have a favorite designer?"

"There were a few she liked. It was a little world she followed. She wore jeans and sneakers, too." He kissed the inner curve of Kate's elbow. "Your arms look pretty in this dress."

Kate looked to see what she was wearing. "Jones New York," she said flatly. Peter rolled onto his back and cupped his hands under his head. "I think Liz appreciated your input on the apartment."

"Yeah, but I'm getting the feeling you didn't."

"What do you mean?"

"I don't consider myself a real estate maven either."

"You were very helpful."

"Then why are you putting me off?"

"I'm not putting you off."

"I feel put off."

From the corner of her eye, Kate could see Peter staring up at the ceiling. "I don't know," she started slowly. "You sounded different tonight."

"How do I usually sound?" he said to the ceiling.

"I don't know, not so Upper East Side."

Peter turned his head toward her with a look of annoyance she'd never had from him. "How's what I said any different from you giving my grandfather advice on interest rates?"

"But that's what I do for a living."

"So I should stick to high school bands and clam up on everything else?"

"That's not what I meant," she said, surprised by how Peter had interpreted her comment. Kate thought he was comfortable with what he did for a living, or what he did because he already had a living. She liked his lack of concern for how others might view his choice. Maybe he was more susceptible than he let on. Inherited wealth had lost some of its prestige, particularly if you weren't parlaying it into bigger and better things, like getting a museum wing named after you or running for a seat in the Senate. "Family money" was a pejorative term when uttered by Wall Streeters, who collected their seven-figure bonuses and considered themselves self-made men, as if they had personally engineered the boom in financial assets.

"Is it a crime to want your sister to like me?"

"No," Kate said softly.

"Then what's bothering you?"

That Peter knew about the environment he had lived in for thirty-plus years shouldn't surprise her, but it was unlike him to reveal his background the way he had at dinner, at least it had been as long as she'd known him. His doing so made her feel displaced. She lived in Peter's neighborhood and worked on Wall Street, but she didn't share his social standing and wasn't a pretender to it. She was from a middle-class beach town in California. If her education and job had given her occasion to mix it up with the East Coast establishment, she was too disdainful of the group to want to belong to it. Not that anyone was inviting her in.

Kate thought all this, but "I don't know" was what she said.

Peter got up, and for a moment she thought he was going to leave. Instead he came around to her side of the bed and sat down.

"This doesn't have to be a problem for us, Kate."

"It doesn't?" She looked at him intently. Why act as if she didn't know what he was talking about?

"I won't hold Wall Street against you, and you won't hold Park Avenue against me. How's that?"

"Your connection to Park Avenue is a little stronger than mine is to Wall Street."

"You've hung in there longer than I did."

"What do you mean?"

"I worked on Wall Street."

"You did?"

"Yeah, at Lehman Brothers, and you don't have to sound so surprised."

"You never mentioned it."

"It was a long time ago. I was only there for a year. My grandfather thought it was a good idea to see if I had any interest in the business. They rotated me around the different departments, but I spent most of my time in commercial paper. I helped the traders and sometimes the salesmen. I wrote out tickets and answered phones, made copies, went for coffee. They let me come to meetings. High-level stuff like that." He smiled archly.

"So what did you think?" Kate said, intrigued by the concept of Peter on Wall Street.

"Lehman was a good outfit."

"What did you think about the business?"

Peter took her hand as if he were about to break bad news. "Don't take this wrong, because I'm sure what you do is a lot different, but commercial paper wasn't that interesting. The guys on the desk were smart, but they seemed like glorified clerks. The traders called the issuers and repeated what they'd been told in the morning meeting. I honestly didn't see where the skill came in, other than speed. You had to be quick. It was like 'Beat the Clock' to get it all done by 12:30. It was fun the first few weeks, but after that it reminded me of Latin."

"Latin?"

"Yeah, Latin. Translating stuff that's already been translated. I mean, what's the point?"

Kate couldn't help smiling at Peter's exaggerated facial expressions. Once he'd gotten started, his description of his year on Wall Street spilled forth, as if he'd been eager to tell her, as if living in New York in 1985 and not being involved in the financial boom required an explanation.

She sat up next to him on the bed and put her arms around his waist. "It just wasn't for you."

"I tried to like it," Peter said, in a way she found touching. "My grandfather would have gotten a kick out of it. When I worked there, he was always talking to me about the market, asking me which stocks I liked."

"Which stocks did you like?"

"Are you kidding? I never said anything. I was terrified I'd give him bad advice, and he'd lose all his money."

"Was he OK with you leaving?"

"Maybe a little disappointed I wasn't coming into his line of work, but he didn't make a big deal of it. He said there were many worthy pursuits in the world, and that I'd find the right one for me."

Kate kissed Peter lightly on the lips. "And now you have." He looked at her and smiled suggestively. "I meant teaching," she said, as they lay back down on the bed.

Chapter 16

The rest of the summer passed euphorically. Kate was falling in love, and though it wasn't the first time, it still felt that way, maybe even sweeter because she knew that this phase of love, when you came together like magnets, wouldn't last forever. She and Peter strolled back and forth between her building and his grandfather's brownstone; held hands in the movies, though not at the baseball game, which suited her fine; danced again at Roseland. In late August, Peter got busy with teachers' meetings. On weeknights he would alternate dinners with her and his grandfather. On the nights Peter had dinner with her, she would arrive home and find him with a bag of groceries in his arms, talking with Frank in the lobby.

A relationship with someone ready and able to spend so much time together was a new experience and a bit overwhelming. One evening after a long day at work and a dinner with clients, Kate had begged off, telling Peter that she was too tired to be good company.

"No problem, I understand," he said, before adding a moment later: "I should still come over though, shouldn't I?"

Liz's move to California had been set for September, a prospect that Kate no longer dreaded. In fact, she liked how their relationship had returned to the more balanced, pre-divorce days. Liz had even gone out on a date, though with the upfront disclosure that she was moving soon and couldn't possibly become involved with someone who lived east of the Rockies. The drama of Ted stopping by faded too. Kate decided not to call him and was more relieved than disappointed when he didn't make a second attempt. Maybe he and Mother Teresa had patched things up.

Life in the trading room settled into a kind of equilibrium. Woody was an unwelcome presence and still very much in charge, a situation that Kate was learning to live with. When Jim went on vacation at the end of August, Woody set up shop in Jim's office. He held the afternoon trading meetings there and used it to make phone calls, putting his feet up on Jim's desk, which obviously irritated Lorraine.

When Jim returned after Labor Day, the relief in the trading room was palpable, especially since Woody took that day off, his first since joining Matheson. Jim filled in for Woody on the trading desk and seemed happy to be back on the line, mixing it up with the salesmen and traders as he had done in the past. Kate had successfully buried the thought that she was being disloyal for not telling Jim about the Fed investigation, but the feeling resurfaced that afternoon when he complimented the bill desk's year-to-date performance.

That night, Peter cooked dinner at Kate's apartment, a recipe for *paella* that one of the Spanish teachers had brought to a faculty dinner the week before. Kate wanted to tell Peter about her quandary at work. She tried to provide context by explaining the auction process and the skill it took to step in front of other bidders, the way she had done in the June year-bill auction. Peter nodded politely but stayed focused on his cooking.

Kate took a different tack when they sat down to dinner. She told Peter how stronger bids saved the Treasury money by reducing the interest it paid on the national debt.

The hint of a smile appeared at the corners of his mouth. "It's really a gotcha kind of business, isn't it?"

"What do you mean, a 'gotcha' kind of business?"

"Every man for himself. Asses and elbows."

It took Kate a moment to grasp the image of people fighting it out on the floor with their backsides in the air. She drew her finger through the beads of condensation on her water glass while Peter took their salad plates into the kitchen. "I can tell you're not impressed with what I do for a living."

"I'm impressed with *you*," Peter called from the kitchen. When Kate didn't respond, he came into the dining room and bent over the back of her chair, circling his arms around her shoulders. "It's that old Wall Street jive. They try to make it sound altruistic when it's really all about making money."

Kate's shoulders stiffened. "Is my being a trader a problem for you?"

"I don't think of you as a trader. That's just your job."

"In a gotcha kind of business. I feel guilty by association."

Peter massaged the tops of her shoulders. "You're all knotted up."

"There's a lot of pressure."

"But you like the pressure, don't you? You're a clutch player. I thought the market was doing just what you predicted." A timer went off, and Peter went back into the kitchen. What a sweet job that would be, Kate thought, watching the market instead of the people she worked with.

Peter set a covered casserole in front of her and lifted the lid dramatically. "*Mira!*"

Kate gazed at the steaming concoction. "I think I'm being investigated by the Federal Reserve." Peter stared at her a moment, then set the lid back on the casserole. She told him what she had learned three weeks ago from Rosemary, and Ernie's advice not to risk Albert's position by sharing the information with Jim.

Peter took off the quilted oven mitts and sat down.

"It's probably something routine. Don't worry, you haven't done anything wrong."

"But you know what people say whenever there's an investigation."

"You're innocent until proven guilty?"

"No one says that, Peter."

"What do they say?"

"Where there's smoke, there's fire. That's what they say."

"Well, I never say that."

They sat over bowls of steaming rice and seafood, the only sound the clacking of utensils against china. Kate knew it wasn't right to be put out with Peter. What did she want him to say? That she was an awesome and scrupulous trader, and soon even the Federal Reserve Bank would know that fact and proclaim it across Wall Street?

Yes, that's exactly what she wanted him to say.

Kate watched Peter eat, feeling guilty for spoiling a meal he had spent hours preparing, but also annoyed that he could enjoy food with the possibility of the Fed coming down on her neck. He looked up and caught her eye. "I have no experience with this kind of thing, but we could call my grandfather. Maybe he'd know."

Kate's heart sank. Telling Peter had been hard enough without dragging his grandfather into it. Beyond being the entirety of Peter's family, Mr. Etheridge was a markets person. Kate wanted him to view her as an accomplished participant and not someone who had problems with the regulators.

"Let's finish dinner," she said, though her appetite was entirely gone.

Peter spent the night. Curled up next to him, Kate quickly fell asleep, but she woke a few hours later to resume worrying about the Fed finding something wrong with her bids, and the fact that she hadn't warned Jim. Ernie wasn't concerned, but in general he was too blasé to be much of a barometer. "Fair and square" was the way he had characterized their success in the year-bill auction, but how fine was the line between aggressive trading and unfair practices in a "gotcha" kind of business? If the Fed wanted to make a point, there was no telling what they might cite you on. It was like a cop pulling you over.

The thought of police and being a co-defendant with Woody gave Kate a chill. She moved closer to Peter and the reassuring warmth of his body, envying how peacefully he slept. He lay on his side, facing away from her, his head more off the pillow than on. The sheet on his side of the bed was pulled out from the mattress and bunched around his middle. He rolled onto his back and laughed in his sleep. "That's so cool," he said.

"What's so cool?" Kate said, but Peter slept on, dreaming his good-natured dreams. Why wouldn't his dreams be pleasant? He loved his job and didn't have to worry about stretching a teacher's salary to cover the expense of living in Manhattan. His keeping an apartment downtown while living at his grandfather's house seemed particularly extravagant. Kate's father had put her through college and paid for her wedding to Ted, but since then money had never been mentioned, the assumption being that Kate would make her own. Maybe money wasn't mentioned in Peter's family either. Maybe the child of a wealthy family never financially left home. Ernie had an expression for people like that: born with a balance sheet.

Kate pictured the prosperous looking house on East 80th Street and the kind but astute Mr. Etheridge. Certainly he understood about auctions, and how a superior read of demand produced a stronger bid. But did he know and like her well enough to agree with his grandson that she'd done nothing wrong?

She rolled away from Peter and flipped her pillow to its cool side. She visualized meeting with Jim the next day to tell him about the Fed investigation. She would get right down to the facts. Her original idea, several weeks old, that a discussion about tracking systems would lead naturally into a disclosure about the Fed investigation, now struck her as far-fetched, as did the prospect of being fired for protecting her source.

Nevertheless, she imagined the various ways Jim might fire her. In his office with the drapes drawn? Over a drink at Delmonico's? Or maybe he would get someone from

Personnel to do it. The whole notion infuriated her.

Let him fire me, she thought defiantly. It didn't matter who had tipped her off about the Fed. If Jim didn't trust her, there was no sense in sticking around. As far as she was concerned, Jim Fletcher was her employer, not A. J. Matheson; any credibility she had at the bank would be on Jim's say-so.

Would she be able to find another job in the securities business? Her best bet might be a job with one of her old mutual fund clients. Several had been impressed by her approach, and encouraged her to move into asset management. They said they would be waiting for her when she burned out on trading, although getting fired was probably not the segue they'd had in mind.

Kate sighed deeply and slipped out of bed, shutting the bedroom door quietly behind her. In the kitchen, she poured herself a glass of milk and took the Oreos down from the cupboard. She was sitting in the living room, mechanically feeding herself cookies, when she heard the bedroom door open. "I'm in here," she said.

Peter came into the living room and stood in front of the sofa, shaking his head with the aggrieved look of an unappreciated spouse. "*Now* you're hungry," he said, eyeing the box of cookies. "How long have you been out here?"

"A little while," Kate said, brushing crumbs from the front of her nightgown. Having trouble sleeping embarrassed her. It felt like an old person's ailment, one step

235

removed from heartburn, and dentures soaking in a glass on the bathroom sink.

Peter crouched in front of her. "There are other remedies for insomnia. You should have woken me up."

Kate leaned forward and put her arms around his neck. "Oh, Peter, what should I do?"

"You've got good instincts. What do you think you should do? Forget what everyone else is telling you."

"I think I should warn Jim. He's been good to me, but so has Rosemary. That took a lot, her telling me what Albert was doing. It would be wrong to betray that kind of trust, but I don't want to be associated with Woody in an investigation that taints the rest of my career. I've worked too hard for people to think my accomplishments are ill-gotten gains. I don't deserve that."

"No, you don't."

"But it's been three weeks. The Fed may have already notified the bank. I should have told Jim a long time ago."

Peter settled next to her on the sofa. She offered him the Oreo box, and he shook several cookies from the cellophane sleeve. "What makes you think Jim will insist on knowing your source?"

"Ernie said he might make it a test of my loyalty."

"Couldn't you respectfully refuse to answer?"

"It's not that easy. When you work for a company,

they assume your loyalty is to them. They get touchy when you don't do what they say." Kate smiled at how basic yet unreasonable that sounded.

Peter looked at her skeptically. "You always do what you're told?"

Kate nodded gloomily, then brightened. She had submitted her trader evaluations in alphabetical order, not numerically as Woody had requested. A minor rebellion, but she told Peter the story anyway.

"God, what an asshole! I never heard of making co-workers rank each other in writing. You went along with that?"

Kate wished she could say that she had been a *refusenik* like Ernie. "No one talked about it much."

"That was his point. Get people looking over their shoulders." Peter twisted the chocolate lid off a cookie and offered her the side with the icing. "What do you think Woody did wrong?"

Kate thought about her own approach in the year-bill auction. She had assessed the interest of clients, encouraging them to bid through Matheson. When she saw how sizeable that interest was, she had submitted a large bid for the bank's trading account, confident that demand would push the market higher. But Woody hadn't been able to drum up much interest in the two-year note from Matheson's clients. Kate remembered the weak book of business reported in the sales meeting the night before the two-year note auction, and how stoic Woody had seemed. She thought he had resigned himself to the situation and recognized the size of the challenge that lay ahead, but perhaps his thinking had already shifted to a different option.

"Maybe he convinced some of the clients he knew from Salomon Brothers to bid through Matheson," Kate told Peter.

"That's probably why he got hired, right?" Peter took her empty glass and the box of cookies into the kitchen.

Peter's comment made her think. Maybe there was nothing more to the Fed investigation than checking out the sudden, dramatic rise in Matheson's participation in the two-year note auction. Once the regulators had discerned the reason—that Salomon's customers were following Woody to his new employer—they had wrapped up the investigation.

"That's *exactly* why he got hired," Kate said when Peter came back into the living room.

"Makes sense," he said nonchalantly, though she could tell he was pleased. Kate's appreciative smile broadened into a grin. There was something compelling about a man who could cook dinner and help you with work problems, all on the same night. He didn't look bad in his underwear either.

Peter pulled her up from the sofa and wrapped his arms around her. They swayed together for a moment, and Kate started to sing an old song softly. "'*My boyfriend's back, he's gonna save my reputation.'"*

Peter pulled back to look at her. "What's that?"

"I think I can sleep now," she announced with a yawn.

"I have that effect on women," he said.

Chapter 17

The next morning Kate got to work at six-thirty, planning to tell Jim about the Fed investigation before the day got under way. To her surprise, he was already in his office; he looked up and saluted when she flipped on the trading room lights. Kate turned on her screens and watched the white numbers come into focus, wishing that a trading position were all she had to worry about. To bolster her confidence, she took out her journal and turned to the entry on the June year-bill auction. She knew it by heart.

The intercom on her desk beeped. "Did you sleep at the bank last night?" Jim was teasing about her early arrival, or maybe he was serious, and referring to the rooms the bank kept for officers who sometimes worked late into the night. Kate had once thought of staying there just for the experience—until Ernie explained about the shared bathroom arrangements.

"Actually, I came in early to see you," Kate said.

"Well, what are you waiting for?" The intercom beeped off.

Kate started to put the marbled composition book away but changed her mind and took it with her. Jim waved her in, pointing to the chair beside his desk. "What's on your mind?"

Kate sat down and quickly came to the point. "I was told something in strictest confidence that I think you should know."

Jim gave her a crooked smile. "So this isn't about the new tracking system?"

"No, it's not, but it is confidential."

"I got that part."

"I wanted to be sure I said that upfront."

"Full disclosure, so to speak."

She could feel her face color. "It's just that..."

Jim held up a hand. "Kate: speak!" he ordered in a friendly tone.

"I heard that the Fed's checking Matheson's bids in the two-year note auction." Kate watched Jim's jaw muscle work slightly, though otherwise his expression didn't change.

"What are they checking for?"

"I don't know. The two-year note has been tight in the financing market, and the arbitrage desk says dealers were getting squeezed. Maybe someone complained to the Fed."

"How long have you been sitting on this

information?"

Jim's words stung, though sitting on the information was exactly what she had done. "I tried to see you when I first heard," she said.

"When was that?"

She felt the heat rise from her neck into her cheeks. "A few weeks ago."

Jim looked at her steadily. "It slipped your mind?"

"We both got busy…and then you were out."

"Lorraine always knows how to reach me."

Kate looked down, unable to hold the intensity of Jim's gaze. "Maybe it's a routine check."

"It isn't routine. They're looking at the June year-bill, too."

She felt her hands start to shake and tightened her grip on her journal. "Ernie says we handled the year-bill auction fair and square."

"Is he your source?"

"No," she said, shaking her head.

"And what do *you* say?"

"I say the same thing. I've got it all here." Kate held out her journal, opened to the pertinent pages. When Jim made no move to take it, she set the opened book on his desk anyway, turning out her pockets to prove she wasn't a thief. "Those bills ran up after the auction, but you could still get them."

"What about the two-year note?'

"I wasn't involved in the two-year note."

Jim raised an eyebrow. "But you had an opinion."

"I thought the risk-reward wasn't there for short-end buyers. I told you at the elevator, remember?" When Jim didn't respond, Kate zeroed in: "Have you checked the list of bidders in that auction?"

"I'm not at liberty to discuss the investigation with anyone." Jim steepled his fingers under his chin, a pose that looked unnatural on him. Maybe it felt that way too, because a moment later he dropped his hands to the desk and picked up her journal. "I used to keep one of these."

"I remember," Kate said.

Jim looked up. "You remember my journal?"

"I remember you saying you used to keep one."

He seemed disappointed and closed the notebook. In the white rectangular space on its cover were Kate's initials and the date of the volume's first entry: *K.McC.M. March 12, 1985—*.

"What does the middle initial stand for?"

"McCord. It's my maiden name."

"I wouldn't have figured you for a name-changer."

"It was ten years ago…it never occurred to me not to."

Jim lifted his chin and smiled. "Now *that* fits." His tone had softened, and his comments seemed layered with meaning, or maybe he was simply wistful. "Did you tell anyone else about Deep Throat?"

"Just Ernie," she said, although Peter crossed her mind.

"Better keep it that way until the auditors speak with you."

"The auditors?"

Jim nodded. "Armstrong's got them all over this." The thought of the bank's gruff chairman made Kate's heart beat out of her chest. Phil Armstrong had probably come down hard, even though Jim was one of his favorites.

"I'm sorry, Jim."

"Why didn't you come see me earlier? Your instincts are usually so good."

"I was worried I'd get my source into trouble."

"Wrong answer. Your first allegiance is always to the bank."

And to you, she thought, heartsick at her own betrayal.

Jim raked his fingers through his thinning hair. "What a fucking way to start the day, huh?"

"Start the day fucking? Now there's an approach worth considering." Woody's voice coming from behind Kate made her flinch. She looked at Jim, then at her watch, surprised to see how little time had actually passed. "Am I interrupting?" Woody belatedly asked.

Well, of course you are, Kate wanted to say, to Woody and everyone else who barged in on that line. How much had he heard? Kate kept her eyes on Jim, who must have been caught off guard too, even though he had been facing the doorway. Kate looked over her shoulder at Woody, who was blocking the exit. She wondered if Jim had discussed the investigation with his head trader. Probably not. Woody seemed too smug.

"Kate and I were just finishing up." Jim stood up when she did, his courteous gesture surprising her. Men at the bank who were Jim's age never stood up for women, not even women clients.

"What were you talking about?" Woody asked, as if it were his right to know. He had a nerve. If Kate had come in on his conversation and asked the same question, he would have responded with a non-answer like "a lot of things," if he responded at all.

"A lot of things," Kate said, maneuvering around Woody like a pothole. She glanced back at Jim, who motioned for her to close the door. Woody had already taken her seat.

At her desk, Kate tried to calm herself, but it was impossible. She had warned Jim too late about an investigation that wasn't routine. As far as he was concerned, there was no excuse for her failure to act expeditiously, the way she handled everything else. Her detailed record might convince the auditors that she had followed proper procedure, but to Jim it simply reinforced how calculated her withholding of information had been.

Kate drew her breath in sharply. In her haste to escape Woody's presence, she had left her journal behind. She looked at Jim's office. Woody was still seated in the chair next to the desk, though Jim was standing and appeared to be talking on the speakerphone. Kate felt incredibly warm, and noticed the small ellipses of darkened blue under the arms of her chambray shirt.

It seemed as if she had worked a full day by the time Ernie came in. How could he be late with all that was happening?

"Train problems?" Kate said sarcastically.

Ernie set down his dripping bag of coffee. "I was at the DAC, playing squash. I told you last night. Do I need a note from Marie?"

"Sorry. You did tell me."

Ernie glanced toward Jim's office. "How long have they been in there?"

Kate told Ernie everything. "Jim says we should keep quiet. The auditors are going to talk to us."

"Is that why you're so jumpy?"

"Well, yeah...and I left my trading journal on Jim's desk."

"Did he want to see it?"

"No, but I brought it with me in case he did." That wasn't exactly true, though close enough.

"So get it when they're finished."

Kate let out a sigh. "I'd feel a lot better if I had it. I trust my own records more than the bank's."

Ernie looked at Jim's office, then back at Kate. "You want me to go get it? I'll just knock on the door, let myself in, take the book off his desk, and be back in a flash."

"You're kidding, right? You'd never get past Lorraine." Jim's secretary had arrived and was dug into her position outside his door.

Ernie made a face. "Lorraine's a pill." But he stayed put.

Lloyd Keezer, coffee in hand, leaned over Kate's desk and asked why Jim and Woody were behind closed doors.

"Probably deciding who to can next," Ernie said.

The intercom on Kate's desk emitted a long beep. Keezer jumped, juggling his cup of coffee and spilling half its contents down the front of his shirt. Ernie laughed so hard he started to wheeze. Whoever was on the intercom rang off, but a few seconds later it beeped again.

"You guys, I can't hear," Kate said. She leaned closer to the unit. It was Jim, asking her to run the morning meeting. Keezer took in the news and scurried back to his desk.

Ernie wiped at his eyes with a coffee-stained napkin. "You running the meeting with Jim and Woody behind closed doors is going to rev up the news junkies. Keezer already smells blood."

"As long as it's not ours," she said.

Kate knew the compliments people paid her as they left the morning meeting had more to do with who *hadn't* presided than with who had, but their motivation didn't bother her. People missed the way the bank used to be, and were nostalgic for the collegial environment that had disappeared with Woody's arrival.

Both the Fed watcher and the economist stood by the speaker's platform, waiting for a private word. Stuart Gerard and Nick Bhattacharya were middle-aged, academic types who worked in the bank's economics department. They researched and analyzed for a living, dutifully showing up on the trading floor to report in meetings and interpret economic data as it hit the tape throughout the day. Though the two men appeared excited by the vibe in the trading room, they were more accustomed to the sedate atmosphere of the economics department, and seemed relieved when the traders and salesmen had had their fill of information and turned back to their phones and screens.

Now Stuart, the Fed watcher, made a chivalrous comment about the benefits of a woman's touch. "People aren't afraid to speak up with you in charge," he added. His expression wavered, as if realizing that the remark could be taken two ways. "It's a more productive exchange.

Lately these meetings have become…what's the word I'm looking for, Nick?"

"Fucked-up?" Nick deadpanned, as if the word were an economic term.

Kate hurried back to the trading room. Through the interior windows of Jim's office, she could see Lorraine, straightening the top of her boss's desk. Kate stuck her head in the doorway.

"Lorraine, have you seen a black and white composition book?" Not waiting for an answer, Kate crossed to the desk, but her journal wasn't where she'd left it. She glanced at Jim's chair and the one she had vacated for Woody, then dropped to her knees to search under the desk, vacant except for the square of hard plastic on which the chair wheels rolled. "Shit," Kate muttered, sitting back on her heels and looking up. "It's this big?" She approximated the dimensions in the air. "Black with white speckles?"

Lorraine shook her head. "I know the entire contents of this office, and there's nothing like that here."

Kate stood up too quickly and made herself dizzy. "Whoa," she said. She sat back down in Jim's chair, hanging her head to clear it.

"Are you all *right*?"

Slowly Kate sat up and surveyed the desk from Jim's vantage point. Her hand started for the desk's center drawer, but she checked herself. "I think this drawer might have been open. Would you mind taking a look?" Lorraine raised her eyebrows, but pulled open the top drawer. A few pencils and a cluster of paper clips.

"Maybe it was one of the other drawers," Kate said, pushing her luck with Lorraine, who opened the side drawers too. They were beautifully organized. Kate's eyes darted to the flat leather boxes on the corner of Jim's desk, but Lorraine planted her hands on the tidy stacks of paper, protecting them like offspring.

"I check everything that leaves this office. If I find your journal, I'll make sure you get it."

"Could you maybe check them now?" Kate indicated the boxes. Lorraine looked exasperated but went carefully through the papers to prove that the journal wasn't there. "I can't do my job without that journal. Do you think Jim might have it?"

"I'll ask when he gets back, but I'm certain he doesn't have it. He never carries anything to meetings. If he needs something, I deliver it beforehand."

"You do?" Kate said, momentarily distracted by the degree of service Lorraine provided.

"Of course!"

"Is he at a meeting now?"

"Yes."

"In the bank?"

Lorraine's prim little smile signaled the end of the line.

Kate got up from the chair. "Sorry to go crazy on you."

"Oh, that's all right," Lorraine said, perky in her particular way. "I'm used to traders going crazy. First Woody, now you."

Kate stopped at the doorway. "What did he go crazy about?"

Lorraine shrugged.

"Was he carrying anything when he left?"

"My job is looking after Jim."

And who looks after you? Kate thought.

Though she was certain the journal wasn't there, she went through her desk again. She slipped the rest of her notebooks into her bag for safekeeping, furious with herself for having been careless with the most important volume. She would have remembered to take it if Jim hadn't stood up for her when she left his office.

"Nice job," Ernie said when he got off the phone. Kate looked at him blankly. "Running the meeting? Ten minutes ago?"

"Oh, thanks," she said. The morning meeting felt hours old.

"You're pretty blasé."

"My journal wasn't in Jim's office."

Ernie mumbled a few reassuring words and went back to work. Again Kate felt a sense of separation that seemed to be forming between them. They were nominally a team, but she was the principal risk taker in bills—even if she hadn't sought the distinction—and the one Jim had singled out for praise the day of the June year-bill auction. *In honor of Kate Munro's successful coup of today's bill auction, she's offered to buy ice cream for everyone.*

Peter called mid-morning. Kate answered his opening string of questions with perfunctory yes-or-no answers, then hunched over the phone to tell him that her journal was missing.

"Maybe Jim took it to check the records," Peter said.

"His secretary says he didn't. I think Woody took it."

"What would he want with it?"

Kate remembered how Woody had laughed when Keezer made fun of her keeping a diary. "It's the only explanation, if Jim doesn't have it."

"Maybe you should look in his office."

"I did! I was rooting around in there like a truffle-sniffing pig," she said, which made him laugh. "It's not funny, Peter."

"I'm sorry. The image is so out-of-character. You're always so dignified."

"I didn't lose my dignity," Kate said, though she probably had.

"I take it back."

*   *   *

Around lunchtime, Kate observed Jim and Woody return to the trading floor. They were empty-handed and didn't speak to each other. Woody sat down at his desk and stared silently at his screens. Jim stopped in front of his office, exchanged a few words with Lorraine, and collected his message slips. He closed the office door behind him and immediately got on the phone.

Please let this turn out all right, Kate prayed. She turned back to her work, though it was difficult to care much about Treasury bills. She responded to inquiries, but she was going through the motions. "They're seeing better prices away," a salesman shouted across the room after Kate gave him a run-of-the-mill bid. It became a refrain throughout the afternoon.

Jim stayed behind closed doors and Lorraine brought him lunch on a tray. In the early afternoon, a man and woman were ushered into Jim's office.

"I wonder who they are?" Kate said to Ernie.

He glanced over his shoulder. "Auditors. The woman is, anyway."

"How can you tell?"

"She lives in Rye. I see her on the train."

Kate studied the well-coiffed woman. "Do you think they'll want to talk with us?"

"Christ, I hope not." Ernie stubbed out a half-smoked

cigarette.

"We have nothing to hide," Kate reminded him.

"Yeah, but that's not how they're going to make it feel."

Kate waited, expecting any moment to be called into Jim's office. But it wasn't until three o'clock, long after the auditors had left, that she heard Lorraine's perky voice summoning her over the intercom.

"I thought I should bring you up to date," Jim said, motioning Kate into his office, "and return your morning courtesy."

She ignored the irony and got right to the point. "Did you check the bids in the two-year note auction?"

"The auditors are doing their work and will present their findings to Armstrong," Jim said. "They report to him, not me."

"But they'll tell you too, won't they? What did Woody say?"

Jim hesitated a moment. "He said we had a big bidder in the two-year."

"Was the trade confirmed with the client?"

"For obvious reasons, we're trying to keep this in-house. It's premature to be calling clients."

Kate tried to sound relaxed, as if this were a routine conversation. "I meant, was the trade confirmed to the client at the time of the auction? Was an actual confirmation letter mailed out? Operations would know if Woody gave any special instructions."

Jim frowned. "The auditors are checking all that. Meanwhile Woody says he won the two-year auction fair and square."

Fair and square. Ernie's description of the year-bill auction. Kate had used the same expression that morning with Jim.

"Was the two-year note bidder a Matheson customer or someone Woody brought over from Salomon Brothers?" she said.

"Look, Kate, I can't get into this. I'm trying to tell you as a friend that Woody has taken a position similar to yours."

Fear spiked in her chest. *A position similar to yours.* Jim made her statement about the auction sound like a claim, her version of the truth. He was linking her defense with Woody's. Perhaps on the advice of the auditors or his own instincts for self-preservation, Jim was distancing himself.

"Are you trying to warn me about something?" Kate said.

"There's a process that has to be followed," Jim said. "The bank has to protect the integrity of its operations. Its status as a primary dealer depends on it."

"Am I under suspicion because I wouldn't reveal my source?"

"I guess you could say we're all under suspicion: Woody, you and Ernie, even me, for failing to supervise you properly. I hope you're all innocent. It'll go a lot better for me if you are."

Kate's tone hardened. "I resent being lumped in with Woody."

"Getting emotional isn't going to help," Jim said.

The old stereotype about women: Kate couldn't believe that Jim was falling back on it. She dug her fists into her armpits to keep from trembling. "I left my trading journal on your desk this morning. Do you have it?"

Jim shook his head. "Lorraine said you were looking for it." He glanced at the spot on his desk where Kate had put it, then looked her straight in the eye. "I don't have it."

She waited a moment to compose herself, but it was impossible to mask her feelings. "You think I did something wrong, don't you?"

"Come on now, Kate."

"No, really, Jim…off the record, if you need it. Do you think I did something wrong?"

Jim stared out the window for as long as ten seconds before facing her again. "Off the record, and if you quote me I'll deny it, but off the record, if you did do something wrong, I don't think it was intentional."

Kate couldn't believe what she was hearing. Jim had still been head trader in June, and knew exactly what she had done in the year-bill auction. He had praised her performance, profusely and publicly. How could he be waffling three months later? Her stomach churned. She gripped the wooden arms of the chair. "Was it something technical? Were we over a limit?"

"I told you I can't discuss it. But if you did err, and I'm not saying you did or you didn't, but if you did, I believe yours was an error in judgment, not principle, and the bank goes easier on that kind of mistake."

Kate smiled sardonically. "That's supposed to make me feel better?"

Jim studied his left hand and picked at the cuticles on his thumb and index finger. He was cutting her loose, throwing her on the mercy of the process and the Matheson tradition. Had the auditors raised doubt in Jim's mind about her conduct in the auction, or was he holding her at arm's-length for self-preservation? Either way, she had been mistaken to consider herself part of the team, someone who would be taken care of as long as she did the right thing.

She thought about Ernie and Rosemary, and wished she had listened to them.

Kate struggled to get through the rest of the afternoon. Emotions kept hitting her like air pockets: anger and resentment, but also humiliation and fear. She felt physically ill, and visited the women's room several times, though she never actually got sick.

"Go home," Ernie told her. "You look like something the cat dragged in."

"You and Woody are still here," she said, and stuck it out till five.

But at home Kate fell apart. She lay on the sofa in the spare room and watched re-runs of sitcoms on local TV. In reverse chronological order, the turning points in her life came hurtling back. She berated herself for taking the notebook into Jim's office; for transferring from sales into trading; for moving to New York; for marrying Ted. She would never have been in New York if it weren't for him. She wanted to move to California with Liz. She wanted to change her name back to McCord, and get a job managing a branch of the Bank of America in Santa Cruz. Within six months, she would have the job knocked and become a pillar of the community, attending Rotary meetings and chairing fund-raisers for local causes. She would catch the eye of management, but refuse outright any offer of advancement.

Kate waited and waited for Peter until she remembered that it was Open School Day at Stuyvesant; he wouldn't be finished until well after nine. She called Liz, who was also out, and then called her father. He let Kate run on about the situation at work, but she could tell he didn't understand what she was talking about.

"You're a good person," he said, when she finally came up for air. "People will see that."

"But the ones who know me best aren't standing up

for me."

Her father was silent a moment. "Could you have mistakenly broken a rule? Could someone have taught you wrong?" He was remembering her driver's license test, when the examiner flunked her for parallel parking the way her father had demonstrated. It was the first test she'd ever failed.

"I don't know, Dad. I don't think so."

"Have you talked to Liz? Your sister can be very resourceful."

"You're right about that!" Kate brightened her tone for her father's sake. She could sense his eagerness to get off the phone. Empathy for his daughter was causing him pain, and he had done all he could from three thousand miles away.

Peter called around ten, still wound up from the evening at school. He had recruited members of the band to perform, which had gone over well with the parents. Kate listened, coveting the satisfaction that Peter found in his work. When he asked about her day, she told him everything.

"You need company?" he said.

"I'm afraid I wouldn't be very good company tonight."

"That's not what I asked."

*   *   *

Peter came over, still dressed in the jacket and tie he had worn for the Stuyvesant parents. He dropped his overnight bag inside the front door and gave her a hug. "I kept my tie on to impress you," he said when she told him that he looked nice.

They sat in the living room. Peter drank a beer while Kate recounted the details of her final meeting with Jim. Her sense of abandonment deepened. Peter listened without interrupting, even when she circled back and repeated Jim's most offensive statements.

"'As a friend,'" Kate quoted Jim. "That really gets me. And the different kinds of error. What's that supposed to mean? That I'm ethical, but stupid? Jim's the one who taught me the business—he and Ernie. I'm not Sacagawea showing white men the way."

"Do you think you should talk to a lawyer?" Peter said.

Kate's eyes widened. "You think I need one?"

"I don't know, the bank's got a lot of lawyers, maybe you should get one, too. It's the American way."

"The only lawyers I know are divorce lawyers."

"I could ask my grandfather."

It was testament to her deteriorating situation that consulting Mr. Etheridge no longer seemed out of the question. "He's going to think I'm a loser," Kate said.

"Unfit company for his grandson."

Peter smiled. "I wouldn't worry about that. He wants me to go to the safe deposit box with him and look at some rings."

The comment caught her off guard.

Chapter 18

To Kate's great surprise, some of her old enthusiasm returned the next morning as the trading day got underway. She transacted a large trade between two money fund accounts, which made the salesmen and customers happy and reminded her of how satisfying competence could be.

"I'm glad you're not letting the bastards get you down," Ernie said, calculating the profits on the trade. He slid the slip of paper across the desktop.

"Nice," Kate said, glancing at the figure. "But I'd rather have my journal back." She followed Ernie's gaze to Woody, who was talking quietly on the phone. "You think he took it?"

"If he did, he probably got rid of it," Ernie said. "Then again, he's the type of guy who might display it in a trophy case."

Kate remembered the antique sideboard and collection of porcelain that Liz had purchased for Woody's apartment. Kate had come along on that buying trip to find a wedding gift for one of her customers. Watching Liz make her selections, Kate had considered the fluke of the two sisters both working for Morehead Woodson.

Kate's heart beat hard against her chest. "I'll be right back," she told Ernie. She walked briskly to the conference room, but it was occupied by a salesman and his customers. She glanced at her watch, then hurried to the elevator. In the lobby she shut herself into a payphone, the old-fashioned kind with a wooden bench and a folding glass door.

"It's like taking a hostage," Liz said, when she heard Kate's suspicions about Woody and her journal.

"I'm not positive he has it," Kate said.

"Oh, he's got it, all right. If he had access and knows it's important to you, he's got it. A guy like him wouldn't hesitate. You want me to go over to his apartment and take a look?"

It was exactly what Kate had in mind, though she slowly circled the suggestion like a hawk. "I thought you were through with that job."

"But I still have a key. It's here in the office."

"Do you have a reason to be there? A legitimate reason?"

"How legitimate was swiping your journal? There are still a few items that haven't come in. This job was so big my boss will do the final walk-through, but it wouldn't be out of the question for me to stop by and check on things before I go. It would make me look good, now that

I think about it."

"But wouldn't the client be present for a final walk-through?"

"Not necessarily. Woody's a busy man. He specifically said that he didn't want service providers crawling all over the place when he's around."

That was like him, Kate thought. Do his bidding, but keep out of his way. "I should probably ask him if he's seen my journal before I send you over there."

"Why don't I just go? I could use some fresh air."

"Better let me talk to him first."

"All right, but when he looks at you like he doesn't know who you are, call me back. Go ask him now, why don't you? If he plays dumb, I'll go right over."

A man in a suit rapped his signet ring on the phone booth's glass door. One minute, Kate mouthed, holding up her index finger. "I'll ask him, if I can get him alone," she told Liz.

"Alone? Don't see him alone! You walk right up to him, stick your finger in his chest and ask him what the hell he did with your journal. Do it in front of everybody. You've got to shock a straight answer out of someone like Woody."

Kate turned her back on the man glaring at her through the phone booth's glass door. "I'd rather not have people knowing my business," she said.

"They're going to find out sooner or later. Your best shot is getting the jump on him. You concede the upper hand if you're afraid to make a scene."

The man rapped his ring hard against the glass and pointed to his watch. "I'll call you later," Kate said and got off the phone.

"Run out of dimes?" the man said snidely as Kate stepped past him.

She looked him straight in the eye. "Drop dead," she said, the words making her feel surprisingly good. She thought she might use them on Woody, but he was gone when she got back to the trading floor and didn't return the rest of the day.

That night Kate had dinner at the Etheridge brownstone. The tranquility was soothing, and she wondered if the home's well-ordered atmosphere had worked a similar effect after the loss of Peter's parents. Or maybe the order and calm were a result of that tragedy. Nothing unpleasant seemed to pass between Peter and his grandfather, as if they had resolved not to cause each other further pain. And so it was jarring when the subject of her difficulties at work came up midway through dinner.

"Peter tells me you've been having your ups and downs," Mr. Etheridge said. He sat at the head of the table, with Peter and Kate on either side, and listened politely as she explained her predicament. The idea of widening the circle to include Peter's grandfather seemed less imperative than it had the night before.

"Do you think Kate should hire an attorney?" Peter said.

"Oh, I don't know," Mr. Etheridge said. "That strikes me as more combative than useful. A. J. Matheson is a fine old firm, and they'll do the right thing. I know Phillip Armstrong. He's gruff but principled."

"Maybe you should give Armstrong a call," Peter said, accepting another serving of roast beef and julienne vegetables from the housekeeper, a woman named Madeline. Mr. Etheridge didn't comment, waiting until Madeline left the room.

"It's unpleasant having your work reviewed like that," Mr. Etheridge said, "but my advice is to stay the course."

Kate smiled wanly at the use of Reagan's campaign slogan from the previous year; maybe Mr. Etheridge knew the President, too. She studied her dinner plate, an old Wedgwood pattern still covered with most of her meal, and regretted confiding in Peter's grandfather.

Peter must have read her thought. "Kate's worked her heart out, and now she's getting a bucket of cold water in the face," he said.

Mr. Etheridge seemed surprised by his grandson's injured tone. "I know what's happening right now isn't something you bargained for," the old man said with belated empathy.

"It makes me not want to work there any more," she said.

"You can quit if you want," Peter said. "There are lots of other places you could work."

"Not with an investigation hanging over my head. Nobody's going to touch me. My record's got to be cleared before I can even think about getting another job."

"I'm sure things will work out," Mr. Etheridge said. He began talking about Peter's childhood, and all the scrapes he'd been in when he was a boy. It wasn't hard to track his thoughts from her brush with authority to Peter's, not that the two were remotely equivalent.

"Having a daughter didn't prepare us for raising a boy," Mr. Etheridge said. "Camilla was quiet and composed, even as a little girl."

So was I, Kate thought, and it gets you nowhere.

Peter walked her home but didn't stay. Maybe he shared her disappointment over the way dinner had gone, with his grandfather offering little more than moral support. Mr. Etheridge's advice to have faith in Phil Armstrong struck Kate as well meaning but quaint. Relying on others to do the right thing certainly wasn't what men who ran big corporations did when trouble arose, at least not the successful ones. Successful chief executives mobilized. They assembled their top in-house advisers and hired the best outside counsel that money could buy, resources unavailable to Kate—though she did have a sister with a key to the head trader's apartment.

Kate knew that Peter would never endorse searching Woody's apartment for the missing journal. She didn't approve either. If she could authorize snooping, what else was she capable of? She pushed the question aside; Liz checking the apartment was the only alternative to letting others determine her fate. Tomorrow at work, Kate would corner Woody and ask if he had her journal. There was a chance, admittedly slight, that he might actually produce the speckled notebook. But more likely he would shrug, a bored expression on his face, and say nothing. If that happened, she would give Liz the go-ahead to search the apartment; Kate had the right to retrieve what belonged to her.

Liz called around ten that evening. *"'California, here I come, right back where I started from.'* What comes after that? Dad never sings past the first line." It was Liz's way of announcing her plan to fly to San Francisco the next morning to meet with a prospective client, one of several that Sally Townsend had promised to introduce.

"Isn't this kind of sudden?" Kate said. Her plan for the apartment search derailed, she slumped against the pillows on her bed.

"Completely," Liz said. "Sally's staying with friends who want to re-do their house in Tahoe."

"You're going to Lake Tahoe?"

"No, Hillsborough. I'd never make it to Tahoe by lunchtime. Sally told them about me, and they said too bad she's not out here, and Sally said I was the type of person who could be there tomorrow. So what could I say? I'm booked on the 8 A.M. flight."

"When are you coming back?"

"It depends. Sally's got another friend in the city who wants to turn her place into Meryl Streep's house. Not her real house, her house in *Out of Africa*. Isn't that bizarre? The woman has views of the Golden Gate Bridge with the fog rolling in, and she wants to drape mosquito netting over her bed. Sally says I've got to talk her out of it."

"Why would you want to do that?" Kate said sarcastically.

"I haven't forgotten about your journal. Would waiting until I got back be a problem?" Liz spoke casually, as if they were rescheduling a furniture delivery.

"I have no idea when the auditors want to see me," Kate said. "It could be next week or it could happen tomorrow, in which case it's already too late to go through Woody's apartment."

"I'm sorry…this just fell into my lap."

"And you shouldn't pass it up. I want you to get the Tahoe job *and* the African makeover."

"It's terrible timing though."

"You can't help that."

"I suppose it's crazy to suggest that you go through the apartment."

"Oh, I don't know," Kate said with a tired laugh. "Desperate measures for desperate times."

"I could tell them you're my assistant and give you something to deliver. Anyone can make a delivery."

"Though there might be trouble if I bumped into the cleaning person," Kate played along.

"Sonia? She'd help you look. Sonia can't stand Woody. He makes her sew snaps in his underwear."

"Liz, I was joking."

"No, really. I saw her sitting there one day sewing a little snap on the fly of his boxer shorts. He marks where he wants the snap with a Post-it Note."

"Please don't tell me this stuff. I'm not going into his apartment. I can't believe you think I'd really do that. Forget about bumping into Sonia. What about bumping into Woody?"

"You go in when he's at work. Make sure he shows up, then you scoot uptown."

"In the middle of the day? I don't have that kind of job."

"People on Wall Street get sick. They go home early. You're the only person I know who thinks perfect attendance is something to aim for."

"What if he has house guests?"

"Are you kidding? The man is an island."

"No man is an island," Kate said listlessly.

"If someone else is there, just go ahead and make the delivery. We'll go to Plan B."

"What is it I'm delivering again?"

"I don't know. There must be something we could lend Woody until I get back."

"This is crazy. I don't know why we're even discussing it. I'm glad you're going to California. You're saving us from doing something really stupid. You could lose your job."

"For letting my big sister have a peek at the penthouse I've decorated?" Liz said sweetly, as if rehearsing for the arresting officer. "A talking-to is all I'd get. You'd be the one taking the risk."

"Maybe I'll just wait and see."

"Wait and see! I hate that expression. That's what Dad said when I asked him when Mom was going to get better. 'We'll have to wait and see.'"

There was silence on the other end of the line, and Kate worried that Liz had started to cry. "You were so little," Kate said.

"It's OK. Poor guy was doing the best he could. But don't you start talking that way. We're too young to be passive."

Was it passive or prudent? Kate wondered later as she lay in bed, but she was too anxious to ponder the distinction. Instead she imagined confronting Woody the next day, a prospect almost as daunting as searching his apartment. She pictured herself marching up to him on the trading floor and jabbing a finger into his chest. "Yo, Woodson! Cut the crap and give me back my journal." The trading room would go silent as everyone stared in disbelief...and respect.

Lately, Kate had focused on Peter as she drifted off to sleep, but tonight she thought about the key to Woody's apartment, which Liz had promised to drop off before heading for the airport in the morning.

Chapter 19

The next day at work, Woody seemed to know that Kate wanted to speak with him alone. He left the trading desk only once and was back before she could complete the trade she was working, and follow him off the floor. He stayed in the midst of people, talking on the phone or chatting with the salesmen who sat directly across from him. As the morning slipped into afternoon, she became increasingly nervous. The auditors could summon her at any moment. She would have to talk to Woody at his desk. From the corner of her eye, she watched him hop from one call to the next. When at last he put down the handset and laced his fingers in back of his head, she jumped up, for a moment on unsteady legs, and forced herself to walk down the row of traders, away from the safe shores of the bill desk.

Her chest tightened as she stood next to the arm of Woody's chair and waited for him to acknowledge her presence. Instead he called out to Scott Pratt, the bank's shoeshine man, as he came through the glass doors of the trading floor. Kate made a space for Scott and his gear next to Woody, who continued to ignore her. It was galling to be treated that way in front of the people she worked with. Watching Woody put his foot on the shoe-shine block, Kate felt the familiar pricks of adrenaline under her arms.

"Have you seen my notebook?" she said, her voice cracking. She cleared her throat and spoke louder. "I left it in Jim's office the other day."

Woody smoothed his knee-high sock under the leg of his trousers.

"It's a composition book this big." Kate held up her hands, noticed that they were shaking, and quickly dropped them to her sides.

Scott Pratt looked up from Woody's shoes. "I think the lady is asking you a question," he told Woody.

"Is it something you can help her with?" Woody said.

Lloyd Keezer spoke up from across the desktops. "Have you checked the conference room, Kate?"

Suspended between the obliging looks of Lloyd Keezer and Scott Pratt, Kate was struck by their decency. She knew that her journal wasn't in the conference room, but Keezer had provided an exit. "I'll take a look," she said and started to leave.

"Don't waste your time," Woody said under his breath.

Kate's head snapped around. "What did you say?"

"Don't waste mine either," he said.

When Kate returned from her cursory search of the conference room, her agitation was so apparent that Ernie asked if it was her time of the month. She gave him a withering look. "How original."

"What's bugging you then? You've been on it all day."

That Ernie could ask such a question made her despair of ever again being on the same wavelength.

"No news is good news," he said.

Kate tilted her head and studied him. "Do you really think that's true?"

"Jeez, it's just an expression."

"No, really. Couldn't 'no news' also mean that the bad news keeps piling up?"

Ernie shook his head. "You're so pessimistic."

Kate went looking for Jim, hoping he might say something to relieve her worries, but Lorraine said he would be wrapped up all day with the central bank seminar. Every year, Matheson rolled out the red carpet for budding central bankers from all over the world in hopes of forming relationships that would lead to future business. Jim would be teaching, Lorraine said, explaining her boss's schedule, and then hosting dinner at the Links Club in Midtown.

Kate recognized the name of the club, which didn't admit women as members or encourage them as guests. The only women's restroom in the four-story building was the one for the help, off the kitchen.

Jim's schedule made Kate feel small and insignificant. She was trying to preserve her reputation with a 99-cent notebook while he networked with future leaders of the world's economic system.

"And they'll be playing golf tomorrow at Winged Foot," Lorraine said. "The clients are thrilled about Woody getting them in."

"Is he playing too?" Kate kept her tone casual, but the news that Woody was involved in client entertainment despite the Fed investigation was startling.

"Woody's a member there. I just hope they can finish their game before the rain arrives." Lorraine wrung her hands, as if ensuring good weather were her responsibility.

"When are they playing?" Kate said.

"They're leaving Manhattan at eight-fifteen. I'm sorry. I don't have time to chat with you now. I have to order the cars." Lorraine picked up the telephone receiver and tapped out the number with the tip of her fingernail.

Back at her desk, Kate brooded over the new information. She was used to being excluded from client entertainment, especially with international clients, whose male chauvinism made their American counterparts seem like feminists. But she wondered if there was a particular significance to Woody's participation in the golf outing. Had the problem with the Fed been resolved, or was he getting a pass because of his membership at the exclusive Westchester club?

"How long does it take to play a round of golf?" Kate asked Ernie.

"Depends on the course," he said.

"How long to play Winged Foot?"

"Who's playing Winged Foot?"

"Jim and Woody are taking some of the central bankers tomorrow. So how long do you think?"

"Four hours, more or less."

"What do you think Woody going along means?"

"That he's still useful," Ernie said. "Can't play the course without a member."

Peter was leaning against the glass wall of the bank lobby when Kate came downstairs. It was the first time he had picked her up at work. He had come directly from school, still dressed in lightly colored slacks and a short-sleeved oxford cloth shirt, his navy blazer slung over one shoulder. He looked refreshingly square, taking everything in like a tourist from the Midwest. She wondered if he was thinking about his own stint on Wall Street, and whether he missed anything about the place.

They were going to the baseball game. Peter had brimmed with enthusiasm on the phone that morning, and didn't mention their dinner the night before with his grandfather. The Mets were fighting to make the playoffs; every game was crucial. It was unthinkable not to be in the stadium as the team headed down the stretch of their best season in more than a decade. Kate hadn't felt much like going until it occurred to her that baseball might be the perfect distraction. Peter would watch the game instead of asking about her day or her plans for tomorrow.

He grinned and straightened up when she came up to him in the lobby. "You're so pretty," he said with discovery in his voice, as if it were the first time he'd expressed the sentiment. "Can I see where you work?"

"Don't we have to get to the game?" The last thing Kate wanted to do was head back to the trading floor.

Peter smiled and took her hand. "We'll do it another time."

The Number 7 train to Shea Stadium was packed with people heading home from work and plenty of baseball fans. The abundance of baseball garb was amazing. Peter struck up a conversation with a Mets fan and his teenaged son, who commented on details from the previous night's game.

Kate's attention drifted back to her last hour at work. Shortly before five o'clock, she had checked the weather forecast, which provided the excuse for a final word with Jim's secretary. "They say the rain will hold off till late afternoon," Kate reported, feeling manipulative when Lorraine's eyes rolled gratefully heavenward. Two cars had been ordered for an eight-fifteen pick-up. Woody would accompany the clients from Manhattan while Jim drove down from Greenwich to meet them at the club in Mamaroneck. Kate estimated that Woody would be away for at least five hours, maybe longer if the dry weather held.

A shiver ran through her shoulders as the train pulled into the stop at Shea Stadium. Peter put his arm around her. "Excited?" he said. "Me, too."

Peter had invited some teachers from Stuyvesant to the game, so there was plenty of chatter. The men's steady stream of quips about the game and everything else taking place in the stadium reminded Kate of the atmosphere in the trading room. When the Pirates took the lead, the stadium grew quiet. The Mets wound up losing, 5-7.

They all rode the subway back to Grand Central, where Kate and Peter switched to the Lexington line. They got out at 59th Street to walk the rest of the way. The night air was refreshing and almost chilly after the stale warmth of the subway.

"Sweater weather," Peter said. "Take my jacket." She put her arms through the sleeves of his blazer. There was a piece of chalk in one of the pockets. "You're quiet tonight," he said.

"Those guys were so funny," Kate said. "They could do stand-up."

"The beer helped." Peter took her hand and gripped it firmly, the way a parent holds onto a small child. They walked along 59th Street and turned north on Park Avenue, traveling the same route they had taken after dinner at Le Refuge, their first date. Soon they reached the spot in front of the Armory where Peter had demonstrated batting stances. Just two months ago, Kate thought, remembering how pleasantly uncomplicated that evening had been.

In front of the Armory staircase, she pantomimed stepping into a batter's box and exaggerated a series of tics and twitches, clenching and unclenching her fingers on the imaginary baseball bat and waggling her wrists in the air. "Who am I?" She puffed out her cheek as though it was filled with a wad of chewing tobacco. "I'm giving it away now."

"Lenny Dykstra. You've been paying attention." Peter smiled and took both her hands in his. "What else is going on?"

In a way it was reassuring that she hadn't fooled him; even during a boisterous night at the ballpark, Peter had paid attention to her. She looked longingly at him, wishing she had been more successful at keeping him in the dark. He tightened his grip. "Did they fire you?"

"No," she said quietly, looking at his large hands covering hers. "They didn't fire me."

"What is it then?"

She took a deep breath before telling Peter about the upcoming golf game at Winged Foot. "I'm left twisting in the wind while Woody cozies up to Jim on the golf course."

"A game of golf doesn't make any difference," Peter said.

"Oh, but it does," Kate said, desperate to convince him. "It shouldn't, but it does. All that after-hours stuff makes a ton of difference, and I don't come by it naturally. I've got to protect myself. I don't think Jim's given my defense a second thought. He's safe, and that's all that really matters to him."

"I wish there were something we could do."

It was an opening as good as any. Quickly, she told him about making a delivery for Liz the next day at Woody's apartment and looking around for her journal while she was there.

"He has your notebook?" Peter said.

"He told me I'd be wasting my time to look in the conference room, which means he knows where it is."

"How do you know he didn't destroy it?"

"It's possible," Kate conceded, "but maybe he didn't. Ernie says Woody might treat it like a trophy."

Peter frowned. "Do you think you might be jumping to conclusions?"

"What other conclusion is there?"

"That he's a nasty, mean-spirited punk, but you already knew that. You're going with Liz?"

"Actually, Liz had to go to California, so it'll just be me."

"The delivery's your cover," he said softly, letting go of her hands.

"If you want to call it that."

Peter sat down on the concrete steps that led up to the Armory entrance. His disillusioned expression made her stomach turn over. "I knew there was something on your mind, but I would never have guessed this."

Kate tilted her head back and stared at the Armory's redbrick façade. "I want my journal back. It's my best defense."

"I hate to see you stoop to his level. You're talking about breaking and entering."

"I won't be breaking. I have a key."

"That's a technicality, and you know it."

"He took something that belongs to me. I need those records to defend myself. No one else is going to do it. It's not important to anyone but me."

"Gee, thanks."

"I meant at work. Checking his apartment would be no big deal if Liz were with me, and it's not that much different without her. I couldn't do this if Liz didn't have the key. I don't know…it seems providential."

"Kate," Peter said, his voice dropping low.

"What?"

"Don't drag God into it. God's got nothing to do with what happens on Wall Street."

"I thought God was everywhere," she said, stung by the way Peter was shaming her. She felt like finding her own way home.

"Couldn't you put this off a couple days? Give yourself more time to think. You've had a rough week, and who knows? Things might be resolved by then."

"It could be too late by then," she said unemotionally, hoping to sound less contradictory.

"I wish I could think of a way to talk you out of this."

Kate touched him gently on the wrist. "It's not like you don't have influence with me."

"No?" He laughed a little. "What's it like then? No job is worth this."

"Funny," Kate said, considering his comment. "It's not entirely about the job anymore."

"Then why do this?" Peter wrapped his fingers around her forearm and made her look at him. "You're not worried about money, are you? You don't have to worry about money."

"It's not about money, but thanks." She turned her head slightly, and he released his hold on her arm.

"What is it then? It's not like you to be reckless."

Kate felt another gap opening: first Ernie, then Jim, and now Peter.

"Is it reckless to stand up for myself?" she said. "There are bad things I can't change. My mother getting sick. My husband leaving. Now some prick wants to screw up my job, but maybe—just maybe—I've got a chance to fight back. I think I'm supposed to take it."

Chapter 20

On Saturday morning, Kate drank a cup of coffee in her kitchen and watched the digital clock on the microwave. 8:40. The cars carrying Woody and the foreign central bankers should be well on their way to Westchester County. In twenty minutes, she would call the club's caddy master, who controlled all tee-offs, and confirm that the Woodson foursomes had begun to play.

She'd had a restless night, waking frequently to check the clock. Around four, she stayed awake, unable to get last night's scene with Peter on the steps of the Armory out of her head. It might have tormented her less if he had continued to argue against her plan to search Woody's apartment. Instead he'd let go of her arm and stared quietly ahead. Sitting next to him on the cool concrete steps, she gazed at his profile, which reminded her of the first time she had seen him, pulling up in the red Prelude to take her to the game. "I'll bet you're sorry you got mixed up with another banker," she told him.

"Nah," he said, but the look of resignation on his face made her heart ache. "I'd better get you home." They had walked the rest of the way in silence. He gave her a polite kiss at the door, but no indication of when they would next see each other, the first time she recalled that happening. Peter's disappointment in her was hard to take, but she was disappointed in him, too. Why didn't he understand that she had to fight back?

At dawn she gave up on sleep and got out of bed. She showered and put on the most dramatic of Liz's selection of green dresses. The padded shoulders and snug bodice gave her a V-shaped torso, like one of the crew on Star Trek. She went downstairs to check the weather. It was humid for September, and she wondered how much different the weather in Westchester County would be. She went back upstairs and, despite the early hour, called Ernie, who lived in Rye, a suburb next door to Mamaroneck, where Winged Foot was located. Besides asking about the weather, she wanted to hear Ernie's voice, to connect to a friend before setting out for Woody's apartment. But it was Marie Mancini who answered the phone. It took Marie a minute to adjust her hearing aid and figure out who was calling.

"Ernie's out mowing the lawn," Marie said.

"Is he worried about the rain?" Kate said.

"What's that, honey? Oh, no, it's beautiful here, nice and hot. The cicadas are so happy." Marie spoke simply, as if she were explaining nature to a grandchild. "Is it raining in the city?"

"No, but there's a chance of rain this afternoon. Are

they predicting showers out your way?"

"Oh, my," Marie laughed softly, the way the hard-of-hearing sometimes cover for missed conversation. "Showers? I hope not! Think of all the brides who picked September to avoid the humidity. That's what Linda did."

Keeping an eye on the time, Kate listened as Marie described the gorgeous weather that had graced her daughter's wedding day. Marie's voice was soothing and made Kate wish that she were spending the day as a surrogate daughter in Rye. She told Marie that she would talk to Ernie at work on Monday, and hung up.

At nine o'clock, Kate poured the rest of her coffee into the sink. She pictured Jim and Woody lining up with their guests at the first tee and discussing club selection with their caddies, or whatever men talked about with the people who carried their bags. She went back to the entry hall and checked the assembled items. Along with the key to Woody's apartment and a letter of authorization for the doorman, Liz had left a small package with a wooden handle affixed with twine.

"Tell Derrick—that's the doorman—you're going to try the lamp in several places but don't leave it there unless you have to," Liz had instructed in a phone call from California. "Look in the obvious places. Remember: Woody thinks he's invincible."

Kate took the authorization letter from the zippered compartment of her shoulder bag. Rereading Liz's chatty note to Derrick was like getting a last-minute pep talk.

The sound of the doorman's buzzer made Kate jump. "You have a delivery, Ms. Munro." Frank sounded especially cheerful. She could hear someone else in the background, and then the familiar sandy voice came directly on the line.

"It's Peter. Can I come up?"

Kate felt a mixture of relief and apprehension. "I was just heading out."

"I'll be right up."

Kate returned Liz's letter to her purse and set it on top of the lamp box. She checked her appearance in the hall mirror, then the time. 9:05. She listened for Peter's knock, always the pickup beat of a drummer. He beat time on the steering wheel, on her back when she hugged him, and gently on her stomach when they were in bed. But this morning his knock on the door came in three perfunctory raps.

Peter stood in the hallway, dressed in a pair of jeans and a khaki-colored uniform shirt. Above the shirt's breast pocket was a white oval patch with "*Pete*" embroidered in red. Kate stared, trying to fathom his attire.

"Can I come in?" he said.

Kate opened the door wider. "I was noticing your shirt."

"It's my dad's. He worked at a gas station when he was in college. It was how my parents met. I guess that's why they saved the uniform." Peter glanced down at his jeans. "I couldn't fit into the pants."

Kate smiled cautiously.

"I borrowed a van," Peter said. "It's parked downstairs. I asked Frank to give us ten minutes." He jammed his hands into his pockets and shifted his weight. "I've thought a lot about this…about your whole situation. I get why you want to do it, and I don't want you going in by yourself."

She felt too much to say any one thing, and her throat ached with restraint. She was grateful that Peter understood and impressed by his resourcefulness, but his resolve wasn't entirely comforting. "I don't want you doing something you think is wrong," she said.

"It's not wrong to make sure you're safe. What are we delivering?"

She picked up the lamp box.

"I'm overkill for something that small." He pointed to the Persian carpet under their feet. "This would be better. Got any twine?"

Kate looked regretfully at the rug with its muted blue and terra cotta swirls, and wondered if Peter was making a point about the high cost of crime. She set down the lamp box and got a ball of twine and a pair of scissors from a drawer in the kitchen. Peter quickly trussed up the rug, then stood over it like a rodeo contestant. "Ready?"

"Just a minute," Kate said. From her bedroom, she

telephoned the golf club and, pretending to be Lorraine, confirmed with the caddy master that the Woodson party was indeed under way. Next she dialed Woody's apartment and let it ring several times. The sound of his voice made her jump until she realized that she had reached his message machine.

Rejoining Peter in the entryway, Kate regarded Liz's lamp box. Was it still necessary now that they had the rug? She started to ask Peter but changed her mind. This was her show. She picked up the lamp box as he hoisted the rug to his shoulder.

Downstairs, Kate got into the passenger side of the van while Peter loaded the rug and lamp into the back. She checked her watch. It was almost twenty past nine. Peter got into the driver's seat and put the key into the ignition. Kate touched his arm. "I'm wondering if I shouldn't go by myself," she said.

He managed a conciliatory smile. "It's all right."

"Maybe I should stick with my original plan." Kate glanced into the back of the van and then at the oval nametag on Peter's shirt. "I don't want to seem ungrateful for all the trouble you've gone to."

"Like I said, I'm all right with it."

"I was thinking that arriving in a van with a delivery man might raise more suspicion than if I went in by myself."

"And what are you going to do when the doorman

takes that dinky cardboard box out of your hands and says he'll see that it gets delivered?"

"I'll say I have to try the lamp in various places to see how it fits with the rest of the décor."

"That'll never fly. A doorman will let a guy haul a rug upstairs but not a lamp box." Peter turned the key in the ignition and looked at her hard. "Where to?"

He had a commanding air for a pacifist, she thought.

Woody's address on Fifth Avenue was truly grand and made Kate's place on East 72nd Street seem like a starter building. A dark green awning, supported on brightly polished brass poles, extended from the curb to the entrance, ensuring that residents stayed dry as they got in and out of their cars.

Peter pulled into a space just past the awning and turned off the ignition. He jumped out of the van, almost colliding with the doorman who had hurried over to them. Kate fumbled through her shoulder bag for Liz's letter, then got out of the van and joined Peter on the sidewalk.

"I have a delivery for Mr. Woodson. Liz McCord spoke with you yesterday?"

"That would have been Derrick," the doorman said, giving Kate an appreciative glance. "He's off today. You'll have to speak to Benny." The doorman's incredibly angled eyebrows produced such a comical expression that Kate thought he might be teasing.

"Are you Benny?" she said.

He smiled wryly, as if he found the notion absurd. "Benny's the front desk manager on weekends. Derrick works Monday through Friday. I'm the swing."

Feeling a trap door rattle beneath her, Kate stared at the envelope addressed to Derrick in her hand. "I have a letter." Her voice trailed off.

"Like I said, Miss, you gotta talk to Benny."

Peter smiled good-naturedly, the rug balanced on his right shoulder and the lamp box in his left hand. "Is Benny inside?"

"He's at the desk. You need a hand?"

"Thanks." Peter gave him the lamp box and checked the name on the doorman's uniform. "We've got the same name."

"Mine's short for 'Peterson'," the doorman said. "First name's Cary, like in Grant, but only my mother calls me that."

Peter laughed. "Say, Pete, can you point us in Benny's direction? This rug is getting heavy."

Kate's legs felt hollow as she crossed the threshold of Woody's apartment building. She walked up to the front desk, where Benny was speaking to a resident. "I have a delivery for Mr. Woodson," she said when she had Benny's attention. "This is a letter from his decorator."

Benny read the letter, his face wrinkling with skepticism. "Mr. Woodson gave you a key?" Kate produced the key, which was tagged with a laminated business card from the interior design firm. She felt a stab of panic. What if Benny called the number on the card?

"Derrick didn't mention a delivery," Benny said. "When did you talk to him?"

"Liz McCord talked to him. She's away on business, but she wanted these items delivered if they came in."

"Derrick didn't say anything to me, and Mr. Woodson walked right past me this morning and didn't mention it either."

Peterson cut in. "You work with Liz McCord?"

Kate nodded, aware of the perspiration forming in the space between her breasts.

"You remember her, Benny. Liz McCord's the lady who brought us the box of chocolates." Peterson smiled at Peter and Kate.

"See's Candy," Kate said. "She brought some into the office too. It's very good candy."

Benny pointed to the letter. "This lady's the candy lady?"

"That's right," Kate said.

"Miss McCord's been working in the penthouse for

months," Peterson said. "She's usually here on weekdays though, which is why you probably haven't met her. Nice of her to remember the weekend crew."

Kate nodded. "She wanted Mr. Woodson to have these things the minute they were available. She doesn't want to try his patience."

"You don't know the half of it," Peterson said, but a glance from Benny silenced him.

Benny looked Peter up and down. "It's the rug and that box?"

"I'm supposed to see how they look with the rest of the furnishings, and leave them only if they're perfect," Kate said.

"I guess it's OK," Benny said, returning Liz's letter to the envelope and tucking it inside his breast pocket. "But you go up with them, Pete. I think Mr. Woodson would prefer it that way."

Chapter 21

Kate's mouth felt dry as she followed Peter and the doorman into the penthouse elevator. She had gotten into Woody's building all right, but what good would it do with the doorman watching her every move?

The elevator door quietly glided shut. "Express service," Peterson said, pointing out the exclusive feature.

"Like the subway," Peter said.

Peterson seemed to enjoy the joke. "Yeah, makes you feel right at home." The elevator door re-opened onto a dimly lit rectangular room, directly opposite a motorcycle.

"Is this the apartment?" Kate said.

"Wait till you see this." Peterson turned up the dimmer on a pair of mini spotlights. The motorcycle's polished metal casings gleamed, as did the fuel tank, which was painted a high-gloss burgundy with the luster of a Mont Blanc pen.

"The guy who lives here must be single," Peter said.

"Ever see *The Great Escape*?" Peterson said.

"About a hundred times," Peter said.

"That's the bike Steve McQueen rode."

"You're kidding," Peter said.

"No kidding. They used two bikes in the movie, and this is one of them. The owner's very proud of it."

"Who wouldn't be?" Peter said. "This is incredible!"

"Does he ride it?" Kate said, curiosity momentarily getting the better of her.

Peterson shook his head. "It's just for show. The owner drives a Porsche."

"Nice," Peter said.

Peterson shrugged. "It's an automatic."

When Peter set the rug down on the marble floor to examine the motorcycle, Kate peeked around the corner into the living room, its elegantly understated design tempering the effect of a motorcycle in the foyer. The streamlined sofa and chairs, upholstered in neutral fabrics, were arranged on a rug of striped wool in varying shades of burgundy. That Woody lived in such sophisticated surroundings surprised Kate, though it shouldn't have. There were plenty of nasty people with excellent taste…or the money to afford a decorator like Liz.

"Is this the bike McQueen tried to jump the wire with?" Peter gripped the handlebars as if contemplating a reenactment. His interest in the motorcycle mystified Kate until she saw him glance pointedly at the lamp box in Peterson's hands.

"I'll take this and let you two admire the Harley," she said.

Peter bent over the bike to inspect the chassis. "I think this is a Triumph."

"Good eye," Peterson said. "They made it look German in the movie, but it's a Triumph all right."

Kate slipped away as Peter began to recount his favorite scenes from the film. In the living room, she took a key from her purse and slit open the cardboard box. She lifted a candlestick lamp from the packing material but didn't bother with the shade. She went through an archway at the end of the living room and into a small library. Her eyes scanned the shelves, but there was no composition book among the leather-bound volumes, books that Liz had probably ordered along with the furniture.

Setting the lamp on a desk, Kate searched each of its three drawers. There were pencils, pens, and a letter opener that looked like a dagger in the center drawer, but the smaller drawers were empty. Fancy accessories covered the desktop: a leather desk set with green blotting paper, and a small bronze statue of a horse. The mahogany magazine rack, tucked between a pair of armchairs, held several back issues of *Fortune* and *Business Week*, but no notebook.

Kate paused, listening to the elaborate diversion that Peter was creating in the foyer. "Do you remember which prisoners actually got away?" he asked Peterson, and started down the lengthy list of characters.

She took the lamp and entered a hallway of stained hardwood floor. Architectural prints hung along a stretch of whitewashed wall opposite a row of open doors. The first room was set up like a gym, with a treadmill and a weight machine placed on tweedy wall-to-wall carpet. Built-in shelves housed a television and a refrigerator. She gave a cursory glance into the smallish bedroom next door, which had a beautiful but empty antique bookshelf, then stopped abruptly at the entrance to the master bedroom. Staring at the unmade bed with its covers turned back on only one side, she finally felt like an intruder.

She clenched her jaw and went in. There was nothing on or under the bed, and nothing but a tube of Chapstick and a Manhattan telephone directory in the end table drawers. She noticed a collection of books in the open shelf space of one end table, all business bestsellers. The fact that Woody read the advice of people like Tom Peters and Lee Iacocca was intriguing.

Next she inspected the walk-in closets, one on either side of a short passage that led into the master bath. One closet appeared to be used for off-season storage, with winter garments in dry cleaners' plastic. The other closet contained the summer wardrobe. A collection of brightly colored polo shirts and sweaters was meticulously arranged on cedar shelves. Woody's business suits were evenly spaced on the rod, with a pair of shoes, toes pointed outward, resting directly below each suit. She knelt on the thick carpet to search the space behind the shoes.

A loud buzzer went off. Kate jumped up, jostling the suits. Her shoulders shook as she crept through the master bedroom, pausing to listen in the doorway. She heard voices but couldn't make out individual words. She glanced at the window and, with a deepening sense of doom, noticed how dark the sky had become. Maybe it had started to rain in Westchester. Maybe thunder and lightning had driven the golfers from the course.

The voices from the foyer went silent. Kate stepped into the hallway and inched her way past the small bedroom. She paused again at the door to the exercise room. Was the sound she heard the elevator door opening?

Sweet Jesus, she thought. Woody had come back.

She felt lightheaded and steadied herself against the doorjamb. She took several deep breaths. She would have to pretend that the delivery was for real and that she was covering for her sister, who was in California on business. Her mind scrambled for a plausible tableau in which to be discovered. She could be trying the lamp out in the library, but where was the lamp? She looked stupidly at her empty hand, then down the hall to the master bedroom. Was there time to retrieve the lamp before Woody came in?

She heard the sound of heels on hardwood as someone crossed the uncarpeted strip of flooring between the living room and the library. Her face went numb, and she touched her cheek, wondering if she could be having a stroke.

"There you are," Peter said loudly, coming into the hallway. "Benny called from downstairs. He wants to know how much longer." Noticing her alarm, Peter lowered his voice. "Are you all right?"

"Who's out there?" she whispered.

"The doorman and me," he said, his voice steady and soft. "Why?"

Kate studied Peter's face, but there were no secret signals in his expression. She let out her breath and pulled at the bodice of her dress, which stuck to her perspiring skin. "It's so humid," she said.

"I think Peterson is a little pressed for time."

"Right, I'll go get the lamp." She found it on the floor next to Woody's bed, by the shelf of business bestsellers. She took a second look at the books, but her journal wasn't among them.

Kate and Peter returned to the foyer where the doorman looked at them expectantly. "I'm afraid this lamp doesn't look right anywhere," she said, shaking her head, "but there's one more place to check. While I'm doing that, would you mind rolling out the rug?"

Peter pulled his hand through his hair and stared at the space in front of the motorcycle. "Here?"

"Those were my instructions," she said.

"I'll give you a hand," Peterson said.

Kate found the kitchen, which looked as if it could support a small restaurant. There were walls of cabinets with mullioned glass doors, and an island topped with gray soapstone in the middle of the work area. Her eye was drawn to a shelf of cookbooks next to the double ovens. *The Silver Palate*; Julia Child and Pierre Franey; even *Betty Crocker's Cooky Book*, but no trading journal.

Tears of frustration stung Kate's eyes. What was she going to do? She didn't trust the bank's records; Woody had obviously tampered with them. The fact that she had kept her own record would do absolutely no good if she couldn't produce the pertinent pages. Providing every journal except the one the auditors were interested in would look suspicious, like the eighteen-and-a-half-minute gap on the Nixon tapes.

She felt a wave of nausea and leaned over the stainless steel sink until it passed. Cupping her hand under the faucet, she drank some cold water and splashed the rest on her face. She blotted her cheeks with a paper towel, and was looking for a wastebasket when she noticed the sideboard at the far end of the room. Woody's trophy case, she thought, and walked over to it, but the only thing on display was Liz's selection of brightly colored china.

"We're ready with the rug," Peter called from the foyer.

"I'll be right there!" She turned and bumped her foot against a wicker basket filled with newspapers and a gym bag. *Home of the Heisman.* An image from work flashed

301

through her mind. She knelt and unzipped the gym bag. Underneath a newspaper and a small racket was her notebook. Her heart pounding, she quickly flipped to the pages recording the June year-bill auction. Everything was still there; not a single sheet had been torn from the binding. She swallowed back the ache in her throat. "Thank you," she whispered. She zipped up the gym bag and re-positioned it on the stack of newspapers. She returned the lamp to its box in the living room, and slipped the journal into her shoulder bag. Carrying the lamp box, she marched into the foyer and pushed the elevator button twice.

"What about the rug?" Peter asked.

Kate turned and stared vacantly at him and then at the doorman, who seemed to be waiting for direction, too.

"Oh, right, the rug." She gave her Persian carpet a cursory glance. "It would be a mistake to leave that rug here. It does absolutely nothing for the motorcycle."

Chapter 22

Peter pulled the van into the traffic on Fifth Avenue and looked across the front seat at Kate. "Did you get it?" She nodded and patted her shoulder bag. "I figured you'd found it, the way you rushed us out of there. Where was it?"

"In a gym bag...with an old newspaper and a squash racquet." Kate shook her head in disbelief. "Just sitting in a basket of newspapers in the kitchen. He must have dropped it there and forgotten all about it." She waited until Peter turned off Fifth Avenue before taking the marbled composition book from her bag and re-checking the entry for the June year-bill. "He didn't even rip out the pages."

"What made you check the gym bag?"

"I remembered seeing it in his office."

"We got lucky with the motorcycle. It was a perfect distraction."

Kate laughed, getting into the recounting. "You two sounded like Siskel and Ebert."

"Peterson was a nice guy. Can you imagine trying to shoot the breeze with Benny?"

Kate shook her head again and silently wondered what other pitfalls she had failed to consider.

"Well, I'm glad you got it back," Peter said. "You can turn it into the auditors on Monday and be done with it."

Kate looked at Peter and considered his comment; she hadn't thought about giving the journal to the auditors before they asked for it. "That might seem strange, don't you think?"

Peter stuck out his lower lip and shrugged. "No stranger than anything else about this morning." He said this pleasantly enough, but the undertone was unmistakable.

"Sorry to have involved you in something strange," she said.

"It was my choice."

"Seems like you're regretting it though."

"I'm glad it's over, that's all." Stopped at a red light, they both stared through the windshield at people in the crosswalk. "You're glad it's over too, aren't you?"

"Of course I'm glad it's over! I was scared to death when that buzzer went off. I thought you were Woody coming into the library." The memory made her shiver. "But I'd do it again, if I had to."

"Well, hey," Peter said, his hands lifting off the

steering wheel. "I've got the van till noon." And just like that, she felt at odds with him, back to where they'd been the night before in front of the Armory. "That was a joke," he added.

"No, it wasn't."

The light changed, and they turned onto Park Avenue. They traveled several blocks in silence. At the next stoplight, Peter reached over and put a hand on her knee. "What's wrong?"

She took a deep breath and let her shoulders drop. "I feel like you disapprove of what I did."

"I might have picked a different way to handle it, that's all."

She turned to look at him. "How would you have handled it? I tried asking him nicely, and he shut me down."

Peter's forehead wrinkled. "I don't want to second-guess you, Kate. You got your book back, so let's just move on."

"But he had my book! You still think it was wrong to take it back? I didn't touch the silverware."

"I don't want to argue," he said, removing his hand from her knee.

"But it's obvious you disapprove. The fact that Woody actually had my book doesn't seem to make any difference. You're making me feel like I'm no better than he is."

"Be fair, Kate. I'm not the one who's making you feel bad."

"I'm in trouble for something I didn't do—that's what's unfair—and you're making me feel guilty about fighting back."

"You want me to praise you for how cleverly we managed to sneak into a guy's apartment? You can't honestly feel good about that."

"But I do! I do feel good about that! Otherwise I'm going into the auditors without a defense. The thing I don't feel good about is being put in that situation, and you not understanding what I had to do. That's what I feel bad about." She looked imploringly at him. The light changed, and he fixed his eyes on the road.

When they pulled up to her apartment building, the doorman hurried over to the curb. Peter motioned for Kate to roll down her window. "Ten minutes to unload, Frank, and I'll be out of here," Peter said.

"You got it," Frank said. When Peter went around to the back of the van, the doorman spoke quietly to Kate. "You have a visitor." She quickly glanced at the building entrance, worried for a moment that someone from Woody's building had trailed the van. "It's your ex-husband. He's been here about ten minutes."

The door at the back of the van slammed shut, and Peter reappeared with the rug on his shoulder. Frank opened Kate's door and took the lamp box. Still clutching her journal, she led the way into the lobby.

Ted sat on an upholstered bench opposite the elevators. He looked distinguished in his white coat, the earpieces of a stethoscope visible in his pocket. He lifted his eyes and studied her intensely, then stood up without shifting his gaze.

"Is everything all right?" Kate said.

"Everything's fine," Ted said. "Did you buy a new rug?"

Kate looked at Peter, balancing the rug on his shoulder and reading Ted's nametag.

"I'll handle the rug," Frank said and stuck out his hand. By the time Kate found her key and handed it over, Peter had disappeared into the recesses of the elevator.

"New rug?" Ted repeated.

Kate watched the elevator door close, then turned back to Ted. "It's a long story," she said.

"Go ahead. I like your long stories." Kate looked at him skeptically; she'd been the listener in their marriage. "Hey, we're all capable of change," he added. "That's what you always told me."

Was that why he was here, to show her how much he had changed? Whatever his intentions, Kate knew that he had prepared for this conversation, and that made her cautious. But his attentiveness was appealing, like their life in the years before med school, when he had made time for her.

Ted stepped back to the upholstered bench. "Sit for a

307

minute," he said. "How have you been? Are you still the top salesman? No, wait, that's wrong. You switched to trading, didn't you?" He smiled as if his confusion was completely understandable. But it wasn't. They had still been married when she moved from sales to trading, and his failure to remember was condescending, reminding her of the imbalance that had always existed in their relationship.

"I remember what *you* do," she said.

Her reaction appeared to surprise him. He opened his mouth as if to protest but seemed to think better of it. "You're right, I should remember."

"It's trading," she said flatly, though his admission placated her. She sat down on the bench.

"So tell me about trading. No, really," he said when she smiled warily. "I want to know."

Kate began to describe her job as a trader, slowly at first so as not to run ahead of Ted's interest. But he listened closely and prompted her to continue whenever she paused. His interest was flattering, if belated, and intensified her curiosity about why he had come to see her.

Peter's reappearance in the lobby and Ted's invitation to lunch seemed to occur simultaneously. "The rug's back in place," Peter said, taking another long look at Ted, who reached for his wallet.

Kate stepped between the two men. "Give me a minute," she told Ted, then walked Peter out to the sidewalk and over to the white van.

"He was going to tip me," Peter said, staring back at the building entrance.

Kate smiled regretfully. "He doesn't realize who you are."

"Has he ever *heard* of me?"

"I haven't talked to him in almost a year."

"But you're going to talk to him now?" Kate looked at Peter and said nothing. He took a deep breath and pulled his keys out of his pocket. "I've got to get the van back."

She put a hand on his arm. "Thanks for all your help this morning. I couldn't have done it without you. I'll call you later, OK?"

Peter seemed to be thinking this over before he nodded curtly, got into the van and drove off.

Kate and Ted walked over to Madison Avenue and turned in the direction of the Magnolia Restaurant, a Greek diner where they always used to go. He spoke about completing his residency in June, a date that had once held importance in her future, too. When they reached the restaurant, he got the door and held his hand briefly against the small of her back. They sat in a leather booth opposite the counter.

"French toast, right?" Ted asked her, when the waiter

arrived to take their order. Kate hadn't eaten all day and smiled instinctively at the prospect of maple syrup flooding thick slices of powder-sugared bread. "I remembered that anyway," Ted said, looking pleased with her reaction.

Again he took up the subject of her job, asking her to explain how a Treasury auction worked. His quick mind grasped the fundamentals with minimal explanation, but he asked about nuances, too. She went into details that she had never discussed with Peter, partly because he had worked in the business, but also because of the negative light they might cast on what she did for a living. Ted reacted as though the work scenarios she described were familiar; he likened the maneuvering at the bank to politics at the hospital.

Kate had listened to Ted's work stories for years, but his focus on her job was new. When he remarked that he had time for a quick walk before getting back to the hospital, she couldn't think of a reason to say no. At the register, she pulled out her wallet, but he took it from her and put it back in her purse.

"What's this?" he said, tapping the composition book.

She pushed the book deeper into her shoulder bag and secured the flap. "My trading journal."

A smiled flickered on his lips. "You carry it around with you?"

As they left the restaurant and walked into Central Park, she found herself telling him about the trouble at work, Woody taking her journal, and how she had recovered it that morning at his apartment.

Ted stopped at a shady curve in the park's winding path. "You went to his apartment and demanded he give it back?"

"No, I asked him about it at work, but he wouldn't admit that he had it, so I went to his apartment and got it."

"Just like that, he handed it over?"

"He wasn't home, but I had a key."

Ted's eyes widened, which made her smile. "It's nothing like *that*." She explained Liz's decorating connection and what it had led to. Kate didn't mention her own apprehension and glossed over the operational details, including Peter's role as deliveryman.

When she finished the story, Ted beamed. "What a gutsy girl you are." He put a hand on her shoulder, a gesture that turned into a hug. She breathed in the aromatic combination of his aftershave and pipe tobacco. Listening to the rustle of the leafy summer canopy overhead, she felt wistful. He must be feeling it, too, she thought, pulling back a little to look at him. Before she knew it, his lips had brushed hers. It seemed almost accidental until he kissed her again, tenderly. Somewhere in that lingering kiss, she responded. The familiarity of their kiss, and the shock that they were kissing, left her breathless.

A helmeted young man on Rollerblades zipped past.

"Hey, Doc, where can I get some of that medicine?" The skater grinned when they looked up, then glided off.

"Is that someone you know?" Kate asked, to have something distracting to say.

"It's the white coat," Ted said. He checked his watch, which she noticed wasn't the one she'd given him before med school. "I've got to get back for rounds."

They left the park and walked briskly back to her apartment; they seemed to have stunned each other silent. *Everyone's capable of change.* Had he come to talk about reconciliation? Her thoughts ran wild about her reaction to such a development. Did Ted have first claim on her affections because they'd been married? Were they one of those couples who split up, found other mates, only to get back together?

Frank was standing outside the building when they walked up, but he stepped inside to grant them the privacy of a Manhattan sidewalk. Seeing the doorman made Kate feel guilty, a reaction that Ted seemed to share.

"I hope I didn't give you the wrong impression back there," he said. He pointed vaguely in the direction of the park. "I wanted to try and put things right."

"But not *that* right," she said, with manufactured composure.

He looked immensely relieved. "I have some news, and I wanted you to hear it from me. I'm getting married next month."

Kate felt as if a cab had jumped the curb and knocked her down. For several seconds her mind refused to turn over. When it did, her first thought was that Ted had managed to leave her twice. She stared at him in his white coat, imagining a wedding boutonnière in the lapel. "To the food services manager?" she said.

"Yes, of course," he said irritably, the old Ted returning. "It wasn't just a fling."

"No, of course not. A fling was what we had back there in the park," she said. Ted looked wounded, but he had nowhere to go. Her pleasure in mocking him was short-lived too. "Sorry. I'm starting to sound like Liz."

"I guess your sister hates me."

"You have bigger fans."

"There were good times, too, though. I supported you too. Not monetarily, you didn't need me for that, but psychologically."

And this was what it came down to, Kate thought, divvying up the blame and consolation. Her head cleared completely, the way it did in the postmortem of a losing trade, when all the unheeded warning signs seemed glaring, and the best you could do was clean the slate and try again.

"Didn't I?" Ted said. Their eyes met for a moment, and Kate was surprised to see that his were filled with emotion.

"Not so much at the end maybe, but the beginning

was good," she said quietly. "It really was." Who suffered most, she wondered, the one left behind or the one who did the leaving? A person could debate that forever.

Ted smoothed his tie and buttoned his jacket; his vulnerable moment had passed. "I've got patients waiting for me. I'll give you a call next week."

"Oh, no," Kate said quickly, putting a hand up for emphasis. "You don't have to call."

"No, it'll be good," he insisted. "For closure."

She stood on the sidewalk for a few moments and watched him walk away. Poor Ted, she thought. There was no such thing as closure.

Chapter 23

Later that same afternoon, Kate sat on her bed, turning the pages of her trading journal. The exultant moment of finding it in Woody's apartment had passed, but she still had the quiet satisfaction of thwarting his attempt to trip her up. She had meant it when she told Peter that she would do it all again, and his disapproval of her tactics in spite of the evidence of Woody's theft was disappointing. Ted had saluted her—all Wall Street would salute her—but those approbations didn't mean as much. Apparently Peter didn't encounter the kind of compromises she kept getting caught up in, or remember what it took to survive on Wall Street.

Thinking that Peter might have gone to the Mets game, Kate watched the final innings on TV, peering closely at the screen whenever the television camera panned across the crowd. When the game ended, she switched off the set and stared out the window. At five o'clock, there was still plenty of daylight, though the days were growing shorter. Summer wouldn't officially end until later that month, but her favorite season of the year seemed long gone.

She poured herself a bowl of cereal, a supper she hadn't fallen back on in several months. Was she returning to the two-dimensional world of work, and waiting to get back to work, which she'd inhabited since the split with Ted? She washed the cereal bowl and spoon and quickly returned them to the cupboard, as if to eliminate evidence of her solitude.

Kate jumped for the phone when it finally rang, but it was her sister calling from California. Liz was elated: she had landed both the makeover in Hillsborough and the *Out of Africa* assignment in San Francisco.

"Are you coming back to New York?" Kate said, half expecting Liz to have her belongings sent after her the way they did in the movies.

"Of course I'm coming back! There's the small matter of packing up and moving 3,000 miles across the country."

"Don't forget I have your lamp."

"My lamp? Oh, the lamp. I didn't really think you'd go to his apartment."

"I went to his apartment, but I didn't leave the lamp."

Liz screamed into the receiver. "Oh my God! You went to his apartment? I can't believe you actually did it! Did you find your journal?"

Kate started to tell the story in a matter-of-fact way, as if Peter were listening. But Liz egged her on and soon

Kate was delighting in the details, warmed by her sister's appreciation for every aspect of the maneuver.

"I'm sorry about the miscue with the doormen," Liz said, "though it doesn't seem to have fazed you any. You went in there and took charge! Should I give Peterson the chocolates I brought you?"

The mention of Woody's doorman gave Kate a start. "Please don't go back there."

"You're right, let sleeping dogs lie. And Peter's the one who deserves the chocolates. He really saved the day. Let me talk to him."

"He's not here."

"He's not? I thought you'd be celebrating."

Kate told Liz about the uncomfortable ride home in the van, and how she and Peter had found Ted waiting in the lobby.

"What did *he* want?" Liz said.

"He's getting married next month."

"Why's he telling you? Does he need to borrow money for the reception?" The disdain in Liz's voice was predictable, soothingly so.

"He said he wanted to make things right with me. He's looking for closure."

"I'll give him closure. Did he actually use that word?"

Kate smiled, imagining Liz shaking a clenched fist.

"He actually did. He said he's going to call next week."

"Get a message machine. I'll buy you one."

"He won't call." Kate realized it would be easier that way, though Ted's failure to follow through even in this regard would still hurt. "I wish Peter would call."

"Was it awkward with him and Ted?"

"It was pretty bad." Kate told Liz what had happened.

"Sounds like you owe Peter an apology," Liz said. "You're not opposed to apologizing, are you?"

"No."

"Then get over there and say you're sorry. Tell him you've never been happier in your life than you are with him."

"I can't say that."

"Why not? That's how you feel, isn't it?"

"I don't think in terms like that."

"You don't think in terms of happiness?"

"I don't measure periods of happiness against each other."

"But doesn't Peter make you happier than Ted?"

Kate thought about the early years with Ted, when the possibility of their love fading away seemed out of the question. She had never doubted him and would have bet everything she had on their marriage succeeding. Now she understood that things happen to relationships, and that complications arise despite everyone's best intentions.

"Peter is more easygoing than Ted, but I'd feel fake saying 'I've never been happier than when I'm with you.' Ernie calls that blowing sunshine up someone's ass."

"What kind of low-class expression is that?" Liz said.

"That's mild by Wall Street standards."

"Well, don't be fake, but get over there."

Kate hailed a cab on Park Avenue. On the short ride to East 80th Street, she tried to think of what to say to Peter. How *could* she have kissed Ted, she thought, though the intensity of that moment was undeniable. How could he have kissed *her*, with an October wedding planned? It was just like her life with Ted had been: romance and grand gesture one minute, arrogance and put-downs the next.

Kate paid the taxi driver and got out in front of the Etheridge brownstone. She tried the entrance to Peter's apartment, tucked under the front steps, but without success. She climbed the steps to the main entrance, rang the bell and waited a full minute. She was debating whether or not to ring again when she heard someone coming to the door.

"Come in, come in," Mr. Etheridge said. "What a nice surprise." The bibbed apron he wore over his dress shirt and tie made him look like an off-duty butler. "I was all the way back in the kitchen. I'm glad you didn't give up."

"Is this an inconvenient time?" Kate said.

"I'm having dinner. Madeline left platefuls of food, and I've got no one to share it with."

Kate let her disappointment show. "Peter's not home?"

"He had to return a van to a friend, and there was talk of the ball game afterwards. Maybe they stopped somewhere for dinner. Have you eaten yet?" Kate paused, thinking about the bowl of cereal. "Sit with me anyway," he said.

She followed him down a long hallway to the back of the house. Mr. Etheridge set out a plate of sandwiches and a bowl of potato salad, urging her to partake. She picked up half a sandwich and took a small bite. "I think Madeline was counting on Peter for most of this food," he said.

They sat at a table that looked out on the walled garden in back of the house. The outdoor lights were already on, spotlighting flowers in earthenware pots around the edge of the brick patio, and a small square of closely cut grass towards the back. Kate touched the vase of purple chrysanthemums on the table. "Are these from your garden?"

"I think those are from Gristedes. Madeline always keeps flowers on this table. My wife did too. She sat here with Peter when he did his homework. You can still see the marks." Mr. Etheridge pointed out the maze of lines and numbers indented in the wood. "There's part of his name."

"Here's a square root sign." Kate looked up, and they both smiled.

Mr. Etheridge poured two glasses of iced tea from a frosty pitcher. "Are things getting sorted out at the bank?"

Kate hesitated, wondering if he knew why Peter had needed a van. "I guess I'll know more next week."

"I wouldn't worry. I have a feeling it will all work out."

Kate smiled diplomatically and took a sip of tea.

"You and Peter give me great confidence in the future," Mr. Etheridge said. "You're not caught up in the wrong things. Did you read the article the other day in the *Times* about all the young women buying mink coats? One woman couldn't decide whether she looked better in the black or the white, so she got them both."

"But she isn't going to wear the white one to work," Kate said.

"You read it too." He laughed softly. "There's no self-consciousness about it either."

Kate didn't own a mink coat, though she wondered whether Mr. Etheridge's objection was to materialism in general or to materialism in younger people. While he didn't live ostentatiously, he did seem to already have a good deal of what others aspired to. Surely his wife had owned a fur.

"I was relieved when they broke off their engagement," Mr. Etheridge said. "Peter told you about that, didn't he?" The comment, seemingly out of the blue, made Kate wonder if the subject of fur coats had brought Peter's fiancée to mind.

"Peter said he'd been engaged, but he didn't go into it," Kate said.

"And I won't either, other than to say I think it was for the best. She was a nice person, but she and Peter didn't hold the same weight." Mr. Etheridge words were kind, but his eyes narrowed, hinting at other emotions he might have felt. "She mistook Peter's gentleness for weakness. I suppose that made her uncomfortable, though I doubt that she could have put it into words. None that Peter shared with me anyway."

Kate kept silent, hoping that Mr. Etheridge would continue. She was curious about the broken engagement, and what he had meant by Peter and his fiancée not holding the same weight. But true to his word, Mr. Etheridge moved on to other topics. He seemed to know all about Liz moving back to California, and suggested a going-away dinner at his house.

When they finished the meal, Kate loaded the dishwasher while Mr. Etheridge covered the leftover food and put it into the refrigerator. She wiped the table with a dampened cloth, looking again at the marks Peter had made in the wood.

"Will we see you at church tomorrow?" Mr. Etheridge asked when he walked Kate to the front door. "It's always quite a party."

The word he selected to describe the church service made her smile. "It *is* a friendly church," she said.

"I meant the luncheon afterwards. It's a birthday party for all us aged churchgoers. Peter is providing the music."

"He hasn't mentioned it," she said, with the growing sense that Peter had started to ease her out.

Chapter 24

The next morning, the social hall below the church sanctuary was at its crepe-papered best. A dozen tables, one for every month of the year, were covered with mismatched tablecloths and cafeteria stainless steel. Decorated cakes served as centerpieces: a heart-shaped cake with pink icing for February, and a replica of the American flag for July.

A woman with salt-and-pepper hair stood at the long buffet table and handed Mr. Etheridge a plate. "Let's see, Arthur," she said, consulting a list. "You're April, aren't you?"

"That's right, Barbara." He turned to Kate, who stood next to him in line. "April Fool's Day," he said with pretended chagrin.

Barbara handed a plate to Kate. "And you're Peter's friend. So nice to see you again." The woman's kindness fanned Kate's hope, in spite of the generic friendliness Peter had greeted her with after the church service.

Mr. Etheridge and Kate filled their plates and took their seats at the April birthday table. Their cake was covered with dyed coconut and jellybean eggs. "Have you ever seen greener coconut?" said the sprightly woman with a bouffant hairdo seated on Kate's left.

Rev. Barlow stood at a table across the room and offered a simple grace. Then Peter and two of his students began to play. On piano, bass, and drums, they made a youthful, jazzy sound that gave the party a lift. It was the first time Kate had seen Peter play with a group. His professionalism surprised her, and she felt guilty that she hadn't given his accomplishment in music its due. He looked handsome in white shirt and tie, and happy, too, chatting with the boys between numbers. They were enjoying the gig, as was everyone gathered in the social hall. They were a community that might never be noticed by someone who had moved to the neighborhood because of a job on Wall Street.

When they were ready to cut the cakes, Peter played a drum roll for Barbara, who flapped her hand in his direction, looking both embarrassed and pleased by the fanfare. She thanked everyone for coming and led the assembly in singing "Happy Birthday." Then she nodded at a crew of volunteers, who fanned out to serve cake and decaffeinated coffee.

Peter stood up from his drum set and headed in Kate's direction, which took some time as people kept stopping him to chat. He spoke to each one, his expression animated, gesturing like a traffic cop. When he reached the April table, he eyed the cake appreciatively. "Jellybeans," he said. "My favorite."

The woman with the bouffant hair got up from the table. "Sit here, Peter. Your grandfather and I will distribute the songbooks." The woman smiled conspiratorially at Kate, but others at the table missed the cue and immediately engaged Peter in conversation about the students in the band. Looking around the social hall, Kate felt sad and out of place, a counterfeit among the genuine article, more alone than she had been the night before in her apartment. She noticed the young musicians at the buffet table, and got up to fix a plate for Peter.

"You read my mind," he said when she set the food in front of him. She smiled and sat down, concentrating on her own plate. "You came by yesterday," he said, his sandy voice so endearing to her now. "Granddad was bragging a little on the way to church."

"He's good company," Kate said.

"He says the same about you."

"Not yesterday, I wasn't."

There was a silent moment in which Peter seemed to take in her comment. "'*Mama said*.' You know the song?"

Kate looked at him uncertainly. "'Mama said not to come'?"

Peter shook his head in musicological horror. "'*Mama said there'll be days like this*.'" His tenor voice unabashedly took up the remainder of the verse: "'*There'll be days like this, my mama said. Mama said, Mama said.*'" Peter's eyes shifted to the junior members of his combo, who were drifting back to their instruments, and to Barbara, waving to get his attention. He took Kate's hand under the table. "Stay for the singing. I'll take you home afterwards."

Peter sank into the red and yellow sofa in Kate's living room. He loosened his tie and pulled open his collar, but looked up before untying his shoes. "OK if I take these off?"

It was the end of a long afternoon. The group singing at the church had gone on for more than an hour. Afterwards, Peter drove his grandfather home and then returned for the bass player and his instrument. While Peter handled transportation, Kate helped with cleanup in the church kitchen. The camaraderie of the volunteers, who carried on a lively conversation over the rumbling of the industrial dishwashing machine, had buoyed her spirits.

"Go ahead, take them off," she told Peter. "Do you want to take a nap?" Looking up from his shoes, he smiled as if he found her question provocative. "I meant, are you tired?'"

"I might be." He pulled her onto his lap. The first moments of their kiss felt strange.

She shifted gently off Peter's lap. "I need to talk to you first. I need to clear the air."

He looked at her for a long moment. "It's clear with me, if it's clear with you."

"You're not just saying that so we can take a nap?"

He smiled bashfully. "A little nap would do us both good."

"You don't disapprove of me?"

"Of course not." He picked up her hand and started to play with her fingers.

"What about going into Woody's apartment?"

Peter shrugged. "We probably shouldn't make it a habit, but there were extenuating circumstances."

"There *were* extenuating circumstances."

"I just said there were."

"It seemed to bother you more yesterday."

"It did and it didn't."

"What part didn't? Helping me out?"

"Yeah, and the excitement. It was fun." He smiled and winced at the same time.

"I'm glad I got my journal back, Peter." She spoke steadily and kept her eyes on his.

"I'm glad too."

Kate's arms went around Peter's neck and she kissed him, but he didn't respond the way she had anticipated. She tilted her head, regarding him lovingly. "Not sleepy anymore?"

"There's something else I thought you'd be mentioning," he said.

Of course, she thought, what self-respecting man wouldn't want to know about an ex-husband in the lobby? "You mean Ted."

"Well, yeah," he said, lifting a shoulder.

"I'm sorry, Peter. It was so awkward. I didn't handle it well."

"I felt like an idiot."

"I'm really sorry. He caught me off guard, and I bungled it."

"That's OK."

"No, it's not. You have every right to be furious."

"I'm not furious. I was, but I'm not anymore."

"He came by to tell me he's getting married next month." It was the second time she had reported Ted's upcoming wedding, and she was relieved that its impact had already lessened.

"I thought he might be trying to get you back."

Peter's vulnerable expression pierced her heart. "I'm sorry you thought that for even a minute." She rested her head against the warm, solid front of him and felt his chest expand and contract. "I wouldn't go back to him, not that he's asking."

"Because you could never forgive him?"

"I think I've forgiven him. It's where I want to get to

anyway."

"Then why wouldn't you go back to him?"

"You mean, if he had asked?"

"Even if he didn't ask."

Peter's insistence on a straight answer made Kate pause. Her relationship with him was so different from the one she'd had with Ted. From the day they first met, Peter had treated her as an equal. She hadn't realized that there were men who considered their partners' aspirations as important as their own. Her parents' marriage had been loving and respectful but entirely traditional, with her mother gracefully accepting whatever her father decided.

Now Kate expected more from her most important connection. She knew that no one person could embody every desirable human characteristic. She would always admire Ted's drive and thrill of accomplishment; those were traits she shared with him. And she appreciated that he had seen the recovery of her journal as a triumph, and not an unfortunate occurrence she shouldn't make a habit of. But if Ted had disagreed with her plan to search Woody's apartment, would he have borrowed a van and shown up to help the way Peter had?

Kate kissed the palm of Peter's hand and pressed it to her cheek. They stayed that way for a moment, the silence settling around them like a soft blanket. "I don't trust him anymore," she finally said.

Chapter 25

The next morning, Kate and Ernie checked in with a receptionist in the waiting area of the bank's auditing department. The atmosphere seemed so tranquil after the trading floor. If not for the brass letters spelling *A. J. Matheson* on the wall behind the receptionist's desk, they might have traveled to a completely different company, one that employed people of calm demeanor and modulated voice.

Two men in suits came through the glass doors behind them. Both carried cups of coffee and looked unhurried, still acclimating themselves to the start of the workweek. Kate was struck by the contrast to her own re-entry that morning, when Jim Fletcher, the head of the government bond department, announced the meeting with the auditors before she'd had time to switch on her screens.

"You two are on at ten," Jim said quietly, leaning over the bill traders' phone turrets. "Don't be late and don't act like they're wasting your time."

"Who's going to trade bills?" Ernie asked.

"I am," Jim said, rolling up his sleeves and leering a

331

little.

"We'll be back in time for the auctions, won't we?" Ernie sounded worried, though not about the auditors. A department head generally lost money when he filled in on the desk, even if he had been a great trader before moving into management. Trading reflexes dulled very quickly.

"I can handle the auctions," Jim said, and for a moment Kate wondered if she and Ernie had been officially barred from participation. "So don't be agitating to get back to the floor. The Chairman expects your full cooperation."

"There goes September," Ernie muttered after Jim walked away, but Kate didn't care. Finally they were getting on with the investigation, which would restore order at work. If Jim trading their position shot a hole through their profits, they would make it up in the fourth quarter. She glanced down the row of trading desks to where Woody sat, still wearing his suit jacket. He must be seeing the auditors too. She wondered whether his meeting was before or after theirs, and if the sequencing made a difference.

For the tenth time that morning, Kate touched the small canvas bag that hung diagonally across her chest, and felt the outline of her journal tucked inside. She had been hesitant about bringing the notebook to work, but now she was glad that she had it. The night before, she and Peter had gone to a 24-hour copy center on Lexington Avenue and made two copies, one for her apartment and the other for him to keep at his place. She had found the canvas bag in her closet—a striped beach bag she used for her swim gear—and worn it all morning, prompting Ernie to ask if she'd gotten a paper route over the weekend.

"It's my journal," she said. "I don't want to lose it again."

"It looks ridiculous," Ernie said, but left it at that.

Kate recognized the woman who now approached them in the reception area of the auditing department: Margaret Finn, Senior Vice President and Head Auditor, the highest-ranking woman at A. J. Matheson. She had been in Jim's office the previous week, the day Kate told him what she knew about the Fed's investigation. Margaret Finn often rode the train in from Rye with Ernie, though she didn't seem to recognize him when she shook his hand in the reception area. Impeccably groomed, she wore Nancy Reagan red and a substantial gold necklace and earrings.

"Thank you for taking the time to meet with us," Margaret told them.

"Was it optional?" Ernie looked momentarily serious before flashing a grin. Margaret smiled stoically, as if expecting that kind of response from a trader. "There really isn't a good time to be away in your business, is there?" she said.

"I guess Mondays are busy for everyone," Kate said, eliciting an eye roll from Ernie.

They went into the head auditor's office, which was sumptuous in comparison to the managers' offices on the trading floor. In addition to the large desk and credenza, there were a sofa and two comfortable chairs upholstered in pale blue damask, not the trader-proof tweed of the bond department. The soft seating was arranged around an oval of beveled glass, supported by curved brass legs. The artwork on the walls was interesting too: silk-screened flowers and water-colored birds. Maybe the bank's highest-ranking woman had enough clout to veto prints of hunt scenes and sailing vessels...or maybe she had done well enough to supply her own decoration.

Margaret took the chair with its back to the window and directed Kate and Ernie to the sofa. There was a copy of the *American Banker* on the coffee table and a crystal ashtray that looked unused, a fact that failed to deter Ernie from taking out his cigarettes. "Mind if I smoke?"

"Go ahead," Margaret said, though her body language screamed an opposite response. "Roger Ward will be joining us. His auditing responsibilities include the bond department." Margaret produced a laminated organization chart with herself at the top of the pyramid. Kate wondered if such a chart existed for the bond department. She glanced at Ernie, whose look of utter indifference made her suppress a smile.

Roger Ward arrived in the doorway, a portly, middle-aged man with a leather folder under his arm, the same man who had accompanied Margaret to Jim's office the previous week. In contrast to his boss, Roger looked harried, as though his morning had already been full. Kate surmised that he was doing most of the legwork on the Fed inquiry.

Taking the chair opposite Margaret, Roger produced a sheet of graph paper from his folder. "I wanted to clarify in my own mind a couple points about the auction process, and then I'd like to ask a few questions about the year-bill auction in June. I'll try not to keep you long."

"We'd appreciate that," Ernie said, ignoring Jim's earlier instruction not to rush the interview. "The boss is trading our position while we're up here, if you catch my drift." Ernie rested his cigarette in the crystal ashtray. Margaret drew back from the plume of smoke, which made Kate wonder about the auditor's predisposition in this case: did she want to clear a fellow employee, or catch one?

Roger spent several minutes reviewing the auction process. He had it down cold, including some back-office procedures Kate had never heard of. With his background in operations, Ernie was well equipped to answer every question. The two men seemed to hit it off. Her nerves settling a bit, Kate slipped the canvas bag from her shoulder and rested it on her lap.

"You know your stuff," Roger told Ernie.

"Kate here is the best proof of that," Ernie said.

"I'd like to ask Kate some questions too." Roger glanced at Margaret. "I guess Ernie could get back to the trading floor now, if he needs to."

Startled, Kate looked at Margaret. "We're trying to be time sensitive," Margaret said.

Ernie checked his watch, and then Kate. "It might save the bank money if I go back." His tone left room for rebuttal, though she knew that asking him to stay would make her look weak.

"Go ahead," she told him.

He got up from the sofa. "All right then, I'll see you downstairs."

The office door had been left open during the interview with Ernie, but now Roger got up and closed it. "The Fed's inquiry mainly revolves around the bidding in the two-year note auction," he said, "but the June year-bill is also being reviewed. Is it fair to say that you're the principal risk taker in bills?"

"Ernie and I have equal trading authority," Kate said.

Roger nodded as he returned to his seat. "That's true enough on paper, but Jim Fletcher says you're the reason the limit is as high as it is."

"Ernie and I work as a team."

Margaret leaned forward in her chair. "But would Ernie be bidding for a billion dollars' worth of year-bills if you weren't there?" Probably not, Kate thought, though the question had never been put to her quite so directly.

"We're not trying to trip you up," Roger said. "We're trying to understand the relationships on the trading desk. You and Ernie, for example, work very closely. Is that unusual?"

"We decide what we're going to bid, and then we discuss it with Jim."

"What about Woody?" Margaret said. "Isn't he the head trader?"

A knot began to form in Kate's chest. "He didn't work here in June."

"You got Jim's approval in the June year-bill auction?" Roger said.

"Yes, of course. A billion dollars' worth of year-bills is way beyond our limit."

"Though Jim's initials weren't on the bid sheet," Margaret said.

Kate gave Margaret a half-smile, one stickler to another, and felt a stirring of animosity.

"Jim backs you up on the year-bill bid," Roger said, "so that's really not an issue. He says you've never exceeded your limits without proper authorization. He told us you keep meticulous records."

"I have them with me if you want to see them," Kate said. Not waiting for an answer, she took her journal from the canvas bag and opened it to the entry on the June year-bill auction. She watched Roger read down the page.

"You have records like this for every auction?" he said.

"Every bill auction." Kate was about to elaborate but stopped herself. *Name, rank and serial number.*

"May we keep this?" Roger said. "I'd like to check it against the bank's internal records, such as they are." The look Margaret shot Roger didn't seem to faze him. "It's helpful to see process adhered to so thoroughly," he continued. "We'll get this back to you as soon as possible."

Kate nodded and smiled cautiously. Maybe she couldn't establish rapport like Ernie, but she did follow the rules, an attribute that had to count with auditors.

"What happened after Morehead Woodson joined the bank?" Margaret said. "Were your auction bids approved by him?"

"I don't think we've bid beyond our limits since then," Kate said.

"Though your participation in the auctions has been strong," Margaret said.

"With customer bids, yes, but not so much for our own account," Kate said.

"Why is that?" Margaret said.

"We haven't been as bullish."

"I see," she said, though Kate suspected that Margaret hadn't grasped the technical details the way her lieutenant had.

"One more from me," Roger said. "Do you ever get involved in bidding in coupon auctions?"

"No."

"How about a coupon bid in connection with another trade?"

"I only bid on bills."

"Are bills ever part of a coupon trade? Maybe a curve-steepening trade?"

Woody's curve-steepening trade, Kate thought, the one he had proposed in July, when he bid so aggressively for the two-year note. Roger and Margaret looked eager for her answer.

"Bills are the most liquid assets in any portfolio," Kate said. "People sell them all the time to pay for other purchases."

"So bill traders could get involved in coupon transactions?" Margaret said.

"We try to give strong prices to our customers," Kate said, "but that doesn't involve us in underwriting coupon auctions, or bidding on coupons either."

"Not directly anyway," Margaret said.

Unsure of the proper response, Kate let this qualifying statement pass.

Roger shifted slightly in his chair. "Do you remember providing those kind of supportive bids in the curve-steepening trade last month?"

"I don't remember specifically. I'd have to look through my records."

"Did you mention the trade at the sales meeting?" Margaret asked.

"I mention a lot of trades at the sales meeting," Kate said, her voice losing some of its even tone. "It's my job to talk about trades that are out there. I articulate pros and cons for the salesmen so they can talk to their clients. But mentioning a trade is different from promoting it."

"You have a lot of influence though," Margaret said, but her statement didn't sound like a compliment.

"Maybe in bills," Kate said, "but coupons aren't my sector."

"So you didn't mention the curve trade?" Margaret said.

"I may have started to mention it, but Woody made it clear that the trade was his idea. Is he telling you something different now?" The auditors went mute, seemingly unprepared for the question.

Kate stared at the artwork on the wall behind Margaret's desk, a study of birds on a green wash background. One bird was only an outline, its shape formed by the absence of color, as if the artist had reserved the space but never filled it in. She looked at Roger, but he was waiting for his boss to take the lead.

"Woody says you worked together on the two-year note auction," Margaret said.

"That's a lie! He knew I didn't believe in that trade. We don't agree on anything."

Margaret's head moved slightly, but otherwise she seemed unperturbed by Kate's outburst. "He says that you both have a large following of clients, and that your combined influence made them bid through Matheson in the auction."

Kate took a silent breath to compose herself. She recognized the cunning in Woody's claim, mixing a truthful statement with falsehood to make it more believable. "Which clients?" she said, assuming the head auditor's calm. "The only client who even mentioned that trade to me said he was passing on it."

"Why would the client give you that information and not Woody?" Roger said.

"Woody wasn't there," Kate said. "Rita and I were having a drink with the client after work."

"Rita?" Roger said.

"Rita Jones. She's the salesman who covers Amalgamated."

Roger's eyebrows shot up. "Amalgamated Asset Management?"

"Yes. Wayne Kimmel is the chief investment officer. He was cautious on the market too."

"Wayne Kimmel specifically told you that he wouldn't be going into the two-year note auction?" Margaret said.

Kate's memory of their conversation at the Hyatt Grand Central came back clearly. "Wayne said that he'd given the curve trade some thought, but he felt more cautious about the market. And I told him that the trade was Woody's idea, not mine."

"Why did you disassociate yourself from the trade?" Margaret said.

"That trade made a lot of money, and I didn't want to take credit for an idea that wasn't mine."

"Did Wayne mention bidding through Matheson in the two-year auction?" Roger asked.

Kate shook her head. "He wasn't bullish."

"How about for a trade?" he said.

Kate shook her head again. "If Wayne had been interested in trading the two-year note—which is not his style at all, frankly—but if he *had* been, he would most likely buy them in the when-issued market, and skip the auction altogether. He'd have more flexibility that way."

Kate's explanation seemed lost on Margaret, though Roger was keeping up beautifully. "That's very helpful," he said, smiling for the first time. "I think we can let you get back to work now."

Kate stood up, holding the now empty, striped canvas bag, its strap trailing down by her side. The atmosphere in the room seemed less charged since her mention of Wayne Kimmel. Even Margaret Finn was smiling when Kate left to go back to the trading room.

Chapter 26

Kate returned from the auditing department in time to hear Ernie broadcasting the early talk on the weekly bill auctions. Pausing on the threshold of the trading room, she observed the bustle in the large, rectangular room, a scene that had always reminded her of a Breughel painting, with dozens of people engaged in various aspects of the same group activity. Ernie hunching over the intercom. Keezer pacing the length of his generous extension cord. Rosemary collecting trade tickets, and Judy taping pink message slips to phone turrets. Rita looked intent, discussing a potential transaction with Adam, and Lorraine seemed contented, tidying Jim's office while he spoke on the phone. It was a homey scene, Kate thought.

Her meeting with the auditors had broken up shortly after eleven. Roger Ward walked her to the elevator, a gesture she interpreted as friendly, though he was careful not to compromise the investigation. When she asked what would happen next, his answer was diplomatically evasive. "Auditors like to establish a working hypothesis and then test it outside the lab." He had smiled and sent her on her way.

Kate slipped into her seat on the trading desk and immediately spotted the message from Peter taped to the intercom. He had called at ten and would call again later. The phone operator had drawn a little smiley face next to his name. Checking the screens, Kate noted that the market had traded off in the hour she'd been with the auditors. She eased the position sheet out from under Ernie's elbow to see what trades Jim had transacted in their absence.

"He bought every bill he bid on," Ernie muttered. "Goddam salesmen picked his pockets."

"When the cat's away," Kate said with a shrug.

Ernie gave her a sideways glance. "Any trouble with Rodge and Maggie?"

"Not after you softened them up." This bit of flattery on Kate's part hit its mark, improving Ernie's mood. She told him about the auditors' questions concerning the curve-steepening trade. "They wanted to know about supportive bids during the two-year note auction in July. Woody told them that we were in on the trade." It wasn't really "we," but Kate thought it might wound her partner to be left out of the accusation.

"Did you tell them we thought that trade sucked?" Ernie said.

"Those were my exact words," she said.

As she added Jim's bill purchases to her position sheet, Kate thought about her session with the auditors. She was pleased with the way she'd handled herself—other than calling Woody a liar—and soothed by Roger Ward's complimentary tone at the end of the discussion. Luckily, Kate had known about Amalgamated Asset Management and Wayne Kimmel's neutral view of the market. She had Rita Jones to thank for the meeting at the Hyatt Grand Central.

The outside telephone line lit up. Expecting it to be Peter, Kate picked up the call, but it was Rita trying to bypass Ernie without being obvious. Kate wanted to ask her about Amalgamated, and decided that the auditors' request for discretion didn't necessarily mean total silence.

"You need anything from the supply closet?" Kate said.

"You're getting your own supplies?" Rita said.

"You're one to talk." Rita regularly distributed trade tickets and pens to the salesmen whenever she replenished her own stock. She said it made her feel bountiful.

Inside Rosemary's supply closet, Kate swore Rita to secrecy and told her about the Fed investigation, speaking without elaboration even when Rita's expression invited it.

"So what I want to confirm is, did Wayne Kimmel bid in the two-year auction?"

"Wayne never goes into auctions," Rita said. "He says he's not paid to be an underwriter. If he wanted to trade, he'd do it in the when-issued market."

Kate pressed her lips together and nodded confidently. "That's exactly what I told the auditors."

"You want me to double-check?" Rita said.

"You'd better not. It might do more harm than good." The women exchanged a cautious look and went back to work, splitting up in the hallway so they could return to the trading floor from different entrances.

Back at her desk, Kate gnawed on the fleshy side of her thumb, replaying her interview with the auditors in light of Rita's confirmation that Wayne hadn't gone into the two-year note auction.

Then it hit her. She signaled for Ernie to get off the phone, leaned in closer when he did, and whispered, "I think Woody submitted an unauthorized bid for Amalgamated in the two-year note auction."

Ernie took off his glasses and slowly polished each lens with the end of his tie. "Interesting."

"But Amalgamated never goes into the auctions. Wouldn't he know that from being at Salomon Brothers?"

"Maybe he figured that made Amalgamated a safe bet."

Ernie had a point. The safest tactic—if submitting an unauthorized bid in a Treasury auction could ever be "safe"—was to use a client who didn't bid in auctions, but one whose substantial interest would be credible. It was a tremendous risk to take…and against every rule in the book.

Kate stared down the row of trading desks to where Woody usually sat. The auditors had spoken to him first, then to the bill traders. Had the auditors called Woody back for cross-examination, or had Kate's input regarding Amalgamated sent Roger Ward back to the bank records?

"Where do you think Woody is?" Kate asked Ernie.

He stifled a yawn; their unusual morning seemed to have tired him. "Maybe he fled the country."

"Could he go to prison for this?"

"They sent Al Capone up the river for tax evasion, didn't they?" Ernie pushed his chair back and stood up. "Lunchtime," he said, and shuffled off.

Kate had always known that her job carried risks like the loss of bank capital and reputation, not to mention her own good name. But the concept of intentionally breaking the law had never entered her mind, and now here she was, working in a crime scene, a few desks away from the perpetrator. It was like realizing you were on a cliff only after the person next to you had tumbled over the edge.

She was thinking about Peter when he called, shouting her name over a background of band music, which brought a smile to her lips. His world seemed so innocent and pure, somewhere she would love to have been at that very moment.

"Where are you?" she said.

"In the gym, rehearsing for a concert. Did you meet with the auditors?"

She checked around her immediate space for eaves-droppers. "Yes."

"Did you give them the journal?"

"I did."

"Were they impressed?"

"I think so."

"Fantastic! What about Woody?"

"I don't know." Kate listened to the strains of music playing on Peter's end of the line. "Is that 'Out in the Country' they're playing?"

"Very good. We're doing an ecology medley. We've also got 'Yellow River' and 'Fly Like an Eagle.'"

"Can I come to the concert?"

"Sure you can. Do you like band music?"

Peter's question stunned her. Had she never told him how much she enjoyed marching band music, the happy, celebratory way it always made her feel?

"I love band music…and I love you too." She winced at the insistent way she had put it, and how she'd made the most important words sound like an afterthought.

"I love you too!" Peter shouted. The band stopped

playing, as if his declaration had brought its members up short. "I've got to get going, but I'll call you later, OK?"

Kate put down the phone and let her conversation with Peter sink in. They had shown the depth of their feelings many times before, though neither one of them had spoken the words, even when they made love. Now they had done so over the phone, with a high school band practically drowning them out. She had been waiting for him to speak first, but taking the lead made her feel strong.

Around three that afternoon, Jim Fletcher's secretary handed Kate a note written on a sheet from his personalized memo pad. *Woodson and Munro in my office at four.* "May I say that you'll be attending?" Lorraine's tone was oddly formal, even for her. When she left, Kate showed the note to Ernie.

"Aren't you supposed to swallow that now?" he said.

There was drama in a showdown, when the principals in a dispute gathered to see who held the better hand. Kate's mind raced during the hour before the meeting: would the miserable reign of Morehead Woodson finally be put behind them? She wanted the atmosphere in the bond department to go back to the way it had been before his arrival. The next head trader would have to come from within the bank; surely Jim wouldn't make the same mistake twice. Even if he was tempted to look outside again,

Phil Armstrong would veto such a move, and Jim was too savvy to invite the Chairman's disapproval, especially now that the bank had been burned.

Letting Ernie handle the trading traffic, Kate contemplated the future. Might she be a candidate for the job of head trader? She immediately dismissed the thought, but it kept returning. She knew she would never be considered under normal circumstances, but battlefield promotions occurred in business too. She had played by the rules and succeeded, which would make her advancement an object lesson for the rest of the department. Alerting Jim earlier to the Fed investigation would have strengthened her position, but she had still come forward, if somewhat belatedly.

Kate drew herself up short; she was getting way ahead of herself. She was happy trading bills, and had never coveted the role of head trader. But if Jim offered her the job, it wouldn't make sense to refuse it. Why take a chance on someone else not working out? Only someone who loved Matheson would make sure that it grew properly, expanding into new businesses without abandoning the culture that had made it the class act in commercial banking.

Telling Ernie that she would be right back, Kate grabbed her shoulder bag and took the stairs up one flight to a restroom where she wouldn't bump into people she knew. She combed her hair, something she never did during the day, and even put on lipstick. Staring into the mirror, she wondered how the other traders might react to her becoming their boss. They would cheer Woody's departure, but would they celebrate her taking his place? "Don't get cocky," she whispered to her reflection.

Back at her desk, Kate noticed that the drapes in Jim's office had been drawn shut. She pointed this out to Ernie.

"Sorry, Toots, I must be slipping," he said, offering her his open pack of cigarettes. "Oh, that's right. You quit."

If Ernie was feeling left out of the drama, he certainly didn't show it. Kate wished that he had been summoned to Jim's office too. Though it was clear that she was now shouldering responsibility for the bill desk, something bad happening seemed less likely with Ernie in the room.

A few minutes before four, she stood at Lorraine's desk, feeling the way she did on the Santa Cruz roller coaster as it cranked its way up the first forty-five degree climb. Lorraine was on the phone. Kate watched her make stenographic marks down one column of a notebook. "Yes, I've got it," Lorraine said, before replacing the receiver. "You can go in now, Kate."

Kate took a few steps towards Jim's office, then glanced back at Lorraine, who was already rolling a sheet of paper into her typewriter. Lorraine looked up and smiled. "Go on in," she said encouragingly. For the first time, Kate felt the bond of being female pass between them.

She opened the door and saw Jim at his desk; he

motioned for her to come in. She froze when she noticed Woody, sitting in a club chair by the window, but he paid her no mind. She sat as far from him as possible, in the corner of the sofa closest to the door.

Jim's thinning hair was wild and his starched shirt-front wilted, but he spoke with control. "I'll keep this brief and to the point. The auditors have made their pre-liminary report to Armstrong, and he's shared it with me. He's informed the Fed, and he and I are meeting with them tomorrow morning. I've already spoken to Woody, and I'll speak with you privately in a few minutes, Kate, but I wanted to get you both in the same room for my own *edification*. Is that the right word?" It was a rhetorical question, though Jim paused as if waiting for someone to answer.

"There was always a chance this wouldn't work out, but I thought it was a risk worth taking," he said. "This didn't have to happen. But now that it has, Phil Armstrong is determined to clear the bank's name and restore our credibility with the Fed. Whatever it takes. Matheson's reputation is his paramount concern."

It sounded like a direct quote, Kate thought, keeping her eyes on Jim. Was he going to fire Woody in front of her? Did Jim want her to spread a cautionary tale in the trading room? She looked down at her hands, waiting for him to continue, wishing he would hurry up and be done with it. The sound of a desk drawer opening made her look up.

"Roger Ward asked me to return this," Jim said, her trading journal in his hand. "The Chairman was impressed."

"He read my journal?"

"The parts the auditors pointed out, what Roger described as a 'well-established pattern of compliant behavior.'" Jim held out the journal.

"Don't you need it for the Fed?" Kate said.

Jim smiled with what seemed like amused regard. "The bank will present its own records, but thanks for the offer. It's good you found it. Where was it?"

Kate perceived movement to her left: Woody had leaned forward to get a better look. His eyes jerked up to hers. She tightened her grip on the notebook, as if even now he might leap up and grab it. She backed up to the corner of the sofa and sat down. She glanced at Jim, who seemed to be waiting for an answer.

"In a gym bag," Kate said, her voice steady and clear. Woody's blue eyes flared and appeared to darken before he slowly sat back, his arms and legs going slack, his expression one of bewilderment.

She looked back at Jim, who had turned toward Woody. "You can leave without escort if you'll go straight out," Jim said. "We'll have a messenger deliver your stuff. Lorraine has a release for you to sign before you go."

Woody stood up, hesitating at the edge of Jim's desk. Woody's humble demeanor, so unlike his usual arrogance, reminded Kate of a moment they had shared shortly after his arrival at Matheson, when they discussed her memo about the traders, and he asked about the biggest mistake he could make.

Jim stayed seated but offered Woody his hand. "Good luck."

Woody mumbled something and moved toward the door, his pinstriped slacks breaking perfectly over the tops of his loafers. He walked right past Kate and out of the office.

She took a deep breath. "What will happen to him?"

"He's hired an attorney," Jim said. "It's an ugly deal."

"Did he submit a bid for Amalgamated without their permission?"

"I'm not supposed to discuss the case. Look," he said, dropping his corporate façade. "You're going to come out of this fine, but the Chairman is pretty steamed."

She forgot all about Woody. "Aren't I fine now?"

Jim fiddled with a slim silver pen, rolling it in his fingers. "Phil wants to clear the decks with the Feds. He can't stand the idea of Matheson being on anyone's watch list."

"What's that got to do with me?"

"The Fed was looking at the June year-bill, too."

Kate felt the pricks of adrenaline under her arms as

Jim came around to the front of his desk and sat in the chair Woody had vacated. "Phil wants to tell the Fed that we've taken action on both situations."

"There's no situation on the year-bill," Kate said.

"It's just for a while, until the smoke clears," Jim said.

"What's just for a while?"

"You moving off the desk. It's not permanent," he said, speeding up his delivery. "The way we're growing, you'll be trading again within six months. For now, I can put you back in sales, or you can transfer somewhere else in the bank. But I recommend that you stay on the floor. You're a natural for this market. I've never seen a better directional trader. Six months will pass before you know it. Think of it as the off-season."

"But I didn't do anything wrong! Why should I have an off-season?" Her voice rose beyond anything that might pass for professional. "I can't go back to sales. That's a demotion and you know it. Everyone will think I'm guilty. Why don't you just fire me?"

Jim looked at her and didn't argue a single point. Completely lost for words, she silently shook her head for what felt like a long time. "I thought you said my journal saved me," she finally said.

"It did save you...that and Roger Ward's comment to the Chairman that all traders should take their jobs as seriously as you do."

"Then why am I being punished?"

The first hint of impatience appeared on Jim's face. "You shouldn't look at it as punishment. Punishment is what Woody's getting."

"But he broke the law and I didn't. Isn't that right? Really, Jim, isn't it? You were congratulating me in June for that auction, remember? You bought everyone ice cream."

There was a knock on the door, and Lorraine stuck her head in the office, addressing Jim without looking at Kate. "You're due in the Chairman's office in ten minutes," Lorraine said. Jim nodded and the door closed silently.

"Was I too late with the warning?" Kate said.

Jim shook his head. "That had nothing to do with it."

"Did you try to change Armstrong's mind?"

Jim looked wounded by the question. "I tried, but there are limits to my clout. I don't exactly come out smelling like a rose on this either."

"But you're keeping your same job."

Jim leaned forward, elbows on his knees. "I hate that it's breaking this way, you being such a purist."

"But you're a purist too, aren't you?"

For a long moment, Jim met her gaze. "Sometimes you've got to get on the train, or you find yourself tied to the tracks," he said. His eyes shifted to his watch. "I've got to go. Think about sales."

Kate remained on the sofa and watched him put on his suit jacket. "I need some time. This didn't turn out the way I thought it would."

"Sure, take some time," Jim said as he opened the door. "So long as you remember that Armstrong's already told the Fed you're off the trading desk."

After work, Kate sat with Ernie in a leather booth at Harry's on Hanover Square. The establishment, located several blocks from the bank, was a sprawling space and heavily air-conditioned, even in September. Kate pulled an old cardigan out of the striped canvas bag, which also held her journal and several items she had grabbed from her desk. A back-up pair of pantyhose, a bottle of Tylenol, and the Mets program that Keezer had given her. She didn't want to leave anything that felt personal behind.

Ernie cancelled his squash game when Kate told him that she had been removed from the trading desk. They didn't speak about it during their walk down Broad Street to the bar, but her reserve dissolved with the wine. She poured out the details of her meeting with Jim while Ernie nodded and smoked and let her vent. After awhile she began to repeat herself: her comeback to Jim when he said she was a purist, and his line about getting on the train before she got tied to the tracks. "I told you that already, didn't I?" she said, her outrage giving way to despondency.

Ernie smiled sweetly. "But you tell it better every time."

She drained her tumbler-sized glass of house red and set it down hard on the table. "Thanks for listening."

"Don't mention it." Ernie motioned to the waiter for another round. He looked tired and sad, his eyes teary behind his bifocals. He had been spared, though to an uncertain fate. Jim would replace her on the bill desk, most likely with a man, and who could say how the new pairing would work? Technically, Ernie should have been removed from the desk, too, and she wondered why that hadn't happened. She didn't want him to be wrongfully punished either, but the way she had been singled out seemed doubly unfair.

"It might not be so bad back in sales," Ernie said, making a teepee of his used matches in the ashtray. "Maybe you could get some of your old accounts back."

Kate took another sip of wine. Returning to sales was unthinkable, and she resented Ernie for trying to put a good face on the idea. He would never do it and neither would Jim, and yet they both seemed to think that taking a step backward made sense for her. But there was no way to pretty up a move back to sales, no matter how carefully Jim worded the announcement. She would forever be associated with the auction scandal, the naïve female who had been duped by Morehead Woodson, then demoted so that Phil Armstrong could feel cleaner than clean.

"I'm not going back to sales," Kate said. The wine was making her plight seem theoretical, as if she were discussing someone else's situation.

"You're not?" Ernie sounded surprised, and she suppressed a cynical reaction to Ernie the Anarchist worrying about toeing the line. "You could move to the buy side," he said. "There are plenty of customers who'd want to hire you. Amalgamated, for one. Kimmel will know that moving you off the desk was bullshit. He'll be mad as hell when he finds out what Woody did." Ernie's suggestion was a fresh blow, an implication that she had no future at Matheson, or with any other primary dealer that valued its relationship with the Fed.

Kate adjusted the canvas bag across her chest, still protecting the journal that had won the respect of Roger Ward, if not the Chairman of the Board. "I'd better get going. Peter will wonder where I am."

They didn't speak during their cab ride up the FDR Drive. The lights in the city were coming on, and the sky was inky blue. Kate had a sense of being suspended between phases of her life, like one of the bridges spanning the East River. Their silence became increasingly uncomfortable as they approached Grand Central. It occurred to her that she didn't know where to report the next morning. Jim would be at the Fed with Phil Armstrong. She thought about posing the question to Ernie but that kind of partner-like consultation was finished. The differing outcomes of the investigation had finally come between them. Kate would remember this day for the rest of her life, but Ernie would go home to dinner with Marie and be back on the bill desk in the morning.

As the cab pulled up to the corner of 42nd and Third, Ernie knocked on the plastic shield between the front and back seats. "Make the turn on Third, and I'll get off there," he told the driver.

Standing on the curb, Ernie stared at the rear of the taxi as if checking the air in the tire. "I would resign in protest, but it wouldn't do any good. Probably make things worse." He glanced at her before slamming the car door. There was a disfiguring look of shame on his face.

When Kate got home, she took her clothes off and crawled into bed, passing out in the rumpled sheets. An hour later she woke up, feeling awful in every way, the scene in Jim's office playing in her head. She tormented herself by searching for nuance in what had amounted to a point-blank demotion. She thought of what she might have done differently, some action she could have taken that would have changed the outcome. But there was nothing she could identify, unless it was her performance in the June year-bill auction, when she'd made a million dollars and shut out Salomon Brothers, the best government bond dealer in the business.

She smiled bitterly into the darkening room and thought about the six-figure bonus that would no longer be coming her way. Did Woody think he had gotten even for the embarrassment she'd once caused him? Would her humiliation be the silver lining to his troubled state?

She showered and put on a clean cotton nightgown, then wandered into the living room to wait for Peter. He arrived with his overnight bag and a solicitous expression that embarrassed her. "You're too good for that bunch," he said after she had talked herself out for the second time that evening. "There's no reason for you to go in there tomorrow." He was probably right, though she hadn't taken a sick day in years. She had gone into work the day after Ted left. She had gone back to school the day after her mother's funeral.

"I loved my job," Kate said. "Now everything about it makes me feel terrible."

"Sometimes I have to feel a problem physically to know there's something wrong," Peter said.

They stretched out on the sofa with their arms around each other. Peter soon fell into a sound sleep, but Kate remained wide-awake. She eased out from under his arm and shifted her position on the sofa. The thought of people finding out about her demotion depressed her. She pictured Lloyd Keezer disseminating the news in record time. There would be no consideration of nuance, even after the details came out. It would be like a story in the *Times*. The shock content would be splashed across the front page, with any analysis buried deep in the business section.

At a certain level, Kate understood that Phil Armstrong wasn't purposely trying to humiliate her; moving her off the trading desk had played only a small part in his campaign to clear Matheson's name with the regulators. As far as Armstrong was concerned, she was inconsequential, the girl who did the Tuesday markets report, someone whose name he didn't mention because he had never bothered to learn it. She wondered if he had finally put her name and face together. Did he realize that the overly aggressive bill trader who kept a detailed journal was the woman he used to address as "Domestic Money Markets"?

But Jim's failure to stand up for her was hardest to bear. In the almost three years that she'd been at the bank, he had become more like a friend than a manager. She would have felt better if he'd put himself on the line to defend her. Even if he had been unsuccessful, it would be a comfort to know that he'd tried—really tried—and that he considered her worth the expenditure of his personal political capital.

Her eyes felt hot but she didn't want to cry. People lost their jobs every day for no good reason. It was a job, not life or death, or even the end of a marriage. But it was the end of a relationship, and a way of thinking about how she fit in. She moved closer to Peter and the warmth of his ample body.

"Are you sleepy yet?" he said in a muffled voice.

"Not really, but let's go to bed."

Chapter 27

The next morning, Kate called Ernie and told him she didn't feel well enough to come into work. "Coke and aspirin," he said, but the advice seemed trite now, and no longer a special cure for her particular ailment.

"I'm not hung over," she insisted, though her head ached and her mouth felt as if it were lined with wool.

"You want me to call if I hear anything?" he said.

In the manner of people who torture themselves with information that only deepens their pain, Kate told Ernie that she wanted to hear everything.

Peter brought Kate coffee before he left for school. "Thank you," she said, taking the cup from him, but she didn't drink the coffee. Instead she lay listlessly in bed, falling into a fitful sleep in which she dreamed she was at work and unable to make sense of the figures on her screens.

Liz's phone call woke her at ten. Kate could hear the wailing saxophone of a Hall and Oates tune in the background. "Are you sick?" Liz said.

"Sick at heart," Kate said. She told Liz everything, starting with Jim's late afternoon announcement, then working her way back in time to the morning meeting with the auditors, a triumph so brief that it seemed not to have happened.

Liz exploded. She lit into the men at A. J. Matheson. Phil Armstrong was a corporate tyrant, more concerned with his own reputation than the truth. Ernie was an incompetent fool living on borrowed time. Liz was less harsh with Woody because he was headed for prison, if a charge of securities fraud stuck. Her most scathing remarks were for Jim, whom she declared disloyal, bad in a crisis, and a man who would have survived the sinking of the Titanic even if it meant throwing women and children out of the lifeboats. Liz railed in a manner that Kate found gratifying, though it didn't change anything.

"Come over and help me pack," Liz said. "You need the distraction and I need the assistance."

And so around noon, Kate found herself picking up sandwiches at a deli and heading for Liz's apartment. The September day was beautiful. The cool air and bright sunshine made her vaguely hopeful, until she saw the packing boxes in her sister's apartment.

Liz was sorting her belongings into three categories: items for the moving van, which she wouldn't see for more than a week; clothes and accessories for her first days in California; donations for the Salvation Army. Her sister kept the conversation light, commenting on songs playing on the radio and her appointment the next day with a psychic named Beatrice, who worked out of a restaurant in Greenwich Village. The sixty-minute session was a farewell gift from Liz's co-workers.

"These people swear by Beatrice," Liz said. "She knows Nancy Reagan's astrologer."

"Now there's an endorsement," Kate said. Following her sister's instructions, she was folding garments around sheets of tissue paper and placing them into a suitcase.

"Beatrice has a large Wall Street clientele, too. Hold on, what am I thinking? You take my appointment tomorrow and ask Beatrice what you should do about work. The timing is perfect!"

Kate smiled in spite of herself. Liz was entertaining, and Kate would miss the way her sister wheedled her into her zaniness.

"You give her a personal article like a lipstick or your keys, and she takes over from there," Liz said. "You could ask her about the sales job. You're not going to work tomorrow, are you? Because Beatrice is booked solid. Taking my spot is your only chance."

Kate didn't want to think about tomorrow. "What about you? Don't you need to consult her?"

"My future's not the one in question."

"I'm not going back into sales."

"Why not? What do you have against sales?"

"I'm not going to spend my day trying to get people to agree on a trade."

"How's that any different from what you've been doing?"

Kate looked up from folding a sweater.

"No, really," Liz said. "I'm not trying to be a smart ass."

"The trader decides on the price, and the customer decides if he wants to trade on it. Salesmen don't decide anything. They're conduits. They don't have any power."

"What about the power of persuasion?" Liz cocked her head, pleased with the question. "You're very good at winning people over to your point of view."

Kate put the sweater in the suitcase. "Not lately."

"Your whole persona is about competence! You've had that forever. Remember how you talked the Camp Fire Girls into letting you be leader of our troop? What were you, sixteen at the time?"

"*Co*-leader. You said you would quit if I didn't."

"And I would have, too." The sisters shared a quiet moment, remembering the time after their mother's death. "You were the youngest Camp Fire leader in California," Liz said. "That took persuasion."

"I think Phil Armstrong might be a tougher sell than the Camp Fire Girls."

"Pretend he's the Camp Fire CEO. Picture him with

a band of merit badges across his chest. Seriously, you should think about talking to him. Be persuasive for yourself, and don't assume that every decision is final. People change their minds...that's what you've always told me."

"When did I tell you that?"

"All the time! These guys have got you cowed. Ask for your job back. They haven't replaced you yet, have they?" Liz stood with her hands on her hips, the picture of confidence. The promotion and transfer to California had already done her good.

"Not that I know of," Kate said.

"So go in there and tell them why they need you to keep trading bills. Put it in dollars and cents. Show them a way to change their minds gracefully. Try it, anyway. If that doesn't work..." Liz trailed off.

"Then what?"

"You'll think of something. Or maybe Beatrice will."

Mid-afternoon, Kate went back to her apartment. She called Ernie but hung up when Judy, the phone operator, answered his line. Kate didn't feel like talking to anyone at Matheson—Ernie included—but there was no other source. She tried him again ten minutes later.

"I was at my sister's, so I didn't know if you'd called," she said when Ernie picked up his line.

"You should get a machine. Marie bought us one, and I'll never answer the phone again."

"Did Jim come back from the Fed?"

"Yeah, he's back."

"Did he say anything?"

"Not to me."

Kate could hear the background noise in the trading room, which made her feel passé. "Has anyone asked where I am?"

"Everyone has asked where you are. You think they like dealing with me?"

"What did you tell them?"

"I said you were having your wisdom teeth pulled."

"My wisdom teeth? How'd you come up with that?"

"It just popped into my head, but it's actually pretty good. You can be out for days with wisdom teeth."

Peter called around four to invite her to dinner at his grandfather's house. "Granddad said he mentioned it to you, and Liz thought it would be OK."

"You talked to Liz?" Kate said.

"I thought you were at her place. Why? Don't you want to come? It might take your mind off things. I got a cake for Liz."

The fact that a congratulatory dinner would be held despite what had happened to her seemed in keeping with the way things had been going. "Did you tell your grandfather?" Kate said.

"Yeah. He seemed surprised more than anything, and sad that you'd been treated unfairly. He said…" Peter stopped mid-sentence.

"It's OK, you can tell me."

"He said they were throwing the baby out with the bath water."

That night, Liz was in her element around the Etheridge dinner table, holding forth on the cultural differences between the East and West Coasts. Kate could tell that their host was charmed, but she found it difficult to socialize. All afternoon she had thought about asking Phil Armstrong to let her go back to trading. The prospect was daunting. She had never witnessed the Chairman of the Board in an actual conversation. At his Tuesday morning meetings he would call on people, and they would say as little as possible, waiting for him to move on to the next person. Armstrong had never even called her by name. She provided more information than anyone else at the meeting, which had undoubtedly been a mistake. She was way too forthcoming to suit the Chairman's aloof style.

Peter left the dining room and returned a minute later with Madeline, who carried a cake on a silver tray. It was a spectacular looking creation: in colorful icing, a cable car climbed a hill with the Golden Gate Bridge for a backdrop.

Liz was overwhelmed. "Where did you get this gorgeous cake?"

Peter smiled proudly. "A bakery downtown."

"I'll be taking that cable car to work." Liz hugged everyone and went on to propose a reunion in San Francisco at Thanksgiving, an appealing weekend complete with a side trip to Napa.

"It's been years since I've seen San Francisco," Mr. Etheridge said. He looked inquiringly at Peter.

"It would be nice to meet your dad," Peter said.

"He'd like that too," Kate said.

"I'd love to take a picture of the cake," Liz said. "Do you have a camera?"

Peter said he had one upstairs, and Liz invited herself along for a tour of the house.

"Your sister has a lot of spunk," Mr. Etheridge said after Peter and Liz left the dining room, the sound of her chitchat receding in the hall.

"Yes, she does," Kate said.

Mr. Etheridge rested his chin against the palm of his hand. "Peter told me what happened at work. It's too soon to tell you not to take it personally, though there would be some wisdom in that."

A polite smile was all Kate could muster.

"It's a difficult position for Matheson," Mr. Etheridge went on. "They're usually the people with the answers. The bank has a proud history of leading the way. After the stock market crashed in 1929, A. J. himself helped the government save the financial system. Now that mantle rests on Philip Armstrong's shoulders."

Kate didn't care about the grand accomplishments and responsibilities of A. J. Matheson or Philip Armstrong, and her expression said as much, though Mr. Etheridge didn't seem to take notice.

"I suspect he didn't think his decision through when he told the Fed that you'd been removed from the trading desk," Mr. Etheridge said. "He wanted the problem never to have happened…so he spoke precipitously."

"That doesn't make it right," Kate said.

"No, but maybe it makes it understandable."

"Not to me." She felt her throat tightening.

There was confusion in Mr. Etheridge's eyes, as if he couldn't quite grasp why his advice was falling short. "I don't want you to think I'm preaching to you."

Kate smiled and thanked him for his concern.

"What do you think you'll do?" he asked.

"Peter thinks I should quit. My sister thinks I should consult a psychic. My boss mentioned going back to sales, which I don't want to do, or he said I could get a transfer."

"Is there somewhere else in the bank you'd like to work?"

"I don't think I'm cut out to be a banker."

"It might not have been a genuine offer either."

Kate looked at him quizzically. "How do you mean?"

"It may have just been something to say, something that wasn't given much thought. If you decide to stay at the bank, you'll need to confirm exactly what it is they want you to do. You probably don't have a choice, even if that's what your boss said."

Mr. Etheridge was right. The sales force reported to Jim, and a position in sales was the only option he could guarantee.

"But if I stay, I'm agreeing to their terms and accepting their judgment," Kate said.

"And that troubles you," Mr. Etheridge said.

"You don't think it should?"

"No one can tell you what should or shouldn't trouble you. I wouldn't even try. But there's nothing morally wrong with accepting the bank's decision. That's what happens in a corporate setting. You do what works best for the company."

Kate might have understood doing what was best for the company if doing so didn't make it look like she had been in the wrong. "Do you think it would do any good for me to talk to Phil Armstrong?"

"What would you tell him?"

"I'd tell him the truth!" Kate knew that her response was naïve the moment she'd said it. Mr. Etheridge was being practical, trying to focus on what she would actually do if she ended up in Armstrong's office. She couldn't just go in there and emote. And the bank chairman had already seen her journal, so there was no point in producing it. She had no credible plan; the look on Mr. Etheridge's face told her as much.

"Yes, there's always the truth," he said, "and talking to him might make you feel better. But I think any effort to persuade him would have to be about the future. It's unlikely that he'll reverse himself, particularly if he's already told the Fed. Your time away from trading might be shortened, but I think that would be the extent of it... and even that wouldn't be guaranteed. I think you need to manage your expectations."

"Maybe I should just go in tomorrow and resign," Kate said.

"Oh, I don't know. I generally try to put off big decisions as long as I can. It gives me a chance to gather my thoughts. You never know what information might present itself at the last minute. Take another twenty-four hours anyway. Your sister's leaving town. Spend the day with her."

Liz and Peter returned with the camera, and Kate's private conversation with Mr. Etheridge ended. But for the rest of the evening, she thought about his advice to postpone her decision and live with uncertainty a little longer, a course of action that went against her instincts. She was in the habit of making quick decisions, especially the painful ones, a practice her job in trading had reinforced. She liked to resolve difficult matters fast and get them behind her. There were plenty of situations she couldn't easily dispense with, which was probably why she got rid of the others so quickly.

With Jim and Ernie bailing out on her, Mr. Etheridge was the closest thing Kate had to a business confidant, someone emotionally uninvolved who could clarify her situation from a corporate point of view. His objectivity was valuable, if not endearing, and she decided to take his advice. In the morning she would tell Ernie that she was taking another day off to conduct personal business. Or he could run with the wisdom teeth story, if he wanted. She imagined the tall tale Ernie would weave about her pain and suffering, which, in a manner of speaking, wasn't far from the truth.

Chapter 28

The next afternoon, Kate walked into a bistro in Greenwich Village. A lone waiter resetting tables looked up and pointed to the back of the room. Kate smiled self-consciously and studied the advertisements for French culinary products that hung over a row of tables pushed up against the wall.

Beatrice sat reading the newspaper at the last table. There was nothing of the occult in her appearance, unless the midnight blue of her silk blouse and the streaks of silver in her short, black hair were taken into account. She wore a pair of reading glasses attached to a braided cord around her neck. She looked a little like Joan Baez.

Beatrice took Kate's hand in both of hers instead of shaking it. "Are you having trouble sleeping?" Kate started to speak, then stopped, wondering if Beatrice already knew the answer. The psychic's comment was more irritating than impressive. Of course Kate was having trouble sleeping! She hadn't had a good night's sleep in more than a week. Her sleep deprivation was starting to feel like jet lag, a persistent, low-grade headache immune to all analgesics.

"Your sister told me you'd been wrestling with a decision, which often leads to sleepless nights," Beatrice said.

Kate wondered what else Liz had said; her sister had probably compromised the session, though it didn't matter. Kate had nothing better to do.

Peter had surprised her by endorsing the idea of seeing a psychic. Then he confessed to an ulterior motive: keeping the appointment in Greenwich Village would place her near Stuyvesant High School in time for band practice.

Kate hadn't been enthusiastic. "I've never looked worse in all the time you've known me."

"Wear that pink and blue dress," Peter said. "You look great in that."

"That's a sundress, and summer's over."

"We're practicing in the gym. It's always hot in there."

It was warm in the bistro too. Beatrice caught the eye of the man resetting tables and motioned him over. "Would you like a cup of tea?" she asked Kate. "It's included, but I don't read the leaves."

"You need a tube of lipstick, right?" Kate said, reaching for her purse.

"Is there something specific you'd like to know," Beatrice said, "or should I give an overall impression?"

"An overall impression is fine."

The psychic held the tube of lipstick up to her forehead and shut her eyes. "Is this your favorite shade?"

"I guess so. I don't wear lipstick that often."

Beatrice placed the tube of lipstick on the table, first horizontally, then vertically, then horizontally again, so that its length was parallel with the table's edge. She picked up the tube and inspected the name on the bottom. "I wouldn't want the wrong shade throwing me off."

The waiter arrived with the tea, which gave Kate the opportunity to get her keys from her bag and offer them in exchange for the lipstick. "Sorry. I should have given you the keys first."

Beatrice put the keys on the table next to the lipstick and looked at Kate more thoughtfully. "I was just fooling around. The shade of lipstick doesn't make any difference. Sometimes people from Wall Street treat a session like a big joke. They seem disappointed not to find me huddled over a crystal ball with a cat on my shoulder. They ask me which stocks they should buy. How high will the Dow go? What's the next takeover target? It's not enough to tell them that markets will be good for some time to come. They want numbers and dates, but I'm not attuned at that level. This isn't about making money. I take each session seriously, and I apologize for assuming that you didn't."

"That's all right. I don't want to know about markets."

Beatrice drank some tea and set the cup down. She placed her hands near the keys and the lipstick. "Life has been swirling around you. You're trying to adjust, which isn't easy, but you're doing all right. Better than the man who's involved."

"My sister told you what happened?"

"Only that a man had done something bad, and they were lumping you in with him. Did I put that correctly?"

"Close enough."

"He's going to be out of circulation for some time, and there'll be plenty of bad press."

Kate had a sinking feeling. "Will I be mentioned?"

"The female angle might be of passing interest, but you're not the story. The press will focus on the outsider. The pollutant in pure waters. The head of your company will be discussed. He's a prominent person?"

"In business, he is."

"He's admired too. That's important to him. It's actually what's driving the whole situation. He's afraid of not being admired, even though he acts like he doesn't care what anyone else thinks. He's a bit of a bully." Kate listened to Beatrice's accurate yet generic description of a chief executive officer. "And a decorated war hero," the psychic added.

Phil Armstrong's stellar military record was part of company lore, though not something Liz would have known about or been able to share with Beatrice.

"I've been demoted," Kate said.

"Demoted in what way?" Beatrice said.

"I've been removed from the trading desk."

Beatrice sat still for a moment before taking another sip of tea. "I don't think they see that as a demotion. They're just moving the pieces around the board, though the man is definitely out. You're familiar with this other work they want you to do?"

Kate nodded. "I was in sales before I moved to trading."

"The job won't be difficult then."

"But going back will. It's a step down for a trader to go back into sales."

"But you liked the work in sales?"

"I used to like it, but then I got promoted, and going back doesn't appeal to me."

"Can you see yourself happy doing the sales job again?"

Kate leaned forward, resting her arms on the table. "Can *you* see it? That's the main thing I want to know. Could I end up happy in sales even though it's humiliating to go back?" She smiled at how absurd her question sounded.

Beatrice picked up Kate's keys, noticing the silver heart shape of the key ring. "This is nice," she said, and set the keys back on the table.

"You're someone who can right yourself no matter what situation you're dropped into, but being able to do something doesn't mean you should do it. You need to ask yourself what you want from it. Money? Status? Feeling good about what you do for a living? There are a dozen different motivations. How important is it for you to keep working at this particular company?"

"They are one of the most female-friendly companies in the business," Kate said. "I know that sounds funny with what's happening, but there really are a lot of good people there. They're just not the ones running the place."

"So if you want to stay, you swallow your pride, take the job in sales, and wait for a better opportunity down the road, when all these good people you mention are running the place," Beatrice said.

"Do you actually see that, or are you using common sense? I mean, as opposed to a sixth sense."

"I tend to look at them as one and the same," Beatrice said.

"I didn't put that very well," Kate said.

Beatrice's expression softened. "My sense is that it's possible for things to work out for you there, and by this I mean that you'll have a job. There will be compromises, but there always are. Whether you'll want to make them is not something I can tell you. I don't predict the future.

I describe what already exists and try to make clients more aware of it." She looked at Kate for several long moments. "Was that responsive?"

Kate was not at all certain that it had been, but she nodded anyway.

"We still have some time," Beatrice said. "Should we talk about your personal life?" Kate smiled involuntarily. "May I ask his name?"

"It's Peter."

Beatrice closed her eyes, and Kate noticed the psychic's short, businesslike eyelashes. "Oh, well now, this is encouraging. Good. I didn't want to send you off on such an uninspiring note. Peter is authentic. He'd do anything for you, and he needs you very much."

Kate tilted her head. "He needs me? He's so optimistic and happy all the time."

"That doesn't mean he's self-sufficient," Beatrice said.

Kate thought about Peter still living with his grandfather, and the vacant apartment downtown that she had never seen. "Will he be faithful to me?"

"Remember, I don't predict the future, but infidelity wouldn't be in keeping with anything about him." Beatrice made her eyes big. "I don't get to say that very often."

"Are we a good match?"

"Well, let's see: he's optimistic, you're pragmatic. He thrives on being with people, all types of people, while you don't mind solitude—in fact, you welcome the freedom from responsibility. He puts himself out there without thinking sometimes, but you're more guarded. You hold yourself in check and study all the angles before you act. He's everyone's friend, but you're more selective about the people you spend time with. I'd say you were very well suited."

Beatrice took off her reading glasses and let them hang from the braided cord. "And you've both experienced loss, though your losses have changed you more. You're more worldly than he is."

"Do you think he's a little naïve?" Kate felt disloyal for how quickly she had formulated the question.

"I'd use the word 'gentle' instead of 'naïve.' It isn't the easiest quality to lead with in New York, but I don't think you'd want to change that about him, would you?"

"Gentle doesn't mean weak," Kate said.

"No, it doesn't, but your strength will always be important in this relationship."

"That sounds a little like a warning."

Beatrice shrugged. "It depends on your perspective." She handed the lipstick and keys back to Kate. "Another man took something from you and Peter helped you get it back."

"My trading journal," Kate said.

"This was something intangible, but I see the trading journal too." Beatrice made a fluttery motion with her hand. "It's all connected."

Around four-thirty that afternoon, Kate entered the Stuyvesant High School Building on East 15th Street. The school's lobby was old and dark. A single box of fluorescent light shone on the uniformed guard, who sat at a desk in the center of the windowless lobby. The only other light came from the brightly lit hallway beyond the reception area.

Kate approached the guard and asked for directions to the gym.

"You want band practice, right?" the guard said. "Mr. Hanley told me to look out for you."

Kate walked through one of the windowed doors that separated the foyer from the hall. The walls were painted a bluish-green, the color of a drained swimming pool. The building was almost eighty years old and it showed. She remembered Peter mentioning plans for a new building farther downtown. In the meantime, the school was operating on double session in order to accommodate academically talented students from all over the city.

Twice Kate stopped students to make certain she was still heading in the right direction. She had worn the sundress to please Peter, but now she wished she were wearing something less conspicuous.

Her pace slowed as she neared the gym. She heard music and then it stopped. She edged closer to the open doorway and peeked in. The gym was a complicated looking structure. Twenty feet in from the walls, a dozen columns faced in white-brick supported the ceiling. An indoor track had been built at mezzanine-level in the space between the wall and the inner perimeter of the columns. A steel railing curved around the edge of the track. Peter was leaning on the railing and speaking to the members of the band, who were arranged in semicircular rows on the floor below. Kate noticed the drumsticks in Peter's hand and wondered if he had been practicing along with the students.

"That was better," Peter said in his sandy voice, "but remember, this is the last song of the concert. The big finish! We want to send them out on a high, so that's how we've got to play it." Much laughter from the band. Peter smiled and shook his head. "You know what I mean. Brass and Percussion, you've got to drive it!"

"Mr. Hanley?" A trumpet player in the section of chairs nearest the doorway raised his hand.

"Mr. Huang?" Peter said.

The trumpet player pointed toward the door where Kate stood. Peter straightened up and grinned. "Perfect timing!" his voice boomed across the gym. "We need an audience." He waved her in with the drumsticks. "Band, this is Kate Munro. Would someone please find her a chair?"

Kate walked into the gym, stopping at the first column she came to. The trumpet player carried his own chair across the gym floor and set it up for her. She nodded her thanks and sat down. She looked up at the mezzanine, but Peter had abandoned his spot on the railing. In the next moment, she saw him, so handsome and unaffected, striding across the floor. She stayed seated, believing that he would kiss her if she stood up. But as he got nearer, she went completely in the other direction, jumping up and startling him a little.

Peter rested his palm on her shoulder. "You look great," he said and gave her a kiss. "How'd it go with Beatrice?" Over his shoulder, Kate could see the students taking it all in.

"It went fine," she whispered. "Go ahead with the big finish. I'll tell you later."

He squeezed her shoulder, then walked over to a rolling rack of folding chairs stationed against the wall. He pulled a chair from the rack and brought it to the trumpet player. "Very gallant of you, Mr. Huang, offering your chair to a lady." Some of the students started to laugh, giving the trumpet player the business.

Peter moved through the ranks of his students, enjoying their teasing awareness of Kate's presence. His easy way of interaction didn't surprise her; she had experienced it since the day they first met. She was proud that someone like him was so devoted to her, and felt grateful rather than apprehensive about Beatrice's comment that her strength would be important in their relationship. Peter had found a job where he was comfortable and where his sensibility had value; he had done the same in his personal life with her. Kate admired the way Peter had put himself into situations where he didn't have to compromise.

She watched him step up to a music stand and wait for his students to settle their music and instruments. He stuck one drumstick in his back pocket and raised the other as a baton. The students fixed their eyes on him. Kate held her breath. A chill of excitement raised the skin on her bare arms as he cued the opening drumbeat.

Chapter 29

For fifteen minutes the next morning Kate had the trading floor to herself. The room was quiet, even tranquil, at that early hour. Jim was usually the first to arrive, and Kate planned to settle things with him before he got involved in his day.

She hadn't bothered to switch on the lights when she came in; the natural light was sufficient for emptying the contents of her desk into a cardboard box. She looked at the vacant rows of sales desks in front of her and tried to imagine sitting on that side of the room every day, ingratiating herself with clients and traders to get business done. She just couldn't. Even her seat on the trading desk felt strange.

On the phone the night before, Ernie had reported Jim stopping by the bill desk to ask where she was. "I told him about the wisdom teeth, but I'll bet he thinks you're looking for a job," Ernie said.

"With the Fed investigating me?" she had responded. "That's credible. Maybe I can get Paul Volcker to write me a letter of recommendation."

Kate looked up when the overhead lights in the trading room came on. Jim Fletcher stood in the doorway, a can of Diet Coke in his hand, checking to see if anyone had beaten him into work. She raised her hand in silent greeting.

"How are you feeling?" Jim said, his voice crystal clear across the rows of desks.

"I took some personal days."

"That wisdom teeth story was bullshit, right?" He stared a moment before walking down the tiered risers, stopping when he reached her row in the center of the room. "You ready to talk?"

Kate followed Jim into his office and stood in front of the sofa while he hung his suit jacket on the back of the door. He set the can of soda on his desk but didn't touch his screens. "I thought maybe you'd run away…thrown your toys out of the pram and taken off," he said.

"I needed a couple of days."

"Fair enough. What do you want to do?"

"I want to trade." Jim's frown warned her to back off if she wanted a productive conversation. "How'd it go at the Fed?" she added.

"It went all right." He sat down at his desk and motioned for her to do the same. "They knew Woody from his days at Salomon. They said he pushed the edge of the envelope there, too, though nothing like this. You could see how much they respect Armstrong. They empathized with him for having to deal with such an unsavory, un-Matheson-like character." Jim looked at her and shrugged, as if absolving himself of the decision to hire Woody in the first place.

"Have I been cleared?" Kate said. Jim seemed confused by the question, or maybe it was the edge in her tone. "Have I been cleared of wrongdoing?"

His expression tightened. "You wouldn't be sitting here if there'd been any wrongdoing."

She felt a cool breeze of relief. Her shoulders dropped, making her realize how tense she had been the past few days.

"It's how aggressive the bid in the June year-bill auction looked that bothered Armstrong," Jim said.

"But that's how you win it," she said.

"Yeah, I know, but Armstrong thought it looked like we were hogging it up."

"Hogging it up?"

"Being un-sportsmanlike. It's not the kind of leadership image Phil wants to convey. That's why he told the Fed you'd be spending some time off the desk. It's a show of good faith."

"Did the Fed ask for a show of good faith?"

"It was Armstrong's idea, though they didn't argue with him. They said the only employee they had an issue with was Woodson, and now he's an ex-employee."

"So let me get this straight. The Fed has no problem with me or with how I bid in the auction, but Armstrong is taking me off the desk for appearing hoggish and unsporting to the rest of Wall Street."

Jim switched on his screens and waited for numbers to appear. "Long bond's down half a point," he said.

"What happened to increasing our market share in the auctions?" she said. "Wasn't that our goal, or does Armstrong have a different take on that too?"

Jim turned away from the screens. "Armstrong wants market share, but he wants it accomplished in a certain way."

"I was doing it the way I was taught. The securities business isn't some genteel industry where people politely announce they want more market share, then wait for the other guys to offer them a piece of their action. You always said we couldn't increase market share without becoming more aggressive."

"I know what I said and I stand by it, but it's Phil's bank. We have to keep him comfortable."

"So I'm off the desk to make Phil Armstrong comfortable?" Kate frowned and shook her head. "This is more screwed up than I realized."

"Listen, don't dismiss going back into sales. It's integral to this business. Distribution is way more important than trading."

"Not at this firm, it isn't."

"Not yet, maybe, but it will be. Armstrong and I talked about it yesterday for three hours."

"You talked for three hours about the importance of distribution?" Kate made no effort to hide her disdain. The Fed had cleared her of wrongdoing, and she could leave A. J. Matheson without a criminal record. As far as she was concerned, she was playing with the house's money.

"We talked about the future," Jim said, "which is all about distribution. Phil told me not to let this deal with Woody get me down. We talked about next steps for the business. Our ability to distribute securities is going to be huge when we get into corporate bonds and equities. You could be a leader in that, Kate. You might just find you like sales better than trading. A salesman's job is evolving into something much more complex. It's moving way past 'how you got the year-bill?' The smartest people in the room are going to have to be the salesmen, if we want to succeed. Armstrong agrees that distribution is key to our future success."

Jim's argument made sense, though Kate believed he was raising it now to cover the injustice of taking her off the desk. Part of her admired him for the spin he was putting on a move back to sales, and part of her hated him for the slick way he was doing Armstrong's bidding.

"So that's what Armstrong thinks," she said sarcastically. Being wrongfully punished had given her license, though the kind that is temporary.

"No, that's what I think. You're working for me, not Armstrong."

"Did you ask him if I could stay in trading?"

"I mentioned it," Jim said, irritated that she wasn't buying his pitch. "But I wasn't going to piss him off about it either. Look, going back to sales for a while is not the end of the world. It will actually help you. Keep you below the radar screen while the dust settles on the investigation, and show Armstrong that you know how to take orders. You can re-up for a trading job later if you want, but my prediction is that you'll like sales so much you won't want to leave." Jim smiled in his old winning manner. "What do you say? Can I make the announcement? I'll write the memo myself." He picked up his silver pen as if to draft it.

And Kate knew that Jim would do a great job with that memo. She had come across a folder of his elegantly worded announcements while cleaning out her desk that morning.

She took a deep breath. "I appreciate what you're trying to do, but I can't resign myself to the injustice of being pulled off the desk."

Jim made a face. "Injustice? Isn't that a little strong?"

"It's how I feel."

"How many times have I told you to leave feelings out of this?"

"I know, but I can't. I never could."

Jim studied her a moment and seemed perplexed by her unwillingness to take his advice. He came around from the back of his desk and sat in the chair next to the sofa. "You know what?" he said with new inspiration. "You need to talk to Armstrong. I felt the same way you did. I couldn't resign myself—that's a good word—to the mistake I'd made hiring Woody. Then Armstrong told me some of the mistakes he's made in his career, and how learning from each of them equipped him to move up in the organization. It's a game of adjustments, and sometimes it's a trial by fire too. Armstrong helped me put it in perspective. You spend some time with the guy, and you'll see what I mean. He really does care about the troops."

Kate didn't point out that she was the one paying for Jim's hiring mistake. And she couldn't picture Phil Armstrong taking an interest in her career when he had never bothered to remember her name.

"I don't know," she said.

Jim pounced on her first waver. "I'm going to call him right now. I'll get something set up for today. Meet with him before you make a decision. You owe me that much. You owe *yourself* that much."

"I'm not promising anything."

"Have I ever steered you wrong?" Jim seemed genuinely unaware of the potential for irony. He was certainly recovering nicely from the Moorhead Woodson affair.

*   *   *

Kate hung out in a conference room until Lorraine told her that Armstrong would see her at eleven. Kate telephoned Liz from the phone booth in the lobby.

"They're bringing in the big guns," Liz said. "That's a compliment. Armstrong wouldn't waste his time on you if he didn't think you were important."

"I guess not," Kate said.

"He probably realizes he bungled it, though I wouldn't expect an apology," Liz said. Kate agreed that there was an element of concession in Armstrong's willingness to meet with her. He could have sent an emissary or told Jim to handle it. Kate wanted to consult Peter, but there was no way to reach him.

She went outside, where there were still plenty of people rushing to jobs with nine o'clock start times. She was both nervous and curious about her upcoming audience with the bank chairman. Would he discuss the future of the securities business the way he had with Jim? She couldn't imagine him describing his past mistakes or explaining how bumps in the road had contributed to his development. But he might ask her opinion on the market. The Chairman's Tuesday morning meetings were, after all, the context in which he had encountered her. She went into a coffee shop and studied the *Wall Street Journal* and the *Times*, making sure that she was current on the markets in case the Chairman brought them up.

At nine-thirty, she walked over to Century Twenty-One, the discount department store on Cortlandt Street, where she and Rita sometimes went on slow afternoons. The experience felt different without Rita and the throngs of bargain hunters who came later in the day.

On the walk back to the bank, Kate mentally rehearsed a defense of how she had handled the June year-bill auction. She no longer entertained hope of an immediate return to trading; Jim had made that much clear. But should she go on record with Armstrong that she didn't consider sales her ultimate goal? She stopped into the women's restroom on the eleventh floor, the one she visited when she didn't want to see anyone she knew. It came to her that the last time she had checked her appearance in this mirror, she actually thought she might be offered the job of head trader.

The receptionist on the 20th floor, where the bank's senior executives had their offices, directed Kate to a formal waiting area. It was almost eleven o'clock, so she declined the receptionist's offer of something to drink. She picked up a copy of the *Economist* from the coffee table, but found it hard to get through even one paragraph. Ten minutes passed, then twenty. She worried that she had mistaken the time, but the receptionist would have informed her of such an error.

At eleven thirty, a well-dressed, middle-aged woman approached the waiting area. Her knit suit reminded Kate of the bright red outfit that Margaret Finn had worn when she interviewed the bill traders.

"I'm sorry," the woman said. "The Chairman's engaged with other business. It could take some time. Would you like to reschedule?"

"That's all right," Kate said. "I can wait."

"It may be a while," the woman reiterated before walking away.

Kate had finished leafing through the *Economist* and was going through the *Financial Times* when the woman returned around noon. Half expecting her appointment to be cancelled, Kate was surprised when the woman said the Chairman would see her now. They walked past the open office door of the bank president, a genial man very much the Chairman's subordinate, who didn't look up as they passed.

Kate's heart rate accelerated when she saw Phil Armstrong standing in the doorway to his office. He seemed shorter than when he sat at the head of the table in the Tuesday morning meetings. The woman handed him a small manila-colored card, which he read and slipped into his jacket pocket. Kate wondered if her name and the purpose for the meeting were noted on the card.

Armstrong made a slight gesture to his right. Unsure of his intention, Kate was relieved when he started to walk in that direction. They went several yards in awkward silence. "Funny thing, the credit business," he finally said. "Our loan to a shipbuilder goes bad, but the price of the collateral appreciates." Was Armstrong admitting a mistake the way he had done with Jim? Or maybe it was a test. Maybe Armstrong made a cryptic statement to see how people handled it. If she said, "Can we sell the collateral?" he might respond, "We're not in the shipbuilding business." But if she said, "We're not in the shipbuilding business," he might say, "How else can we recoup our losses?" She decided to keep quiet and hope for a clue.

They walked another thirty feet down the longest hall she had ever seen. Were they going to meet in a conference room somewhere? Maybe Armstrong would start his pep talk once they reached their destination.

They came to a single, private-looking elevator. Armstrong pressed the button. "A. J. Matheson had this elevator put in. It connects to the hall outside his old office. Saves a lot of time."

"I see," Kate nodded. They must be heading to the room where the Tuesday morning meetings were held. She appreciated the symbolism of meeting in that room, where she had often briefed the Chairman and his lieutenants during the past year.

The elevator door quietly opened. "There are people waiting for me," Armstrong said. He turned slightly toward her, though they didn't make eye contact. "Good luck in your new assignment." He turned back to the elevator and stepped inside. The door silently shut between them.

Kate felt like the wind had been knocked out of her. She looked around, hoping there had been no witnesses to the Chairman's brush-off. Hot, angry tears stung her eyes, and her throat ached. She had an overwhelming urge to find a bathroom. She located the women's restroom at the opposite end of the hallway and had to check the door closely to see the word "Women" microscopically engraved on a brass plate above the door handle. The room itself was small, too, but apparently adequate to serve the female population on the 20th floor.

She let the cold stream of water wash over her hands. Surely that exchange wasn't what Jim had in mind. Phil Armstrong had kept her waiting for an hour and then given her a minute. His offhanded comment about shipbuilding made no sense. The dismissive way he had treated her was insulting. She felt small and completely insignificant.

She splashed water on her face and blotted her cheeks with one of the linen towels stacked next to the sink. She knew it was unwise to act too quickly in a situation like this one, and that it was better to wait until the flood of emotions subsided. But she had stewed long enough about her decision. It was like nursing a bad position, torturing yourself as you watched the market drift lower, holding on even though you knew there was nothing on the horizon to bail you out.

Jim was in his office when Kate got back to the 10th floor. His door was open and she walked right in.

"Should we shut the door?" he said, gauging the look on her face.

She shrugged. "It's up to you. I won't raise my voice, if that's what you're worried about."

"Did you meet with Armstrong?"

"There really wasn't a meeting. I waited an hour and then walked him to the elevator."

"Did he say anything?"

Kate felt a moment's satisfaction: the normally unflappable Jim was actually taken aback.

"He said something about a loan to a shipbuilder going bad, and that the price of ships had risen." She glanced out the window where, ten floors up from Wall Street, a pigeon walked along the outside ledge.

"Maybe he had you confused with someone else."

She looked at Jim. "That must have been it."

"Don't get that way."

"Don't get what way?"

"Look," Jim said, his flat-footedness over. "I'm sorry Armstrong treated you like that, but you can't judge your future at this company on him."

Kate drew her head back. "How else should I judge it?"

Jim sighed with exasperation. "Shut the door." She stayed put. "Please shut the door and sit down for a moment. You're making me nervous."

She did as he asked.

"Listen, Armstrong's not the future of the firm," Jim

said. "He'll be retiring in five years. It's mandatory at sixty-five. It's the next generation who'll move this firm ahead."

Kate thought about five years, a significant period. A year longer than college. Half as long as her marriage to Ted. And the next generation of the firm? Was Jim referring to the men who attended the Tuesday morning meetings, the ones too intimidated by the Chairman to make more than a peep? The thought of that group holding its collective breath for the next five years seemed ridiculous.

She smiled lazily, surrendering to a moment of clarity in which she could see what sticking around the bank would mean to her day-to-day life. She had done what she could to salvage her position, but the terms for survival were too unattractive. Her work problem went beyond a move from trading to sales. She didn't buy into the Matheson vision anymore.

Jim misread her dreamy expression. "You could be part of it, Kate. The first woman in securities to make senior vice president. If you stick around, I'll bet that happens. I'd consider it a personal goal."

Her smile broadened, partly at the compliment Jim was trying to pay her, but also in recognition that she had made her decision. Still she was touched by Jim's efforts to keep her in the fold, and she didn't want to seem ungrateful for what he obviously considered an awesome opportunity—for what *most* people would consider an awesome opportunity. Jim was a true believer. He would never understand why anyone who had broken into the securities business would choose to give it up.

How could she explain her choice without making herself sound self-righteous? When you came right down to it, she did not meet the criteria for a flourishing career at A. J. Matheson. She could see that now. Of course she had some of the skills, but not all of them, and not even the most important ones. She could figure out the market and work with its participants. She could take risk and hold up under the unavoidable pressure that comes with a high stakes game. But she wouldn't accept blatantly unfair treatment, at least when it came to herself, she thought wryly. And she wouldn't knuckle under. No amount of time on the job was going to change that.

Or maybe the opposite was true. Maybe time on the job would change her, altering her judgment about what she would accept to preserve her position. It might not always be a matter of principle either. She thought of Lloyd Keezer, clinging to whatever scraps they threw him because his family needed the medical insurance.

"I appreciate your saying that, Jim, and everything you've done for me. I really do. But I think it's time for me to take off."

"Take off all the time you want. You've earned it."

"No, I mean, take off for good."

"Don't make that mistake, Kate. Don't leave all this on the table because you're pissed off with Armstrong."

"It's not that, though he really was incredibly rude."

"Then don't take off because you have to go back into sales."

"It's not that either."

"Bullshit. If I told you to go back to your desk and start trading bills, you'd do it in a heartbeat."

Kate took a moment to consider the comment. "I don't know that I would," she said philosophically.

"You sat there this morning and told me you wanted to trade."

She smiled, as confused as Jim by her change of heart. "You're right, I did," she laughed.

"Your feelings are hurt because Armstrong didn't give you the time of day. That's understandable, but don't turn it into a Federal case." Now even Jim smiled. "You know what I mean."

Kate grinned. "That's a good one, Jim." Her body felt light, her mood oddly cheerful.

"You can't quit. You quit now and you'll leave a lot of money on the table."

She arched an eyebrow.

"All right, not a huge amount, not this year, but there'll be something," Jim said. "Forty or fifty thousand. And then there's the fifteen per cent profit sharing and your medical benefits."

"Don't forget my five weeks' vacation," she said.

"I'll give you a leave of absence, that's easy to do. You'll be back. I know you will. You're like me: you just keep coming. You want to win." Jim smiled confidently.

Kate looked at him and then down at her hands, folded modestly in her lap. Jim was right. She did want to win, and leaving the biggest game in town would not be easy. "There are other games," she said softly, beginning the process of convincing herself.

"Not like this one," he said. "Sure, you could work ten, eleven, twelve hours a day at some other job, but you'll never make what you can in this business."

"It's not just about money."

"No?" Jim inflected the word comically. Then his eyes widened. "Are you getting married? Is that what this is all about?"

"I'm not getting married," Kate said, though her full, rich blush would probably convince him otherwise.

"Ernie mentioned there was some guy."

"There is some guy, but we're not engaged."

Jim grinned. "Not yet, you aren't. Who's the lucky man?"

That's right, she thought; let Jim think it's about a man. It was sad that this was how their conversation was ending. There was so much more she wanted to convey, about fairness and bargains honored, and the path the bank must adhere to if it wanted to succeed with its integrity intact. And it was depressing how everything about a personal life seemed to count against a woman. But Jim's assumption about Peter wasn't her principal grievance. Her disappointment with how everything had turned out went deeper than that.

Suddenly she felt exhausted, too weary to argue. Jim's suggestion that she take a leave of absence offered them both a gracious way out, and she took it.

Ernie was busy on the phone and barely looked up when she came to get her shoulder bag from the emptied desk drawer. She noticed the cardboard box into which she had put her things, and decided to have it sent to her apartment rather than make a scene. I'll call you, she mouthed to Ernie, and left before he got off the phone. As she walked up the tiered stairs on the sales side of the trading floor, she glanced at Rita, who was also on the phone but signaled for her to wait. Kate stood self-consciously on the middle stair until Rita rolled her eyes, shook her head, and pointed to the receiver, making the yak-yak sign with her hand. Kate shrugged and held up her hands in commiseration: what are you going to do?

She walked up the remaining stairs and stopped at the glass doors. Feeling the weight of the moment, she turned to take a last look at Ernie and Rita, at Keezer and Rosemary, and everyone else on the trading floor. How long would it take for them to realize that she was gone? What would their reactions be? Would she be missed?

A management trainee carrying her lunch tray back to the cafeteria approached the glass doors. It took Kate a second to realize that the young woman was holding the door open for her.

Acknowledgments

Because this is my first published book, I'd like to thank people who contributed to my development as a writer. Linsey Abrams tops the list. She has the remarkable ability to help writers achieve within their own context and style. I am also grateful for the insight and encouragement of other teachers: Carla Hills, Suzanne Hoover, Fenton Johnson, Brian Morton, Lucy Rosenthal, Joelle Sander, Steven Schnur, and Candy Schulman.

I thank writing workshop members at Sarah Lawrence, the Housing Works, and Candy Schulman's nonfiction workshop: their input has been invaluable.

I thank family and friends who took the time to read and comment on early drafts of the manuscript: Wendy Becker, Kate Bell, Joel Cohen, Ellen Culbreth, Kim D'Amico, Virginia Faulk, Maribeth Finn, Steven Gherini, Stuart Gherini, Scott Gherini, Sandra Haskin, Coreen Hester, Emily Irving, Luann Jacobs, Jean Griffen Kerr, Ann Kirkham, Nancy Osborne, Jackie Purcell, Eileen Smith, and Paul Zintl. Thanks to later readers for fine-tuning and support: Beth Andrews, Elizabeth Augustin,

David Fisher, Stephanie Hanbury-Brown, Janet Hanson, Laura Holson, Ruth Lenrow, and Susan Smith.

I thank Molly Cross, Stuart Gherini, and Jill Martin for proofreading and Nick Sargen for technical advice on the government securities market; Tracy Brown, David Ebershoff, Gunter Nitsch, Eduardo Santiago, Irene Seltzer, and Peter Spiegelman, for advice about publishing; Reverend Richard Martin for the use of his sermon; Maura McCaw for editorial suggestions and empathy throughout the process; Liz Liscio for confirming the description of Stuyvesant High School; Elizabeth Ackerman Valins for the cover design; Joseph A. Gutierez for marketing expertise; Jim Staudt for the author photo; and Jaine Eney for unflagging optimism.

I thank my parents, Allan and Royle Gherini, and my children, John and Liz, for their love and excellent company.

Last but not least, I thank my husband Sam for being a stalwart ally and for his inimitable one-liners, which appear throughout the book.

Breinigsville, PA USA
05 November 2010
248700BV00001B/1/P